TOM PAINE MARU

L. NEIL SMITH

PHOENIX PICK

an imprint of

ARC
MANOR
Rockville, Maryland

Tarikian, TARK Classic Fiction, Arc Manor, Arc Manor Classic Reprints, Phoenix Pick, Phoenix Rider, Manor Thrift and logos associated with those imprints are trademarks or registered trademarks of Arc Manor Publishers, Rockville, Maryland. All other trademarks and trademarked names are properties of their respective owners.

ISBN: 978-1-60450-260-2

www.PhoenixPick.com
Great Science Ficstion at Great Prices

Visit the Author's Website at:
http://www.lneilsmith.org

Published by Phoenix Pick
an imprint of Arc Manor
P. O. Box 10339
Rockville, MD 20849-0339
www.ArcManor.com

Printed in the United States of America / United Kingdom

For Cathy, my Butterfly Princess

જાજી

I would also like to thank those who made the 2005 e-edition possible, beginning with Ken Holder, its publisher, "cyberarcheologist" William Stone, whose intrepidity unearthed it from a tomb of obsolete software, Scott Bieser, more and more my good right arm in creative exercises, my wife Cathy and my daughter Rylla who suffered through my cranky absent mindedness, and Jeff Barzyk, who rescued me on the very last day of the rewrite.

CONTENTS

A WORD FROM THE AUTHOR

Tom Paine Maru was intended to be my first "big" novel, with twists, sub-plots, otherwise admirable characters working to cross purposes, and all that there kinda literary stuff. It also contained my ideas about why so many people struggle to gain and keep power, and why others (or sometimes even the same people) bow down to it. I also tried to make sure that it had "enough sex and violence to satisfy even the most apolitical reader", but the book was badly cut by its first publisher, and languished until it fell out of print.

For a short time, after a kind friend painfully extracted it from WordStar 3.0 for CP/M in which I'd written it, I tried to make it available to readers through my website as an e-book, but that never really quite worked out. To proclaim I'm delighted that it's now being offered by Arc Manor would be an understatement.

So here's _Tom Paine Maru_, fully restored to the novel I meant it to be, and readers may judge for themselves whether my theories encumber or enhance it. I only hope that they enjoy reading it as much as I enjoy seeing it in print again.

L. Neil Smith
FORT COLLINS, COLORADO
AUGUST, 2008

PROLOGUE: ASPERANCE DOWN

A SOFT, FRAGRANT wind heralded the coming of darkness. It brought with it the distant murmur of thunder.

"*Asperance* Re-entry Command to Lifeshell Four, come in?"

Silence.

"*Asperance* Re-entry Command to Lifeshell Five, come in?"

The radio operator's pleas were rewarded only with an empty static crackle. Eyes streaming, he backed away from the flames as the breeze shifted suddenly in my direction. What is it they say about smoke following beauty?

Beside him, standing over the smoky fire, the Lieutenant shivered, thrust his hands in the pockets of his uniform, demanding impatiently, "Any luck at all?"

Still coughing, the operator looked up from where he squatted, trying to coax a signal from the unit in his hand while heating a can of emergency rations at the same time. The expedition's cook—along with most of our supplies—had been aboard the missing Lifeshell Four.

"Not a whisper, sir. They might be having problems with their own communicators."

"Both units?" The thunder was a great deal louder this time, forcing the Lieutenant to repeat himself. "Both units?"

"Then again," the operator held up his own radio, "it might be this one. I would not have any way of knowing—sir."

That made a certain sense. The officer squatting by the fire was a botanist. Our regular communications expert was aboard the missing Lifeshell Five, the second of two re-entry vehicles we could not reach. Things would begin to get really interesting when it came time to erect the microwave array for sending a message home. That gear was aboard one of the four ablative-surfaced globes that had managed to—no, it was not quite time, yet, to say "survive". We did not know whether the others had indeed perished, nor were we certain that we had succeeded at surviving.

The Lieutenant shook his head, silently mouthing unprintable words.

The blurry copy-processed expedition manual had ordained a landing at dawn, allowing one full period of daylight in which to establish ourselves on alien, possibly hostile territory. The planet's searing primary had decreed that we re-write those ineptly-collated pages. Even the few hours that we had spent in orbit, shielded behind nearly-opaqued photo-responsive plastic, had blackened the hardiest of us, covering some in weeping blisters. Thus we had chosen a landing site in the high northern latitudes, prayed, then triggered the retro-igniters.

The landing had not been quite as bad as the scientist had said it might be. I had fractured a bone in my foot in two places. Four lifeshells had grounded violently within a few klicks of one another. We had not as yet located the other pair, although there was a fresh crater nearby. Where there had once stood eighteen intrepid Starmen, select of nation-state, pride of an entire planet, there now trembled a dozen frightened, homesick souls, variously shattered, unanimously bewildered.

Again, that low mutter of thunder toward the horizon.

I checked my makeshift splint before attending to the other wounded. The aluminum pistol cleaning rods kept slipping off my instep to a position either side of the arch, where they could not prevent the flexing of my twice-broken foot. It was growing dark rapidly. Thunder boomed with increasing regularity until it threatened to become a continuous, intimidating roll. I should already have broken out the expedition's arsenal. But so many wounded needed help—our medical officer, with his precious supplies, was lost in Lifeshell Five—that there had not been time so far to think about my regular duties.

Dazzled, shaken though we were, the surface of this planet seemed like heaven: rich with life, moist. Even here, on this twilit winter hemisphere the soil was warm, darkly aromatic. Four small moons blazed overhead, their reflected glory unbearable to look upon directly. It was a place to build a new beginning, to love a woman, to raise a family.

Not a square centimeter was uncovered by green growing things. Ordinary birds, extraordinary in their numbers, filled the trees with music. Pale, day-bleached grasses whispered with the hasty passage of tiny, furry, four-legged creatures, or sparkled with half-hidden multicolored scaly life. Insects swarmed in myriads. Even as we cursed them, we laughed with delighted astonishment while they pricked away at us.

Not a hundred meters from the landing site there was a brook with a small pond behind a barrier of mud-caked branches made by some broad-tailed swimming mammal. For a solid hour, earlier in the day, I had sat at its edge, dangling my ruined foot, more running water trickling between my bare toes than my family had used throughout my lifetime.

Now the thought gave me a feeling of guilty apprehension.

As a precaution, I crawled back into Lifeshell One, fumbling through the litter at the bottom. I began uncrating hand-weapons—eight millimeter Darrick automatic revolvers—getting them loaded, ready in their racks. Even through the thick walls I could hear the thunder now. Our telescopic survey from orbit had betrayed sparse signs of primitive settlement. On the one-problem-at-a-time principle we had chosen to land as far away from those as possible. Still ... Finding a pair of oblong, foil-wrapped packages, I stripped off the wrapping, exposing a pair of reloaders, tipped one of them into the port of a weapon, then thumbed the triangular plastic cartridges into its grip-magazine. Repeating the procedure, I then fastened two issue holsters to my equipment belt. Now, if something unexpected happened, there would be at least one pistol ready for each of the mission commanders.

Carrying another half-dozen Darricks, still in their corrosion-proof containers, I crawled out of the lifeshell toward the rack I had erected earlier beside the fire. Already the least injured men were trying, under the Lieutenant's direction, to inflate our microwave dish, spreading the limp plastic it was made of in a circle safely distant from the sparks being whisked into the air by the twilight breeze. Like one of those sparks, our home star would drift across the sky sometime tonight. Our signals would take two years to get there from here.

No time like the present to start.

Thunder boomed!

This time it did not die. Suddenly ... *they were upon us,* half-lit figures out of a horror story, come to do their bloody business under the broad light of the moons, night-raiders riding us down from the sweat-foamed backs of tall, long-legged beasts whose disminded screams mingled with those of the helpless victims they helped to slaughter.

At the edge of the encampment, I watched as an officer was was lifted, impaled on a lance-point, tossed away like refuse, smashed against the hard ground. The frail plastic of the microwave dish, our only link with home, was shredded beneath the monsters' hooves. Beside the fire, the botanist/radio-man went down before a single, crushing sword-slash.

The sun had not been down an hour.

The Lieutenant ran at me, his mouth agape with terror. I struggled with a holster-flap, freed the gun, stretched it toward him. He never touched it. A rider, firelight reflecting blood-red off half-tarnished armor, overrode him, cutting him down with a vicious swipe of his sword.

The Lieutenant stumbled, grunting with surprise as much as pain, then collapsed. The rider swept past him, aiming his broadsword at me. Before I realized what was happening, the Darrick's sights were on the grill-slotted front of his helmet. I pulled the trigger. Bloody flesh exploded through the helmet's seams. The beast went on without its rider.

In a stride, unconscious of my wounded foot, I was standing over the Lieutenant. Above the bellowing clamor of armor, hooves, men possessed by the exultation of killing or the terror of dying, the Darrick's blast had seized the attention of our attackers. Someone galloped toward me, a huge plume bobbing atop his helmet. He stopped his mount half a dozen meters from me, dipped his lance, kicked the animal's sides.

Aiming for a helmet again, I fired, then cocked the Darrick. The empty triangular plastic casing fell at my feet to join the first one I'd fired.

A second nearly-headless rider toppled, spilling his life over his animal's neck. I heard a war-cry close beside me. For the first time I was aware that I had the other pistol out of its holster. My front sight found its own way to the mark. Another skull exploded within its steel jacket.

My right-hand Darrick spoke again. Another alien fell, dashing his bullet-churned insides on the ground. A red haze formed before my eyes as the universe became the sound of my guns, the shadow of both front sights against firelit body-steel, the clash of bloody-edged metal, the flashes of my pistol muzzles in the dark. Men fell, shouting with surprised anger, screaming with agony, gibbering with fear.

What seemed to take hours must actually have been over with in seconds. Ten star-traversing "heroes" now lay mangled, everything that they had ever been, everything that they had ever done, gone to feed the warm, rich soil. Almost unopposed, the enemy had hacked us to pieces.

I glanced down at the litter of white plastic cartridges between my feet. The Lieutenant's arm was all but severed from his body. I found myself standing over him, with a pair of slowly-cooling empty-handled pistols.

With a merciless *swoosh!*, the battle-nicked flat of an ancient, carbonless iron swordblade slammed into my head from behind. It did not take my consciousness away altogether, only a certain amount of interest in what was going on. Sullen, pock-marked, bearded faces seemed to swim around me under dented helmets, gabbling words I almost understood.

Rolling my body aside, they stopped the Lieutenant's bleeding arm with a rough clot of manure, binding it with twists of something resembling burlap. Quarrelsomely, they divided our pitiably few belongings, stripping what was left of the lifeshells, no doubt, to chink the leaks in peasant hovels or decorate the walls of a crudely-hewn fortress. They hauled us away on a wood-wheeled cart drawn by animals different, stockier than those the metal-suited warriors had ridden.

My last sight of the encampment was a tower of greasy, roiling smoke.

I would never return to Vespucci, my home planet.

I would never see my fair Eleva again.

PART ONE
THE STARMEN

DUNGEON, FIRE, AND SWORD

THREE WHOLE WEEKS for my eyes to adjust.

A person would have thought that I could see better by now, even in what little torchlight managed to squeeze through the tiny window, with its three stupid bars, in the rusty iron door of the cell we shared.

Just as well: that made it lots easier, eating from a crock of half-frozen slush they pushed in at us whenever they remembered. You could ignore the fuzzy stuff growing on its surface, hold your nose, pretend some of the lumps did not squirm as they began to thaw in your mouth.

Darkness got to be a kindly friend.

From where I sat, I did not need any floodlight to smell the Lieutenant's arm rotting off. Why he was not dead already ... Maybe I should have thanked our pre-flight immunizations, but the shots they gave us simply let his nightmare—mine too—stretch out that much further.

Eleva would have called that defeatism.

But then, Eleva was not here.

Of course it could have been that my perspective was all screwed up. In the last month it had shrunk, by abrupt increments, from the sun-filled universe—perhaps too much room out there, too many hard chips of starlight pressing in on us—to this underground kennel, hip-high, only two meters square, lit by the leavings from a jailer's passageway.

The Lieutenant—my lieutenant—Lieutenant Third-Rate Enson Sermander, sprawled unconscious in one corner, gradually surrendering to gangrene, provided hypothermia did not claim the both of us first. He had never been much to look at, even in the best of times: tall enough that his scalp had crested through his hairline; a least a year's eating ahead of his calorie-quota. The man's face was a brown plastic sack full of stale pastries. He inevitably dressed like an unmade Army cot. Incarceration with infection was not improving him any.

Another corner was mine.

A third corner I had crawled to a couple of times every day in the beginning, back when I had still cared. It smelled worse than either one of us. At least that helped attract most of the scavengers away.

I wondered what Eleva would have said to that.

I kept thinking that the fourth corner would have been perfect for a table-model ColorCom. But reception was probably terrible down here, even if they had invented CC—or electric lighting, for that matter—on this putrescent alien mudball the natives for some reason called Sca.

At that, I would have gratefully settled for my button mandolar, with which to play myself to death, but it had no doubt burned, along with everything else from the *Asperance*. The idiots who believe that olden times were wonderful ought to try living in the real thing for a while.

A place for everything—with everyone in his place.

Each midday, somehow, when the nastiness seeping frozenly out of the rough stone walls began to drip, marking high noon, I would summon up the energy to belly over to the Lieutenant to check him out. Aside from shivering all the time, it was the only exercise I got. I was not strong enough to stand any more, but the Scavians had taken care of that: there was no room in which to do it. If the torch outside was fresh, I would try picking some of the blind, white, writhing things out of the Lieutenant's decay-blackened arm to squash on an already-slimy floor. He would struggle feebly at the attention, out of his head.

I was especially careful not to drop any of my own load of vermin into the wound. It took real character to move away from him afterward. His rotting infection was the only source of warmth in the place.

He would lie there, breathing raggedly, occasionally moaning, but for the most part leaving me alone with my thoughts, my dreams of home, such as it was, of fair Eleva, which were a subtle torture in themselves.

As thoughts go, they did not amount to much, a stagnant, circular trickle of regret. Three horror-attenuated weeks still had not been enough to accommodate me to my probable fate. A day from now, a week—or never, if they really had forgotten about us down here in the dark—His Excellency the Bishop, His Grace the local Baron, would finally settle between themselves who got to dispose of us and by what means.

Lieutenant Sermander was lucky. He most likely would not last that long.

Me, they would drag to a secular gibbet in the "town"—a thatchy pile of animal-droppings rucked up against the soiled skirts of this castle—or to a more highly sanctified burning-stake in the greater filth-heap that passed for a metropolis, seventy-odd klicks north of here.

Either way it ended here, back home on dear old Vespucci, they would never find out what had happened to their eighteen intrepid Starmen, the flower of the Naval Reserve. With encouragement—not to mention sufficient distraction—the citizenry would eventually forget.

Everyone but Eleva.

Bureaucrats would breathe a discreet (but hardly unanticipated) sigh of relief. It would have been nice, they would tell themselves, to have found a paradise world, ripe for exploitation. Even so, they would remind each other, now there would be seventeen fewer obsolete heroes to worry about. Never mind that it had been the most expensive liquidation, per capita, in the history of Vespucci, simply raise the tax on protein, or on birth or death or water. The warriors who had recently helped batter our beloved planet into political submission—pardon, make that "solidarity"—presently figured in the official mind as nothing more than the likeliest source of counter-revolution: once-convenient nuisances to find a place for, of honorable exile, of dryrot.

The eighteenth?

No hero, certainly, obsolete or otherwise. Just a humble Navy corporal who was good with certain kinds of necessary machinery. I guess you could say I was the single real volunteer aboard, the sole enlisted man, the only one with dirt under his fingernails, therefore, in the view of my superiors, a sort of machine, himself. My reasons are none of your business, but—well, Eleva wanted to marry an officer.

They had promised me ...

The only other individuals neither forgetful nor relieved would be the scientists. But they would be *quiet*. It was their expertise that had landed us here. Unless they managed somehow to contain their angry curiosity, they would make perfect scapegoats for our failure. Modern Vespuccian methods are more technically certain (for which read: considerably more painful) than any medieval hanging-tree or pyre.

Eleva, dearly beloved, where are you tonight? Are you thinking of me?

Or will you find an officer to marry, after all?

THE LIEUTENANT GROANED, stirring fitfully.

With what amounted to a supreme moral effort, I managed to lift my good foot, to bring it down on the rat nibbling at his fire-streaked fingers.

I missed, of course.

The jar of my boot on the muck-coated floor sent a shock through my sick, cold-stiffened body. The shaggy, naked-tailed creature scrambled back to its hole between two ill-fitted stones, to chitter away displaced frustration among less-venturesome but equally greedy companions.

They could afford to be patient.

Rats were only one surprising familiarity awaiting the Vespuccian expedition to Sca. Since the founding of our (then) Republic, two centuries before, natural philosophers had been accumulating evidence that humankind had originated elsewhere. There was never enough air to breathe, except at the lowest altitudes. There was never enough water to drink. There was never enough food to eat. There was never enough light.

17

Animal species on the planet were divided sharply: those like us, oxygen-invigorated, bilaterally symmetrical; or those constructed on a radial, seven-lobed architecture that lived by extracting chlorine from the lowland salt-sinks. The latter species predominated, perhaps because they did not lose three or four out of five newborn at every generation.

Each was thoroughly poisonous to the other, a phenomenon that made the ceaseless competition for environmental niches very interestingly deadly.

Recent republican emphasis on reasonable individual liberty, a resulting prosperity, a stable peace wholly unprecedented in the fifteen hundred years of written planetary history, had allowed the philosophers leisure time, among other resources, to dig up—quite literally—astonishing confirmation of a thousand ancient, bitter tales.

We did not belong.

How else could we have realized, from our remotest prehistoric beginnings, that Vespucci was nothing more than a frigid, barren, dried-out husk of a world, circling a dull amber clinker of a primary, never much of a home to anyone, totally without a future? That is what folk-wisdom had always maintained. That is what modern day science had corroborated. If Vespucci had been our natural place in the universe, we would have fit in, like the seven-legged crawlies of the chlorine marshes.

Vespucci would have fit us.

As the planet's shifting sands were probed, it began to appear that we—some of us, anyway—might try our luck elsewhere. Maybe that bright blue-white star, companion to our own, "merely" two light years away. For the dessicated books, the incredibly well-preserved artifacts the scientists found revealed that there was an abandoned starship orbiting Vespucci somewhere overhead, fashioned by the hands of human beings, our ancestors, who had known more than us, but who had nevertheless marooned their helpless unhappy posterity in this wasteland.

Yet we scarcely expected to find human beings here on Sca, nor ordinary rats. Nor powerful Barons ruling a degenerate barbarism, nor the Bishops of the Holy Order of the Teeth of God, who, in an uneasy alliance with the feudal aristocracy, held their sun-bleached world in a double grasp, one fist of terrifying faith, the other of naked brutality.

Something slithered out from between the mortarless stones behind my neck. I had been hearing the creature off and on, with its bristly sound of stiff body hairs or countless legs, for the past several days, halfway hoping that it was large enough to eat—the rats were too fast for me—or poisonous enough to bring this insanity to an end.

Perhaps I would have time to use it on the Lieutenant, as well.

I moved. It gave a dampish bubbling squeal, then vanished, leaving silence.

FOLKS BACK HOME had seen us off grandly. Eleva had 'commed me at the skyport quarantine. Military bands blared loudly over every channel as our clumsy shuttles one by one grumbled aloft toward the new, half-completed vespucciostationary satellite, assembled around the remains of an older technology. Fully finished nearby lay the *Asperance,* product of our two most important sciences: physics; archaeology.

The World State (no longer a republic) had decided to call her a "starclipper".

Eighteen Starmen (that being what the World State decided to call us) bound themselves into position alongside the flimsy framing, where they would work, eat, sleep—while exercising grimly in place for months. Fireworks followed the speeches; personal interviews were ColorCommed to a grudgingly united world below. Ranks of heavily armed peace-forcers were not shown on camera in the crowd scenes. We floated free of the station, powered the inertia field-generator, spread our sails.

Mankind was free of Vespucci for the first time in their recorded history.

Technically sophisticated as they may once have been, practicing sciences long lost to their grandchildren—our ancestors—we had learned nevertheless that they had arrived a Vespucci by desperate accident.

Their lifeless, dust-filled ship lay in orbit, lifeslip stations gaping, empty. Within, in addition to their records, the scientists had discovered the "Thorens Broach", the means by which they had ducked *around* the laws of physics, hemstitching through an unreal continuum where every point in distance-duration is geometrically common with every other—but one's destination was uncontrollably random. They had definitely had a destination in mind but had not reached it. Their electronic log held horrific stories of a dozen panic-stricken random leaps until, at last, a marginally-habitable planet had been stumbled upon.

It was still only marginally habitable, which was why we were leaving.

I wondered at the time we read the papers, saw the unfolding story on the ColorCom: what had these people fled to take such a chance? What horrors had they willingly traded for the parched nubbin they named Vespucci? I sincerely did not want to know. Neither did anybody else. It was new worlds we looked for, a future for ourselves, for our children.

Generations of desperate hard figuring, plus a leg-up from what had been rediscovered amidst buried shards, orbital trash, propelled *Asperance* starward on a newer principle, one that made us feel we had won a certain measure of superiority over our unlucky forebears. Her quarter-meter-diameter hollow core was a paragravitic "antenna" spinning out a field rendering everything within her billowing plastic folds inertialess, no longer subject to the normal laws of accelerated mass. *Asperance* would not try to evade the speed limit, as

19

folk-tales held that those before us had been "punished" for doing; she would remain in normal space, to ignore the theoretical speed limit altogether.

Half of that capability had been achieved by the time I was born. We Vespuccians—in this case meaning the citizens of the single most advanced nation-state that had ultimately forced their country's name upon an reluc- tant entire planet—were old hands at navigating the local system, pushed by photon sails kilometers in width, but merely a single molecule thick. We had explored a dozen lifeless, hopeless balls of baked or frozen rock, often taking months or years to travel a few astronomical units, discovering nothing for their effort in the end.

A sun-system, a planet, a nation-state, all known as Vespucci. It betrayed, I thought even as a little child, a certain narrowness of perspective. It was not the sort of insight I could talk about, even with Eleva. By the time of Con- solidation, there were even those who wanted to rename our capital city, Volta Mellis, Vespucci. It was easy to understand: our options were as limited as the imaginations of our geographers.

Not particularly coincidentally.

Asperance might make all the difference. We had learned our ancestors' physics from the textbooks they had unwittingly left us. The sails of our ship were meant to billow before the interstellar tachyon winds, faster than light itself. She could traverse local distances in seconds. Two light years to the nearest star—a little over ten trillion kilometers—would require something under nine weeks.

GRIMLY, WE HUNG on.

Daily, we forced down our inedible rations. Dully, we exerted our bodies against elastic cradles to prevent the void from devouring our bones. Under those merciless, cold pin-points of light, we slept only fitfully. Scarcely ever crawling from the racks to which we had been assigned, each of us tried to forget—or at least not to remind one another—that we would have to find some haven in which to survive the two years it would take for our puny sig- nals to carry home the news of whatever we had found. Eventually we might even be followed by other vessels like *Asperance,* even possibly get back home someday ourselves.

Home.

Eleva.

If.

So, the officers played CC games, watched our meager stock of entertain- ment tapes until the brown oxide wore off the plastic. I chorded the button- fretted mandolar, wondering what was to become of us, seeing pale blue eyes, coppery hair, the delicate red bow of a mouth, where they had no right to be, against the ebon canopy of space.

Sixty-two days after our departure, we orbited a promisingly cloud-swirled marble hanging before its overwhelming primary. It was green down there, vastly greener than Vespucci, even to the naked eye, heartbreakingly blessed with water, so inviting it stirred primordial caution deep within a company accustomed to less charitable handling by nature. Yet, with a little finagling, perhaps, this paradise was—ours.

We were prepared to pay.

Asperance shut down her inertialess field generator, to shed her filmy wings in free-fall. We eighteen Starmen huddled together in half a dozen tough, spherical lifeshells of carbon filamentized polyresin that she had carried at her stern. During the all-but-endless journey to this place, they had been our only refuge from the pale, frozen stars.

Or from one another.

Now, under the blinding blue-white brilliance of a foreign star, Sca's thick mantle of atmosphere began to abrade their skins, filling their bottoms with human sweat. Each armored lander became shrouded, isolated from the other five within its own tortured curtain of ionization. We cowered inside, isolated equally, despite the inhuman crowding, each man alone with his thoughts, his fears. Our homeworld, niggardly as it may have been, was out of touch, lost to us perhaps forever.

THE BARON, AS heavily-scarred by some nameless infection as the merest of his vassals, enjoyed a complete ignorance of the geography of his own planet. He refused to believe the "superstitious nonsense" I managed to communicate to him: that we were from that bright light in the sky, right there, where I am pointing. We were all invaders, he decided, foreign vandals, common brigands, breakers of his benevolent peace.

He wanted to hang us.

The Bishop, through a live-in delegation at the Baron's castle, was all too ready to believe, naming us sorcerers, non-human demons, unnatural purveyors of some weird (but, it appeared, not very potent) magic.

He wanted to burn us.

The Bailiff, a squat, evil-eyed old ruffian with a short axe in his belt, did not much appreciate being caught between two absolute powers. I recognized his type immediately: a retired head-trooper, the kind of battered career non-com who has seen it all, done most of it himself, a little of it twice, but still does not believe a word of it.

He was very enthusiastic about my daily interrogation, however. That did not call for divided loyalties, no sir, not at all. He soon discovered my shattered instep, along with the fact that I screamed quite satisfactorily when he ordered it twisted, grinding the broken bone-ends together. Given such "incentives", I found learning a new language ridiculously easy. Scavian seemed to follow familiar rules, varied from my own Vespuccian more in pronunciation than vocabulary. I began to wonder whether Sca might be the hell-hole my ancestors had fled. Yet how could these savages have constructed even the absurdly unreliable star-drives we had discovered abandoned in orbit above Vespucci?

I became a lot more fluent—also less curious—when they began displaying tongs, pincers, obscenely-shaped irons thrust into buckets of glowing coals. For the most part, however, the Bailiff preferred simply having my foot exercised. It was much less expensive than good charcoal.

I told them everything I knew, plus plenty I did not know I knew. I remember at one point offering pathetically to go back home to find out more. None of this seems very real, somehow, although many of the scars, inside or out, I will carry to the end of my days. I passed out frequently during those sessions. With no memory of the intervening period of relief, I would often wake the next day to find some poxy minion wrenching my ruined foot again. Eleva's eyes, her smile, began elude me, abandoning me when I needed their recollection to sustain me.

Naturally, most of what I had to tell the Scavians did not make sense. Even sane, physically whole, how do you explain air-power or overlapping fields of machinegun fire to some primitive in knitted iron underwear whose notion of leading-edge martial arts is to poke at his enemies with a metal-shod stick? At last they gave up, dragging me away until some agreement could be arrived at about what to do with us. The Bailiff personally saw me bolted into a hole in the dungeon wall.

The Lieutenant had remained completely unconscious during the eternity—perhaps a week—that I had been put to question. That had not stopped them torturing him. The forms must be followed, after all.

They had not invented locks on Sca. The door, a crudely-hammered meter square of iron sheet, was fastened at its hinge-like hasps with soft metal rivets a centimeter in diameter, quite beyond reach of the palm-sized grating in its center, or the slopping-slot below. These were the castle's lower-class accommodations, at the literal bottom of the heap. Down here, the walls dripped constantly, when they were not frozen solid, with seepage from the luxury dungeons high above us. We were fed occasionally. Someone came to replace the torches in the passageway.

I estimated three weeks' passage by making small tears in the edge of my flight jacket every time I awoke to the drip, drip, drip of the polluted stone around me. Very rapidly I became too weak to keep such a calendar, except that my uniform jacket obliged by getting easier to tear.

Twenty-two rips in the rotted fabric later, the Hooded People came.

FAREWELL TO ELEVA

THE HEAVY WOVEN synthetic restrainers cut painfully where they rode across my midsection. It was hardly noticable after the grandly hollow send-off we had received, or the crushing four-gee eternity from the desiccated surface of our native Vespucci up to stationary orbit.

Nighttime reigned in this position. To the right, several kilometers away, the new space station lay, still under construction, a wild hodge-podge of beams, containers fastened to the hull of the ancient colonial ship which had brought our ancestors here. Between the interstices in the new construction, she could still be seen, a micrometeorite-pitted dull metal sphere, dozens of meters in diameter, dead, cold, empty for fifteen hundred years—until lately rediscovered by her creators' children.

Already copies of her fusion powerplant were being installed in Vespuccian cities all over the planet.

Reflexively, I smoothed the creases from the trousers of my special, fancy, useless uniform. Tailored just for this occasion, they were a violent shade of lavender to photograph well on CC, tricked out with silver braid, a deep maroon stripe running down the pants leg, a short, waist-length jacket which kept riding up, exposing the place where the shirt crept continuously out of the beltless waistband of the trousers. The knee-length silver boots were clumsy, would have to be jettisoned for weight's sake before the *Asperance* shipped out.

At least I sat unburdened, as were the rest, with the awkward matching pistol belt. As the sole enlisted man among the crew, I was not entitled to carry a sidearm, merely charged with keeping them all in good repair, making sure the officers did not shoot themselves in the foot before I could stow the ordnance aboard-ship. I carried my mandolar in its collapsible fabric case; it used up every gram of my personal freight-allowance—luckily I do not grow beard enough to need a razor desperately—but I counted on the mandolar to keep me sane during nine weeks' endless voyage.

I shifted the safety-straps once more, trying vainly for comfort, peered forward to the end of the long, cylindrical transfer-canister where they were showing the festivities on a large ColorCom screen. At least they were interrupting the blaring military bands, the posturing politicians, long enough to give us a clear view, for the first time, of the *Asperance* where she lay a few klicks off the new space station. She looked like nothing else in Vespuccian history, not like any kind of vehicle at all—certainly not like this stubby, heavy-winged orbiter which had flung itself down a long, long runway earlier this morning, into the purple sky from the port just outside the capital, Volta Mellis.

From some vantage-point, probably another shuttle, we could even see ourselves approaching the starclipper, the shuttle's bay doors opened already, exposing the tube which temporarily, uncomfortably, housed seventeen officers, along with their single, general-purpose flunky.

No, the *Asperance* resembled a huge antenna of some kind, A single long, extruded titanium mast no larger in diameter than a big man's thigh, crossed perpendicularly at intervals with complex, tightly-guyed spars. At her forward end were the shackles for her photon sails, kilometers-wide umbrellas she would unfurl to catch the solar winds which would sweep us to our destination. Aft, she bulged with a half dozen multipurpose spheres, heavily armored for the landing, stuffed full of consumable supplies for the voyage.

The entire fragile assemblage resembled a child's toy. Draped from end to end in tough, loose, transparent plastic tenting, at the end of every cross-spar, there clung either a skeletal one-man seating-rack, or cluster of instrumentation.

The *Asperance* gleamed dully in the reflected light of the sun, her titanium core housing the inertia-canceling field-coils, the re-entry spheres concealing the field-generator/power-plant. Thirty meters long, not counting her sails, she would prove far more uncomfortable than the shuttle we now occupied.

Four more exactly like her were under construction. We could see the torches flaring, the spacesuited figures swarming over them off to our left.

Asperance was the first completed. If something went wrong with her, something which came to light—perhaps fatally—during our "shakedown cruise", it would be too late to make significant changes. The design—along with the four other ships—would have to be scrapped. Something else newer, undoubtedly more expensive, would have to be undertaken, all over again.

The freshly-conquered provinces, the ordinary citizens who had conquered them, would groan a little more under the increased weight of taxation. Perhaps another division or so of peacekeepers would have to be sent to quiet the groaning.

Or perhaps a flotilla of Navy aerocraft might be dispatched on another "good will tour" to drive the point home unmistakably.

We would not care. We would be far away.

Or dead.

"I just do not know, Corporal O'Thraight, three years is a long time..."

I watched Eleva Dethri through the smeared transparency, hating the quarantine procedures at the base, wishing I were on the other side of the plastic where her voice would not come to me through an electronic filter, yet, deep inside, a little grateful for the regulations which saved me from potential humiliation.

I never touched her; I never knew if she would want me to.

Behind her on the corrugated metal wall of the shed, garish posters proclaimed the glory of our coming leap to the stars, informed visitors of the many rules governing their brief, highly-supervised stays, exhorted them to tell their friends, their co-workers, their families, how their voluntary tax contributions were building a magnificent future for unborn generations of Vespuccians.

"Yes, I know, Eleva, darling, if you could only...besides, when I come back, I will be an officer."

Dim red sunlight trickled through the windows on her side of the barrier. The shed stretched forty or fifty meters. At the door, a heavily-armed Army guardsman stood at parade-rest, watching each conversing couple closely. There were a dozen stations like this one where we Starmen could have a short, unsatisfactory glimpse of those we loved, of the lives we were leaving behind.

She was right, of course. Women generally are about these things. Three years is a long time, a lifetime, almost the same amount of time I had loved her, since an Officer's Club dance where she arrived come on the arm of some slavering lieutenant. Since I had last played the mandolar in public. Even then it came as a temporary assignment, an unlooked-for break in my regular duties.

Changing my life.

"An officer?" Her pale blue eyes brightened a little, she licked her lips uncertainly. "Why, Corporal, how wonderful! An astronaut, one of the first eighteen...but three years?"

Eleva the beautiful: fair, lightly-freckled skin, tightly-curled copper- colored hair, taller than I by a centimeter or so, unless I stood up very straight. I stood up very straight. Combat boots helped, except when she wore high heels. I suppose, as the only offspring of a warrant officer—worse yet, descended from an upper-class family whose demotion, after a lost battle, had been the scandal of the previous century—she never fitted, either among the enlisted class of my beginnings, or the officer class she desperately aspired to rejoin.

I shifted uncomfortably on the tractor-seat bolted in place before the counter they had divided down the middle with a plastic partition. We eighteen would spend two weeks here, with our alternates, until we proved to carry no diseases which might compromise the mission. Air pressure measured slightly higher inside the buildings to insure our isolation. We communicated with the outside world by wire.

Eleva looked unhappy. "Corporal..." She glanced around to see whether anyone listened, a futile gesture, as, in addition to the guardsmen, our conversation would be line-monitored by the psychiatric staff. "...Whitey, I—I do not know what to say. I, well, I had my plans, my life sort of laid out in front of me. Now you..."

Now I... I had thrown her an unpinned grenade by promising to become the officer she wanted. What else could I do? Did I want a commission for its own sake, for my own sake? I knew I wanted Eleva. Like most individuals of my class, I had learned not to want much of anything else.

"Say you will wait for me, Eleva," I answered, trying hard to cover the anger, the frustration I felt, "Or say you will not. Either way. You will not say you love me. We have never... But let me know, now."

"Please do not force the issue, I do not know what to say! Whitey, I do not know what I feel. Three years? Why, by then, I will be..."

"Three years older. Eleva, go marry a captain. I will learn not to care. Anyhow, it is too late, I am stuck here with this mission, all on account of—"

"Do not dare blame me!" she pouted. The door-guardsman looked our way, raised eyebrows under his titanium helmet. "I never asked you to volunteer for the *Asperance,* did I? I did not ask you to do anything at all—except let me alone!"

This was turning out all wrong, not at all as planned, as dreamed about. Saying goodbye to the only girl—woman—I ever loved, I had expected something different from her, something warm to take with me to the cruel stars. Now I watched myself ruining it, heard myself say all the wrong things, helpless to stop myself saying them.

"Then what the Ham are you doing here, Eleva Dethri? Why did you come?"

"I do not know!" she cried, flinging herself off the stool. She ran out of the room while I could think of nothing to say but "Eleva! I love you! Please do not go like this!"

But of course she could not hear me. The press-to-talk switch popped up the moment she released it.

THREE YEARS EARLIER, I stood before the battered desk of my CO/conductor, Colonel Gencom, trying hard to understand what they were doing to me. The office walls were lined with photographs of the band over two generations, half a thousand men in uniforms of varying obsolescence, half a dozen wars of varying unbearability. On the window sill behind his desk lay a tarnished trumpoon with a bullet-hole through its bell; the unit color-cords hanging from it were stained with something which matted the braids together. Something dark, nearly black.

"Whitey," the Colonel shuffled through the sheaf of paperwork as if he, too, could not comprehend the reasoning behind this order, "You are the best damned mandolar player in the band. I hate to see this happen; you know how it is: 'Ours not to reason why...'"

Never mind that, in an orchestra, nobody hears the mandolar except the other musicians who rely upon it for harmony, chord-progression, rhythm even the percussionist depends on.

Never mind that the papers on the Colonel's desk were reassigning me to training as a field-armorer, a sort of meatball gunsmith—something I knew nothing about, possessed no background for. There was a war on; there was always a war on; war imposes its own reasons, its own demented logic. There existed a greater need, in the eyes of the State, for field-armorers than for mandolar players no one except the other musicians could hear.

Never mind that I had been trained to play the mandolar, by edict of the same government, since the age of seven.

I doubled as company supply-clerk, meaning in the first place that I was in charge of spare reeds, mouthpiece-covers, mutes, assorted junk like triangles, ceram-blocks, train whistles, sand whistles, slide whistles. In the second, it meant I billeted with what I was in charge of, spending my days—except for rehearsals, performances—among endless shelves of odd-shaped semi-musical detritus, inventory forms, the storeroom dust of a hundred military years.

In the third place, I was de-facto repair officer: if a thumb-key broke off a picconet, if the bass saxonel got dented, if the xylotron threw burnt insulation all over the xylotronist, they brought it to me, for soldering, hammering, emergency rewiring—even a little first aid. I got to be pretty good—undoubtedly the reason I had been chosen for retraining.

"It is not all so bad," the Colonel shattered me of my reverie, although I thought he spoke more to himself than to me. "While you are in training, you will be available should we need you. I suspect there will be no replacement, not in a hurry, anyway."

I nodded. Nothing he said required—or justified—a reply.

"There may be other opportunities, even after you are rotated out into the field. I shall try to see there are, if it would please you, Whitey."

"I would like it very much, sir."

"Good. Also, you will always have your musical talent to fall back on, as a comfort to yourself, your comrades. It could be worse, could it not, Corporal?"

I saluted, snapped my heels. "Yes, sir, Colonel, sir, it could be worse, sir."

He gave me a very unmilitary grin, shook his head ruefully. If one thing the Navy—or the Army, for that matter—could arrange, it was for things to be worse. He knew it. I knew it.

I turned smartly, started out of his office.

"Whitey?"

I turned again, curious. He removed his spectacles, rubbed his eyes, looked back up at me. "Since we will not be getting a replacement, take your mandolar with you. You will need to stay in practice, anyway."

"Yes, sir. Thank you, sir."

"Do not thank me, son, I am not authorized to give away Navy property. I do not know what happened to Corporal O'Thraight's mandolar, just before he got reassigned. Thank the Navy, boy. I do it every day. You could never print the words I use to do it."

THE VOICE IN the corridor outside said, "Here it is: YD-038."

Nobody knocked. The door opened. Miss Sixte, ninth-floor mother for the local Navy Reserve creche stepped inside.

I snapped to attention.

It was a gray room, three meters by three, with a gray door, six little gray bunks, YD-036 through YD-041 inclusive, smoothly tucked to regulation tautness. Miss Sixte kept pretty much to herself. Sometimes you could hear her sobbing in her own room after lights-out. None of the kids ever managed to discover why.

Everybody else had gone to calisthenics that morning; I had been told to wait. It made me nervous. I had never spent much time here in the daylight. Behind Miss Sixte, a tall, thin man carried an odd-shaped plastic box by the handle. "Whitey, this is Sergeant Tenner of the Twenty-third Aerofleet Band. He is going to be your teacher."

I had teachers, plenty. Tenner looked okay, though, if kind of weird: cadaverouslike, with slicked-down hair, olive skin, a good smile. Good hands, with long, thin fingers. "Whitey?" He offered me one of the hands.

"Sergeant," I answered, gravely adult as I could be, "What is that you are carrying, sir?"

"Not 'sir', 'Sarge'. Take a look." He handed me the case. I fumbled with the spring latches. Inside, in a tight-fitting bed of bright yellow plush, lay the most beautiful object I had ever seen.

About the length of my forearm, it had a long tapered neck on the flat face of which six inlaid columns of square brightly-colored buttons touched each other at the edges, like mosaic tiles, each about the size of a thumbnail. They marched down the neck in twenty-four rows, until it blended with the body: not much larger than the neck, very slightly ovoid. At its bottom was a cluster of tiny knobs. Six long plastic vanes stuck out from the face, centimeter-high, six centimeters long.

Tenner took the beautiful thing from my reluctant hands, arranged the fingers of his left on the neck-buttons, just-so, fluttered his right thumb down across the hinge-springed vanes.

A chord more wonderful than anything I had ever heard. E-minor-seventh.

"What do you think, Whitey?" Nobody had ever asked me that.

"What is it, Sarge?"

"A mandolar. From now on, it will be your life."

THE SKY DEMONS

SLOP, I REMEMBER thinking, is a bit early today.

I had heard the barred doors slamming open along the length of the hall-way. Now a shadow eclipsed the only light in my severely atrophied universe. To my immense astonishment, a heavy mallet rose, fell, rose again, fell—exactly as it had done when we were sealed into this purgatory, this time miraculously splitting the soft rivets in the hasp.

The rust-blistered door grated open noisily. Out in the hallway, forms moved erratically from side to side, throwing bizarre shadows into my world. I cringed backward, only partly in terror of renewed torture, mostly because my fear-filled eyes were painfully blinded by the raw, unfiltered glory of a smoky torch in the sconce across the passage.

"Ye're of a certes as these be the ones ye're wantin'?"

His harsh voice seared forever into my memory, the Bailiff stood before the door, visible from the waist down. I recognized his boots, the hem of his mailed shirt over its padded vest. A hammer with chisel dangled from one of his sword-callused hands. A hatchet hung from his belt.

Other figures, completely anonymous in their floor-length hooded robes, bent down nearly double to examine us, each in turn averting its hidden face as it did so, from the ghastly sight, from the vile stench of two once-human beings being slowly converted into piles of putrescence.

The rats skittered back into their niches.

The last of these hooded apparitions, in a dialect of Scavian that was al-most unintelligible to me, spoke to both of us in a low sibilant crackle betray-ing not a hint of personality, or of gender, or even of humanity.

"You are the sky demons?"

Backlighted by the flickering torch outside, the vapor of its breath hung menacingly before my face within the frigid cell. I tried to look it straight in the face. Firelit shadows gave the impression of a brown-robed man, arms folded into opposing sleeves, faceless, terrifying.

"What is it you want from me now, torturer?" I managed to croak a question of my own in response. They were the first words I had spoken—besides Eleva's name—in what seemed like centuries, "Yet another confession?"

"With the right truth, demon, yet may you live to see the moons rise."

I had almost forgotten that this planet had two pairs of natural satellites. It had been very scenic, four moons, until the animal-riders slammed down on our half-built camp, shattering our dreams forever.

"I will see them—just before you light your bonfire! Now get out ... "

The comparative fresh sweetness of the air outside our cell seemed suddenly unbearable. For some reason I began coughing uncontrollably, huge tears streaming down my face. Fever, followed by chills, passed through my body in waves. I was suddenly ashamed of the filth that covered me, worse of being humiliated before my captors. What would Eleva—

"Silence! Silence!" the whisper demanded. "Your silence or the truth! Now listen carefully! Do you hold the reins of the star-flying machine?"

It was another minute before I could speak. At this rate, I would not last much longer. The figure bending before me, after its brief tirade, remained mute. When my voice came, it was a hoarse sobbing rasp.

"What are you asking me, priest?"

"Guide you the star-flying machines?"

Burning, I reasoned dully, is probably better than being hanged. Once the flame sears your nerve-endings, I am told, you can not feel a thing. It certainly beat outliving my inoculations, as I seemed to be doing now, eventually contracting leprosy or perhaps something equally attractive.

Or being eaten in my sleep by rats, for that matter.

"Sure," I lied. "Naturally. Of course. Also, 'of a certes'. I piloted one such star-flyer here myself." I paused, adding, "But it will not now return to the sky. It was not ever intended to. It has been burned, the ashes scattered by warriors. I have explained this before."

Queerly, the anonymous form squatted on its robe-draped haunches, frozen for a long moment as if in deep meditation. Then one of its identically-clad companions still out in the passageway approached the Bailiff.

Coins clinked within the silence of stone walls. The Bailiff appeared to look both ways, then withdrew. Almost as if a switch had been thrown, the hooded figure halfway into our cell came to life again.

"Demon," it hissed, even lower, even more threatening than before, "If you wish to return to life, tell us how your thunder-weapons are fashioned."

So that was it.

In the furious one-sided battle at the landing-site, I had somehow managed to kill or wound a handful of the animal-riders, their thin metal plating being worse than no protection against my fast-moving eight millimeter slugs. Staging single-handed gunfights with barbarian warriors had not been part of my job-description when I had signed onboard the *Asperance*. I was supposed to prepare the arsenal for the officers. Had I done so, perhaps we Vespuccians might have fared better.

Instead, I had sat on a streambank, paddling my toes in a little brook. I had fiddled with my music, daydreamed about my girl, watched a couple of the moons rise, while, all the time, the enemy was coming to murder us. As an armorer, I had been much more useful playing the mandolar.

In any event, my guns had been emptied in due course, confiscated by the brawling killers while I lay unconscious, the remainder of our ammo surely destroyed. Back home, in the Final Vespuccian War, I had done what the field-manuals told me, employing a fancy kit of gauges, drift-punches, screwdrivers, confident in the certain knowledge that replacement parts were never further away than our field resupply depot.

I might be able to hand-make certain of the tools—screwdrivers are easy, even good ones—what I knew of manufacturing the Darrick 8mm Revolving Magazine Pistol could have been engraved upon the tip of the Bailiff's back-up dagger with the chisel he had used to open the door.

Naturally, I said: "Of course I can tell you. Nothing to it. I know all of the proper incantations. Burn me, I cannot teach you a thing."

The hooded speaker froze again, its companions likewise ceasing all movement in the hallway. Praying, maybe. Or thinking about a New Improved Holy Order of God's Teeth, augmented with a little advanced military hardware. Old Vespuccian fairy tales told about such things: how, for example, Kalvan the Boss traveled back in time to teach the Olden People about modern machinery. That was before we learned that our Olden People had forgotten more about such things than we had ever known.

The Baron would not be happy, I thought. Then again—I started trembling at the idea—perhaps these "thunder-weapons" of mine were religiously illegal. Perhaps the Bishop only wanted to assure himself that, by disposing of us, he was eradicating dangerous or forbidden knowledge.

Well, either way, at least I would die warm. The cold down here, the vile dampness had seeped into my very bones. The insides of my lungs felt coated with the same fine mildew that garnished the cuisine. I would not last very much longer at this rate, whatever I chose to say. When they discovered the true extent of my technical education ...

The faceless figure came back to reality.

"This other demon—" Like an image of Death itself, the dark apparition gestured with a long, empty sleeve. "Knows it these things as well, the making of thunder-weapons, the guiding of sky-flying machines?"

I coughed again, this time to give me time for thought. Lieutenant Enson Sermander, in these late, great days of the Vespuccian State, had the finest military career his family could buy him—one of the old Command Families, with a real name. Do him credit, though: he had spent another fat half-dozen years purchasing even more status on his own.

In the War, he had flown (or so he said) a ram-fighter against the Shirker States. Certainly at the launching ceremony nine—no, twelve—weeks ago, his chest had been ablaze with ribbons. I was glad Eleva was not there to see him in his glory. Five confirmed kills, three probables. Feats of arms against clumsy blimps, fragile biplanes. He was only here in this dungeon only because he had not thought quite quickly enough to buy himself into favor with the current regime. Being too slow on that kind of uptake clearly defines one as a threat to national security. So, he had been volunteered for the *Asperance* expedition.

As for flying the starclipper to this place, even the Lieutenant had admitted with a chuckle that the computer was the best pilot aboard.

Nevertheless, he had not been too bad a fellow, for an officer. A cheerful cynic, the only one of seventeen crew members who had ever spoken directly to me outside the line of duty. I had come to like him, in a way. Those who actually knew what they were doing, he left strictly alone to do it. That is what constitutes a good officer these days.

The Lieutenant was a good officer.

"This sky-demon is the great-grandfather of all sky-demons!" I announced, with as much enthusiasm as my weakened body would let me muster, "I am only his humble apprentice—but he is sick. He needs help!"

"He does, indeed." A nod from beneath the hood, then that eerie, hackle-raising whisper again. "This may be arranged. Able are you to stand?"

"Not in here."

The hooded figure backed out, straightened.

Its companions reached in swiftly to drag me out by the armpits to my feet. Agony tore through my right leg as I set weight on my much-abused foot. I bit my lower lip, choking back nausea. Tears squeezed from between my tightly-closed eyelids as the priests half-carried me across the narrow corridor, propping me against a comparatively dry wall where sooty cobwebs powdered my excrement-soaked uniform. I clung, breathing heavily, to a torch-sconce, my heart hammering like a machinegun.

They slid the Lieutenant's body out of the cell.

He moaned, even fought them weakly, trying to speak. Restraining him with a surprising gentleness, one of the hooded figures extracted a relatively clean swatch of the ubiquitous burlap material from its robe, dabbed at the Lieutenant's enormous pustulent wound until fresh blood broke through the crust. A new rag was then wrapped around his arm.

"Nothing can be done for this one ... " the hooded figure whispered chillingly (was it the same one I had spoken with in the cell, or was this another one?) then, to my relief, added, " ... here."

Fighting dizziness, I croaked, "Then let us go where something can!"

They nodded; it almost amounted to a bow. The trip upward through seemingly endless underground corridors—there was no sign of the Bailiff nor of any other castle personnel—was a hazy purgatorial nightmare, reminiscent of the period, eons ago in some sense, of my daily torture-sessions. My foot was now three times its normal size, swollen up to the knee. I was queasy, half-conscious, weak. Terribly weak.

It seemed to be a busy place, this dungeon. Screaming issued out of every cross-corridor, pitiable moaning, the rattle of chains in their wall-rings. The priests looked at one another whenever this happened, their faces hidden from me in the shadows of their cowls, then looked resolutely straight ahead. The endless upward march went on.

I did manage distantly to wonder if it were day or night outside. This was no trivial matter on Sca, where all life was active during the well-lit nighttime hours, only to scurry from the dawn as if from an enemy horde. Already, in the higher-rent dungeons, my eyes smarted from the more numerous, better-trimmed torches. Outside, a naked blue-white sun would burn the optics out of my head, then start for the brain.

Suddenly we passed through a pointed stone arch to an outdoor court I recognized from our arrival here. Around the yard were railed places for the riding-animals, great piles of dried vegetation in long tied bundles, ragged servants busy with shovels. Near the gate stood another of those wooden-wheeled carts, hitched to four big pulling beasts.

It was nighttime.

Under the gentle light of a single risen moon, armored soldiers loitered about the yard, a great many of them. The Bailiff was among their number. He approached us as we slowly crossed the flagging. He was an old man for his culture, I suddenly realized, perhaps forty, white-haired, his face the usual Scavian battlefield of smallpox scars, fleabites, the marks of hard-fought mortal duels. He coughed as he spoke to us, a nervous hand fingering the pommel of his two-edged hatchet.

"Now tell me where ye might be taking these here captives?" he demanded, very loudly, "They be property, duly held for My Lord the Baron!"

Something official was happening here: he wore a breastplate over his mail now, a crested helmet, bearing the local symbol of authority, a gibbet—rampant or gules or something—on what looked like a field of bloodsoaked mud. The hooded folk gently placed the Lieutenant on the courtyard flagging. The priest I had been leaning on stepped out from under me. I swayed a little bit but managed to stay afoot. Soldiers all around us lost a bit of their transparently artificial nonchalance.

"Here is our warrant and seal!"

My guide had answered in a stage-whisper, nearly as loud as the Bailiff's bellowed challenge. It was equally intended to be overheard. I let my eyes roam the high walls of the courtyard, looking for a noble face observing the proceedings through a narrow slit, but saw nothing.

From the broad trailing sleeve of a hooded robe, there appeared a parchment. With arthritic fingers, the Bailiff laboriously untied the ribbon, unrolled the document, skipped over the writing—which he likely could not read anyway—to the heavy wax seal affixed at the bottom. He eyed us, a swat-trickle escaping from under his dented iron cap.

Then he decided: "Why, may God blind me, this be but yon little Bishop's seal! Where be that, and the written word, of My Lord the Baron?"

From all quarters, his men began sauntering oh-so-casually toward us.

"Here, thou treacherous canine, is word enough for the Baron!"

This was spoken by another of the hooded people—in that same low, threatening whisper—who had slipped up beside the Bailiff. Steel whispered from hidden leather. Something dark was thrust into the fellow's undefended armpit, out of sight beneath the Bailiff's arm as two of the priests picked the Lieutenant up. We marched past the bewildered guardsmen to the cart near the open gateway. The Bailiff waved his men away, beads of sweat decorating his unlovely cratered face.

"Th-the w-word of God be the Supreme Law..." he stammered loudly, "Thy Holiest of Orders rightfully acc-acc—b-bows to no temporal authority."

"Why, you learn canon law quickly, villain," the weapon-holder whispered, almost sounding amused. "Now you may help us with the oxcart!"

Abruptly one young guardsman stepped forward as if to block our progress, his fire-hardened wooden pike at the ready. With a casual swipe, the free hand of the priest lashed out. The guardsman took a stunned step backward with a ruined face, blood gushing onto the pavement. He collapsed, his pole falling to the flagstones with a clatter.

The tension in the courtyard turned to fury in a wave that swept around its walls. More guardsmen took a step, lowered fire-blackened spearpoints. Swords, daggers, battle axes were loosened in their scabbards.

"No!" cried the Bailiff, his shoulder rising several centimeters under the impetus of the upthrust steel in his armpit, "Stand ye all where ye be! Have that guardsman broken if he lives!" He pointed at the wounded and unconscious youth, but his face had turned to that of the priest. A murderous hatred now raged behind his small, bestial eyes.

Together the two pulled at the harnessing of the animals, turning them toward the gate. With some difficulty they managed to line up the crude planked wheels of the cart to fit between the raised beam-edges of the narrow drawbridge. I very nearly fainted on the spot, only the idea of how Eleva would despise such a display of weakness sustaining me. They half-carried me to the cart, handing me up where I could lie gratefully in clean straw. Remotely I felt them lift the Lieutenant up beside me. Two robed figures took hold of the straps on the animals' faces, pulled them through the gate onto the suddenly fragile-seeming bridge.

It groaned under the strain.

The other priest now trudged behind us, close enough to touch, had I been able, keeping a hidden eye on the Bailiff who had somehow been persuaded to perch his broad rear-end on the lowered tailgate of the vehicle. As if at an afterthought, the priest jumped up beside the man.

"I yield to thee for now," the Bailiff hissed between clenched teeth. It was easy, there were so many missing. Veins standing out on his scarred forehead, his voice began to rise as we passed beneath the rust-pitted portcullis. "But we shall all see anon who bows to what authority!"

The outer walls of the castle were now lined at their tops with soldiers, each with a sheet-bronze cap, a leather vest closely sewn with iron rings, a sharpened wooden pike. Each young, disease-marked face peeked out over the high collar of a thick batting of cotton under-armor.

"The Baron," continued the Bailiff, "Shall hear of—!"

There was the briefest of motions under the man's arm, no noise at all. The Bailiff stiffened momentarily, lost interest in what he had been about to say, then slumped, propped against the hooded figure beside him as we rumbled off the end of the bridge onto a rutted dirt roadway.

Gradually, miraculously, the Baron's castle grew small in the distance.

I struggled to an upright position on the pile of straw in the swaying cart, looking at the priest whose weapon had been tucked away again.

"Just what is it that you are you planning to do with us?" I asked, almost surprised that I was beginning to care again—about anything.

We turned a corner, finally losing sight of that hateful pile of stones behind a line of tall trees. The priest was a long time answering.

"First you teach us," the figure said at last in a loud crackling hiss. It gave the Bailiff a shove. His body tumbled off the side of the road into a ditch, vanished from sight. "Then you disappear, as well!"

ESCAPE TO CAPTIVITY

SCAVIANS NEVER SEEMED to have discovered that wheels should be round.

The man-tall weathered pair on the cart might possibly have begun that way. They were constructed of heavy parallel timbers, bolted together carefully with iron strapping. But apparently it had never occurred to the wheelwright to apply some of that iron strapping to the rims, as tires, so the end-grain had worn less quickly than the rest of the circumference. Ah well, perhaps in another thousand years ...

The straw-covered bed lifted, dropped, lifted, dropped, with every half-turn each of the wheels made, perfectly out of synch with one another.

The Lieutenant did not notice. He lay even more deeply unconscious than before, although he seemed to breathe more regularly. His uniform was as tattered as mine. In addition to his wounded arm he was covered with sores from our long confinement. I wondered what they had done to him, what kinds of torture his unconscious body had endured. Whatever it had been, it did not show—which made me shudder with grisly speculation.

Although nominally winter, only a few hundred kilometers from the planet's northern pole, it was much warmer here, aboveground. My toes, my fingers had started aching as they thawed. I itched furiously all over, the vermin I unwillingly carried with me stirring from their torpor.

Fellow escapees.

How long it would take the Baron to catch on that his Bailiff was never coming back from this excursion, I could not guess. The hooded people seemed altogether too relaxed about it to suit me. My "Pistols, (Darrick), 8mm, Magazine, Revolving, (one each)" were Vespuccian history's most sophisticated handweapons, fabricated directly from specimens discovered aboard the abandoned colony starship. But even they, I had found, could not hope to stand up to a sufficient number of mounted men, primevally equipped but unafraid to die. If the Baron sent his minions after us, I was half-prepared to wake up in my cell again.

Or dead.

Despite such grim considerations, well-shaken by the irregular rocking of the cart, I dropped off into an uneasy sleep at least a dozen times before we made our first stop. I would wake up, startled, remember where I was, assure myself the Lieutenant was okay, watch the hooded figures plodding silently behind us ... silently behind us ... Then awake again, repeating the whole heart-stopping process until it seemed that I had been doing this same idiotic thing for all of my life.

Two of the moons were high now, painfully bright. Sca's star, its sun, is an unbearable blue-white fusion torch, the temperature, the color, of metal being welded in front of your face. Animals, humans, plant-life, all seek refuge from the full deadly light of day, some in burrows or by bundling themselves in thick, reflective, toughened leaves.

Scavian nighttime calls forth life again, illuminated much more brilliantly by the planet's satellites alone than the high-noon summer surface of my own world ever is. Birds sing. Flowers bloom. Peasants stumble from their caves or their tightly-shuttered huts to till their masters' fields. The rare desperate individual forced to travel abroad by daylight does so closely-robed—as these mysterious strangers who carried us with them—even so, at the risk of nasty burns, no matter how many layers of primitively-woven clothing he simmers and sweats in.

A thought struck through the pain-filled fog swirling inside my head: mankind could not have originated here, either! Unless it was this sun they were escaping, just as we, in our own way, had tried escaping the ungenerous star of Vespucci. I could not picture human life evolving on this planet, the place was far too inimical to it. Then again, perhaps the star itself had changed, at some time in the past. Perhaps it burned hotter now than in the early days of Scavian life.

The cart lurched to a stop.

I very nearly slid off the slick yellow straw into the dirt-track of a road, but one of the trailing hooded people steadied me. The one up in front made clucking noises at the animals, wrestling them into a right-angle turn. We trundled into a narrow cavern between two great growths of shrubbery, several meters tall. As the pulling-creatures fed themselves from bags of grain tied to their faces, the hooded ones directed their attention first to the unconscious Lieutenant, then to me.

The Lieutenant they stripped naked, efficiently, dispassionately. They turned him, carefully examining infected cuts, sores, abrasions he had acquired in our short, eventful stay on Sca. They were gentle with his deeply-injured arm, working together in a monastic silence that was perhaps appropriate, somehow generating an atmosphere of calculated haste, cutting away the crude bandage with its sickening cargo.

I had rolled over to watch them work on the Lieutenant, when a sudden lance of pain shot through my broken foot. I stared down at myself with agony-gauzed eyes as a robed figure busied itself at my trouser leg, with what was left of my stocking. The moment the mangled foot was exposed, I had to look away. It was as bad, I thought, as the Lieutenant's arm. Without question I was going to lose it, counting myself lucky if that was all that I lost. In any event, I would never again—

—abruptly, everything froze.

As one, the three hooded people turned away from the cart. Two of them crossed the narrow roadbed, crouching down behind a big clump of slowly-opening nightbrush to conceal themselves from the direction we had just come—the direction of the castle, of the Baron, of the Baron's murderous riders. The remaining figure hid itself on the near side.

They waited.

How they had detected our pursuers was a mystery. All I knew was that, eventually, there was a sound, a cascade of hollow noise quite unlike any other. It was terrifying, especially since I had heard it for the first time when our camp at the *Asperance* landing site was being overwhelmed. It was the sound of hard-shod animal-feet, pounding in their hundreds on the ground, audible through the very soil itself. Gradually there came, too, the metallic jangle of the mounted warriors the animals bore, their weapons, heir equipment, rough shouting, the peculiar hair-stirring high-pitched screaming of the riding-beasts themselves.

As the mounted warriors thundered into sight, I had a plain view abreast from the tiny clearing. Casually, the hooded people stepped into the roadway with a smooth silent motion. The mounted column braked to a dusty, disorganized stop. Archers twisted their arms over their mailed backs for arrows. Axes were loosened in their belt thongs.

Swords were drawn with a ringing whisper.

This was followed by a brief unpleasant exchange of words, an even briefer silence. Then the officer heading the column happened to glance for moment to his right, straight at me. He began to shout a command.

All at once, a broad fan of white-hot energy leaped from the burlap sleeve-ends of the robed people, showering the column, flaring into a wall of flame where it struck the mounted men. In a single horrifying instant the entire troop was engulfed, consumed where they stood, animals, men, without so much as a final scream of terror or pain.

The heat of the thing baked itself onto my face.

When the flames died out a scant few seconds later, exactly as if someone had turned off a gas valve, all that remained in the road were a few blackened, irregular smoky lumps which might once have been saddles.

Even the bones had burned.

As quickly as it had begun, it was over. The three robed figures calmly returned to the cart without looking back. They gave me water, flat-tasting, mildly bitter, drugged. I was not particularly surprised to awaken, swaying, bumping once again, with Sca's four moons about to set.

Daylight was about to arrive.

Daytime on Sca is just about twenty-five hours long, Vespuccian.

What's unusual is that so are the nighttimes.

I had been unconscious for quite some while, apparently, wrapped up in a heavy robe like those worn by these strange people who had either captured or rescued us, but with the hood thrown back on my shoulders. My right foot was bound to the knee in clean local coarse-weave concealing something else, some other dressing, comfortable, yet firm.

All right, then, what was missing? What bothered me?

Lying on that pitching wagon, I discovered with a little shock that I had forgotten completely, somewhere in the past few nightmarish weeks, what it was like not to be in constant pain, waking, sleeping, or floating dazedly suspended between the two states as I had been most of the time. It was a peculiar sensation, like being thrown out of a high window. Pain had come to be the hidden foundation of my existence.

The Lieutenant, too, wore a robe, but its long brown sleeve was slitted open to reveal the same rough burlap bandaging where the crude alien sword had nearly cut him through. He was snoring loudly. It was contagious.

What felt like only moments later, I awoke again, the moons apparently still setting. This time, something felt very wrong, deeply disorienting. Perhaps it was a remnant of the drug. I twisted around, glancing reflexively at the Lieutenant, but his color, if one could judge in this slantways light, was steadily returning to normal. He breathed easily, if a bit loudly. The hooded people marched onward, two behind us, stolidly, mutely, any faces they might have possessed hidden away deep within the shadows of their clothing. A third guided the pulling-beasts who could scarcely have been more stoically unresponsive.

Then I had it: the moons were actually rising! I had slept one entire hellish day-period through. To all appearances, our little traveling company had simply kept marching, when I had half expected we would take shelter somewhere, to wait for another night to travel. No wonder I was warm; it was residual daytime heat that I was feeling. This—

—then another thought struck me: what had fooled me was that the moons were on my left. If they were rising, then they should be on my right.

We were traveling south,

Not northward to the city of the Bishop—or the burning-stake.

Another night passed.

In one of my mother's ancient folk songs, there is a passage about some place "where the dawn comes up like thunder". On Sca, it comes up like a fission-bomb explosion. At the first excruciatingly brilliant bead on the clut-

39

tered horizon, the hooded ones halted the cart again. There had been a false down over there for some hours. It is never dark on Sca. Now the strangers stopped to drape heavy fabric over the animals, snugging string-drawn coverings down over the beasts' placid eyes.

The very air had an expectant smell to it. Insects were suddenly silent, birds nowhere to be seen, nothing rustled in the day-bleached grass.

The Lieutenant's sleep-disheveled robe was bound closely about his body now by gentle, competent hands, his limbs carefully covered, the hood slipped up around his ears. They closed the front with a draw-cord, fumbling deep inside the face for some time until they appeared satisfied. I got basically the same treatment, every square centimeter of my exposed flesh cloaked, everything accomplished in total eerie silence. Once the hood came over my head, one of the robed figures reached in, pulled a dark interior netting across my eyes, reducing my point of view to a small, increasingly brilliant circle. Soon it was like peering out of the mouth from deep within a darkened tunnel.

Creaking into motion once again, we plodded onward under the near-lethal sun, meeting no one, seeing no one, not a single living thing except for trees, bushes, other foliage, their leaves clenched tightly into little knots to resist the deadly glory overhead. Time after time, half dazed, I would move to loosen the heavy stifling robe—my body was drenched in sweat that only made the itching worse—only to have my hands pulled gently away from the fastenings. Then I would remember what the sunlight on this planet could do to human flesh.

On Sca, in addition to the gibbet, in addition to the pyre—as if the rulers here really needed another form of brutality—exposure to daylight was a third form of execution, reserved for miscreant nobility.

Within an hour, everything around us appeared to be washed out, lit only in shades of glaring white, impenetrable black, like an old, over-exposed photograph. The Lieutenant mumbled, tossed, struggled fitfully with his smothering protection. They propped him up, gave him something to drink through a small plastic tube thrust into the face of his hood. Afterward, he rested quietly. Within my own sweltering discomfort, I began to yearn for a sip from the same potion, probably the drugged one they had given me the day before, but it was never offered.

We continued southward.

Slowly, I began to have an idea about what might really be going on here. Growing up, I had been warned never to jump to a conclusion prematurely in the absence of reliable data. This is very good advice. However the human mind—mine, at least—was designed to jump reflexively, on the basis of partial information, whether its owner wants it to or not. Mine was doing that right now. Since nobody else would talk to me, I thought I would give it a chance, at least to explain.

Say that these mysterious characters were from the Church. They dressed the part. They had the Bishop's seal. I do not believe that anybody but a monk, accustomed to long years of suffering in silence, could have endured the journey thus far as these individuals had, without so much as a sneeze, a hiccup, or a lame joke. I knew less about religion than I had about the manufacturing of weapons, but I knew a little history. The Church of Vespucci, compulsory in the nation's schools, largely ignored by everyone in adulthood, was a transparent prop for the State. It had not always been so; in earlier times it had been active, powerful—divided into a half dozen schisms.

These hooded people might be renegades of a kind, representatives of some faction that wanted neither the Bishop nor the Baron to kill us. Perhaps they wanted our technology—not that they appeared to need it—perhaps they simply wanted to dispose of us themselves. This was not pleasant speculation, but it was the only conversation I had.

Whenever it got boring, I drifted off to sleep.

Exactly as I had done during church services in school.

Nighttime came at last, almost reluctantly, it seemed to me, as if the cruel blazing star overhead somehow enjoyed what it did to the land that lay beneath its hammer-blows. They pulled the cart off of the road again. The animals were fed, then watered lavishly from some nearby source. The Lieutenant was unbound, his vile wounds carefully tended to. His eyes actually opened for a moment. He looked at me with what might have been recognition, perhaps the same mild astonishment that I felt at still being alive, then the man lapsed once more into oblivion.

Gratefully, I unfastened the face-netting before they got to me, undid the hood, spread the robe wide open down the front. It was still breathtakingly hot. It would be several hours yet before the outside temperature dropped appreciably. Sca is lucky that its atmosphere is not thicker. Getting rid of all that insulation helped a good deal anyway.

I almost laughed at the memory of nearly freezing to death in a dungeon only day before yesterday. Now, sweat soaked my hair, ran into my eyes, dripped from the end of my nose. My body vibrated with the heat.

Somewhere over the past several hours, probably in my sleep, I had somehow regained a trace of self-respect, as well. Hooray for me, then. Feeling painfully distended below the beltline, I arose stiffly from the bed of straw, beginning to slip off the end of the cart with the idea of trying to limp over to one of the more inviting-looking shrubberies.

Firm hands restrained me.

"Look, friends," I told them, "I have to go to the little boys' bush!"

The two stepped back, giving me room.

I slid the rest of the way, putting weight on my bad foot. It held without much pain, but I was weak, as if my body were made of warm gelatin. Dizzy, I hobbled over to do what a man has to do, trying to ignore three pairs of unseen eyes fastened on my every move. I could not help, however, noticing how careful they were to stand upwind of me. I could not very well blame them for that, all things considered. If I could have avoided standing downwind of myself, I surely would have.

This time, the animal cart had been brought to rest close beside a shallow, sandy-bottomed stream. Attempting to reorganize the remnants of my clothing underneath the burlap robe, I began to have another idea—maybe not a very sensible one, but only the second idea I had enjoyed in a long time. I decided to savor it. However crazy it might be, it was certainly better being burned at the stake by second-string inquisitioners.

Several yards away, two of the hooded figures were at the cart, fussing with the animals. The third seemed to have been delegated to watch me, staying within a few arms' lengths. I addressed this nearest one.

"Say, are we going to be here for a while?"

There was the very slightest of nods.

"Then how about letting me wash some of the prison out of my clothes?"

No response.

"Look here, Your Reverence, I saw what you people did to a hundred armored troopers. Believe me, I am as harmless as a man can get. I am not going any place you do not want me to go. But I have been steeping in my own filth for a solid month. More, if you count ship-time. Just consider it a last request: maybe it will help your box-office at my witch-burning!"

The swaddled form turned toward its companions at the far end of the clearing. The biggest of them nodded, although it was plainly much too far away for my voice to have carried. On the other hand, they had heard the late unlamented cavalry long before I had. Maybe they were just aliens with good ears. In any case, the nod got passed along to me.

"Thanks, I will do the same for you sometime—in the next life."

I glanced around without being obvious about it, making certain of my surroundings in a manner I had been taught, laboriously drilled in, since earliest childhood. Especially, I made sure of the Lieutenant's location. I had been pleased to see my personal hooded chaperone touch reflexively at its waist at the mention of the troopers it had helped massacred.

Nice of it to show me where the real power was.

I turned, stumping with only half-feigned weariness over to the stream-bank, making an exaggerated production of my crippled weakness. Dropping my borrowed robe onto the grassy bank, I removed my poor old rip-fringed jacket, peeled off what scraps remained of my uniform shirt, unfastened my pants. Underneath, my shorts were in worse shape than the shirt. Both garments were scarcely distinguishable from the filth, the unsloughed flesh, that seemed to be all that was holding them together. They began coming apart in the blood-warm stream the instant I attempted to rinse them. I let the rotting fragments slip away in the current, started scrubbing at my body with clean yellow sand.

And thinking.

Nakedness is an odd thing. Different people certainly react to it differently. I had been acquainted with another lieutenant once, back home on Vespucci when the Navy Reserve had been "temporarily" handling routine urban police work under martial law in one of the first of the Holdout Kingdoms we had overrun. We had been idling on the stone steps of a police station, waiting out our change-of-shift, talking about burglars.

"Corporal," he had told me, if you ever hear a noise in the night, always take time to grab your pants before you grab your candlestick or crowbar or whatever to confront the thief. Otherwise, you will be at a severe psychological disadvantage. Nakedness equals helplessness. You will know it. The burglar will know it. You will lose. He will win."

Or something like that.

Later on, my CPO observed wryly that an attack by a stark-naked crowbar-wielding householder might just be a perfect burglar medicine. At the least, it would startle the dickens out of the intruder, maybe even run him off, or at the least, buy you a little extra time for maneuvering.

Personally, I had agreed with the Chief. I had always thought that that lieutenant—exactly like all lieutenants everywhere—was just a little on the prissy side. *College boys!*, as the CPO often snorted with contempt. I was willing to bet, on this oppressively-religious planet, that these hooded people (if someone had thought to ask them) would be likelier to agree with that lieutenant than with my old Chief.

That would be their mistake.

I rinsed out my pants, rinsed out my jacket, enjoying the air on my clean, freshly-abraded skin. Like the Lieutenant, I was covered head to toe with ugly lesions, but they seemed to be healing already. I thought about things some more, like what to do about him. I looked around as unobtrusively as I possibly could, considering the tactical situation.

My guard appeared to be paying more attention to its comrades than to me. Its back was turned. Peripheral vision, I knew from experience, was completely blocked by those hooded robes. I stepped carefully toward the bank, avoiding any telltale splashes or ripples, keeping an eye on the other figures at the cart, as well as the one nearest me. If I could just get hold of whatever weapon had blasted that armored column ...

I put off trying to figure out where the Holy Order of the Teeth of God might have gotten such a thing. Or plastic sipping tubes. Maybe there had been a higher civilization here once, maybe the one that had exiled my poor ancestors to Vespucci. Or, for that matter, there might even have been a previous landing from some other—no, no, stupid, concentrate!

Even in the miserable condition I was in, surely I could overpower one small monk who seemed more interested in meditating on the Great Whatever than in me. I had an advantage—I was desperate. Surely, if I stayed close, they would hesitate to incinerate one of their own, if only for the second or two I needed to puzzle out how their weapon worked.

I had to keep the Lieutenant out of the line of fire.

My foot found the stream-edge where the grassy turf hung over. I glanced down. The sodden burlap on my leg had slipped. Beneath it lay something rubbery, something almost alive in appearance, silvery-gray, like the reflective underside of Scavian leaves in the harsh four-moon light.

I lifted my bad foot carefully up onto the grass, my good foot on a large rock just above the waterline. I balanced, my weight over my good leg which felt like a spring coiled beneath me. Crouching, I breathed in slowly, silently, deeply, trusting to the lifelong martial arts training I had suffered through from gradeschool to bootcamp. I had been good at it, my only "sport", the only one they give no letter for...

I sprang! Charging across the freshly-opened grass, I threw myself into the air for a flying—then *slammed!* to the ground in shock, the breath blasting out of my lungs. I shook my battered head, looked up at my hooded guard, crouched low in a tense combat stance, hands extended, ready for more trouble any time I was foolish enough to start.

No longer hooded.

I was looking straight into the eyes—aflame with fury at the moment—of the most beautiful pale-haired blond female I had ever seen.

WINDOW ON INFINITY

"HAD ENOUGH, ASSHOLE?"

The weirdly lovely creature circled warily, stepping sideways, one small fist extended, one drawn back like a coiled spring, ready at her waist. Her hair tossed wildly as she moved, lashing at her shoulders like pale fire, enveloping her face, golden highlights, glints of copper, struggling for dominance in the moon-reflected glare of Sca's primary.

I sat on the grass in the dent I had made, keeping my mouth shut.

"Don't be too hard on him, Cilly," another of the priests shouted suddenly, throwing back his hood. "He must have thought we were going to—"

"Stow it, Coup!" she spat, not once taking her eyes off me. They were green, with undertones of that deep bluish glow you find in the heart of a nuclear reactor. "Anybody who sneaks up behind Lucille Olson-Bear better be prepared for what he gets! *And don't call me Cilly!*"

Then to me: "How about it, jerk, ready to behave?"

I blinked, trying to absorb everything that was happening around me. To my surprise, I was feeling halfway healthy. Without thinking, I braced myself to rise—when a light sweep from a small foot kicked my hand out from under me. I was down again, liking it less every minute.

The man this Lucille Olson-Bear had called "Coup" interrupted once more, coming toward us suddenly in long unmonklike strides, abandoning the bantering tone he'd started out with, for one of warning, of command.

"Quit playing with him, Lucille, that's an order." He pointed a big finger at me. "We're supposed to be on his side. He's a customer, remember?"

This "Coup" may have been the largest man I have ever seen, with a close-cropped, nearly shaven head that could have been chiseled from a mountainside, a big ugly nose, ears that would have looked like cargo hatches on anyone else. One of his hands was the size of both of mine together.

"Yeah," I added from flat on the back of my lap, some confidence beginning to return at the prospect of having such an ally to protect me from the little blond, "The customer is always right. Can I get up now?"

I had deserved that second knockdown, a white-belted boot knows better—

"Give us your parole, first!" Lucille had not relaxed from her combative stance, not by a fraction of a millimeter. She still stood over me, tense-muscled, breathing hard with meanness, rather than exertion.

I could match it if I had to: "What the hell good would that do? You do not know me. Maybe I lie a lot." I was starting to get mad, all right—about a month's worth of mad, or maybe a lifetime's. "You tell me what is going on, Goldilocks, then maybe I will give you my parole."

Perhaps. If she was lucky.

A gentle breeze stirred the trees around the clearing, lifting Lucille's hair softly. Her cheeks were flushed, tiny dampish curls stuck to the smooth curve of her forehead. The girl was absolutely beautiful.

Terrifying, but beautiful.

"Goldilocks, is it? Well, buddy-boy, what's going on is a long, complicated—"

"You are not from Sca!" I interrupted suddenly. Here accent was different, more like mine. There was not a mark or a blemish on her gorgeous face. "Nor from Vespucci, which means that there must be a third—"

"Slow down, son." Coup loomed tall as an airport con-tower over Lucille. "Let's start with polite introductions—preferably vertical ones!" He leaned down, took my hand, lifted me to my feet like a child.

"Whitey O'Thraight," I answered the big man reflexively, giving it the official pronunciation, "Armorer-Corporal, Vespuccian Naval Reserve."

All at once I realized I was standing at attention without benefit of any command to do so. "Coup" affected people that way. Also without benefit of my uniform or any other clothing at all. Oh well, the rank designations tattooed on my arms should be enough uniform for any real Vespuccian.

"There's a formula we've heard before," Lucille observed to our companion, "Name, function, rank. Buddy-boy, the only thing you left out was your serial number. Haven't been reinvented where you come from?"

She added, "—And are you ever going to get dressed?"

Lucille appealed to me. Embarrassingly enough, I was beginning to show it. Two long months in space, another month—or an eternity in prison—if that is any excuse. Hastening to the river-bank where I had left my remaining clothes, I called back over my bare shoulder, "Do you people never ask one question at a time? That *was* my serial number."

"What?" Lucille and Coup said it together.

"Whitey O'Thraight; YD-038. Five digits. Almost a real name."

It *was* something to be proud of, after all.

Lucille whitened, muttered in a grim, low voice, "Sweet Lysander Spooner's baby buggy bumpers, what kind of a sick, twisted, rotten culture—"

"Not in front of company, Cilly."

"Don't call me Cilly!"

The big man laughed hugely, patted Lucille on the head, tousling her hair. "Corporal O'Thraight, I'm Geoff Couper, and this impolitic and violent young female has already introduced herself, I believe. I take no responsibility—nor does anybody else, including herse—*Whoops!*"

As good as Lucille was, Couper was blindingly better, casually blocking her intended sidekick to the belly with an iron forearm, then seizing her extended foot. He held it for a moment as if contemplating twisting it off, then released her with a little push so suddenly that she had to hop for balance. Tension, half a second's pause, then they laughed. It was like watching a pair of giant mountain predators at play.

Self-consciously, I gathered up the tatters of my uniform, along with what little of my dignity was left. I put the pants on, then the jacket, both wet. While Couper continued sparring with Lucille on a verbal level, I hesitated with the robe they had given me, folding it over my arm. Then, changing my mind, I sought privacy behind a bush, for some reason of irrational modesty. I removed the sodden clothing again.

This was my first real chance to examine the hooded garment. The outer shell was about right for what one might laughingly call the technology of Sca, but it was a deception. I should have noticed it at once. That rough-woven fabric next to my much-abused skin would have hurt. But the robe was lined with the same odd material that was still wrapped around my game leg. Except the silvery-gray stuff was buffed up into a velvety nap, the surface noticeably warmer than the night air.

The front edge of the robe slipped between my exploring fingers. I felt a cylindrical lump sewn into the hem. Examining it, I squeezed an end. Instantly the lining cooled to the touch. Dew began to condense, running off in tiny diamond droplets. Frost started to form. It took several tries, twisting, pinching, before the lining began to dry again.

Who were these people, anyway?

"**Who are you** people, anyway?" I demanded as I emerged from the semi-privacy of my dressing shrub, uniform draped over my robe-covered arm.

"There you are, Corporal," Couper was massaging the leg of one of the draft animals, "For a moment there, I thought you'd decided to go AWOL on us. I guess we didn't finish the introductions after all, did we?"

Lucille was not in sight.

Couper turned to the last of his traveling companions, a portly, gnomish individual, robe open and hood thrown back. He had a broad face, featuring black bushy sideburns that merged at the bottom of his chin.

Couper put his big hands on our shoulders, "Corporal, say hello to Owen Rogers, our weapons tech. Rog, this is Armorer-Corporal Whitey O'Thraight."

Rogers raised a skeptical eyebrow at my title, as if he had just been introduced to a genuine flint-knapping savage. He nodded civilly enough, then went back to tinkering with one of the group's incredibly small, impressively potent handweapons. This had wiped out a hundred cavalry? I opened my mouth to speak, but Couper went right on without me.

"I suppose that I ought to add that Owen is also our expedition praxeologist," he observed, "A very busy citizen indeed, our Mr. Rogers."

"Don't call me a citizen, Coup," Rogers replied in a voice higher, more nasal, than I had expected, "I'm too tired to undertake a duel tonight."

Rogers took a stiff paper packet from his robe, extracting what appeared to be thin brown twig. With his thumb, he flicked a small mechanical firestarter, placed the twig in his mouth, lit the end, drew smoke, puffing it out again. He peered critically at a part he had removed from the weapon, polished it on his robe, peered at it again.

I asked for lack of a better topic, "What is a 'praxeologist'?" Lucille was still among the missing. "More importantly, who in Hamilton's Holy Name are you people? What kind of 'expedition' is this?"

Both men stiffened slightly, as if at something I had said.

"We might ask the same of you, buddy-boy—omitting the damned obscenity."

I whirled. Lucille was right behind me, having come from another section of the little brook. Her wet hair was plastered down, bunched together into a knot at the back of her neck. Even that way she looked good.

"There ain't no such thing as a free lunch," she said, "Tell us something we want to, we'll tell you something you want to know—maybe."

I was just about to ask what obscenity, when the Lieutenant began stirring on the cart. He groaned, babbled a few words, tried to sit up against his good arm. Couper hurried over to him, gently pushed him down again, while continuing to address me as he examined my ailing officer.

"Corporal, where we come from, there was once a primitive people who had time and distance somewhat confused in their cosmology." He glanced over at Rogers. The praxeologist/gunsmith nodded professional confirmation. "You see, they figured that, if you came from far away, then you also came from the distant past. A decidedly odd point of view—"

"Which has its merits," Rogers interrupted, looking up from his work.

"In this instance, perhaps," acknowledged Couper.

He peeled the burlap from the Lieutenant's arm. Underneath was the same rubbery gray dressing I wore. Set into the resilient substance was a small rigid panel of the same color, two centimeters by five, decorated with tiny lights, miniature switches. One by one, as Couper labored over my friend, the little lamps blinked from red to yellow to green.

He returned his attention to me: "Where you come from, Corporal, there will be legends. Stories of a beginning, or an arrival." It was a statement, not a question. He gave me an evaluative squint that seemed to broadcast, even at its friendliest, that he was not a man to lie to. "There always are. Have you ever heard of a place called 'Earth'?"

"'Earth'?" I rolled the unlikely syllable around in my mouth. "Why would anybody name their world 'dirt'? Is that where you people are from?"

Couper went back to the electronic panel on the Lieutenant's dressing. Rogers smiled, but it did not disguise a worried look that had accompanied his transformation from artisan to professional—what?

Praxeologist.

"In a manner of speaking, Whitey. Tell me, now, is this Vespucci of yours a city-state, a nation-state, a planet, a planetary system, or —"

"All four by now, most likely. What do you mean by, 'in a manner of speaking'? I would think that you are either from a planet, or you are—"

"Is that so, Corporal?" Lucille sat on the—what do you call it?—the part of the wagon that is connected with the pulling animals, helping Rogers now to tend the weapons with a sort of absent-minded contentedness that I have seen other women reserve for knitting. I looked down at the ground, suddenly self-conscious, for a variety of reasons.

"What if," she began, then stopped. "Okay, say a child had been born aboard your ship while you were in transit to this mindforsaken place?"

"He would be a Vespuccian, er ... citizen." I glanced at Rogers briefly, wondering if the word still offended him. She answered for him.

"I see. Rog, hand me that orifice gauge, will you" This thing sprayed a little light against the cavalry out there, after I stopped it down for the torture-master. Must be some play in the control ring."

She might have returned to her work without further comment, but I spoke again. "I meant to ask about that. You did not have my reasons for hating the Bailiff. I realize he was about to shout for help, but why—"

"Constitution! I'd planned to fry the scum whether he made a peep or not!" Lucille answered cheerfully, tightening some adjustment at her weapon's muzzle-end, "That's standard policy with us—for his kind."

I must have goggled.

Rogers stepped in: "Lucille's standard policy, she means. Still, there's something to be said for that, too. It's a reliable method of measuring how civilized an individual—or an entire planet—really is. Savage cultures encourage torturers. Merely barbaric ones tolerate them, sometimes torture them back in revenge. While a truly advanced culture—"

"Attempts to rehabilitate them?" I asked, beginning to feel that possibly I understood this fellow. The Vespuccian educational system warns everybody against the few like him at home, overrationalizing, sentimental—

"Just another word for torture," Rogers replied evenly, jerking my assessment of him out from under me, "Or a subtle variation on it. No, we kill them, as Lucille says, like any other vermin, swiftly and humanely. And it's also lots cheaper than rehabilitation or any other alternative."

"A plasma-gun under the armpit," Lucille added before I could readjust, "simply does wonders for the local rate of cultural advancement."

Rogers chuckled, "Not to mention underarm odor!"

Suppressing a grin of his own, Couper grunted, wrapped the burlap back around the sleeping Lieutenant's real bandage, fiddling with the temperature-adjusting lump at the edge of the unconscious officer's robe.

"Corporal, if I let this conversation go any further without ..." He stopped, started up again: "Son, bloodthirsty comments to one side, we're basically a scientific exploration team, assigned to study this garbage-dump of a planet. Other questions—and answers, do I make myself clear, Lucille?—had better wait until we get where we're going."

Lucille stuck her tongue out but remained silent.

"Which is where, scientifically speaking?" As I watched, the girl reholstered her weapon somewhere underneath her robe. Rogers began putting his gunsmithing tools away in a fabric roll, took the feed-bags from the animals' faces, tossed them into the cart beside the Lieutenant.

"That, Corporal, is a pretty good example of a question that'll have to wait," Couper replied, "Anyway, doing something is better than just being told about it. Saddle up, scientists, we've got miles to make!"

THUS IT WAS back to the same plodding journey as before.

Only this time, there were certain differences.

I sat up on the end of the wagon, having had the little control panel on my own dressing examined, the burlap cover drawn back over it. All of my lights had been green. Except for the negligible weight of the thing—the burlap on the outside weighed more—plus an occasional surprising deep healing twinge, my broken foot felt good as new. The—Earthians?—did nothing to discourage me from walking on it.

Of course they did nothing to discourage me from doing anything else, either, including lying down beneath the wheels of the moving cart, or blowing my brains out. (Although they did not offer to lend me a pistol.) The subject of parole had not arisen again. They did not seem to care, now, whether I escaped or not. They simply assumed that I would come along with them meekly. They were right about that, too: wherever they were headed had to be a lot better than where I had been.

But now, at least, they talked to me, Also to one another, joking, arguing, even answering more questions that I sneaked in from time to time, almost as if trying to catch up for their earlier stoic silence, the purpose of which remained unexplained. We ate emergency ration bars not terribly different from those I had "enjoyed" on the way from Vespucci.

Theirs actually tasted like something.

Chalk, I think.

Mostly, they asked me questions.

"We haven't any record of this planet of yours, Whitey, although the name 'Vespucci' is certainly familiar enough," Owen Rogers was explaining to me as he trudged behind the wagon with Couper. Lucille was taking her turn at guiding the animals up front. "It isn't too surprising, I suppose. This is the farthest we've reached into your particular stellar neighborhood so far. About how far is Vespucci from Sca?"

Was the query as innocent as the way it had been put? Or was there some deceit behind the fellow's open, questioning eyes? I looked over at the unconscious Lieutenant. "I am not sure I should answer that, question, sir. You must understand, I—" The memories of brutal interrogation rose unbidden inside me, choking off the rest. I guessed that now I would find out what sort of people these Earthians truly were.

"Please don't call me sir, Whitey, call me Owen. And I understand your reluctance perfectly. 'Leinster's Dilemma', we praxeologists call it. For the sake of your home planet's survival, you dare not take the chance of trusting us, no matter how you may come to feel about us personally."

Personally? I preferred to watch Lucille, her emerald eyes alert, glittering with intelligence and passion for living, her golden hair drying now, streaming behind her in the quadruple moonlight as she strode purposefully along. With that cascade of hair and the hooded robe, she looked like a ancient witch of yore, a bewitching ancient witch.

"Something like that, sir, I mean ..." Scientists were officer-caste to me. It was hard addressing him by his first name. I wondered what her body was like under that bulky— "What did you say, er, Rog?"

"I said okay, then tell me about the Navy, Whitey, your Vespuccian Navy."

"Naval Reserve. Mine—everybody's, unless they are in the Army Reserve."

Rogers' already worried-looking forehead wrinkled further. "You mean that everybody on Vespucci has to spend a certain amount of his life—and her life, too, I'll bet—we call the practice universal conscription."

"Ah," I breathed. "So you have it, too?"

"Absolutely not." He seemed offended at the idea. "We abolished it long ago, with every other form of slavery. So how old were you when—"

"I was born into the Navy," I said with what almost amounted to pride, "just like my father before me. That is why Vespucci—the nation state, I mean this time—was able to consolidate the entire planet so easily. Other countries were flabby, undisciplined. We are not."

A sour expression flashed over the praxeologist's face for just an instant, then it was carefully rearranged away, although not without some visible effort. What is it about nosy strangers that makes a person want to stand up for all of those familiar, stupid things that he hates the most? I had always despised compulsory service, military rule, as early in my life as my discovery of the carefully-censored fact that other people, other countries did things very differently. I had always wondered afterward what was so wrong with being flabby or undisciplined.

At least occasionally.

"Meaning that in your nation-state of Vespucci, the trains run on time? Well, that would certainly explain the nature of your name, anyway."

"What is so wrong about my name? I have the name that my father left to me. We were a Gold Nova family, I will have you understand. My father died earning us two extra digits posthumously at the Battle of Kahl's Pyre. You could not have a better name unless you were born into one of the old, original Command Families, like the Lieutenant, here."

Couper, lightfooted like a predator, unlike Rogers plodding beside him, spoke, his narrowed eyes never leaving their suspicious sweep of the countryside all around us. "And what would the Lieutenant's name be?"

The Lieutenant had been a half-corpse so long, I realized I had failed a little in the introduction department. "Enson Sermander, sir. He—"

Couper began laughing. "One of the upper upper crust, hunh? That's just swell! Corporal, your lieutenant here doesn't have a 'real' name, any more than you do!" He stopped for a moment as we plodded onward, wiping tears from the corners of his eyes, then had to skip to catch up with the cart. "Great Albert's ghost, the things you run into out here!"

"I do not get it, er, Coup."

Rogers maintained a hard-won neutral expression.

"Well, let's see. You're a corporal, right? And in the Navy? Son, 'ensign' is an old time military rank back where we come from—in the ocean navy. About the equivalent of a shavetail, do you savvy? Never mind. Now tell me, son, does your friend here outrank an Army captain?"

"The Army Reserve" I corrected automatically, "Yes, sir, he does." I was puzzled. What was Couper's status? "He ranks just below a Navy colonel."

"Death and taxes, what a world! Nonetheless, I'll wager you a tall stack of chips that this 'Sermander' is nothing more than a corruption of a pair of old-fashioned titles 'sir'—or maybe 'sergeant'—and 'commander'."

"I never thought about that before," I replied, not really wanting to think about it now. I wondered what all of this was leading to. If there were no such thing as a free lunch, when would they answer my questions?

Rogers leaned in, smiling his sad old praxeologist's smile again, obviously wishing that he were back repairing guns. "People seldom do, not about their own cultures. For example, at one time Coup's name was a title, too: 'barrel-maker'. And there are ancestors back in Cilly's family tree named after a huge furry animal. Tell me, Whitey, what do you know about the first settlers to reach your world, Vespucci, the Hamiltonians?"

Shock: who were these people? Who were these people? Who were these—?

"How in the Holy Name of Absolute Authority do you know about the Hamiltonians? We have only recently discovered our past ... I never mentioned ... Rog, do you know where all human beings originally came from?"

Embarrassed silence all around.

"The stork brought them!" Lucille snorted finally.

Rogers grimaced, picked up his pace, trudging forward to take his turn at coercing the animals. He never did explain what praxeology was.

In the middle of that long, bright night, we came to yet another clearing, indistinguishable from any other that we had encountered. All evening we had been paralleling the same stream I had bathed in before. Since my first sketchy wash, my skin felt loose, as if it were about to fall off in ragged sheets. I itched. It was a form of torture itself.

"Well," I said casually, presuming on my apparently cordial new acquaintance with these still mysterious individuals. "If there are no objections from anyone, I am going for another long, sandy scrub. That is, if we intend to linger here for that long." I slid easily off of the straw-slick cart-bed, marveling all over again at how good my leg felt.

Couper helped Rogers guide the wagon under a low-hanging tree. To my surprise, he began unhitching the animals. Searching through the straw, Lucille produced, unwrapped, then unfolded a small mechanical device resembling a portable electric fan. Rogers began sliding the Lieutenant down with my enlisted help. We placed the unconscious man on the ground, propped securely against a boulder. The Lieutenant mumbled, his eyelids fluttering a little, but he went directly back to sleep.

"Only one objection, son." Couper drew his plasma-gun. My heart skipped, believing that this was the end, until I saw that he was glancing warily about the clearing. He reholstered his little weapon, then began replacing the daytime shade fabric over the animal's backs. Using a section of flat harness, he slapped each of the beasts on the rump, driving them out of the clearing. "Some peasant is in for a very profitable surprise," he said. "The objection, Corporal, is that we're here."

Lucille had set the odd collapsible device on the same rock which supported the Lieutenant's slumbering head. She stared at it intently for a moment, then glanced suddenly at me. Almost as if she had been caught doing something naughty, she hastily threw a switch on its base.

"Rapunzel, Rapunzel," she intoned, "Let down your hair ... "

I took it for some kind of code, like fighter-pilots use.

" ... Rapunzel, Rapunzel, this is Lucy Bear!"

The machine spoke: "Cute, Cilly, cute. Are you people ready? We're running late." Involuntarily, my eyes lifted skyward, searching for some superadvanced starship coming to pick us up. I almost began to cry. I had believed that I was going to die on this miserable dirty planet.

Couper's crew gathered round.

"We're ready, Ev, with two guests," replied Lucille, "Non-hostile, more or less, and both severely wounded. They'll need some special arrangements."

"Congratulations to one and all, then." the little communicator replied, "and a hearty well-done. Which is how I'll have 'em waiting for you and your guests, unless they're vegetarians, or you prefer yours rare. Okay, computer's got the fix ... it shouldn't be too much longer ... "

I found myself straining to hear rocket-thunder, or maybe even the almost supersonic warbling whistle of some weirdly wonderful alien drive. Rogers folded up the communicator, tucking it under one robed arm.

"There it is!" Lucille cried. She pointed. A minuscule spark of utter brilliance, electric blue, had appeared in front of us, about a meter from my nose. It quickly widened into an azure-edged hole—right through the very air in front of us! Through it, impossibly, I could make out a complex metal-plastic interior where the light was softer.

One at a time, they stepped through the hole, avoiding the lower edge.

I helped Couper carry the Lieutenant. Behind us, the azure circle shrank again, to no more than a blinding dot, brighter than Sca's sun. It disappeared with a pop! Plastic-upholstered benches fronted a circular wall. Above them were curved windows, reaching to a domed ceiling.

Through them glowed the stars, undimmed by atmosphere.

Below, the surface, deeply curved at this altitude, of the planet Sca.

We were in orbit!

"Welcome aboard the Little Tom, my friends," said a voice I knew from Lucille's little radio transceiver. "Dinner is about to be served."

I turned—nearly fainting with surprise—to confront my first real alien: over a meter tall, man-shaped, but completely covered with fur!

LITTLE TOM

"DINNER IS ABOUT to be served."

Thus spake the alien monster.

The thing was little, man-shaped, a couple of heads shorter than I am, spindly, almost frail-appearing. It nonetheless spoke with a deep, rumble-toned authority, its humanlike voice seeming to emanate from a wristwatch-sized electronic instrument it wore strapped to its hairy wrist.

Couper bundled the Lieutenant away, mumbling something about "medical stasis", "Basset coils", other meaningless arcana. I went on staring help-lessly at the non-human pilot, while Rogers, following Lucille's example, shucked his monkish robes with every indication of relief.

Underneath, each of them was attired in a close-fitting overall of the now-familiar silvery-gray material, sleeves equipped with an inset control panel similar to those on our bandages, only larger, sporting perhaps ten times as many tiny controls. Ev (was that the alien's real name, or simply one adopted for the convenience of human tongues?) preferred the "summer issue" version: abbreviated sleeves, shortened legs, the gadget-panel situated where his belt-buckle ought to have been.

Each of my new acquaintances was armed, the ubiquitous small plasma gun slung in a highly unmilitary variety of manners: under the arm, at the waist, in separate holsters or pockets integral with the suit.

Almost immediately, Rogers provided further demonstration of the strange garment's capabilities, intently pushing sleeve-buttons as a rainbow chased itself across its surface, stabilized, settled into a garish green-yellow checkerboard. For some reason, this aesthetic outrage seemed to please him. He looked up, asked Ev, "When do we eat?"

The pilot's stubby muzzle wrinkled, displaying an intimidating collection of long yellow fangs. "Very likely never, unless you tone down that vomitous tartan of yours. In any case, we'll wait for the boss." He flipped a furry thumb in my direction: "So who's the supernumerary and who's paying for his room and board, dinner and drinks?"

I kept wishing that he would turn around so I could see whether he had a tail to go with the pelt. I wondered if there was not perhaps a hole through the seat of his pants for it, like a character in a cartoon.

It did not seem polite, however, to ask.

"Ev Williamson, captain of the *Little Tom,* meet Corporal Whitey O'Thraight, from the planet Vespucci," Lucille answered before Rogers or I could do more than open our mouths. "He's an armorer, if we're to believe him, and an accomplished musician, late of something called the 'Vespuccian Navy'." She rolled her eyes ceilingward in mocking disbelief.

"Just add him and his Lieutenant to the Survey Service tab," said Rogers. "My guess is that the investment will prove to be well worth it."

"Naval Reserve," I corrected Lucille stiffly, then, before I could stop myself, I said, "A standing army is the age-old instrument of tyranny."

"No shit, Corporal," Lucille said sarcastically. "How about a navy treading water? Two tenth-bits says you learned that in a government school, the *ultimate* instrument of tyranny." Before I could summon up a suitably acid comeback, she yawned, "Well, this seminar has been fascinating, but I'm headed for the showers. That mudball down there is more than a mere smartsuit can handle, the remotes don't tell the half of it. And you simply wouldn't believe that pile of rocks and garbage they call a castle. I'll be having unsanitary nightmares for a week!"

Without waiting for a reply from any of us, Lucille took a step backward, then seemed to melt into the floor. She vanished without a sound.

There was a chuckle from behind me. "Well don't just stand there rubbernecking, Admiral," Williamson seemed to be addressing me. "And don't take it personally, she treats everybody that way. Gonna be a fine human being someday, if we let her live. C'mon park it somewhere. Can I get you something to drink?" He turned slightly. No tail. I was disappointed.

I picked a spot on the continuous, well-upholstered sofa running completely around the room, beneath the windows. Covered in some warm, supple plastic, it was the only article of furniture in sight. It was embossed with riding-animals like those we had seen on Sca. These were carrying men in broad-brimmed, floppy hats, twirling cables of some kind above their heads as they pursued creatures not unlike those that had pulled the cart. The plastic was darkish tan in color, contrasting with the polished metal window-framing, or the deep, soft-colored carpeting that covered the entire circular floor-space from wall to wall.

"Thanks, er ... Ev. Say, would you mind my asking you a nosy question?"

On Vespucci, we are given to doing even the smallest things with elaborate ceremony, public rituals where the masses mass, officials officiate, where everybody is highly aware that something important is happening—such as laying a new section of sidewalk in a residential area, your tax dollars at work. All this chit-chat seemed incredibly, almost scandalously flippant, informal, considering what was actually transpiring.

56

It kept coming back to me, over and over again, that I was aboard an authentic alien starship, beginning a perfectly polite, extremely trivial conversation with a genuine Creature from Outer Space! (The Scavians, somehow, I did not count as aliens, perhaps because they had been human enough to torture me.) Who were these people, anyway, who appeared to take my presence among them for granted, as if they made a habit of encountering heretofore unknown human civilizations every day?

"Ask away." He turned back to face me, amusement in his big brown eyes, as a small section rose from the thickly-carpeted floor behind him, seemingly of its own accord. "Depends on how nosy you make it, Kilroy."

Kilroy?

Glasses of various types, bottles of different sizes, shapes, and colors, other universal alcoholic paraphernalia nestled in plush lined recesses in the side of the extruded column. A small deep-pile divot rested on its upper surface. The furry bartender fumbled with the drinks.

"Well ..." (I fumbled for an honorific, uncomfortably settling for a given name in its place.) "Geoffrey Couper tells me that he is from a ... from some place called 'Earth'. I am curious about where you are from, er, what sort of ... person you are." How the Hamilton do you put a question like that courteously? What species are you, sir?

He paused, what might have been a grin on his face, staring out at the stars for a moment in contemplation. "I suppose you might say I'm from Ceres—the central core city—take a right at Earth and keep going for another hundred megamiles. I'm a Chimpanzee, which means my people are originally from Africa. But then so are yours. Scotch okay, Kilroy?"

Rogers had done something to one of the windows. It had become a mirror in which he was critically examining his garish programmed suit pattern. He glared resentfully over his shoulder at Ev, then gave it up as an incomprehensible difference in tastes. He slumped down on the sofa a few feet away from me, with his arms folded across his chest.

"Chim-pan-zee," I muttered, getting a feel for the exotic word. All these planets I had never dreamed existed: Earth, Ceres, Africa. "Scotch is fine, whatever it is. I will try anything once. What is a mile?"

"Five thousand of these." Williamson held his oddly-shaped hands twenty centimeters apart. "Rocks? Water? And what're you drinking, Rog?"

What did rocks have to do with anything? More importantly, who the devil was Kilroy? The gunsmith looked up from a contemplative study of the boots built into the legs of his—what had she called it?—'smartsuit'.

"Anything that burns. I'm hitting the showers when Annie Oakley's done. She wasn't kidding about conditions planetside—no offense, Whitey."

"Listen," I protested. "It is not my planet!"

They both laughed. Aside from an only partially psychosomatic outbreak of furious itching, this second mention of showers in five minutes made me realize that: a) water falling downward; plus b) rear ends adhering to sofas by themselves; must mean that c) we were under acceleration.

A glance through the windows confirmed it spectacularly. Sca was slipping steadily away. I was not heartbroken. I looked at Williamson. The so-called pilot handed me a tiny glass of innocent-looking amber fluid.

I wondered who was driving.

I had been thinking, ever since I had understood the nature of our present location, of asking another question. I had even begun framing it several times, but backed off, partly out of fear of the likeliest answer. Now, with trepidation, I asked, "Can you people take me, take the Lieutenant, home in this machine?" The two gave each other an odd, almost embarrassed look. Williamson blinked. Rogers opened his mouth, then shut it. There followed a long awkward pause I did not much care for.

"Let's talk about that after we've had something to eat." My head jerked around: Couper rose through the carpet, stepped forward without leaving a hole behind him. His smartsuit had been adjusted to a dull, non-reflective gray with the look of a uniform about it, abetted by a rank of colorful campaign ribbons on his left breast. "How about it, Ev? The Lieutenant is tucked away safely, and Lucille's right behind me."

So she was, oozing weirdly out of the floorboards just as Couper himself had done. I remembered the drink that I had not touched, took a big gulp of the "Scotch". It *burned,* all right. I gasped, wheezed, started coughing as I watched a sizable portion of the floor in the middle of the room begin to get taller. The carpet-pile on its surface dwindled somehow until there was a smooth, table-like surface it its place. Then, up through that surface, places settings rose, complete with silverware, also substantial servings of food, steaming in their containers.

Who were these people, anyway?

More drinks were produced as the company politely waited through Rogers' turn to freshen up. It was loudly hoped that the man would reprogram his suit. We were five for dinner. If there were any more crew aboard the *Little Tom,* they failed to manifest themselves. Couper paternally headed the irregularly-shaped table, our pilot, the Cerean/African/ Chimpanzee, occupying a seat more or less at the end opposite.

They honored me with the place on Couper's right, directly across from Lucille. With a thorough shampoo, some imaginative tinkering with the push-buttons of her suit (it now had a somewhat daring neckline—from a Vespuccian point of view, I suppose—and was a medium shade of violet with a single bright diagonal band of green), she looked exactly as she had before: a soldier of whatever kind she was, who happened to be a remarkably beautiful young woman. That is, if you could overlook the pistol she carried slung cross-draw at her left hip.

The women I had known all of my life carried babies there, not guns.

Rogers sat beside me. They heaped their plates as if it had been they, not I, who had been living on Scavian largesse for several weeks; I surprised myself by not being particularly interested in food. The stars outside drifted like faraway cities glimpsed from a high-flying aircraft. What must our velocity be? This had never happened aboard the *Asperance*. I am not sure it is ever supposed to happen. "Aren't the stars supposed to bunch together, turn blue, or something?"

"Or something, right enough," laughed Williamson. "The inertialess field around this ship is thick enough to warp the skyscape out there into a full-color 3D portrait of Lysander Spooner himself, beard and all. What you're seeing isn't even a computer correction, Corporal. It's a holomural, entitled ... now, let me see, something historical, something literary, I forget. Oh yes! *Stardate*. Personally, I think it's very silly, but the passengers always seem to like it. Pass the radishes, please—*excuse me*—the little red things in that bowl there?"

I took another sip. Wine. I certainly found it more to my taste than Scotch, although, compared to potables available to the enlisted classes back home, even that was smoothly agreeable to the palate. I wondered: were we eating alien-food, or was Williamson politely dining Earthian tonight. Or was it some eclectic mixture? I had not heard of a single thing on the table before me. Each bite was a new adventure. Or a risk, as I discovered when I tried eating one of those little red things.

Embarrassing afterward, too.

There were thick, savory sections of grainy-textured protein they called "beef", rather akin, they told me, to Scavian pulling-animals, but bred by Earthians for slaughter only. Their culture had no need for beasts of burden. The most highly-valued varieties of beef came from two planets, as I understood it, one called "Alamo", one called "Newer Zealand". Nobody thought to mention what had become of Older Zealand.

I was given a creature about the size of a roof rabbit (familiar Vespuccian fare I would have welcomed as a relief from culture-shock), but shaped much differently. "Squab". Ugly name for such a delicious thing.

There was another menu item, too, served in impossibly monumental slices. lightly spiced. It was the correct pinkish-orange color, too, but ... Well, if ham does not come from a hamster, where does it come from?

Many vegetables, none recognizable, took the place of Vespuccian turnips, palmetto, or cabbage. Salt was offered in perfectly ordinary shakers. It was seemingly inseparable from some black-white speckled substance that felt worse on the tongue than Williamson's little red things. However, exactly the same flavoring, somehow formed into a thick crust that was cooked onto the beef in an oven, was absolutely wonderful.

Beside a gigantic bowl of sugar, double-fist sized, grand enough to grace an Admiral's table, rested a second, delicious powdery-brown condiment that some of my companions stirred into a hot black bitter drink, along with enough milk to dry up the community hutches for a week. "Coffee", they said of the black drink, some of it brewed with cinnamon, a spice greatly favored on a planet they called "Mexico", as was the brown powdery "chocolatl" they used with it. Couper vied with Williamson expressing delight in an even more esoteric substance, "chicory", at which Lucille wrinkled up her pretty nose, simply at the mention.

What she said of it, oddly, were things I had been thinking about her.

I AM NOT certain what I had been running on, thus far.

I had drifted through all that had happened so far rather numbly. Matter-of-factly. Now, reality was catching up, giving everything that occurred at that table a dreamlike quality. It all required effort, concentration, to focus on any given object, or any specific moment in time.

Conversation was lapping around me like that stream on Sca, words, phrases, sentences making no more sense than its babbling waters. Even my palate was overwhelmed. So many new things, so much of it. If these people were nothing else, they were fabulously rich. This holiday feast was nothing more to them, I realized somewhere along the line, than a hearty farmhand's supper. At home, for example, custom reserves milk for babies or toothless ancients. These people fairly swam in the stuff.

Having tried coffee without satisfaction, I somewhat diffidently asked them whether they might ever have heard of something called tea. They answered me with a list of thirty or forty different varieties, enumerated on a ColorCom screen that somehow oozed out of the table's surface.

"Just tea," I pleaded, beginning to shake all over.

Williamson brought me "liptons", inoffensively sweet, wonderfully aromatic. I accepted the cup from him, then found that I had drifted off somewhere again. When I went to sip at it, the tea was already cold.

I do not believe that I will even mention dessert. Back home on Vespucci, they arrest people for things like that. I am not entirely certain how real any of it—or anything else that evening—was, anyway.

Toward the end, the dishes, fine delicate porcelain embossed with the name of the little starsailing vessel we occupied, mysteriously cleared themselves away somehow, along with the silver, when I was not looking.

Geoffrey Couper, still resplendent in his quasimilitary attire, poured himself another glass of wine. Others had been passed around without my having noticed. Following Rogers' earlier example, he chose a small white paper tube from a container on the table, placed it in his mouth, set the free end afire, drawing smoke from it with obvious relish. The container was passed. Lucille, with the praxeologist—his suit still garish plaid, his bushy hair and beard parted formally down the middle—joined their commander in this weird ritual. Not all of the little paper tubes were white, nor of quite the same size or shape. Some of the fumes smelled roasty, nutlike, some of it grassy-sweet.

"Now, son," Couper began once these postprandial ceremonies had been attended to. He exhaled smoke. "You have a lot of questions to ask us. I know you're tired, but—well, we have a lot of questions, too."

"Yeah," Lucille chimed in. "Like what in Hamilton's Hades were you and your people doing on that medieval scumball in the first place?" She flicked a cylinder of accumulated ash from the end of her burning tube into a small glass dish. Hers was one of the sweet-smelling variety.

I blinked. "Why, I had been planning to ask you exactly the same thing!"

She inhaled another lungful, trying, for some peculiar reason, to speak while holding her breath. "Yeah, Corporal-baby, but we asked first!"

Couper gave her a low, fatherly growl of admonition, then grinned, letting it fade. "Lucille is right, I'm afraid. If you don't mind, son."

So, to the faint but welcome accompaniment of unfamiliar recorded music drifting down from somewhere in the area of the ceiling, I told them all about the voyage of the *Asperance,* the shocking massacre at its end, how we wound up in that cesspool of a dungeon where they had found us, the mission's only survivors. It did not take very long. I did not tell them about Eleva. To my somewhat guilty astonishment, it was the first time I had thought of the Lieutenant in a couple of hours.

I caught a riffle of melody from the overhead speakers that might have been composed especially for the mandolar. Suddenly I realized that I had not heard music of any kind, aside from the inside of my own head, or my demented humming in the dungeons, for what seemed an eternity.

Couper sipped at his wine contemplatively. It was a thick, sticky liquid whose flavor seemed to crawl all over the tongue like lukewarm fire. "What surprises me is that they let you live, after what you did to—"

"But we never did anything to them! I told you, we all tried to avoid—!"

"What our peerless leader means, Whitey," Rogers laughed, "is that you— second person non-plural you—singlehandedly disposed of ... what did it come to in the end, Boss? You did the field-interviews for me."

Couper shook his head with what appeared to be rueful admiration. "Well, it all depends on which village the information came from. I make it seventeen heavily-armored knights, with weapons not terribly more primitive than your own, Corporal O'Thraight. Yes, no matter what you or those Scavians may think, not terribly more primitive at all. Understand that administering steel by hand, or lead by means of expanding chemical gases, largely comes down to a matter of aesthetic preference."

He took—a sip?—from his smoking-tube, tapped ashes off of its end into Lucille's bowl. "You're something of a legend back there already, son, one I fear is going to prove troublesome for us in the future."

There was a lapse in the conversation that lasted for several heartbeats.

"How many projectiles," asked Rogers, demonstrating professional interest at last, "do those quasi-rotary slug-chuckers of yours carry, anyway?"

I felt the temperature rising in my cheeks. "Er, fifteen apiece, in the magazine," I mumbled, keeping my eyes down on the tabletop. "Seventeen—I suppose that I could have used them to better effect. I had two of the weapons, all I could manage to get loaded before we were attacked. If only I had been more conscientious when we first landed, my people might have ..." I found it hard to choke back the tears that threatened to humiliate me even further in front of these strangers.

Couper leaned over to place a big hand on my shoulder. "Those fancy-britches with their boughten commissions wouldn't likely have been much help, even if you'd loaded a hundred weapons for them, son. You still don't realize, do you? Great Albert's ghost, boy, half the reason those Scavians tortured you was simply to reassure themselves that you were really human!" He crushed his smoking-tube out in the ash-bowl. "You'll be a legend all over again when we get back to the ship!"

"He's right," the Chimpanzee agreed. "Find yourself the right pubcaster, and you won't have to worry about no free lunches for decades!"

"Get back?" I looked all around me: this wonderful spacecraft of theirs was at least twice the size of the late *Asperance*. All I had seen so far was the upstairs. "You are trying to tell me that this is not—"

"This is *Little Tom*, son, a private auxiliary with some amazing capabilities, but an auxiliary nevertheless. Begging your pardon, Captain."

The furry alien lifted a negligent paw. "A small thing but mine own, as I told a young female acquaintance recently. Everyone to his own vine and fig tree, whatever the crap that's supposed to mean." He fumbled with the container on the table, extracted a very large green burning tube. The smell, different from Couper's or Lucille's, was horrible.

"But how—" I began.

"Wait and see," Couper answered, not answering anything at all. "As to what we were doing on Sca," he looked around the table, they looked back at him. "In a manner of speaking we were—still are, for all that—conducting a preliminary survey of the planet and its many and—"

"—and not-very-diverse—"

"Thank you, Lucille, when I desire your help, I'll lift up your rock and ask for it. Yes, its not-very-diverse cultures." As if his own smoke had not been enough pollution in his lungs, he took the smaller tube from Lucille's fingers, drew from it, closed his eyes, held it for a while before expelling it. "Not very damned diverse at all!"

I thought about that guilty-looking glance they had all shared. "Preliminary survey? Preliminary to what? With exactly what object in mind?"

Rogers the praxeologist spoke: "Need there be any particular purpose for scientific inquiry? Isn't knowledge valuable in and of itself?" He ground his own burning-tube out, then immediately lit another.

"So sayeth the guy who doesn't pay the bills!" Lucille retorted, "We're free-roving traders, Corporal-darlin', privateers desperately looking for a fast ounce any way we can get it, by hook or by ..." She patted the weapon on her hip suggestively. "You know you can get more with a smile—and a plasma gun—than you can with just a smile."

"Arrh!" agreed the gunsmith in a funny croaking voice. "An' Oi'm the Jolly Rogers hisself!" He covered one eye, rolled the other one and leered obscenely, folding his free hand into a big fist, except for the middle finger which he crooked, clawing half-blindly at the girl.

She giggled, looked suddenly startled, then peered suspiciously at the tube between her fingers. It was the first time I ever saw her relax.

Williamson shook his head. "Oh, for Spooner's sake, Coup, set the poor devil straight before these two have him thinking that we're going to make him walk the plank. You know he isn't a bad guy for a Kilroy."

Most of what he said was utterly meaningless. Kilroy again. I had to struggle with that drowsy, drifting feeling stealing back over me. In addition, I was becoming increasingly self-conscious about the fact that I was the only one here who had not bathed recently. I did not count the sketchy washup in the creek. What was so bad about walking on a plank, anyway? If Lucille was trying to make me think that they were all cutthroats of some kind, the fact that they had gone out of their way to rescue me—also the Lieutenant—spoiled her story a little.

"They manufacture a wine on Sca," Couper declaimed with sudden incongruity, holding his glass to the light, "remarkably disgusting in every respect, except that it possesses peculiarly potent antibiotic properties against a disease that dolphins frequently contract in Europa."

I could see that. I could see anything. "What is a dolphin?"

This time they all blinked somewhat foolishly at one another. One of them muttered something about "impossible things before breakfast". This conversation seemed to be making less and less sense to me all the time. I began to suspect it was the wine. Or possibly the burning-tubes.

"Another kind of non-human intelligence," Rogers supplied finally, giving Williamson a courteous nod. "Good friends of ours, for a long time."

"Yeah," said Lucille, "some of my best friends are dolphins." From a well-hidden pocket, she took what looked like a small flat stone, inserted the last centimeters of her smoking-tube, drew heavily on the other end. There was a sharp *crack!*, sparks flew from the object.

"Seed," everybody said at once.

"Bet you think I did that on porpoise," she winked.

Music continued playing. Unable to think of anything better to say, I asked, "This planet the dolphins are from, this 'Europa' you mentioned ...?"

Couper ignored me: "The point, son, is that we explore sinkholes like Sca, hoping to discover new materials, new ideas, manufactured goods occasionally. We heard about you two—the 'sky demons'—in marketplaces for two hundred miles' radius around that pile of dung and incompetently-chipped rock where they were keeping you. At first we thought you might be one of our own we'd somehow lost track of. There are quite a few of us out here. Later, when it developed that you couldn't be, it was even more important to pull you out in one piece."

"Why was that?" I asked.

More embarrassed silence, then: "Because," said Rogers, assuming his grim professional expression (I liked him better as a gunsmith), "yours is the first independent star-traveling civilization we've ever discovered."

"Human." Williamson rose, excusing himself to attend to some technical matter. He took three paces, sank right through the floor, disappearing.

"The first independent human star-traveling civilization?" I asked.

None of them seemed very delighted at the prospect. Watching the pseudostars drift by "outside", gave me something else to ask about. Now seemed as good a time as any. Or bad. "Speaking of star-traveling, I ... I mean I have sort of been wondering what your plans are. You see ..."

"He wants to go home, Coup," Rogers interrupted, "A perfectly natural, easily-understood request. We should have talked this over earlier."

"I told you—" Lucille began.

Coup stopped her. "Son, I admit I've been putting this moment off for as long as I could manage. There are reasons, all of them highly sensible although I don't expect you to see it that way, why we can't just—"

"Orders." Lucille stated suddenly, flatly.

"Hunh?" responded the older man, a whole flock of uncomprehending wrinkles furrowing the space between his eyebrows. She had surprised him.

"The Corporal is a soldier, Coup—or a sailor. I'm not sure I've gotten that part quite straight yet. Anyway, orders are something he understands."

She turned to me, addressing me as a human being for the first time. "Whitey, we're expected at a Rendezvous. We just can't take any unexpected sidetrips until we report in." She paused, looking from me to Couper in an expectant manner. "I don't think it'll hurt anything to tell you this much about it: the discovery of another culture with faster-than-light capabilities was a severe shock to us all. And it's a matter of very serious concern to us. Policy has to be generated, dig?"

I nodded, all too familiar with being on the receiving end of "policy". "So what does that make me, then, a prisoner-of-war or something?"

"Hardly!" Lucille guffawed. It was a startling thing to witness. "Coup here is right: what it makes you is a celebrity. Think you can stand that for a while? Cocktail parties, media interviews, virtual book signings, endorsing royalty checks, empty-headed news-sluts pretending to hang on your every word, then distorting them beyond all recognition?"

Couper said, "I'm not sure I could."

"Well I might just give it a try," offered Rogers. "For the heck of it, I mean." He winked broadly at the young woman sitting across from him—who returned a suspicious stare—licking his lips. "Groupies."

"Groupies?" I echoed the alien-sounding word, perplexed all over again. Groupies. Groupies. Sounded dangerous. What planet were they from?

"It's nothing more than a disgusting expression that we stumbled over in a disgusting place." Lucille wrinkled her nose. "The 'United States of America'. Could be the most alien civilization that we've ever—"

"Excuse us, folks, is it too late to set another place?"

Everyone at the table turned to watch the furry Chimpanzee pilot, rising slowly, straight through the wall-to-wall carpeting. Beside him, grinning in apparent perfect health, stood my Lieutenant, Enson Sermander.

RENDEZVOUS IN SPACE

"I AM SOMEWHAT fatigued, Corporal, since you aren't kind enough to inquire."

The Lieutenant was dressed from collar to shoe-soles after the fashion of our hosts (or captors) except that his wounded arm was sealed inside the silvery-gray suit, folded across his chest. "Nor shall I be using this—" he indicated the missing sleeve, "—for quite some time, I gather. Aside from that, well, I consider the alternative."

His skin-tone was good. His movements seemed powerful. There was a healthy sparkle in his eyes—especially once he caught sight of Lucille.

"Well, well! Pardon me, Corporal—you were through with that chair, anyway, were you not? What have we here, gentlemen, a veritable cactus-blossom among the thorns?" Rosy fingers seemed to brush along Lucille's white, graceful neck, well up into her cheeks. She stared down with apparent shyness at the table-top, nervously fingering a napkin.

Me, I must have eaten too much at dinner. I suddenly wanted to regurgitate.

"More likely just another thorn, Lieutenant," answered Geoffrey Couper before the girl could speak. "A more decorative one than most, admittedly. Sir, allow me to introduce my colleagues. Owen Rogers; I believe that your term is 'armorer', also Sc.D., Praxeology, Mekstrom University Limited, Titan—one of the habitable moons in our system. Captain Williamson you've met. I'm Geoff Couper, Mission Supervisor. This is Lucille Olson-Bear, Security and Defense—our principal thorn, in fact. And now I think that's quite enough of titles for the moment."

The Lieutenant bowed low over the table, scooped up Lucille's hand, kissed it as he clicked his heels. I'd seen him do this before, back home. "Miss Olson-Bear, gentlemen. You have my deepest gratitude. My life is indeed yours, for you have preserved it in the face of the bleakest—"

"Thank the Corporal, here," interrupted Rogers, "He kept you in one piece, in the face of the bleakest, long enough for us to find you."

"Why, yes, er ... well done, Corporal. It shall be so entered in my report when we return to Vespucci." He straightened, turned to face Couper with a shrewd expression. "We are returning to Vespucci, are we not?"

Suddenly I could understand all of the previous embarrassed pauses I had encountered. Nor was there anything I wanted to say, about this, either.

"Um, directly, Lieutenant," Couper answered.

"Make that, um, indirectly," Lucille corrected, "Lieutenant, we were just explaining to your Corporal, here, that our standing orders call for checking in with our primary vessel now. Not until that's accomplished ..."

He spread the palm of his good hand outward. "Say no more, my dear girl, you have my complete understanding—my thoroughgoing sympathy. I, too, have impatient superiors to whom I must deliver an account of myself and my regrettably diminished command. I would impose that much further upon your gracious hospitality. Have you a microwave capable of—"

"Microwave?" Lucille was plainly puzzled.

"Microwave!" Couper was amused.

"Not even for cooking," answered Williamson. "And even then, it wouldn't—"

"The man is talking about radio," said Rogers. "Electromagnetic spectrum. Lieutenant, I'm sorry to tell you it would take—what, Ev?"

Williamson rolled his eyes back in thought. His muzzle twitched slightly. "*Little Tom* tells me we've gone four-point-two-three light years."

"It would take four-point-two-three years for an electromagnetic message to reach Sca," Rogers explained. "Let alone Vespucci, even if we happened to have the equipment, which we don't—you'd have to look in some museum somewhere. And even if—well, your Corporal's been pretty closed-mouthed about telling us the location of your planet."

"Four ... light years!" I couldn't help myself, It took superhuman effort not to scream it back at him. "You say we have come that far in only—"

"Steady on, son," said Couper. "We don't communicate by radio wave any more, Lieutenant. And, without belittling any of its considerable accomplishments, I rather doubt that your civilization could make much sense of the paratronic transmissions we might send them instead. Even so, the EM spectrum transmission-reception lag would be lessened by a factor of only ... let's see: just a whisker under e squared times pi ..."

"Sixty days," supplied Williamson, who seemed to be an instant mental calculator, in addition to being the underworked pilot of this machine. "It would take two months, and, long before then, we'll be at the Rendezvous. Face it: there's nothing faster in the known universe for transportation or communication, than a spaceship like *Little Tom*."

"**Look,**" said **Rogers,** in the impatient tone of a someone explaining ColorCom to a blind man. "I've keyed the colors so you'll understand, okay?"

"Okay nothing," I objected. It was getting harder to concentrate by the minute. "What do colors have to do with sinking through the floor?"

Dinner was long over. Couper, Williamson, the Lieutenant were all conferring. Lucille had gone below, which is where I would be going if I could ever get the hang of it. I, alone among the company, was still unshowered, unshaven, extremely unslept. That fact was being brought home to me now as I struggled to comprehend what my fellow armorer was "explaining".

"Look, Whitey, this little ship isn't keyed to your ... call it brainwaves, I guess you'd say. There's no point in correcting that now, since we'll be at Rendezvous pretty soon. So I've adjusted this section of the floor—right over your quarters—to let you through."

I puzzled over this for a moment. "Very thoughtful, of you or the ship. What keeps me from breaking both ankles when I hit the floor below?"

He snorted, "That's what I'm trying to explain, Corporal! I've marked the section yellow. The deck below is blue. You step onto the yellow section, the ship senses that it's you—never mind how it knows ..."

"Great. Then what?"

He rubbed his eyes with one hand. "You saw how the dinner-table came up? The molecules that the floor's composed of simply expanded, readjusting themselves to take up a little more room, and *viola*, a table!"

"That's *voila*," Williamson commented from across the room. The alien had incredibly sharp hearing, I thought to myself. "No strings attached."

"Whatever," Rogers replied. "Where was I? Step on the yellow part, a piece of floor belowdecks expands until it reaches the ceiling. Its blue molecules then interlace with these yellow ones, and you get green!"

"I am getting that way already." I sighed, shaking my head. "You're telling me that the molecules of the two floors actually intermingle?"

"There isn't a cubic inch of this whole ship that isn't smart that way. Then the yellow upper floor molecules get out of your way, while the blue lower floor molecules contract again, lowering you gently to the—"

"Hold it! That may be perfectly all right for carpet molecules, Rog, I don't know. But I am not mingling my personal molecules with any—"

"Of course not! No mingling. They get completely out of your way, leaving a perfect Whitey-shaped hole—actually it's the shape of your latitudinal cross-section—as you sink sedately through the floor."

I looked at the yellow pentagon he had adjusted for me, observing that his taste in interior decor matched his sartorial taste. The rest of the carpeting up here was maroon. "Sorry, Rog, it just seems like magic ..."

"Right," he replied smugly, "Any sufficiently advanced technology will—"

"Resemble advanced technology," Couper finished for my mentor as he approached us, "And nothing more. That theory you're quoting, Rog, is a crock. Once a civilization gets the idea of technology, per se, into its collective head, it eventually stops believing in magic at all."

Rogers protested. "But Whitey just stated—"

"I heard him. He's obviously tired and probably didn't mean it literally."

I opened my mouth to agree with him—also to comment that his hearing was fully as acute as that of the furry pilot—but yawned, instead.

"All this palaver is keeping him from a hot shower and a soft bed."

I shut my mouth, stepped onto the pentagon, not caring much what happened.

"Sweet dreams, Whitey," Rogers told me as I began to sink through the floor, "And remember, whatever else you do down there, don't push the button in the john marked 'TR'. Hey, cut it out, Coup, I was only kidd—!"

THE CEILING CLOSED neatly over my head, depriving me of further byplay between the two. I found myself descending into a small, tidy compartment with a pair of single beds. It connected with a compact head.

Shaking off my robe, I peeked at the shower stall, expecting more of Rogers' "magic". I was not disappointed. The curtain consisted of a rigid but elastic membrane, perfectly transparent, with no opening visible. On a hunch, I pushed a hand against it. The hand went through exactly as I had expected, immediately followed by the rest of me. The membrane then changed from transparent to translucent, offering me privacy.

There were no faucets. Instead, a colored band, ranging gradually from blue to red, crossed one wall at chest level. I touched it in the middle. Water began to flow, by which I mean *flow*. The stinging ultrasonically-propelled mist I was used to at home was replaced here with a torrent that nearly knocked me off my feet. I had touched the broad colored band at its top edge—no savage Whitey; Couper was right about technology—now I placed a finger nearer the bottom; the pressure slackened. I ran the finger up again, enjoying a Vespuccian-bred reflexive guilty feeling as liter upon liter cascaded all around me.

Soap: there did not seem to be any. I glanced around the stall. Not so much as a tray. At least I could scrub as well as possible, as I had in the stream, learn the secret of the missing soap tomorrow. Finishing up, I noticed that soap was not the only amenity lacking. There had not been any towels hanging outside in the bathroom, I was certain now. Nor any in the stall (they would be soaked through in any event). Possibly there was a cabinet outside. I stepped through the curtain—

—coming out dry as the sands of my native planet!

Clean, as well. I recalled suddenly how my hair had squeaked in the shower, how the flaking film of unsloughed skin had been blessedly absent. The shower was a stall, all right. Purely for recreation or relaxing purposes, I guessed. It was the transparent membrane-curtain that—literally—did all the dirty work. I stepped back into the bedroom, pondering Couper's argument with Rogers about technology and magic, wondering for just a moment after all, who had really been correct.

Another notion stopped me. According to my new acquaintances, *Little Tom* was only an auxiliary ship. Wait until we reached the other—

Surprise! On the right-hand bed, rolled up in their Vespuccian-issue fabric belt, lay a pair of 8 millimeter Darrick pistols. My pair, it appeared, in their regulation holsters. Unsnapping the flap of one holster—they were adjustable for wearing on the right or left side—I checked the grip. I was empty. Well, either Earthian technology had its limits, or they wanted me to have my weapons, but did not trust me with live ammunition. Nevertheless, it was good to have these pistols back. I wondered how they had been retrieved. I would hate to be the Scavian nobleman holding them if Lucille did the retrieving.

Turning, I noticed a bare spot in the blue carpet. The robe I had discarded there was gone. Working my way around the walls, pushing my hand against them as I had done the shower curtain, I finally found a closet whose "door" vanished upon penetration. Sure enough, there was the robe, hanging right beside the remnants of my uniform—also that of the Lieutenant. Do not ask me how the robe had gotten into the closet.

Magic?

Really good room service?

I was not fooled. All of this was great fun, it was interesting, but Couper had been correct. Magic it was not. I folded down the soft, clean blanket, climbed into bed, cradling the double pistol belt in my arms. The lights began dimming on their own. I was not afraid, not of the darkness nor of the power these people possessed. I simply envied them their wealth, their knowledge, hoping hard that someday, my own people ...

My last conscious thought: "There ain't no such thing as a free lunch".

I AWOKE FROM a dreamless sleep, better rested than I had felt in months. Beside me, in the other bed, Lieutenant Sermander lay snoring, still wearing what Lucille had called a "smart suit". Rogers had used a similar expression, attempting to explain the weirdly cooperative carpet.

Untangling myself from the bedclothes, I moved quietly out of long habit, so as not to disturb the Lieutenant, stumbled into the bathroom to discover no particularly magical surprises where the rest of the plumbing was concerned, except that all of it seemed to use a lot of water.

I decided to test that gimmicky shower curtain again.

Into the stall, out again.

I definitely felt different. Clean, not particularly refreshed. I think a person needs hot running water to wake him up, to shake him out—not to mention doing something about what a good night's sleep does to his hair. I fiddled around some more with that red-blue shower control, deciding to ask about toothbrushes later. Yes, if you happen to be morbidly curious, there was also a shower curtain-type membrane stretched across the toilet seat. These people may have spent water like it was going out of style, but they certainly did not waste paper.

In the closet hung my tattered uniform, the burlap-veneered robe I was thoroughly tired of. Also what looked like a brand new smartsuit. With widened eyes I took it off its hanger (still wondering how the robe had hung itself up the night before), began slipping my legs into the—

"Don't try that without some help the first time, Whitey, you may hurt yourself." I jumped at the voice from above me. Owen Rogers' head protruded down through the ceiling like some ghastly trophy. He caught the startled look in my eyes, rolled his own backward until only the whites were visible, let his tongue hang out one corner of his mouth. "Hold on," he laughed, finally breaking the pose, "I'll give you a hand."

He withdrew his head; there was a pause while a section of the bedroom floor grew up to meet him, bright colors flashing on its sides to warn anyone who might have stepped on it by accident. Then his feet appeared, his horribly-patterned suit-legs (this morning it was purple locked in mortal conflict with two shades of orange), then the rest of him. I signaled for him to be quiet on account of the sleeping Lieutenant.

"Constitution, Whitey," Rogers answered in a voice only slightly quieter than an orbital shuttle taking off, "I was supposed to wake him up, too. Say, if you fit the catheters in that way, you'll wake him up with your own screaming." He was referring to certain of the suit's inner arrangements. Very personal. Very embarrassing. Brushing my clumsy hands aside, he did what had to be done efficiently, without fuss.

"Now at least you'll know whether you're coming or going, Whitey. Just pass your hand along the diagonal seam, that's right, hip to shoulder. You're all done—except for selecting some real snazzy pattern."

"I believe that I will pass, Rog, thank you." I had noticed that the others preferred solid colors, or simply the natural silvery-gray hue of smartsuit material. Then, catching my old bedraggled Navy uniform in the corner of one eye, I asked him, "What could you do with that?"

"Fascist-modern," he murmured appraisingly, then imitated Lucille by wrinkling his nose. "Oh well, you fish on your side, I'll fish on my side, and nobody fishes in the middle. Is the color right, or has it faded? I assume that sleeve originally ended in a cuff, like the other one ..." Pressing buttons on my arm, he eventually created a very impressive facsimile of my Navy Reserve

71

uniform, complete to the chevrons. Campaign pips decorated one counterfeit breast pocket. On the "collar" were displayed the hard-won crossed pistols of a field armorer.

"Great," said Rogers, standing back for a look, "Sure you won't have any jackboots? Sam Browne belt? We're having a special on both of them this week. How about your hoglegs? I cleaned 'em up the best I could. Sorry there isn't any ammo. The Dardick was a fine old design, and—oops! Forget I let that slip, Whitey, have mercy on a fellow peon."

I looked at the man closely, then turned, retrieved my pistols from the bed, belted them around my waist, unaccustomed to the extra weight on the left side. "What are you talking about, Rog, 'a fine old design'? Where in Hamilton's name do you know Darricks from?" About a hundred extremely odd notions were flitting through my mind at once. Now I knew what Williamson had meant by "impossible things before breakfast".

"Honest, Whitey, I can't tell you—why, good morning, Lieutenant Sermander! Glad to see that you slept well. We're docking in about ninety minutes. I'm here to invite you to breakfast." News to me, too. Sermander blinked stupidly, hoisted himself upright, blinked stupidly again.

The Lieutenant said, "I shall have rock-lizard eggs on toast, four strips of crisply-grilled hamster, plenty of tea. You need not bother setting a place for me. My man, here, will serve me in my quarters." Looking first up then down, his eyes settled on the pistol belt. "We shall be discussing those, later." He stretched, threw his legs over the edge of the bed, arose, waddled off to the bathroom. Behind him, the door dwindled, leaving a blank wall. I had not known it did that.

Rogers appeared to be in deep thought. Then he, too, blinked at me, focusing again. "Lieutenant's an uppity son-of-a-bureaucrat, isn't he?"

Before I could reply, the carpet started doing odd things again. Couper was descending into our midst. The little cabin was getting crowded. "You fellows go on upstairs. Get yourselves something to eat," he suggested. "You've got a big day ahead of you, Whitey. I'll stay behind and straighten Lieutenant Sermander out. That arm of his needs looking at, anyway. And Whitey? Nobody gets waited on around here, especially by the individual who saved his life. How's that leg?"

"I had completely forgotten about it, sir."

"Then git—and don't call me sir, I work for a living!"

We got, me wondering what it was like to live in a culture where nobody gets waited on. How he had known to come straighten out the Lieutenant? Who were these people, anyway?

STRANGE FOOD, STRANGER drink, strangest conversation. Only I was awake, now, fully rested. This morning Lucille smoked what everybody else did. Nobody said a word about my Darricks. I felt conspicuous, although the others were all carrying weapons of one kind or another. Couper came upstairs with the Lieutenant twenty minutes later. My fellow Vespuccian was red in the face, not looking pleased. He changed all that for Lucille's sake, however. He was even mildly civil with me.

"You actually piloted that flimsy box-kite across two light years? Nine weeks—how horrible!" Lucille never looked at me, but smiled, flirting with the Lieutenant, fascinated by everything he had to say. The man glanced my direction before answering, warning written on his face.

"We had a good computer system, my dear, not like in the bad old days, when it was seat-of-the-pants flying against a grimly determined foe."

"You're too modest. I've never known a real aeroplane fighter before!"

You still do not, I found myself thinking, then shut it off: It is an officer's world. There is nothing any NCO can do about it. I was mentally debating whether to be annoyed—the Lieutenant had adjusted his suit to duplicate his own, rather grander, Navy uniform—when Williamson stopped in the middle of an unlikely fable he had resumed about an old lady blowing up an entire planet to make a philosophical point.

"Ammonium nitrate, she told me, soaked down with Number Three diesel fuel—although where she got it in the Asteroid Belt—excuse me a moment, will you?" He generated an expression of mild concentration.

Suddenly, the computer-generated mural wrapped around the room faded, replaced by a more accurate frozen starscape in the midst of which blinked a solitary light. The brilliant point seemed to explode into a solid object, a blazing upper slice of a hemisphere, hanging in the void before us, swelling to occupy our entire field of vision. It seemed to rotate as we swung around to approach it from its flat underside.

There was nothing to convey any sense of scale, but the thing was possibly six or eight times larger than the *Asperance*, at least three times greater in diameter than *Little Tom*. Its curved upper surface was featureless, seemingly lit from within by an eerie, grainy scintillation. Underneath, near an edge, a bowl-shaped opening yawned, one of seven: six deep cavities around a seventh in the center. Each, save the empty one we closed on, was neatly filled with a smaller craft, miniatures of the giant ship, identical to the *Little Tom*. The seams were nearly invisible—our pilot outlined them for us on the viewscreen—the lower contours of the small ships matched that of the mother vessel. Their colors matched, too, a brilliant sparkly blue-white.

"Last chick home to the nest, as usual!" Williamson relaxed again as the great form closed over us. The original starry screen display was restored. He pointed a broad-nailed finger ceilingward. "In case you two Vespuccian gentlemen are wondering, that baby up there is *big*. Eight hundred sixty-nine Jeffersonian metric feet across. Dunno what that would be by your reckoning." He rose. "Well, it's been a barrel. Thanks for traveling *Little Tom*. If something profitable ever comes from that benighted dustball—which I misdoubt sincerely—kindly let me know. Whatever it turns out to be, I've got three percent."

General laughter around the table.

I got up, started belowdecks to collect my few belongings. Behind me, despite the finality of his words, the pilot lingered, perched on a corner of the table as the conversation continued. "You can be sure, Ev," Rogers told him, "that whatever policy is ultimately decided on, with regard to this discovery, we'll be doing the Confederacy—the entire galaxy, for that matter—a real favor. Besides, there's bound to be something—organics, minerals, handicrafts—that we can use."

Buried to my shoulders in the floor, I could not see the pilot, but I heard his scorn-laden reply. "Easy to say! Since when were you an expert on planetary exploitation or sterilization? Rog, I've seen dry planets before. Don't con a starship, I won't run herd on your pet savages!"

Savages?

My head sank below the carpet, while my heart was sinking deeper than the dungeon on Sca. So we Vespuccians were savages, were we? No wonder, then, this run-around about going home. I gathered my uniform, left the robe behind, rode the pillar of extruded floor back upstairs, knowing I would have to discuss this with the Lieutenant as soon as possible.

The breakfast table had been put away when I returned. Couper, Lucille, their "pet savage" expert, all stood together in the center of the room, a few small items of hand luggage scattered about their feet. The Lieutenant, chatting with the girl, turned to me as I approached.

"Ah, Corporal O'Thraight," he proclaimed. "Enough is enough. It is time to hand those play-toys over. I am the ranking survivor, after all."

"Sir?" I knew perfectly well what he was talking about, but I intended making him come out with it plainly, in the hearing of the others.

"The sidearms, Corporal, give them to me." I sighed, draped my tattered uniform over a travel case, reached for the quick-lock of the belt.

Couper stepped between us.

"Wait just a second, son. Lieutenant, we've got a long-standing tradition where I come from. We don't permit self-styled authorities to badger a man out of his rights." I would not have liked being on the receiving-end of that scowl. The Lieutenant, in turn, looked confused.

"Permit?" he demanded stiffly. "Rights have nothing to do with it at all, sir. Those pistols were issued by a state of which I am the highest-ranking representative present. O'Thraight, give me that belt now!"

I reached for the buckle once again. "As you were, son." Couper ordered. I sighed, dropping my hands. "Lieutenant Sermander, you're in my—what's the word, Rog?—jurisdiction, now. Whitey earned those rotary popguns preserving your self-important carcass. Moreover, no state has the right to issue weapons or reclaim them—no, nor any rights at all, even to exist! This argument's over, unless you want everyone you meet from now on to know the true color of Vespuccian gratitude."

The Lieutenant's face reddened, veins stood out on his forehead, he trembled a little. Then, abruptly, he relaxed with a big shrug. I unclipped the left-hand scabbard from its eyelets on the pistol belt, extended the holstered side-arm. "Take this one, sir, that way we will both—"

KLANGKLANGKLANGKLANGKLANG!!!!!

Abruptly, a blood-curdling alarm filled the ship. The Lieutenant froze in place. I looked around, heart racing, wondering what it all meant. The Earthians each stood at alert attention, their eyes on Ev Williamson.

That individual, his own eyes closed momentarily, his head cocked as if listening to something, stood rigidly for a few seconds. When he opened his eyes, he was almost a different person. His deep voice rumbled:

"Rendezvous is aborted. Take your places.

"We're under attack!"

MYSTERIOUS STRANGERS

SURPRISINGLY LITTLE ACTION filled the next few moments.

Lucille followed Couper, huddling with the pilot Williamson as if in conference. However none of the three uttered a single word, nor even seemed to be looking at the others. Each stood in eerie silence, eyes closed, consciousness apparently directed inward. Owen Rogers glanced their way, then started shouting orders. "Whitey! Lieutenant! Come with me—no, never mind your stuff, it'll be just fine where it is!"

Three long steps, he dragged both of us by the elbows, to the center of the room, the Lieutenant emitting an indignant, "My good fellow—!"

"Lie down—right on the floor. No, not that way, on your back so you can see what's going on! There's gonna be a little shooting, and you'll be out from underfoot. I know, Lieutenant, I know. You're Snoopy, Lando Calrissian, and the Red Baron all rolled into one. You wanna be in on the action. Me, too—but as a praxeologist or even as an armorer, I'm strictly a supernumerary in this dustup, just like you."

Without waiting for us to obey him, he threw his bulk onto the carpet. I should not have been surprised. He began to sink, a cavity forming around his body, until all but his rounded belly lay flush with the surface. "Well, you guys, what the state are you waiting for?"

We followed his example, the Lieutenant somewhat reluctantly. The versatile flooring molded itself around us. Only the handles of our luggage showed; it, too, was now part of the deck. Lucille, Couper, Williamson the pilot, also lay on the floor, in it, as the overhead showed the Rendezvous-ship spitting out vessels similar to *Little Tom*.

Suddenly: "Here they come!" A bright ferocity rang in Lucille's voice. At an eyestraining distance from the *Little Tom*, a cluster of small dots showed infinitesimal against the starry background. Our craft pulled away from the mother ship, all of the other auxiliaries taking up positions of their own in a loose sphere about the larger vessel.

76

"I guess we might as well let our two passengers see what we're up against," observed Williamson. No excitement was audible in his voice at all. Many of the dots turned to scarlet—rather more than had been immediately apparent. Hundreds of "stars" now stood revealed as an attacking fleet, growing as it approached, individual craft still too small to be discernible except as pin-pricks of blood-colored light.

"Lee, *Tom-squared*, here," crackled a voice in the ceiling. "I've got 'em on instruments at twenty, closing like a revenuer on a widow's homestead."

Another voice, not one of ours, answered, "Acknowledge, *Tom-Tom*, twenty-thousand and closing. Hold your position and engage as you bear."

The first voice was tinged with masculine excitement, the second serenely feminine. Rogers said, "*Tom-Tom*'s another auxiliary. He's the closest. These bandits don't show on radar, it's what makes them so—"

"Bandits?" squeaked the Lieutenant, a beat ahead of me.

Blamm! The little ship shook with the impact, our makeshift acceleration nests cushioning what must have been a titanic shock. "Where the state did he come from?" swore Williamson. The starscape reeled momentarily as *Little Tom* regained headway and maneuvered sharply. In an instant, we could see the enemy, headed straight for us again.

Peculiarly, the object resembled *Asperance*, not streamlined like *Little Tom*, yet different from our Vespuccian ship, too. With nothing to give us an idea of scale, it consisted of a central shaft, a lozenge-shaped nodule at one end. Where the shaft met the presumed crew-cabin, half a dozen hydraulic-looking landing-jacks sprouted, angled slightly outward toward the stern. Our adversary had sustained some collision damage. A couple of his legs were bent, fuselage dented badly.

But he was persistent.

As the enemy loomed nearer, its shaft-end pointed menacingly toward us. What destruction had *Little Tom* suffered? Closer ... closer ... tension filled the room until it seemed the hull would burst. The Lieutenant ground his teeth. His corporal suppressed a whimper.

"Right on, baby," our pilot growled from his own gravelike depression, "Come and get your medicine!" A brilliant flash washed out the sky-display. The enemy fighter reappeared, damaged worse, its body charred, its legs burned away to stumps. "Son-of-a-bureaucrat! I got him!"

Williamson's cheer was a bit premature. Despite the punishment, our adversary swiveled until we saw it base-on, swelling as it bore unstoppably closer. The heavens flashed again—an explosion, a shower of debris. "Just in time, too," the pilot observed, "Let's see how many of these vermin we can burn before they punch us full of holes!"

"Rogers," demanded the Lieutenant—the tip of his nose just visible as he talked, "You said we Vespuccii were the only space-traversing—"

Flash!

He was cut off by another brilliant, frightening display. To the right, a saucer-shaped vessel, sister to our own, confronted two of the strange enemy craft. Each of them was at least three times larger, shaft-end to lozenge-tip, than the diameter of the scout. Suddenly, the smaller vessel's underside pulsed blindingly. Energy spat from the entire surface, crashed against the alien antagonists. Both retreated, severely hurt. The saucer pursued, firing its peculiar keel-batteries again and again. One oddly-shaped attacker dissolved in a greasy cloud of scattering scrap. *Little Tom* swerved again, blasting away at an unseen opponent, losing sight of the other ship, the outcome of its battle.

"Yes, in a way," Rogers offered from his dugout. "And then again, no."

"What?" I beat the Lieutenant to it, this time.

BLAMMM!!

The ship shook from side to side as if hungry predators were tearing at her substance. "You guys sure have short attention-spans," he continued, "I meant, yes, you're the only space-traversing folks we've run into so far, but, looking at it another way, you're not, exactly."

"How informative," the Lieutenant sneered. I paid attention to the praxe-ologist, rather than our impending doom. Hideous ripping-noises made it difficult. "What, in the name of everything authorized, do you mean?"

"Rog is a social scientist," offered Williamson across the room. He should have been preoccupied, unable to hear our conversation. "It doesn't have to mean anything!" Blinding light flared again. Another alien vanished in swarming wreckage. "Gotcha, you hyperthyroid ant-grunt!"

There was a short lull, as if between strokes of heat-lightning: "Owen's referring to his pet Gunjj," Couper sighed, "Nobody believes a word of it, understand, but—Bandits, Ev, two o'clock low!" The ship dipped, swerved; light again flared blindingly. "But he still burdens defenseless strangers with the story on occasion." A low shudder ran through the fabric of *Little Tom*, threatening to shake my internal organs from their fastenings. Every cen-timeter of the vessel groaned—a pair of bristly-jointed alien limbs lashed briefly across the view-area.

Rogers said, "I actually meant these things—ouch! Take it easy, Ev, I've got a tender stomach!" For a moment, we lost our orientation. It seemed as if we were hanging from the floor, looking down at the ceiling.

"Not with your taste in clothing," the pilot replied.

This was insane: five-sided bantering while fending off a deadly enemy. At least Lucille was keeping silent. "What are these things?" the Lieutenant contributed, "Or is that another of your precious secrets?"

"Not at all, Lieutenant," Rogers told him. "They're virus."

"What?"

"As near as we can tell," the praxeologist said, "they evolved in deep space, out of huge clouds of formaldehyde and interstellar—oh, boy!"

Miraculously retaining my stomach contents again, through yet another violent loop, I gulped bile. "Why do you call them—'gunge'?"

The praxeologist wrinkled what I could see of his face, then tried to shake his head. Even at this angle, I could see the sweat beading on his somewhat greenish features. "We don't call them ... I mean, these aren't the Gunjj." He spelled it out. "They're an intelligent species."

"Maidez, maidez!" the communicator crackled at the limit of intelligibility. Outside, a vessel struggled with six gigantic organisms worrying her like desert scavengers. *"Tom Swift Maru* to anybody listening! They've penetrated my hull! It's filling up with—Oh, yech! I've set autodestruct. We're bailing out. Stand by on pickup!"

Lucille spoke: "Gotcha, TSM, relaying. We'll—Great spirit of Osceola!" *Tom Swift Maru* exploded in a blinding ball of flame. "At least they took six of the bastards with them!" Lucille said grimly. Our ship swerved suddenly, its batteries snarled, another super-virus vanished.

More insanity: "The truth is, Whitey, until recently, we—the Confederacy, that is—never had full contact with another sapient species—nobody counts the Gunjj. We call them that because, when we first began to explore, we kept running across their 'calling-card'. Given a nice, clean, uninhabited planet, oxygen and greenery, sooner or later we'd find, carved into a tree, or painted on a rock, a characteristic inscription." Rogers lifted an arm above the floor like some weird insect buried in the sand, used a rubber-coated finger to trace a sign in the carpet; the pile obligingly turned contrasting blue.

"Mind you, we never found it on any occupied planet. Just what it indicated, no one had the slightest idea. Sometimes the symbol appears ancient, weathered, only about half-legible. Others are fresh, as if the grafittist just left minutes ago. It's associated with artifacts, empty plastic containers, other kinds of refuse, occasionally a broken tool."

Groaning loudly again, the little ship wheeled, blasting, pivoting once more for another shot. The hull *clanged!* harshly. I wondered how Rogers could go on with this lecture of his so calmly, having watched a sister ship destroyed with her entire complement aboard. Then I saw his eyes roll at the noise. This was his way of keeping his nerve.

I listened for the same reason.

"Some of the inscriptions were tiny; they could hardly be read. Others, gouged across entire continents, were naked-eye visible from orbit. Each instance was exactly like this, cursive stylized emblems appearing to spell out the word 'Gunjj'. Of course it had to mean something else in an alien language. Except for showing up on planet after planet, I suppose it might have implied no more intelligence than the dried-up slime-track of a snail—you do know what a snail is?"

There was a screeching, tearing noise. A section of the viewing dome went black. I said nothing about snails. The praxeologist would not have heard me anyway. The poor fellow's voice rose half an octave, increased its pace by fifty words a minute, but went on. "It was as scientifically disreputable a mystery as the Loch Ness monster or the supposedly lost planet Lucifer. It might have gone on the same way, unsolved, if it hadn't been for a near-disastrous adolescent practical joke.

"An individual Gunjj resembles a bunch of asparagus—no asparagus on Vespucci? All right, a bundle of semi-flexible tubes, bound in the middle by a bit of string. Only they're twelve feet tall, a sickly pale gray, and the string supports a belt pouch for personal effects and weapons. They don't stand their full double man-height, but droop the tops of their stalks over, like the tentacles on a sea-anemone—which I can see that you don't know anything about, either."

The missing viewscreen sector flickered fitfully to life again. It did not present a pretty picture. The enemy virus were much reduced in number, but so were Confederate ships. The ruins of a dozen littered the void, some with tiny figures managing to escape from them, some without. I looked at the Lieutenant. Either he was more courageous than I had believed, choosing to catch up on his sack-time, or he had fainted.

"There are a number of theories," Rogers continued, cultivatedly oblivious to the awful scene before us, "concerning extraconfederate life-forms..." He seemed to lose his place for a moment—perhaps due to a catastrophic explosion on the rim of the mother-ship. Then he went on. "Some see evolution as convergent, every intelligent species we find should resemble humans, simians, or cetaceans, because they'll inevitably occupy similar niches in the ecologies of their respective planets ... "

Again Rogers tapered off. For a terrible moment I was afraid that he had fainted, too. I could not bear the thought of his joining the Lieutenant in peace, leaving me alone to face this nightmare. "Yes, praxeologist," I imitated Sermander's peremptory tone. "The opposing theory?"

"—Er, the other position ... holds that evolution is never that convergent, not enough to make up for an isolated beginning, billions of years of independent development, on an entirely different planet. By this reasoning, which has so far been confirmed by the few glimpses we've had, the lowliest Terran slime-mold colony is a vastly-closer relative to us than any outsystem organism, and resembles us more nearly."

Terran? So I was a Terran, if Rogers had actually meant to include me in his "us". I thought about the obviously alien organisms native to Vespucci. No mistaking them for anything our ancestors had brought along.

From Terra, it would appear.

"Most praxeologists will agree that intelligence can't differ very much, from one species to another. The parameters for its existence are just too narrow. Consequently, we'll be able to play chess, swap horses, even tell dirty jokes, in any civilization we ever encounter. Our semi-contact with the Gunjj seems to confirm both theories—of physical difference and psychological similarity. They look weird, but they're no more alien in outlook than, say, the Japanese seem to North Americans. Lost you again, didn't I? But it's true. I know, I was there."

"It was a dark and stormy night ... " Williamson interrupted in a melo-dramatic voice. He was interrupted himself, when another small squadron of giant virus zoomed toward *Little Tom,* requiring rapid action. The attack appeared to be slacking off, but it was not over yet.

Rogers snorted: "Some people just don't appreciate a good story when they hear one. It was aboard the old *Tom Smothers Maru,* a small scout, not un-like this one. The pilot was Koko Featherstone-Haugh, before she ascended to ... call it a higher plane of existence, and I was fresh out of school, myself. We were exploring the masked region between a pair of nebulae, not looking for anything in particular except a potential profit, when the long-distance rangefinders began squawking.

"Heavy metal ahead ... "

Captain Koko Featherstone-Haugh (Rogers pronounced it "Fanshaw") nodded, putting the helm hard over. "Not one of ours—see what magnifica-tion the traffic will bear, will you, Rog?" Koko was an imposing individual, nearly two meters tall, almost as wide, heavily muscled. Not human. She was in charge. For a young man with the ink still wet on his diploma—even wet-ter on his contract—it was enough.

He obliged. In the overhead viewscreen, an apparently empty sector of space ahead of them broadened suddenly, the dark spaces from star to star widening, more stars becoming visible between. To each side, vast clouds of gas blanked out the stars, leaving only impenetrable blackness.

A tiny point of light appeared, swelled into a pair of closely-associated points. Little more was visible; trailers of gas limited visibility. "Captain, Ma'am, any more and we'll be looking at microbes clinging to the roof, in-stead of objects, er ... fifteen light-minutes away."

Abruptly, the floor dilated around the odd, rising figure of a creature that was neither simian nor human. It stood—on all fours—approximately half a meter high at the shoulder. It was perhaps a meter in length. It sported a pair of sharply-pointed ears, a matching nose, a thickly-bushed tail. It answered to the name "G. Howell Nahuatl".

Rather articulately.

"I say, fellow beings, why have my ablutions been interrupted? Aren't you as distressed as I am that I actually found a flea upon my person after our last planetside outing?" The animal sat down on its haunches, began scratching at one of its prominent ears with a hind foot.

"It wasn't a flea, Howell" answered Koko, "but some other form of bu-goid—more like an isopod, I thought, and when it got a taste of your iron-based blood, it died a horrible death. Look what we've got here."

81

Howell's eyes were not particularly good, yet he had a quick, analytical intelligence his companions valued. "Could it be, at long last?"

Rogers nodded vigorously. "One for the books—a genuine alien spaceship."

"Or just as likely, a pair of rogue asteroids, fused together," replied Koko. Her simian heart was beating rapidly, hoping, hoping. But, after all, she was the captain—if only of a tiny scouting vessel.

"Whatever it is, it's dead in the water," Rogers observed. "No signs of powerplant emissions, life-support operations. With our luck, it's been here for half a billion years, and everyone aboard is a mummy."

"No jokes about motherhood, you two!" Koko warned, "A starship built by another sapient species. Mummies or not, it would still be fascinating."

"For everybody but the mummies," Howell replied blandly.

"Well, enough consultation. We're never going to find out this way." Koko took a determined hitch in her pistol belt. "We're going in, gentlebeings. You two want to settle into the floor, just in case?"

"I'm going to meet my first alien civilization stuck up to my armpits in broadloom? You must be kidding." Rogers readjusted his smartsuit to what he considered its cheeriest configuration. "That's better!"

Even the colorblind coyote shuddered.

Nevertheless they approached the object with a degree of caution. Soon it became unmistakable. It was an artifact, two spheres fused together, their hull plates, their riveted seams plainly visible. There seemed to be no drive-tubes, no masts or shackles for photonic or tachyonic sails, no broad surfaces for the generation of propulsive particles of either kind, such as their own little ship employed. In short, the mysterious vessel must be powered in some manner completely unfamiliar to the Confederacy or the crew of the *Tom Smothers Maru*. Portholes followed a peculiarly skewed line about the equator of each globe.

There was light showing in them.

Koko halted her command a thousand kilometers away. A thin mist from the surrounding nebula concealed nothing, but it lent an eerie quality to the scene. At her order, *Tom Smothers Maru* began sending every customary form of energy ever used for communications in known space.

"Here it comes!" cried Rogers. He pointed to the bright image of the alien ship on the screen. Overlaying the picture—it was hard, sometimes, remembering that one was seeing what the computers were seeing—was a brilliant reddish aura, pulsing, dancing, pulsing, dancing.

"What I should like to know," said the coyote, "is how we're expected to make sense of this without any referents. And don't give me any of that nonsense about counting up to ten—how do you ask for flashlight batteries, first aid kits, or frostberry sodas with mere numbers?"

Half an hour later, Howell's question had been answered. The alien vessel repeatedly communicated: "529, 529, 279,841 ... 529, 529, 279,841 ... 529, 529,

279,841 ... " Noticing that the third number was the square of the first two, it occurred to Koko this might mean they intended sending a picture, five hundred twenty-nine pixels high, by the same number wide. "A good thing," she muttered to herself, "they don't have triangular telecom screens—I'd never have figured it out!"

The Gunjj turned out to be harmless—as harmless as intelligent life ever gets. They, too had been worried—more so than the crew of *Tom Smothers Maru*, since it developed that they were marooned in what they considered the middle of nowhere. None of this became clear very quickly. Having pictures helped. So did actually traveling over to the alien ship for more direct communications. Slowly, a context was built up in which understanding, cybernetically assisted, became possible.

Becalmed might have been a better word than marooned. The best translation of their ship's name would have been the *Disgruntled*. She was nominally a warship, long since decommissioned, presently being used as a training vessel for several hundred young Gunjj on the equivalent of a midshipman cruise, in the middle of their educational period.

The Gunjj breathed an oxygen-nitrogen about the same ratio as Terrans. It was fairly easy to tell the relative ages of Gunjj: when they were "born", they were a single stalk or strand, fully as tall as their elders. In time, the stalk split—although not altogether away from the individual's body—resplitting again until the adult, in its prime, resembled the collection of vegetables Rogers had referred to.

It was at this point that reproduction began occurring. The single stalks would complete their development, then separate from the parent to begin the life cycle all over again. The diameter of the original being began to shrink. In their old age, Gunjj adults resembled Gunjj babies, except for differences in color or texture, minor, cosmetic, which were not immediately apparent to Earthians. Then again, the Gunjj probably could not tell a human teenager from an octogenerian, either.

The practical joke?

Midshipmen will be midshipmen. The Gunjj used a peculiar system to "drive" starships faster than light: the mathematical/metaphysical principle of non-simultaneity. Over interstellar distances (in theory, over any distances at all) it is considered nonsense to speak of two events happening at the same time, without a way to synchronize their time-scales.

No such method exists—or supposedly can exist. All right, then, reasoned the Gunjj, why not work it backward? If a ship departed the Gunjj home world, headed for Colony A (the Gunjj did not actually establish colonies— no one knew why), despite the fact its velocity can be measured, plus the distance between the two points is known, there is no guarantee it will arrive at any specifically given time. Such would imply a synchronicity that physics holds to be impossible, nonsensical.

Suppose the voyage is supposed to take a hundred years. It makes as much sense, from this abstruse standpoint, for the traveler to arrive a hundred thousand years after takeoff, or a hundred million. Likewise, a mere hundred seconds, or nanoseconds is equally logical, accomplishing, in effect, travel vastly faster than the speed of light.

Except that Gunjj ships have no actual velocity. Their transition between two points, for all practical purposes, is instantaneous. Thus obvious, widespread traces of their planetary explorations everywhere one looked, while at the same time (not speaking scientifically, of course) no Confederate had ever encountered any of their ships in flight.

Until *Tom Smothers Maru*.

All intelligent life, no matter how different in appearance, will be psychologically similar. Young Gunjj, no different from humans or chimpanzees, liked to have their fun, particularly at the expense of nominal superiors. Everyone is nominally superior to a midshipman cadet.

Thus another principle of physics was brought into play. The Gunjj non-simultaneity drive could not be used immediately upon leaving a planet. Something about the gravity fields. Neither was it actually instantaneous. (Although how anyone could actually testify to that is a question.) As a joke, half of the midshipman class aboard the *Disgruntled* arranged to calculate, to twenty-three decimals, their velocity during transition. They performed all of the calculations but one, ready for the last read-out at the tentacle-squish of a computer-button.

Meanwhile, the remaining half of the Gunjj midshipman class was equally prepared to state, with similar precision, the *Disgruntled*'s location.

Unfortunately, Werner Heisenberg—along with his equivalent in the culture of the Gunjj—says you cannot do this. You can either know, with great precision, the velocity of a particle (or a ship) or its location. Not both at the same time. The ship took off, exceeded the necessary number of planetary diameters for her transition across the galaxy, prepared to go hyper—then two buttons were pushed. The ship froze dead in space where she was found, full of frightened midshipgunjj.

They had been there for almost a decade when *Tom Swift Maru* had discovered them, a handful of grownup officers with a hundred overaged cadets. Naturally, they were highly grateful to have been discovered. Koko puzzled over the problem, then consulted with Rogers, who had a chat with Howell. Learning the Gunjj language, with some computer assistance, they found that, as cultures go, these odd aliens were very shy. They would never have contacted the Confederacy, left to themselves.

But they made a wonderful, highly salable brandy. Their discovery of chocolate, thanks to the crew of *Tom Swift Maru*, was practically a religious experience for them. There would be future contact, with trade.

It was Howell who, knowing little of physics, but plenty about logic, hit upon the solution. The Gunjj vessel was latched onto—a bit of a strain for a little ship like *Tom Swift Maru*—then towed away toward a random destination at a carefully uncalculated velocity. Of course they vanished in a wink, resuming what was supposed to have been their instantaneous voyage to wherever it was they had been going.

"Do you actually expect us to believe this blatant nincompoopery?" the Lieutenant asked irritably, when Rogers appeared to finish his story.

"Oh, Lieutenant Sermander. Glad to see you're with us again." Rogers laughed. "No, I don't expect you to believe it, Nobody else does."

"Excuse me, Rog" I said, beginning to notice that the shooting was over. There were no more supervirus visible on the screen. Ships had begun returning to the mother vessel, including *Little Tom*. "I do not understand how this Howell creature's idea was a solution to anything. Did it not simply render the Gunjj more lost than to begin with?"

Rogers laughed again. I noticed that the others, relaxing now from their battle posture, were standing by to watch us take the punchline. "But Whitey, they were never lost. They were the least-lost travelers in history, which, of course, was their problem. Howell's solution worked because it restored the Heisenbergian uncertainty they needed to travel. They were no longer caught on the horns of a metaphysical contradiction. They were able to move, after ten years of being frozen there."

I blinked stupidly. Then it occurred to me to ask, "Did anybody ever find out what their symbol—the 'Gunjj' marking— really meant?"

This, apparently, was what the praxeologist had been waiting for. He looked about the room, making sure that everybody appreciated it properly. "Sure they did, Whitey. It turned out to be not much of a mystery at all. It meant nothing, more or less, than 'Kilroy was here'!"

At least the Confederates all enjoyed a good laugh. Kilroy again. Who in Hamilton's Holy Name was this Kilroy? The Lieutenant, rising from the floor with a weary look, scratched his head, but said nothing.

I said nothing, but scratched my head.

"Don't let it get to you," Couper grinned, then gave Rogers a dirty look. "I never could decide, myself, about that story, although Howell backs it up. I've never known him to be a liar—hold on, elevator going up!" The floor began rising, taking us nearer the phony stars. It required courage not to hunch claustrophobically as the ceiling approached. Then we were through, presumably the hull of *Little Tom* as well, standing in the mother ship above the docking bay.

"Welcome aboard *TPM3C*—informally known as *Tom Lehrer Maru!*"

I stared, mouth agape. The source of this welcoming female voice seemed to be half animal, half machine, a sort of man-sized legless lizard wearing a smartsuit, its own exposed rubbery gray-black skin surrounding a pair of wise brown eyes above a roguish, protruberant muzzle. The creature rested in the gleaming frame of a four-wheeled conveyance, mechanical hands responding to her wishes as she greeted us.

"Armorer-Corporal Whitey O'Thraight, Lieutenant Enson Sermander: I am LeeLaLee Aukorkauk S'reen. Kindly consider yourself at home, good landlings, we dock with our own mother-vessel in six and one-half hours."

PART TWO
THE PRIVATEERS

THE GARDEN OF LEELALEE

IN THE GRAY salt marshes of the Vespuccian Low Desert, there live certain rare, minuscule, fin-scaly creatures without legs, breathing water instead of air. A porpoise is something like that, but it is bigger, uses lungs like human beings, pointedly claims possession of a mind, as well as a central nervous-system more subtly complex than any human's. It also considers itself the hottest space pilot in the Known Galaxy.

I was not certain, at the start, which of these quirks was true of porpoises in general, which peculiar to LeeLaLee Aukorkauk S'reen. She was the only porpoise I had ever met. It was equally true that only six-plus hours were not going to be enough to get well acquainted, even if I had wanted to. It was not really time enough to absorb anything.

Around us, people (here I use the term as loosely as they did, themselves, taking into consideration the variety of finned or furry folk within eye's reach) were busily rising or sinking through the floor of what appeared to be a broad green shallow valley. The virus attack seemed to have generated some urgency or excitement among them, which I thought was natural enough. I recalled the damage I had seen being done to this ship by the creatures, wondering what its condition was.

It was difficult to say. From wall to unseen wall, a thick carpet of vegetation lay before us, randomly punctuated with trees, sometimes sparsely, often in thick copses interwoven with a complicated network of brightly-colored rubber footpaths. Also fin-paths, as I was to discover. If there was appreciable battle-damage, it was not in these quarters.

Lost to everything, to everybody else, the Lieutenant stood where the deck extruded him, deep in thought. Or culture-shock. By default, the task of carrying his luggage with my own was delegated to the lowest-ranking representative of the Vespuccian State present at the time.

Couper smothered my hand in his own giant paw. "I'm afraid I've got some chores waiting. Have a good time, son, take a sightseeing tour. We'll round you up when it's time to transship again, right, Rog?"

89

"I'll take care of it." The praxeologist hiked a big shoulder-bag closer to his chest, shook my hand when Couper had released it, then clapped me on the back. "Hoist a couple for me. We'll see you in a few."

They turned their polite attention to my superior, all of them but Lucille. She looked at me as if she were seeing me for the first time, a puzzled expression on her pretty face. Then she shrugged, shook her head ironically, took a step in my direction. I barely avoided the reflex to shrink away from the tense ferocity she always carried with her.

She stood briefly on her tiptoes, to brush her lips across mine. "That oughta hold you for a few hours, Corporal, until we get the fire put out." There was a sharp nip at the end of that semi-kiss she gave me, rather painfully, on the lower lip. It throbbed for a long time afterward.

It was not the only thing that throbbed.

As the company from the *Little Tom* dispersed, we Vespuccians followed the porpoise LeeLaLee, at her suggestion, walking briskly behind her shiny mechanical trundler. I did not even think to ask her where we were going, being a bit worried about the Lieutenant, who had not yet said a single word. He had to be nudged before he started moving.

"What? Oh ... yes ... let us go, by all means. There is a good fellow." Immediately he fell silent again. I was more than a little dazed, myself, but this had more to do with the tiny blood-blister forming on my lower lip than with any scenic wonders the *Tom Lehrer Maru* might have offered. Lucille was a girl who believed in fighting a fire by starting others, elsewhere. Nonetheless, I made admiring noises at what seemed to be the right places. It seemed the politest thing.

"How very gratifying it is, young landling," The porpoise pointed one of her spindly metal manipulators at some object of interest, "I am extremely fond of this vessel myself—and do not like having her attacked—albeit she is merely the material consequence of certain gross human and simian manipulatory capabilities that a kind evolution seems to have bestowed upon them, in lieu of truly adequate cognitive faculties."

I did not follow half of what she said, but was aware that it was not particularly nice. "However in plain truth, if you wish to be impressed," she went on, "wait until you see the ship we're about to meet!"

LeeLaLee's wheeled contrivance began to slow as it approached the bank of a narrow canal that paralleled the footpath. I stopped right behind her, then had to take the Lieutenant by the elbow until he halted, as well. The man looked up at me blankly, blinked down at the swift current that he had nearly stepped into, then returned to his thoughts.

In one respect, I was impressed. Unlike *Little Tom*, no one was rising or sinking through the ceiling here. It may have been fifty or a hundred meters high, difficult to tell in the mist-diffused glare. LeeLaLee steered her gleaming contraption down into the water. With a gleeful *splash!* she left it, then continued by swimming along beside us.

Occasionally the pathway would dip or the canal would rise, then her sleek form would be visible through a transparent retaining-wall. In some places, usually encompassed by privacy-creating leafy bowers, there would be a table with chairs, set on the synthetic flagging before the water-windows. "Landlings" conversed with porpoises through the glass, the inevitable topic being the combat action that had just occurred. There did not seem to be much concern for the safety of the ship or of its complement, rather the atmosphere resembled a break in the ordinary routine, a holiday of sorts. I would attempt to remember that, the next time I found myself cowering in a foxhole in somebody's carpet.

Some distance ahead, I could make out a complicated double looped figure-eight, where several converging footpaths suddenly vaulted over the water. Unbelievably, a transparent aqueduct arched over them, in turn.

Meanwhile, sharing the overhead with the birds, many chimpanzees, humans, other bipedal sentients less clearly discernble, hung from fabric-covered wings, swooping, soaring, kicking at the treetops with laughter. Occasionally a land-dweller, plastic extensions on his hands or feet, a large lens on his face, would meet LeeLaLee in the canal, nod, pass her by. This seemed equitable: not every marine being we observed had abandoned its wheels. I had to dodge several on the footpath, pulling the Lieutenant out of harm's way before he was run down.

Finally we reached the rim of the vast park-like chamber, almost needing the reminder of familiar oval-doorwayed bulkheads that we were inside a gigantic starship, moving through space at incomprehensible velocities.

I said something about this to LeeLaLee.

"You'd remember, my fine shore-grubber, were we not moving!" the Captain observed as she swam into a waiting set of wheels to join us on the walk. "Each precious drop of water, every clod of carefully-cultured soil, would be swirling overhead in a muddy maelstrom, did we not allow a calculated inefficiency in the inertialess field, enough uncorrected acceleration to give us one-half of a gee, if that means anything."

Walking around the garden perimeter, now, I looked at storefronts, cafes, other shops with fancy, interesting window displays. Was this a spacecraft or a shopping-center? Experimentally, I bounced a little on the balls of my smartsuit-shod feet. "The gravity feels about right to me, Captain." Among its other virtues, dense-cored Sca was a great place for the development of bad backs, fallen arches. "Which would be closer to your own standard," I asked her without thinking, "Sca or Vespucci?"

"How would the creature know?" The Lieutenant's derisive snort caught me by surprise. "It has not been anywhere near either planet." He gave the porpoise a look of apologetic embarrassment, "Enlisted people!"

LeeLaLee's wire-spoked wheels rolled nearer, leaving diamond-patterned tracks on the tile that vanished quickly in the warm, dry atmosphere. "On the contrary, pompous officer, this Sca where you were found falls within three decimal places of possessing an Earth-like gravity. Your own—Vespucci? You actually call it that?—appears to be a rather small, tired world, of approximately seven tenths standard."

The Lieutenant stared at her in astonishment. "But how could you possibly—"

"How could I possibly? Because I make it my business to know these things, Lieutenant." She fell silent, then: "After all, I am the Captain."

Now there was an answer that made sense to the Lieutenant. He shut up again. We three continued along the esplanade, looking into shop windows.

"HOW ARE WE supposed to pay for this?"

LeeLaLee had left us at a colorful open-fronted restaurant nestled in a shop-cluster at the margin of the park. Where we were seated, we could gaze out over the landscaping or into a rippling blue-green tunnel courtesy of a transparent canal-wall passing directly through the cafe. Both thoroughfares bustled with passers-by of a half a dozen species.

The waiter was a short, wiry, bald-headed human male attired in a dark green two-tone pin-striped smartsuit that might have nauseated even Owen Rogers. He rolled his eyes ceilingward a moment as if for divine inspiration. "There ain't no such thing as a free lunch. It says here you're on a Survey Service account. Funny, you ginks don't look like no Survey rowdies. Where'd y'get them fancy suit-patterns, anyway?"

He indicated our Vespuccian Navy Reserve markings.

I opened my mouth, but the Lieutenant held up a hand. "I believe, sir, that we are specimens. Now tell me: does one choose a white wine with this repast, or a red?" I wanted to ask him how he suddenly knew that two strangers who had just walked into his establishment were on an account of any kind. Also, who was he to talk about funny suit-patterns?

He goggled at the Lieutenant's inquiry. "With lobsterburgers? How 'bout a Coke, buddy? It's the real thing, y'know. Fresh shipment today all the way from New Atlanta. A very good month." He busied himself at a fountain tap. "Specimens, are you? Thought those came in a bottle, too."

"Please, my good man, not at luncheon! We shall, with certain self-explicable trepidations, accept your culinary recommendation. Now leave us, if you please." He eyed the food before us with suspicion, then looked up at me with very much the same expression on his face. "Corporal, I would be interested in hearing your impressions thus far."

"Um, well, I cannot tell whether these little things on the bread are insects or seeds of some kind. I do not think I am going to eat them."

Outside, an enormous dark chimpanzee-like animal knuckled past our cafe, gliding on tiny wheels that were somehow attached to its huge feet. One of its massive arms was in a silvery rubber sling. Abruptly, a bright pink balloon blossomed from its mouth, swelled nearly to the diameter of the creature's head, then collapsed, leaving sticky pink remains across its leathery muzzle. The monster blinked, cleared its eyes, its nostrils, looked around to see whether anyone had witnessed the accident. Then it stuffed the peculiar substance back into its jaws, hitched up its heavy pistol belt, rolled onward on its little wheels.

"No, you dimwit! I refer to our situation—to our experiences—to our putative hosts, their society, their technology. I realize that you are scarcely the trained observer I am, but ... what are your reactions?"

I thought about his question, sipping at the bubbly brown liquid the waiter had brought us. So far, I had been too busy gawking to do very much processing. "Well, sir," I finally told him, "I do not much care for the cavalier manner in which they shuffle us around. Oh, they are polite enough about it, but just the same the disrespectful way that Geoffrey Couper treated you. About the sidearms, I mean, I could have—"

"Nonsense, my dear boy, nonsense!" He waved a hand negligently. "I understood entirely. Chain of command, et cetera, et cetera. Come to speak of it now, I rather liked his keen, decisive manner. Beneath the facade of sloppy—one might almost say civilian—casuality that we see all around us here, there is a core of steel, a center entirely unembarrassed in the exercise of power. Confidence. Discipline. These combinations do not occur often enough in our military, let me tell you!"

He took a bite of his sandwich, got a very odd expression on his face.

"Lieutenant!" I glanced wildly around. "Never say things like that!"

"Come, Corporal," he replied around the bite of food, "Have you never entertained the thought yourself?" He gave me a knowing, cynical look.

I kept my eyes on the tabletop. "If I had, sir, I would not voice it out loud. Certainly not in public." I made a gesture that, for generations in Vespuccian enlisted society, has meant, "The walls have ears".

"A very wise precaution, Corporal—Whitey. There is something profoundly wonderful about these people, reaching further than bland explanations involving scientific research." He lowered his head along with his voice until he resembled a Vespuccian carrion-bird. "It is obvious that our expedition—what is left of it—has accidentally stumbled across the cutting edge of a vast, wealthy, expanding empire."

What I wanted to say was that they did not seem very imperial to me.

"They are ultra-cautious at their frontier, or follow a velvet glove policy in general, but the power is there, mark my word. They make us Vespuccians look like, how do the ranks have it? Like 'tiny turnips'."

"*Lieutenant!*" I do not think I had ever been so shocked.

"Hush! I swear that am going to get to the bottom of this. When I do ..."

"Yes, sir?" I was almost afraid to hear what would come next.

"Well, now is scarcely the time for making irrevocable decisions, is it? An opportunity will present itself eventually, Are you with me, Corporal?"

"With you, Lieutenant?"

"All I mean is, are you prepared to follow my leadership in this matter?"

"You are the Lieutenant, I am only a corporal, sir." Which was as noncommittal an answer as I could think of with a second's notice. He was either an acute judge of the political realities, or verging on paranoia. It is often difficult to tell, even at the best of times. In either case, it did not sound as though he were all that anxious to return home immediately. Fingering my bruised lip, I agreed with the man mentally that now was not the time for making any irrevocable decisions.

Then I thought of Eleva.

"Whitey?"

Suddenly, right beneath my sandwich-plate, the tabletop lit up to speak my name. I started, coming close to upsetting the Lieutenant's half-finished drink, then cleared away my empty dishes. I found the image of Owen Rogers, live in three-dimensional color, staring back at me.

"I finally got out of that federated staff meeting! Our little mini-war today made trash of every schedule we had. Thank Lysander's intransigent shade that armorers don't make policy. Otherwise. I'd be stuck in there until Rendezvous-after-next. You got any plans right now?"

I looked across at the Lieutenant, chin resting in his palm like one of the statues in Hierarchy Park. He gave me an irritated glance of dismissal, went right back to his thoughts. "No, Owen, apparently not."

"Well, then," Rogers said, "follow the edge of the park about a quarter-circumference, to a place called 'Chuck's'—I'll meet you there. Oh yes, and bring your boss along. Got surprises for both of you."

The image faded, vanishing behind its sprinkling of bread crumbs, salt-shakings, those little seed-bug things I had carefully scraped off my food. I glanced at the Lieutenant again, raising inquiring eyebrows.

"Oh, very well, Corporal, by all means! Let us go see what the fellow wants." He rose. I realized then that Rogers had not mentioned which direction we should turn, leaving the restaurant. I interrupted the waiter who was clearing a table in obvious ill humor. He flapped his dampened cloth, refolded it, then smeared it around the plastic a little.

"It's atmosphere they want, do they? Antique electric lightbulbs right outa the Fission Age, and dumb, dumb, dumb appliances! Which means I gotta do medieval chores like this one! Too bad those goo-squirtin' virus didn't fill this whole place up! What I wouldn't give for modern, sanitary, self-serving, self-cleaning—what? Chuck's is it?"

"That would be helpful," I told him.

"Turn right, and it's more like a third of the way around." He snapped the cloth at the floor, folded it again, began to return to his task, then took a good look at my gunbelt with its double burden. "Shucks, Kilroy, don't look like you need t'do business at that place—but death an' taxes, the customer's always right. Or so they tell me."

Except when he is confused.

Nonetheless, we followed his instructions out around the colored sidewalk, dodging trees, canals, pedestrians, wheeled fish, until we came upon a broad plaza with a fountain in the middle. Imitation sunlight poured down over the scene, several dozen people strolling, standing, talking dangling their feet in the water. The emergency seemed to be over with. I wondered when or if they ever worked for a living.

Strange what you will not notice in unfamiliar surroundings. Now, when I was looking for something specific, I suddenly realized that all the shops lacked an important, commonplace feature. Not a single written word was displayed on any of them. Often there was something that resembled a sign, a simple, more or less self-explaining graphic. Otherwise, there was nothing but empty space where there should have been a company ident, the name of a prop. I filed this with other odd-shaped data: the fact LeeLaLee had known all about Sca, even about Vespucci, without contact with the returning crew from *Little Tom.* Or how the waiter, after a moment of conspicuous cogitation, suddenly knew whose cuff it was we were eating on, but neither who nor what we were.

Except that we were Kilroys.

Rogers met us at the fountain. "Right over here, gents. Come on in."

The sign bore the holographic image of an unfamiliar handgun, but did not say "Chuck's". The entity behind the counter was an enormous, broad-shouldered powerful-looking being with a dark shaggy pelt, much the same as I had seen a while earlier on tiny foot-wheels. It wore a strange hat, two partial hemispheres of tan canvas, different sizes, the smaller hemisphere atop the larger. Some sort of sun-helmet, I guessed.

"Jambo, B'wana!" he said. "Long time no ungawa! What can I do you for?"

Rogers shook his head tolerantly. "Can the Swahooie, Chuckles. Got a couple of new customers for you. This is Whitey O'Thraight and Enson Sermander, both late of the planet Vespucci. Gentlemen, I give you Charles C. Charles, a valued professional colleague and the hairiest, if not the hugest, gunsmith in the known galaxy. He's an eccentric genius, in his safari mood just now. Be careful not to step in the usunga."

Charles accepted the Darrick I unholstered for him, examining it minutely, cocking a huge brown eye at the gun, his huge black fingers surprisingly dexterous. "Vaguely familiar. Looks like an old-fashioned soldering gun. Probably pretty anemic. What is it, about thirty-two caliber?"

"Eight millimeter Darrick," I told him.

"A thinly-veiled alias in both senses. That's Dardick, son, with a second D." He glanced significantly at Rogers. "Something lost in the translation?"

"At a guess," the praxeologist replied, "two and a half thousand years."

The gunsmith whistled, shook his head, then got back to business. "Let's see, now: full length plastic casings, I suppose, triangular in cross—"

"Trochoidal," I corrected.

"Whatever. Something with a polymeric memory, most likely, for obturation and extraction. Feeds here with a stripper—fourteen, fifteen, maybe sixteen of them. Rotor lifts when you cock the hammer or cycle the trigger, forming two sides of a chamber with the topstrap forming the third. Bang! Next cycle, the empty comes out this little slot, no deposit, no return. An automatic revolver, by Albert, or a revolving automatic. Handy for mystery writers who don't know the difference."

I nodded enthusiastically, enjoying the first conversation I had fully understood in days. "Surely you do not have ammunition for it, though."

"Don't call me Shirley," he replied. "And I can order it custom fabricated."

The giant paused, with that same look of deep thought on his face that the waiter—along with many others we had recently met—had displayed.

"There. I'll take a few measurements, send them on ahead to the Rendezvous, and they'll be waiting for us at the mother ship with any luck."

He thought again. "Will five hundred trounds do you?"

"I, er ... " Five hundred cartridges represented real wealth back home.

Rogers stepped in. "Put it on my Survey Service account, Chuck. And make it a thousand trounds. The Corporal here is a bit out of practice." Looking at me, he shrugged. "I know, 'There ain't no such thing as a free lunch,' but occasionally you can find one that's awful cheap."

I gulped, unable, at first, to frame a suitable reply. Then: "The Darrick employs a double-base nitro pistol powder, about medium fast-burning. The bullet is ten grams of a cast lead alloy, ten percent tin, ten percent antimony. There is also an over-powder wad, a disc three millimeters thick, made of the same plastic as the casing. The primer—."

"Gotcha." The gunsmith winked. "Make yourself t'home while I'm out back."

He disappeared through a curtain. I wondered whether it laundered him as he passed through it. He looked pretty clean for a gunsmith, I thought, although a bit singed around the edges of his fur, probably from tinkering with plasma-guns. Meanwhile, Rogers thumped a broad finger jovially on the transparent display case he leaned against. Once again I noticed the lack of signs, posters, price tags, all around the shop. It was as if writing had never been invented in this culture.

"What's your pleasure, *Herr Leutnant?* We can't let you go around all socially nekked like that. Pick yourself out a roscoe. It's on the house—or on the ship, if you prefer. Like I just said, 'There ain't no such thing as a free lunch', but you'll earn it. You will, too, Whitey."

The Lieutenant blinked, suspicion wrestling with amazement across his jowled countenance. The walls of the place were lined with racked pistols. There were five more big display counters full of weapons in bewildering variety. Only about a quarter of the machinery visible was immediately recognizable as firearms, the remainder being unfamiliar technology.

Some were obvious projectile-throwers, but with what source of energy? Others apparently emitted some form of pure energy, similar to lasers, or the plasma guns I had seen used to grisly effect on Scavian cavalry. Not a single long-arm—no rifle or shotgun—was visible, however. Like writing, Earthians did not seem to have stumbled across the concept, although they had a couple of unique notions of their own.

One of them seemed to be about color. Vespuccian weaponry tended to be blue-black, occasionally silver, or some combination of the two. Sometimes—very rarely—they were finished in locally appropriate camouflage. Confederate weapons could be any color: bright red, green, orange, bilious yellow, lizard-egg blue, purple, warm tan, or even hot pink.

Apparently private individuals, private companies, were permitted to produce weapons, sell them, even compete with one another at the business. On Vespucci, this highly restricted article of hardware was exclusively created, also stringently distributed, only by official government arsenals, to those whose duty it was to protect the State. Attempts had been made to limit their use to a designated individual, with a special magnet ring or fingerprint recognition, so far without success.

Uncomfortable, the Lieutenant cleared his throat: "I appreciate the gesture, praxeologist, truly I do. However, a sidearm is merely insignia, a badge of authority. It serves no other practical purpose. No one can hit anything with a handgun. Thus, in circumstances where just anyone is free to purchase, possess, to actually carry one of the things ..."

He let the implication go unstated.

Rogers did not: "What you're saying, then, is that an officer and a gentlebeing might be mistaken for one of the peasants? Okey-dokey, Lieutenant, it's your life and a free galaxy—will be, anyway—just keep in mind that in the Confederacy such officers as we permit don't have any flunkies to do their killing for them. You may want to reconsider."

The Lieutenant's face began turning that same alarming shade of purple-red as before, the veins standing against on his forehead. He opened his mouth, no doubt to blast Rogers into some netherworld when Charles C. Charles reappeared just in time to prevent the eminent catastrophe.

"Okay, Whitey, here's your piece. We'll hold the chamber pressure on the first lot at twenty-five kay, just to be on the safe side, but if you ever feel the need for more power, this weapon's structural material can be ionically treated—and there are better plastics available."

He tapped a broad nail on the Darrick—the Dardick's—upper receiver as he said this. Rogers waggled his eyebrows, rolled his eyes dramatically, as if restraining himself mightily from asking what is the point in gilding some stinkweed that will never be a cactus-blossom.

"Uh, thanks," I said. "Where ... when can I—"

"Right here, after Rendezvous." The furry giant stood still for a moment, his attention elsewhere. Then: "Which should be coming up a little ahead of schedule, I think. We got into trouble, and Mama came arunnin'."

We walked out of the shop just as darkness fell.

It took a moment to recall that we were not outside on a planet's surface. Occurring overhead was a display like I had seen aboard the *Little Tom,* although on a vastly grander scale. Soft lights came on across the wooded park, stars glittered down at us for the first time. Two of them swelled, grew into perfect replicas of *Tom Lehrer Maru* or its small auxiliaries: glowing white inverted bowls, featureless, smoothly-contoured, yet somehow seeming to vibrate with vast pent-up energies.

" ... should see Chuck when he's trying to be Nanook of the North," Rogers was saying as we watched events unfold overhead. It must be an old story to him, I thought. He scarcely seemed to notice it. "A gorilla with a harpoon and an extra fur coat is overdoing things."

Outside, the pair of ships began to grow again! One of the vessels came nearer, or we approached it. These things are relative, or so I have been told. Just as *Little Tom* had nestled in its recess beneath the vastly greater *Tom Lehrer Maru,* so now *Tom Lehrer Maru* found herself dwarfed almost to insignificance as she maneuvered toward one of seven docking bays on the lower surface of a monstrously larger vessel.

I estimated that this "mother ship" everybody had been talking about had to be in the neighborhood of three or four thousand meters in diameter. Three or four kilometers! Why, monstrous was hardly the word—

"Two point one zero Jeffersonian metric miles," Rogers observed as if he could read my mind, a possibility I was beginning to take into serious consideration. The second ship, twin to the first, stood off as we maneuvered into place. I wondered why it was here, why it was waiting.

"Wait," cried the gunsmith-praxeologist, "you ain't seen nothin' yet!"

The stars dimmed briefly, blotted out as we docked. Then they reappeared as if we were seeing through the mother ship—as if we were now a part of the mother ship, seeing things from its point of view.

Ahead still lay that second vessel, swelling with every moment that passed, expanding, growing, engulfing the universe from rim to rim.

I gulped as my battered sense of scale underwent another dizzying reorientation. Beneath the impossibly vast ship, seven giant docking bays awaited! The first ship had been only intermediary. Now we were preparing to link up with *its* mother ship, riding up into a vast bowl, a featureless, brilliant white caldera. Overhead, the stars went out once again. They stayed out this time. Daylight was reinstated, sound, motion returned to the garden—the tiny backyard garden—of LeeLaLee.

"This is where we get off!" Owen Rogers exclaimed, grinning so hard I believed that he would crack his face in half if it went any further, "Before you ask, she's seven and one-half miles in diameter—a little better than twelve of your kilometers, if I understand right.

"Gentlemen, I give you *Tom Paine Maru!*"

POOL OF INFORMATION

IT DID NOT resemble a classroom; it did not sound like a lecture.

G. Howell Nahuatl called at my assigned quarters first thing the next "morning". I was already up, from lifelong habit. The door became transparent—at least in one direction—revealing the furry, four-legged creature as he sat in the companionway outside, one hind foot scratching absently in the vicinity of his brightly multicolored collar.

"Alexander Hamilton!" I entered the main compartment from the bathroom, freshly showered. "Do you have any idea what time it is?" These people had struck me as being more relaxed about rising in the morning.

I needed to ask someone about shaving, although Howell was not the one to ask. My beard itched, although it did not look terribly bad—somewhat unmilitary, but then so was the pattern that I had hastily programmed into my suit: eight or nine subtle shades of gray-brown hairy-textured illusion, closely matching the natural coloration of my visitor.

Unable to see me, the coyote rolled his eyes back, considering: "Why, yes," he answered over the door-communicator. "It's just after six A.M. That's oh-six-hundred, to you, Corporal. I thought that you might appreciate an opportunity to have some of your many questions answered."

Almost immediately upon our arrival the night before, pleading urgent business, Rogers had introduced the Lieutenant and me to this remarkable creature from his remarkable story. The coyote was quite unlike the simians or cetaceans I had met thus far. There had scarcely been time—I had scarcely had the energy—to do more than simply be guided to my billet, to fall into an exhausted unconsciousness. Dimly, I recalled something about the Lieutenant being similarly seen to. Also a promise of more guiding-service tomorrow, issued by the canine.

He nipped suddenly at the base of his tail—the canine, not the Lieutenant—then turned with sedate dignity to wait. Thinking that my foremost question—when could we go home?—never seemed to get answered, I wrapped my pistol-belt around my middle, then checked each magazine and the pair of stripper clips I carried. Sixty trounds. It was good to have enough ammo. Sealing the final suit seam, I asked, "What is the drill this morning, Howell? Can we have some coffee, first?"

The door dilated, or whatever it is called. Howell sat in the hallway outside, exactly as before, no sharper nor apparently real than he had been, courtesy of the door's sophisticated imaging electronics.

"The drill?" He looked puzzled. At least I think he did. Facial expressions are somewhat difficult to figure with non-humans. I could not tell whether he was confused by the question, or by my smartsuit pattern, which was supposed to be a joke. "Ah, yes!" he replied at last, "You mean, 'What are we about to do?' Well, we shall obtain the coffee to which you have become so rapidly habituated. Very briefly after we meet your comrade-in-arms, I shall conduct both of you to 'school', for your first formal lesson in privateering for fun and profit."

He blinked, pausing to scratch at an ear, "I do believe, Whitey, either the vermin are growing immune to my shower curtain, or I shall have to get my circuits examined for an altogether different sort of bug."

WE WALKED DOWN the corridor a few meters to something he called a "transport patch". We must have used it, or one like it, the night before, but I had no memory of having done so. I was still a bit dizzy at the casually-mixed colors in the decor, along with the consistent absence of written signs. I hitched at my gunbelt, fastening it a notch looser. Life aboard the Confederacy's ships was already having as unmilitary an effect on my waistline as it was on my grooming habits.

"Privateering?" I asked.

Howell replied, "A small jest. Wait a moment before you follow me."

The coyote hesitated himself, then trotted onto the scarlet carpet covering a two-meter square. An area of about the same size covered the wall behind it. He walked directly toward this, as if it did not exist, then was gone. I began dimly to remember. Even in the full (if artificial) light of morning, I did not believe I would ever get used to this particular sight. It had only been my fatigue the night before that had allowed me to accept, as in a dream, that it was happening. Howell's head popped back out of the wall, looking like a hunting trophy.

"Well, Corporal O'Thraight, are you coming?"

"No, but my eyes are getting glassy." He didn't laugh.

Suppressing a shudder, I shut them tightly, stepping into the wall exactly as Howell had done, There was no sensation. Blackness, silence surrounded me, then we were both on a mustard-colored patch, facing the opposite direction, away from a wall, Hamilton knows how many floors from where we had started, or how many thousands of meters away.

The coyote cocked his head, regarding me with what my unpracticed eye took for sympathy. "I know just how you feel, Whitey. It requires some getting used to, being squirted around like the contents of a small intestine. If it's any comfort, I had to be carried through the first time, drugged and semi-comatose, while the electronic portion of my consciousness decided that the walls weren't really eating me." He sighed. "It would appear that some of my inborn canine instincts are more difficult to suppress than others. Count yourself lucky in this regard."

"Now where did we put your Lieutenant, last night?" He blinked, gave a cheerful flip of his tail, trotted to a door not far along the corridor.

"... in the name of Authority do you want?" bellowed a familiar voice as I caught up. This side, the door was opaque, preserving the Lieutenant's privacy. "Oh, it is only you. Wait while I get something on."

He had not yet learned to sleep comfortably in his smartsuit. The door vanished, he stood before us arrayed in Naval Reserve pattern, employing his usual vice-regal tone. "Have you any idea what time it is?"

"Everybody thinks I'm a chronometer this morning. What d'you think I have, ticks?" He glanced at me to see if I had appreciated the joke, then enjoyed a desultory scratch. "It is six-seventeen precisely, Lieutenant Sermander, of a beautiful artificial dawning in the season of your choice. Will you have some coffee, or will you just eat us here?"

The Lieutenant shot a look of hatred or something at the little canine, then gained control. "Coffee—yes. Something to eat as well, I think. What is the agenda today, Nahuatl? Another round of endless, profitless philosophizing?" Together we left the compartment, began walking back a few dozen meters to the transport patch we had arrived by.

"Profitless? Scarcely, Lieutenant. In the Confederacy, that would practically be a mortal sin. As I was explaining to the Corporal, this morning you're finally going to begin to grasp the function of this ship ..."

Sermander's eyes lit, but he kept his peace as he stepped into the wall.

Blackness, silence.

"Coffee and breakfast for two," Howell requested as we stepped through the carpet onto another patch. The chimp who met us nodded, turning away. Howell called, "And a brace of tender lamb-cutlets, rare, while you're about it, will you, with an iced mocha cappuccino. Gentlemen?"

I blinked. This was not another of the narrow corridors housing transients, nor the restaurant I had expected, but a broad, outdoor space, lit by an artificial sky. We were surrounded by jungle foliage, the bustle of multispecies traffic somewhere in the background, far beyond.

The resilient lavender walkway skirted the edge of a wide meadow. At its other end, looking as small as insects to us, several teams of individuals ascended or descended a rocky cliff-face, on ropes strung between them. There was a faint shimmer in the air around them. The area had been partitioned off somehow, forming its own climatic zone. On the other side, sand was blowing, a brisk wind fanned it into a wispy pompadour at the top of the cliff. The place almost resembled home.

Howell noted my interest: "That's for Sodde Lydfe," he observed. "A most difficult place, indeed. These conditions you observe are meant to duplicate the equatorial wet season. Certainly not my idea of recreation."

We stopped to peer at the cliff-base, where a pair of humanoid figures fired at an orange multi-legged beast clawing its way toward them. Its furious screaming was audible even on this side of the barrier. As the plasma hit, the hairy thing gave a cough, rippled, vanished.

"Hologram," Howell explained. "Keeps them on their toes. Shall we continue?"

Abruptly, the sidewalk plunged into a forest, through a clearing where a dozen chimpanzees were throwing flat steel knives at the butt of a log propped between the trees. The weapons stuck with a *thump!* Chatting gaily, the non-humans walked forward to recover their hardware.

"Also for Sodde Lydfe," Howell offered. "They really ought to be practicing in burnooses, with a desert gale howling. Elsewhere you'll find others, learning the knack of diving in water that's slushy with crusted salt, or attempting to control an ultralight plane in a dust-filled tornado. Now the Captain has returned, the training will double its pace, I'm afraid. Not my lid of tea, even if I do have a built-in sand-repellent coat. Let us betake ourselves, then, to moister climes, whatsay?"

The Lieutenant scratched his thinly-covered scalp, offered not a word.

I could see that he, too, was greatly impressed with the technical achievement *Tom Paine Maru* represented. Who would not be? There was discipline apparent here, as well, a purposeful order both of us could admire. Nonetheless, I continued worrying over the lack of clocks. Not a single book or sign, presented itself, nor any labels on products or artifacts. No thermometers or barometers to be seen. No one, at least in my sight, had consulted any written reference, nor written anything down.

If anyone had started a dossier on us, they were keeping it well hidden.

People aboard this ship simply seemed to *know,* without any of the effort that implied, without any source for the knowledge. It sent chilly fingers up my spine each time one of them halted to contemplate the insides of his eyelids for a moment, then produced data he had not possessed before. I wondered what the Lieutenant thought of it, all, but had not yet had a chance to ask him. Now might be the opportunity. Howell had continued walking along the path, while Sermander hung back preoccupied.

"Discipline, you say, Corporal?" He almost whispered the words. "Try asking one of these people about it. Its existence will promptly be denied! I have small patience for all this affected leaderlessness. There is an imperial iron fist hidden somewhere in the Confederate velvet glove. I am determined to know who wields it—and much more importantly, whom they will choose to wield it for them when they take Vespucci!"

Shock surged through me. "Lieutenant! You do not think—!"

"Be obedient to your orders, Corporal, if only for lack of a more substantial course. Be mindful of your duty. Accept my lead. Refrain from any unsolicited comment or unguarded opinion. I am aware that you are just as curious as I am about this 'Sodde Lydfe' planet, about all of these careful preparations being made. Still, I would caution you: accept only those answers that are volunteered to you. Ask no question yourself. That way we both may live to understand what is really going on."

WE CAUGHT UP with Howell along the purple walk, just as the sound of carefree laughter came splashing at us like sunlit droplets from a fountain.

The Lieutenant addressed the coyote. "If your community operates so equitably upon good will," he gave my pistol-belt a contemptuous look. "Tell me, Howell, what purpose is served by all these warlike preparations."

"Lieutenant, you couldn't possibly be more mistaken!" Howell laughed, an eerie sound in the mouth of a dog-creature. "Good will hasn't got a thing to do with it. And—you said equitability?—that's utterly irrelevant. Self-serving behavior of the productive, benevolent variety is simply more consistently successful than the aggressive or self-sacrificial kind. The Confederacy runs on nothing more than common greed. But won't you be seated so they may bring our food?"

Greed? I refrained from unsolicited comment.

The rubbery sidewalk had become a red brick court, centered on an enormous blue-tinted pool. Sprawled on the sunlit tiles everywhere, sitting at a dozen tables, lolling in the water, was a collection of sentients that made it look like the revolutionary committee at the zoo.

It was even possible I was seeing my first Orca.

That imposing individual lay at anchor in the pool, magnificent in black-on-white, rolling majestically, keeping a sensitive hide moist, exposing himself evenly to the warm rays of a non-existent sun. The pool was a miniature lake, not at all crowded by the herd of porpoises who enjoyed the water. There was a salty tang in the air, Chimpanzees, humans, the larger simians I had learned to call gorillas, lounged about, having their breakfast (lunch, dinner—you could never tell what "shift" someone was on), conversing quietly, doing any one of a dozen other things, none of which seemed connected with going to school.

Across the water I glimpsed Lucille. My heart jumped inexplicably. I had trouble breathing. She scowled back, then turned toward a tall, bronzed, sun-blonded male sitting at her table, laying an affectionate hand on his forearm. It was clear enough by now that she did not like me much. The compliment was heartily returned. Whenever Lucille and I began conversing, it invariably ended at high volume. Which made that twinge of—what, jealousy?—I felt toward the tanned muscle-man annoying.

It as just as well that we happened to be on opposite sides of the big pool just now. We appeared to be on opposite sides of everything else.

A small female chimpanzee stood at a whitewashed metal table under a gaudy umbrella. She began abruptly, "On Earth, the development of vocal speech from simple pack-hunting calls initiated a period of what might be termed 'catastrophic physical evolution' among the prehuman species. That period has left a contradictory legacy to this very day."

She spread her hands. "The question before all of us this morning is whether this catastrophic pattern is inevitable elsewhere, as well."

Taking a step toward the pool, she looked disdainfully into the water, unconsciously fingered her bracelet speech-synthesizer, her only article of clothing, as she waited for the background noise to die.

"We are speaking," she said, "of evolutionary changes occurring with hyper-rapidity, for the first time under the impetus of the evolving species itself, yet only partially so. And therein lies the tragedy: those involved had no idea whatever of what was happening to them."

The killer-whale pivoted on his tail, ribboning around to face the chimpanzee, regarding her with a docile brown eye that belied the ferocity of his teeth. Waves splashed over the edge, darkening the brick flooring. The fastidious female hopped backward, avoiding damp feet.

"Can this be?" demanded the Orca in a ridiculously shrill voice, "Can something be under control, as you suggest, and yet be out of control?"

"Understand, friend waterlog," interrupted a naked human dangling his toes at the pool's margin. His neatly rolled-up pistol belt lay on the sun-warm tiles beside him. "They thought they were doing something else!"

Laughter all around. I did not see anything funny.

Our table was near the water. One ear cocked to the conversation, Howell hopped onto a screen-seated chair. The Lieutenant dug into his breakfast without saying a word, ignoring what was going on. I sat down absently, forgetting my food, trying to make sense of things. I thought about Eleva, wondering if whatever I learned here might help get us home to Vespucci. Next to us, a gorilla played backgammon with an unfamiliar orange-furred alien draped in swollen purple rolls of fat.

"Quite correct," this unattractive individual offered through her wrist-talker. "Young Miss Lakebones simply felt that Mr. Flintchip told more amusing stories than any of his rivals. Which, from the typically human viewpoint, automatically made him better husband material. Unless he demonstrated his virility by raping her first, of course."

"Cynic! Maybe Mr. Flintchip simply whispered sweeter nothings," grinned a woman lounging in a suit adjusted to conceal everything but her skin. A huge pair of tinted spectacles perched atop her nose. She had laced her fingers together across her middle, a dozen centimeters too high (or too low) to salvage anything resembling modesty. She was even beginning to sunburn a bit, or was of a naturally red-pigmented subspecies.

"We've gone over this before," said the orange-purple alien.

"And we'll go over it again. The fact that humans evolved language at all refutes the image of our species—of its males, anyway—as inherently brutal, or that rape is instinctive, or that it's even particularly widespread! Believe me, we wouldn't be sitting here now discussing it. None of us humans would carry the genes to make that possible!"

At her feet, a pair of tiny black-haired children braided colored string complexly through their fingers. One of them gave a double flip of her wrists. The pattern changed completely, at which the other child giggled with delight. Children were present everywhere, in fact, human, non-human, many paying rapt attention. Others (in this respect they did not differ from their elders) variously ate, drank from tall, frosted glasses, dozed in the increasingly-hot sun, knitted, cleaned weapons, tanned, played table games alone or with companions. A blond bearded individual mercilessly stropped a huge curve-edged knife on a peculiarly-shaped stone as he listened to the conversation, testing its edge periodically on the fine golden hairs of his heavily-muscled forearms.

It was utter chaos.

Worse, I could not tell who was who. The chimpanzee I had taken as the lecturer, who had begun the session in what seemed the middle, had gone back to her table to ponder a chess problem, uttering not another word through the morning. Three meters away, a blonde, blue-eyed girl child with black skin sat on the warm brick tiling. She could have been no more than nine. In one hand, she held a loop-ended stick, in the other, a bottle of liquid, foamy at the top. She wet the loop, extracted it, blew through it, releasing dozens of glistening bubbles wafting on the still air over the pool, shimmering with iridescent color.

"Back to the point," the girl dipped into the liquid again. "Prior to this, Blind Nature had conducted evolution through a never-ending series of random mutations, winnowed for viability by environmental stresses. It was an excruciatingly slow, but excruciatingly thorough procedure ..."

The words sounded odd, delivered across a soft palate, through the merest beginnings of her second set of teeth, She blew again, making more bubbles. "Then, suddenly, folks began selecting themselves—rather, each other—for a narrow list of attributes, without any idea what they were doing, or of the likely consequences." Producing another impressive stream of bubbles, she subsided to let someone else talk.

This someone was a large gray dolphin sloshing around in the slanted shallows, delicately nibbling on a rack of freshly-grilled fish.

"Quite so," it whistled through its blow-hole while it ate. "Quite so. And yet before we speak to the frequently disastrous consequences of overly-selective processes, it is vital to realize that language, during this period and afterward—is only secondarily a medium of communication. It was and is vastly more important as the substance of rational thought, software for the mind, as will be the case wherever we—"

"There he goes again!" laughed a chimpanzee behind me. She waved a long cigarette-holder at the porpoise. "Needlessly belaboring the obvious!"

It was not that obvious to me. If speech is not primarily a means of communication, then in Hamilton's name, could it be what they said it is? Brain software? I leaned to whisper this question to Howell. Before I could, the Lieutenant grumbled, "So this is what you dragged me out of bed for, a midshipman squat-session at eight o'clock in the morning!"

The fellow sharpening the knife strode to the pool's edge, He was younger than I had taken him for, angrier, somehow. "Norris," he growled a sketchy introduction, "Just off the *Peter LaNague,* fresh from Obsidia!" He pointed the blade at his ankle, thickly bound in gray-silver. "I'll be disabled for two weeks because speech on that rotten mudball is neither communication nor thought!" He stood, the huge double-edged dagger in one hand, the odd Y-shaped stone in the other, feet spread in a combat-stance, daring anyone to contradict him.

The gorilla with her arm in that familiar-looking sling lounged beside the pool in a long reclining chair across from young Norris, "I got this day before yesterday, Charlie, just practicing for Sodde Lydfe."

For some reason, laughter rippled through the crowd. Somebody at a near-by table murmured something about "roller skates". Another said, "Clumsy!"

"I heard that!" I think the injured simian would have stamped her foot, had she not been lying down. "You ever try rappelling down a cactus-covered sand-mountain? Or diving in water so salt-saturated you need a hundred pounds of weight to keep you down? The whole planet is like that, and the operations we've planned are a lot more complex than anything we'll be doing on Obsidia the next few days. Sure it's a primitive world. There are lots of them, precisely because almost none have discovered the 'obvious' facts that this class is supposed to cover."

Norris nodded grudgingly, then turned to sit where he had been, but never stopped honing his knife, I wondered what would be left of it by the time we reached this "Obsidia" that he had spoken of so bitterly.

Now that it had been called to my attention, quite a few of those present were recovering in various stages from injury or disease. One person, a dark brown man with black, tight-knitted hair I had first mistaken for a cap, was covered with greenish blotches of some exotic infection. He lay in the "sun", soaking up energy as if it were a cure. Perhaps it was. In addition to casts or splints on every kind of limb possessed by these highly-varied beings, some wore flat bandages, eye-patches, back-packs, all constructed of the same basic smartsuit material. I wondered about the backpacks—then made myself stop. They would be an excellent place to carry an artificial heart or liver.

As before, the Lieutenant paid no attention to any of what was going on, but went back to his breakfast as mine grew cold while I gawked.

There was plenty to gawk at.

"Howell," I whispered at the coyote, "I thought that all of your Confederate ships were named 'Tom-' or 'Bob-' something, 'Maru'. That means 'ship', somebody told me. Now Norris says he is from *'Peter LaNague'*—"

"'Maru' is Japanese," said the coyote, "one of many languages of Earth."

"Okay," I said, "but—"

He interrupted me. "The universe that we live in is vaster than most individuals know, my young friend. It is vaster than they *can* know, ever. Not only is space itself infinite (or as near to infinite as makes no difference), so is time, you see. And in more ways than one."

"You are saying that there's more than one kind of *time?*"

"I cannot explain all of this at once, Whitey. I wish I could. But we have three fleets, altogether. *Tom Paine Maru, Tom Edison Maru,* and others of what we term 'Tomfleet', operate in one kind of space. *Bob Shea Maru, Bob Wilson Maru,* and all the other 'Bobs', operate in another kind of space, which is nearly identical, but separated from the first by a kind of time. A different kind of time than ... well, you lack the basic vocabulary, I'm afraid." He paused as if in thought.

"Peter LaNague is part of a ranger fleet that traverses the distance—or rather, the difference—between the two kinds of space."

"I see," I lied.

"You don't," Howell corrected cheerfully, "but you shall, with due effort."

He returned his attention to the larger conversation, still going strong. Something about "birth trauma", evolutionary cul-de-sacs. At least that is what it sounded like. We were not alone in having our own private colloquium. There seemed to be no rules, no discipline, no leaders. If it was indeed a "class", it was the strangest I had ever attended.

Everywhere small knots of people spoke quietly among themselves, seeming not to disturb others. In a corner near the pool, on a stretch of thick grass, a pair of human males sparred—some sort of karate—trading blows, grappling, stopping to contribute to the class discussion.

Madness.

"Right!" spoke an all-too-familiar voice, replying to the injured gorilla's comment about 'obvious' facts. Lucille said, "We've wandered off the subject. I was born on Earth, where this problem started. My mother was one of the Healers who had to deal with it when cross-time immigration began. My dad was an immigrant, fleeing a government fully as nasty as our Vespuccian 'guests' over there represent. Dad was a sort of pragmatic praxeologist who, for some strange reason was never afflicted—"

"It's you who're wandering now, my dear," said Howell politely. "And I believe that I, of all beings here, may speak to the subject of genetic predisposition with the greatest authority, having borrowed civilization from the human race, as have all you simians, without paying the evolutionary price. The origins of cetacean culture are lost in the mists of an antiquity so ancient as to be irrevocably untraceable."

He climbed from the chair seat to the tabletop.

"The real conundrum before us is: will a different evolutionary history, that of the Sodde Lydfens, engender a markedly different attitude toward authority? Will a different physical placement of the generative organs—at the opposite end of the body from those of elimination—have a salutary effect on their view of procreation? Most importantly, how will a broader birth-channel affect their fundamental psychology? Not to speak of their rather novel number of sexes ..."

It went on a full six hours, until noon, people arguing, joking, debating points I could not comprehend. We had breakfast, lunch, and something called "tea" that was more than something to drink. Now and again someone with no reason to know would announce news of this or that expedition to this or that planet. Occasionally scores were given for games called baseball, hockey, fencing, and metallic silhouette. I estimated that I understood an average of one word in ten, At last the session began to break up—perhaps "melt away" was a more accurate term. Increasingly fewer sat around the pool or were interested in the talk.

Abruptly, the blue-eyed child with the bubble-pipe jumped up to run in our direction. Without prelude, she threw both her arms around Howell's furry neck, then unhesitatingly kissed the coyote on the muzzle.

She looked and sounded normal until she said, "I gotta go now! Koko promised t'show me some United Statesian video flatties of Carl Sagan, for the History of Xenopsych lecture I hafta give tomorrow morning."

The coyote nodded, once he had been released, used his right front paw to poke a lock of the little girl's golden hair back into place. "That should be amusing, my dear. I believe I've seen those old tapes, myself, I needn't caution you not to take the fellow too seriously, Mowgli?"

"Aw, Daddy, please don't call me that!" The little girl blushed. "Anyway, Carl Sagan was practically a Kilroy, himself, wouldn't you say?"

Howell gave his odd laugh. "A few decades before the fact, and in a galaxy far, far away. It's a state of mind, sweetheart. See you at dinner."

She picked up her toys, said goodbye, ran full pitch away from the pool. He turned to us, pride in his electric voice, "Elsie, gentlemen, my daughter. She's the only xenopsychology student on our praxeology staff. Until lately, it was a discipline in search of subject matter. Now she finds herself the resident expert at a time of crisis, I'm afraid." He nipped at a knot in his fur. "Well, would you like to see something else, stir up the circulation a bit, perhaps think about a meal?"

"It will amount to nearly the only thing I shall have gained from an otherwise wasted morning," complained the Lieutenant. But he rose, following the child down the path with a confused expression on his face.

"Howell," I asked diffidently, as we left the brick-floored clearing for the deep woods again, "there is one thing you could explain ..."

He laughed. "Surely not that Elsie is adopted ... ?"

"No." I admitted how little of the morning's intellectual exercise I had understood, He assured me once again that, in time, all would become crystal clear. I had not believed it the first time he had said it.

"But Howell, I am most embarrassed to confess that I do not even know who the teacher at this morning's session was supposed to have been!"

The coyote stopped on the path, looking up at me. "Whitey, the principle focus this morning was on you—and the Lieutenant, of course."

"On us?"

"And you did perfectly splendidly. Take my word for it!"

NOBODY HEARS THE MANDOLAR

IT IS ONE thing to look at water, to appreciate the miracle of it, to sit on a bank dangling your feet luxuriously as it slips between your toes. It is quite another to ride on top the stuff, piled dozens—hundreds—of times higher than your head, grimly pretending you are enjoying yourself. In that respect, I shared the prejudices of chimpanzees.

"Wahoo!" a voice from somewhere shouted, as a curved, glistening, transparent wall of liquid threw itself against our boat, trying to overturn it. Overhead, a great white bird made noises like a rusty hinge.

"I knew you'd like this, Whitey!" said the same voice.

"Ulp!" I answered politely, giving the voice a sickly smile.

The wave passed—the water-wave, not the wave of nausea it had provoked—depositing cold salt spray down the neck of my borrowed nautical jacket. Koko Featherstone-Haugh, my sailing-companion for the afternoon, worked mysteries upon a bunch of ropes, then hollered at me to *duck!* The spar at the bottom of the sail swung suddenly around, just brushing the top of my head with only a hint of its potential for destruction.

The boat pitched over in the opposite direction.

As did my stomach. I threw up.

A strapping female who wore pink ribbons in her dark, curly hair, Koko kept a small four-stringed "ukulele" in a waterproofed custom smartsuit-fabric case somewhere belowdecks in this seagoing deathtrap. On a stout belt at her waist, replacing the plasma pistol favored by most *Tom Paine Maru* personnel, she lugged a monstrous antique reciprocating bullet-gun. It was a fifty-caliber Gabbet-Fairfax, she told me—about twelve millimeters—a gift from "a dear and trusted friend".

Oh yes: Koko was also a gorilla.

This might be why she quickly became one of the few individuals I felt sure about aboard ship—the big star-traversing one, not the wallowing marine disaster of this afternoon. Koko had been the person with the sling on her arm that morning beside the swimming pool. She was also the roller-

110

skating gum-bubbler I had seen aboard *Tom Lehrer Maru*. Off on a "mission simulation" somewhere else, she had returned to her own vessel, after having broken her arm during a practice climb.

With nothing but Vespuccian experience to guide me, never having met people like these, I was uncertain how to read them. Couper seemed like a man you could lean on, big, tough, ugly. On Vespucci, officers like him routinely ordered other men to certain death, all the while assuring them that everything was just fine. Owen Rogers was a fellow artisan, but with a distinctly Confederate attitude, whatever that ultimately implied. Howell, just like Koko, was not human, but I liked him.

On the other hand, I trusted that little witch Lucille no further than I could throw her. Probably not far at all, the way she had been trained.

Earlier that terror-filled morning, I spoke with the Lieutenant once again. He was fascinated with this great ship, with everything aboard her, with her obvious dedication to a cause. He seemed avid to possess what Rogers called "a piece of the action". How could a mere corporal insist that his superior consider more carefully what little we actually knew about this "action" that he so badly wanted a piece of?

"**CORPORAL, DO NOT** be a fool."

We were in the Lieutenant's quarters—a four-compartment suite featuring tall, broad windows overlooking *Tom Paine Maru's* answer to an ocean. Up to my ankles already in his sandy-colored wall-to-wall carpet, I looked down several dizzying stories, onto that dangerous, foam-flecked, shattered mirror, dazzling under the ship's artificial sun. Already I was anticipating this morning's new experience with dread.

Even this early, coming here, I had run across groups of people taking inhuman-sounding language lessons under the brilliant sky. I had seen peculiar equipment being manufactured in rooms I passed, or clothing being fitted or tried out. Repeatedly I had been told, "Oh, that's just for Sodde Lydfe—" Followed by an abrupt change of subject.

I needed to compare notes with my boss, to learn what he had discovered.

Lacking any artistic bent of his own, Sermander, whose talents lay more in persuading others to do things, had badgered Howell's little girl Elsie into selecting a 360-degree hologram of some less deadly desert than Sodde Lydfe, from a lengthy Confederate catalog of such images. This, apparently, was a planet called "Wyoming". Three walls were given over to it, creating an illusion of furniture grouped amid sandy scrub. They had dimmed the sun, edited visible vegetation, until it was indeed like the Central Oasis at what passed for springtime on Vespucci.

I cannot say it made me feel homesick. I had seen a battle fought in this place, during the Final War. Ten thousand dead. The facsimile only made me feel guilty—mainly for not thinking about Eleva all morning.

Koko, I had met formally last evening at a "dinner theater" my praxeologist friend had insisted attending, *Tom Paine Maru's* amateur musical production of *Loose Lips,* based on an ancient classic about a young mutant, the physician who taught her to capitalize upon her peculiarity, the many men whose problems her unique talents helped solve.

I blushed through the entire performance.

Recognizing Koko, I made the mistake of telling her how much I had enjoyed the swimming pool schoolroom. Her broken limb was fine now, in only a few days' time, thanks to the Confederacy's medical technology. She intended to celebrate by risking its integrity all over again, on the high seas. Distracted by the play, I found myself conscripted into going sailing along with her. Before keeping my dubious appointment with the ocean-going gorilla this morning, I was grimly determined to convey my doubts to the Lieutenant, in order to ask him what he thought.

He told me.

"Corporal O'Thraight, this vessel is over twelve kilometers in diameter. Twelve kilometers! These people—if we must call them that—are only a small part of something unthinkably more enormous. Just imagine the industrial establishment capable of such construction! Imagine the energy sources! Simply the place-names that we hear, the products that we sample, betray an empire vaster than Vespucci ever dreamed!"

He strode to a cabinet built into the bulkhead beside the door, poured himself a drink, tossed it back, then poured another. "This is so much larger than your petty misgivings, Corporal, so much larger than you are, yourself. But it is not, I assure you, larger than Enson Sermander!"

For some reason, he seemed uncomfortable on the glass-fronted side of the room. The view was somewhat daunting. Far across the water, cloaked in haze, nearly at the horizon, there appeared to be a city, with tall buildings gleaming. He paced the carpet in front of a sofa near the claustrophobic safety of the hallway door, one hand thrust into his pants pocket, the other locked around his drink. He seemed to mutter at the floor, rather than at me: "Yes, yes, I know what that must sound like. But let us try to face the facts, Corporal, let us be realistic."

"Yes, sir," I answered, my gaze distracted momentarily. Outside, several individuals of at least two species, wearing big multicolored triangular wings, soared above the pounding waves. "That is what I am attempting to do, sir. I am not comfortable, being friends with people I do not understand. I wish to know if you believe that they can be trusted."

"Entirely immaterial, Corporal—Whitey. They can be trusted to be whatever they are, to do what they have already done, to create a stellar hegemony with unimaginable resources to draw upon. Think, man: when they confront our puny world-state, Vespucci will not last a microsecond!"

"I admit I have been thinking much the same thing, Lieutenant. But is that not scandalously disloyal, shamefully unpatriotic, maybe even treasonous?"

"Think, Corporal!" the Lieutenant demanded again. "What does true loyalty to Vespucci demand of us? We must survive. We must learn what we can. We must return upon the day of confrontation with a complete understanding of these people, an ability to negotiate, to intercede, to ... "

To *rule*, he was thinking. The Lieutenant imagined himself the Confederate viceroy on Vespucci, destroying our independence to save it.

"But, sir, I—!"

"But nothing, Corporal!" He sighed dramatically: "Oh how true the observation is, that it is invariably the underclasses who defend the system and their place within it most vehemently. However, Corporal—Whitey—I am attempting to make an appointment with the captain of this vessel, whoever that may be. I await his call at any moment. I shall offer my knowledge of our planet, offer my wisdom in promoting peaceful contact between the two civilizations. Vespucci needs her strongest minds at this moment, her strongest hands, her strongest resolve—"

Her strongest stomachs. I had first heard a speech like this at the age of five, when they announced a reduction in the milk ration. I told myself that he could not help himself. He was an officer, after all.

"—in order to survive!" he was going on. "Trust them? In the long run, it is an investment. Work with them, relax with them, eat with them, sleep with them, if that is your inclination. I shall see you are awarded a medal for duty beyond the call. You can remain my aide, if that is your desire, or be a provincial governor, once we get home."

Once we get home.

Already, it had begun to sound like an unattainable fantasy. The Lieutenant was correct about one thing. We were helpless on our own, totally dependent on Confederate generosity for our eventual return to Vespucci, for our day-to-day survival, even for the clothes we were wearing.

"Yes, sir," I said, "If you say so, sir." I think I actually meant it. He scowled at me, then winced when his line-of-sight took in the far horizon, the vast agoraphobic chasm outside the floor-to-ceiling windows.

"Sir," I offered. "You can shut these windows off, if you want to. Just turn this knob at the base. They showed me how to do it when I was given my room downstairs." I demonstrated. The windows quickly faded to opaque. Just as quickly, the desert landscape wrapped around the room, enclosing us securely in the pseudo-familiar. The Lieutenant seemed to breathe easier. He finished off his drink, poured himself another.

"Thank you, Whitey. Now get out of here. Go—what did you call it?— 'sailing'? Perhaps it will take some of the starch out of that overly-stiff collar of yours. And while you're sailing, Corporal, think upon what part you might play in a New Confederate-Vespuccian Order."

I could actually hear the capital letters.

I got.

For days, sitting around, I am waiting for your call,
Hope my face won't fall—off the wall.
And the daisies in the ground are around ten feet tall,
Though they started pretty small, half-past Fall ...
Butterfly, how come why I never see ya?
Have your fun, when you're done,
I wouldn't wanna be ya!
'Cause I'm through sitting around, getting rusty on the shelf—
I can be lonely, by myself, without your help ...

Koko started over again at the bridge, "Butterfly, how come why ... ", repeating the final line. By the finish, I had figured out the chords—you mashed your fingers down on the strings between the inset wires, just as if they were buttons. Primitive, compared to the mandolar I was used to, but satisfactory. I was anxious to try it for myself.

She passed me the little box. It was a remarkably unsophisticated artifact for so technically advanced a culture. I found that I could omit the fingering-positions for the last two mandolar-columns, to play a creditable C, F, or G_7, strumming the strings where they passed an acoustic aperture in the body, just as if they were control-vanes. The resulting sound was crude, yet somehow wistfully appealing. Koko promised to show me a tune called "Ukulele Lady". As I experimented with her ukulele, the lady extracted a cigar from a pocket on her gunbelt, lit it, then lay back in the sand, watching the waves roll in.

We sat on a dune at the margin of the water. The "shore". It is only called a "beach" when there is sand. Her little boat was hauled up, its brightly colored sail furled. In the "west", the artificial sun was setting as spectacularly as any ever did, except, perhaps, on Sca.

I was still thinking about my earlier conversation with the Lieutenant. A year ago, perhaps even a month, I would have found his blatant opportunism normal, if not exactly admirable. Half of the conquests in Vespuccian history had been initiated in the name of advancing "international understanding". The pragmatism offered afterward—often in the name of the legendary philosopher MacVelly—as an excuse for duplicitude and treachery was standard classroom fare.

Now, having met these people of *Tom Paine Maru* and the Galactic Confederacy, I was no longer sure. They were powerful, accomplished, wise, but naive. The Lieutenant's intentions would have disappointed them.

Koko and I were not alone on the beach, although Confederates give each other lots of elbow-room unless otherwise invited. Other people watched the sunset. Several were assembling scraps of water-worn wood, for a fire—deliberately set aboard a starship, I reminded myself. A larger number stretched a net between poles thrust into the sand, then batted a ball over it, using their hands, their heads—even their feet.

One of these impressive kickers proved to be the injured Norris from yesterday's "class", late of the *Peter LaNague*. Blond, bearded, stocky, he was also short, almost tiny. Despite the dressing on his leg (I shuddered to contemplate what sort of wound required two weeks to heal in this society) he gave a good account of himself, spinning, twisting, lashing out with a good foot that was probably a lethal instrument.

I turned to Koko: "Tell me about Obsidia."

"Zzzzz—what?" She started awake in time to avoid a cigar burn to her pelt. "Where'd you hear about that? Oh, yes. It's just another primitive planet, Whitey, our next stop, according to the scientists. The name is one we assigned it, appropriate to its tech-level. People there don't know what a planet is, let alone that they live on one. There's about a zillion tribes, nations, empires, all of which call the place "Dirt" in their native languages. Conditions there are your standard 'nasty, brutish, and short', thanks to widespread sapient sacrifice, and a ruling priesthood in what we laughingly regard as the leading culture, very similar to the ancient Aztecs. If that means anything."

It did not.

"In any case, our work is almost done there, and it's our final visit for a while. Then on to Sodde—hold on, isn't this Howell coming?"

Koko must have had fantastically sensitive hearing. It was many seconds before I heard their voices, coming from the other side of a dune behind us, even longer until they were in sight. It was little Elsie I noticed first, chattering gaily, skipping barefoot alongside her father. Then I could not help but notice Lucille. Her costume may have begun as a smartsuit. Opaque here, transparent there—mostly transparent there—it was a tribute to Confederate technology. A while later, I remembered—with some annoyance at myself—to breathe.

They stopped, Koko exchanging greetings with the females. Elsie ran off at once to play in the water. The gorilla scratched the coyote behind an ear, careful not to disturb the dark glasses he was wearing. He extended a friendly paw to me. "Well, old fellow, how did you like sailboating?"

I reddened. "The porpoises would thank me if I gave it up."

I did not think until later to ask myself how he knew what we had been doing. Something inside me had begun to grow accustomed to the way these people seemed to read each other's minds, to know things without perceptible reason, to share information, experience, without speaking.

Koko laughed, not without sympathy. Howell admitted that he felt much the same about the sport. Lucille sat gracefully on the sand beside them, as far away from me as possible. She took a cigarette from a small case she carried—somehow it dispensed itself already lit—then gazed out, wordless, past its orange-glowing coal at the slowly darkening water. Less than a dozen yards away, someone set the head-high heap of wood afire. I felt its radiation on my face almost immediately.

Or maybe it was just my imagination.

"I'm glad we can offer something to offend everyone, Corporal." Lucille peered around the gorilla's impressive bulk, also the lesser obstruction of the coyote, to give me one of her most malicious grins. "You know it may surprise you to learn that there are individuals aboard this ship—the two legged kind and otherwise—with exactly the same instinctive reaction to your kind as you say you have to sailing."

She expelled smoke as if it were a bad memory. Then she took in another deep puff, let it drift from her half-open mouth, and inhaled it into her nostrils. For some bizarre reason, I found it horribly attractive.

But I was rapidly getting tired of her attitude. "Precisely what is my kind, Miss Olson-Bear, or are you not prepared to be specific?" My hands shook to match the racing of my heart. My words came from between gritted teeth—with anger or with what, I could not have said.

"Oh, our little Lucille is always prepared to be specific," Howell offered blandly. "Although somewhat less often to be courteous to our guests."

"Guests?" snorted the girl. "Is that what you call them, Howell? I'd use another word, myself! Your kind—since you ask, Corporal O'Thraight—is the uniformed, goose-stepping soldier-boy kind who wants to 'fight and bleed and kill and die', in the words of the poet, for an evil institution that hasn't any more right to exist than he has!"

Koko watched, her eyes mild, as fingers of heat felt their way up into my face. Howell shook his head, a very human gesture. "The 'poet' she cites was a satirist, after whom the shuttle you arrived on was named—blast!, there's just no way to end that elegantly without a preposition!"

I repeated Lucille's words. "No right to exist? I understand, then, how you could slaughter a whole company of men in the name of some stupid abstraction. On Vespucci this would make you a great politician!"

Her face redder than mine, Lucille was erect suddenly, threw her cigarette away, snapped into a combat stance. "Get up and say that, stormtrooper!"

"Why?" I asked her. "You only want to hit me for expressing my opinion."

"Oho!" Howell exclaimed, "Hoist by her own petulance, I believe! Have we suspended free speech when I wasn't looking, my dear, or is somebody—I won't mention her name—simply being unethical and rude?"

"Sit down, Cilly," Koko drew smoke, patted the ground with a hand as large as both of mine placed side-to-side. "You'll get sand in my ukulele."

As always, the furious girl glared sharply at the speaker when the name "Cilly" was pronounced. But she subsided somewhat: "All right, Koko—for you. For now! But somebody's got to give this Kilroy an education!"

116

"And aversive conditioning," replied the coyote, sarcasm dripping from the tiny holes in his collar-speaker, "is such a very effective means!" Koko offered him a drag on the cigar. He took it, inhaling deeply.

To my utter amazement, he actually got through. "Howell, please don't be mad at me. Can't you see? These Vespuccians are military. They represent a government!" She thumped back to the sand as Koko had suggested, this time only one space away from me, to the left of the talking coyote. My own reaction—whether to her anger or proximity—amazed me just as utterly. I folded an arm across my lap to conceal it.

He grinned, "I'm not angry, Cilly, say you're sorry, it'll make it square."

"I never apologize," her lower lip was trembling. "It's a sign of weakness!"

He laid his muzzle on her lap, looking up at her with big brown eyes. "On the contrary," he sighed, "it is partial payment of a moral debt."

There were tears in her voice, rather than her eyes, "I'm sorry, Howell ..."

"No, my dear, you must apologize to the Corporal, here. He's the one you've been riding. My back wouldn't have stood it for this long. I'd have to've done something about it." He gave me a significant look.

"I'd rather die!" It was almost a whisper, jaw tight, lower lip trembling.

"Somebody may eventually arrange that for you," I growled. "I will not be made to feel ashamed of my country. Sure, if everybody was like Howell or Koko, here—rational—then this anarchistic system of yours might just work. But if even one of them is like you, Lucille, then everybody needs the protection of the military or a government!"

Heaving my sea-tired body to its weary feet, I frowned down at the girl. "Now threaten me again! This time you will not throw me by surprise!"

Lucille's eyes grew large. She moved back a little. Howell shook his head, then looked at Koko as she reached up with a long arm to pat me on the shoulder with an astonishingly gentle hand. "Please calm down, Whitey," soothed the gorilla. "Nobody's going to hurt you, here."

A trickle of sweat ran down between Lucille's breasts, for some reason driving me half crazy. Beneath the upper portion of her virtual bathing suit, Lucille, too, was betrayed by an involuntary reaction very nearly as embarrassing as my own as hard points showed at their tips.

"Nobody will hurt you," Howell agreed with Koko, "Even if they wanted to. But what ever gave you the idea that rationality is a prerequisite to liberty? There's a sapient right to be free, period, whatever condition we find ourselves in. We do not need to earn it. Nobody has a right to withhold it from us until we do. Nor does a society operate on reason—which is an individual attribute—any more than it operates on kindness. As I recently explained to your Lieutenant with regard to criminality, in the Confederacy, stupidity and ignorance have just been priced out of the market, made too expensive ..."

"Whitey," Koko interrupted—these people seemed to do a lot of that— "In all of sapient history, there are only three ways that people have ever discovered to organize themselves. One individual can tell everybody what to do—that's called monarchism. Or everybody can tell everybody else what to do—that's called majoritarianism. Or—"

"Or nobody," Lucille almost shouted, although I could tell she was horrified at her bodily response to the idea of fighting with me, and trying frantically to calm down. "Nobody tells anybody what to do! Always the best way, Corporal. My sister Edwina and I were raised on the old Confederate Solar frontier, in a place called the Venus Belt. I—"

The girl stopped talking suddenly. There was another of those odd, lengthy, prescient silences. Then, even more voices came to us from behind ...

"But you cannot have it both ways," the Lieutenant bellowed. "Do you not see?" Koko, Lucille, turned in the direction of the noise. Howell's ears perked, but he kept his eyes on Elsie, playing in the surf.

"Three ways, you mean, Enson. Perhaps that's where you've gone wrong. It is Mindkind's second oldest argument: is the universe chaotic, as it often appears to be, or is it rigidly determined, as cause-and-effect seem to imply? Wait, now. Does free will truly operate, as we intuitively feel, or does determinacy eliminate any such possibility? And back around, does free will necessarily imply chaos?"

"Grrr!" The Lieutenant did not actually say that, but it was something close. "These are childish semantic games! Of *course* the universe is determined, my good doctor. Free will is a pathetic illusion!"

"Well," chuckled the other voice. "You could have fooled me. But then, I suppose that's what illusions are all about. Hello, darling. Hello, everybody! I'm attempting to introduce Lieutenant Sermander to the many wonders of praxeology, but he's resisting my blandishments manfully."

"Darling" turned out to be Koko. She reached a big hand upward to an even bigger one, while its owner bent down to give her a peck on the cheek. In the rapidly-gathering darkness, it was difficult to see precisely who this friend of hers was. A gorilla, certainly, male to judge from his size. He wore a sleeveless short-pantsed outfit in pale green with a large red circled cross on the left shoulder. He also wore light, wire-rimmed spectacles. He held a brown cigarillo in one hand.

He plumped down on the sand beside Koko.

"Francis," the gorilla began, "you know everybody except for the Corporal, here, Whitey O'Thraight. We went sailing this morning, while you were in surgery. Whitey, this is Francis W. Pololo, H.D., my husband."

Transferring the cigar to his left hand, he swallowed mine with his massive right. "Pleased to meet you, Corporal, did you like sailing?"

I was glad he could not see me blushing in the dark.

"Francis," said Koko, "you've made him blush! He did very well, for a first-timer. Where he comes from, they haven't any open water at all."

Now how had she known that? The people of *Tom Paine Maru* seemed almost telepathic at times, clairvoyant at others, sharing information and experience with each other without speaking, gazing at the ceiling and suddenly knowing. Now, apparently, they could also see in the dark.

"Nor praxeologists, I gather," Pololo observed, looking at the Lieutenant.

"That's obvious!" snorted a sarcastic voice the other side of Koko.

"Hello there, Lucille, how have you been?" Pololo responded, "I take it that you've been teaching Corporal O'Thraight the finer points?"

"Only of 'feudin', fussin', and fightin'," Howell scratched himself idly with a back leg, "They haven't gotten to praxeology, yet."

"What in the name of Hamilton's ghost is praxeology?" I demanded. I had been trying to get Lucille to answer that very question for days.

"Properly," intoned the gorilla, "it's the study of human action—and by extension," he brushed a hand over his pelt, patted Howell, "of the actions of all Mindkind, taking in everything from ethics and epistemology, through sociology and anthropology, to politics and economics."

"Are you a teacher of this subject?" I asked.

"Dear me, no," said Pololo. "I'm a physician, Corporal, a Healer, which is not a praxeological discipline, but a physio-mechanical one. It's simply an interest of mine, as it is with many—otherwise, soap operas would soon lose their lucrative appeal. I met your Lieutenant, here, while he was attempting to find the ship's captain." He grinned at his wife who looked down at the sand, shaking her head. "I've been trying ever since then to explain to him why that's such a difficult undertaking."

Even in the dark, I could sense the Lieutenant's exasperation. "The good doctor assures me that there is, indeed, a captain. Yet no one will conduct me to the bridge, to the control-room, or even to the captain's cabin. I have been assured that this personage may be found at unpredictable times in private quarters—which do not appear to exist—or in a certain forest. I wandered that forest for three hours this morning, witnessing nothing more than several groups of picnickers!"

Koko laughed. "You might have seen me there, any morning. I like picnics."

BEFORE US ON the beach, the fire burned low, no longer reflected by the moon-glistening waves rolling up onto the sand. One by one, the celebrators had departed, first the strangers who had built the fire, played games, eaten primitively-cooked food, sung several songs as we listened to them. Then Koko, her husband, the Lieutenant, muttering about "getting an early start". Finally the Nahuatls, Howell and Elsie.

The evening was warm. Breezes off the water were moisture-laden. Even Lucille, who had remained behind, seemed not at all unpleasant, breathing close beside me in the darkness. She graced the air with a fragrance all her own, that had everything to do with being female, and nothing at all to do with perfume. Eleva, Vespucci, the Navy, my duty, all seemed very far away at the moment. Thoughts of witchery, dangerous, often unbearable—but oh, so stirring—crowded into my mind.

"What?" I asked, jolted out of my reverie.

Lucille, however, could never just leave things alone. "I said, 'a permanently powerless underclass'. Why don't you ever pay attention Corporal? That's what you come from, you know, without hope, without a future. What's it like to spend your whole life, cradle-to-grave, *in grade?*"

I began to feel different, less pleasant emotions. "This is not strictly correct, Lucille. I am a corporal, now, but we are all born privates." Except, of course, for officer class children like the Lieutenant.

She said, "I'll refrain from the dirty double-entendre that inspires."

"That is uncommonly decent of you, Lucille. Are you sure you feel well?"

"Aha!" she exclaimed. "The worm turns at last! You're learning bad habits with us here, Whitey. Sassing back. Disrespect for authority. Hell, I thought you were actually going to hit me, back there for a minute."

"I do not hit women," I told her. Not even small, nasty-tempered ones who needed it, I thought to myself. Despite the edge in her words, Lucille's had softened with the last few phrases, dropped half an octave. It was the first time she had ever called me by my given name.

I wondered what she wanted.

She snorted: "I understand. It would be discourteous. Unmilitary. 'Duty, Honor, Country'. Is that all you really want out of life, Corporal?"

Even in the darkness, I could imagine the arch of her eyebrows. If anyone could manage a come-on sneer, it would be Lucille, I thought. Me, I wanted to go home to Eleva. Now, more than at any other moment, even in the dungeons of Sca, I wanted—I needed—to go home to Eleva.

"Come on, Corporal, tell us what you really want. To save glorious Vespucci—what a name!—from us bad, nasty anarchists? Is that what you want? Well, I've got some news for you. It'll take a better man than you are to do it—and he won't want to! You'd have to do a heap of growing, all in the wrong direction, as far as your culture's concerned."

"What do you mean by that?" I snapped.

"Nothing much. Except that at this moment, in order to serve the best interests of Vespucci as you conceive them, you're going to have to overcome what it created in you: passivity, resignation, overawe for the high and mighty. It's ironic, but far from surprising. To save your precious culture, you've got to become what it least wants you to be."

"What is that? You were going to say 'a man', were you not? Not very original. Nor very true, although I do not expect you to see it. Your friends are all afraid to say it, but you do not see very much of anything, Lucille, except the mixed-up angry garbage inside your own head."

Craaack!

My mouth stung where she had backhanded it. I had known it would happen, sooner or later. Grinning, I spat out a drop of blood, feeling as if my arteries were charged with something carbonated. "What is the matter, little girl? You can ration it out, but you cannot take it yourself?"

Lucille leaped up, turning to stamp away. In the last flicker of firelight, I seized her by the ankle, twisting my wrist. She slammed back onto the ground, spitting sand as I had been spitting blood just an instant before. In the heat of the moment, she seemed to forget what she knew of real combat, raining ineffectual blows on my chest and shoulders as I crawled alongside her, holding her down. I grabbed her wrists, held them together with one hand. Her face was flushed—I could feel the warmth of it on my own—her breath came in harsh gasps.

Then she composed herself: "Okay, let's do something military," she said sarcastically. "How about a little rape to round out the evening's—"

I pressed my free hand hard over her mouth—her eyes had gone wild— "Lucille," I told her, "with you, I suspect that would be impossible."

She would have hit me again, but by then I had skinned her suit down over her upper arms, binding her. In another moment, she was free again, completely, as was I. Her small, naked breasts were crushed against my chest. Her mouth half open, her eyes rolled back in her head, she moaned, almost screamed as I penetrated her. Her back arched, her arms locked rigidly around me, pulling me deeper inside her. She thrust her flat, hard belly against me, climaxing before I did.

An unbearable light flared within my brain, a brilliant, all-consuming white light that left little violet sparks behind when it faded.

Eventually, they faded, too.

For a moment, it had felt to me as if I knew the secrets of the universe, the answer to every problem men had ever confronted. As she lay in my arms, breathing hard, her voice, very low now, husked in my ear.

"What took you so fucking long, Whitey?"

THE WRATH OF KOKO

"MORE COFFEE, CORPORAL darling?"

The swimming-pool session, the Lieutenant's argument with Pololo, were neither the first educational experiences I was subject to aboard *Tom Paine Maru*, nor by any means the last. There were moments when the entire ship felt like some vast stargoing campus, but it was always difficult distinguishing teachers from students, or schooltime from recess. Maybe that had something to do with the utter absence of books.

Recess did have its moments, however. "No, thank you," I answered her. "I believe that I will just lie here for a while, gathering my strength."

The low buzz of something called a "bumblebee" distracted me for a moment. As it faded, I could hear the trilling of something called a meadowlark.

I leaned over to kiss Lucille in the hollow of her beautiful collarbone. She ducked her head—it turned out she was very ticklish—grinned, then grabbed me around the neck, wrestling me down on my back.

Everybody seemed quite anxious that I should learn ... whatever it was they wanted me to learn. I was aware that the Lieutenant was going through much the same thing. I liked most of the individuals I came to know, human or otherwise, very much. They were almost unanimously warm, kindly, generous with everything. How they could embrace a cold, unfriendly, discredited philosophy like capitalism was beyond me. But if I had heard "There ain't no such thing as a free lunch" once in my first few days aboard *Tom Paine Maru*, I had heard it a thousand times.

Of course, it was possible that one pose or another was a lie.

"Well, you lazy bum," she shook my shoulders. "I do!"

"What? Oh—coffee—please go ahead without me."

One consistency remained. The focus of nearly every conversation was the planet Sodde Lydfe. Every anthropology seminar I was pressed into attending by Howell, Elsie, Koko, or Lucille, lectures about psychology, geography classes, economic dissertations, all were aimed at analyzing strange cultures

122

that, in turn, were compared to others I had never heard of: Nazi Germany, Stalinist Russia, Socialist England—a similar place called Denmark—Nortonian California, Occupied Hawaii.

Occupied by whom?

Lucille tried to help: "Nazis are a local brand of fascist," she explained with ill-concealed impatience. Coffee or not, I felt she had something other in mind that morning—again—than discussing politics. "From that first place I ever told you about—remember 'groupies'?"

Unselfconsciously naked, she rolled onto one side, ran a finger in a circle over the middle of the bed between us. Not for the first time, I thought that I had seen celebrated paintings at home that were less heartbreakingly beautiful than Lucille was, with her small but perfectly formed breasts, her slender waist, her narrow, almost boyish hips, her long, flawless legs. The surface firmed between us. She took her cup off the nightstand where it had filled itself, set it on the mattress, then reached back for a cigarette rising through the tabletop.

"I remember." I tried to avoid sneezing when the first tendril of tobacco smoke drifted toward my face. "Also that you called my uniform 'fascist modern'." I thought back over the history lessons inflicted on me over the last few days. "The Nazis were United Statesians, then?"

It was strange, waking up in a forest clearing. Breezes stirred the evergreens a hundred meters away, rippled uncut grass that lay between them and us. The field was littered with upjutting boulders, covered with gray-yellow lichen, outcroppings of prickly-pear whose blossoms were attended by flying insects. Our bed was being circled, high above, by a broad-winged raptor that passed overhead as if he could not see us—which he could not, since he was a holographic recording, just like everything else displayed on Lucille's apartment walls.

She wrapped the sheet about her, depriving me of the room's most scenic view. "Good memory, for a Kilroy, Whitey, but in that era, the entire world was controlled by fascism: Nazis in a nation-state called Germany, *Fascisti* in Italy, Shinto in Japan, the New Deal in the United States. similar things elsewhere, though people didn't always realize what philosophy was in the driver's seat. Check into Zionism sometime."

She dragged deeply on her cigarette, then ground it out in a glass dish she'd taken from the nightstand. "A provincial governor—Huey Long—was asked whether fascism would ever take his country over: 'Yes, but we'll call it anti-Fascism'. And he was right: everybody was election-bent to make the trains run on time, just like on Vespucci, Efficiency and discipline are the keywords, am I right, Corporal O'Thraight?"

Lucille could never resist giving me the needle. I was learning to ignore it. "Damn it, is no one ever going to tell me what a Kilroy is?"

She laughed: "By coincidence, an expression from the very period we're talking about, a sort of a fragment of a joke. Millions of conscriptees battled

123

all over the planet as politically identical nations struggled for control. Wherever the slave-soldiers went, they saw a chalked-up drawing of a little man—" She held the sheet up, fingers curled over the edge, her nose resting between them. "—and the legend, 'Kilroy Was Here'. Me, I always thought it was a pretty black piece of establishment humor: countless men and women bleeding and dying, thinking that they were fighting the dragon, when, all the time ..."

She trailed off a moment, then, "Anyway, when we Confederates finally had a reliable stardrive—as opposed to the engineering nightmare that got your ancestors into trouble—we burst out into space, expecting an endless, open frontier. Instead, you—the Vespuccians, the Scavians, the Obsidians, everybody else—were here first."

She pulled another lighted cigarette from the bedside table. Taking it from her hand, I drew on it experimentally, then made the horrible mistake of inhaling. When I was through coughing, I said, past streaming tears, "So we are all of us Kilroys—also we are fascists."

"Right," she nodded, dropping the sheet. Paralyzed by the reminder that this beauty had been mine to take and hold and play with, and would be soon again, I nearly forgot what the conversation had been about.

"Somebody once observed," she said, "that the word 'Kilroy' might be interpreted—in a language of Earth called French—to mean 'Kill the King'. Now that's a joke of a different color. Maybe it's us who are the Kilroys, since it's our solemn, sacred duty to kill off the very concept of a king! Well, are you about through dogging it, Corporal-baby?"

Ah, the endless joys of courting a military woman. My spirit was more than willing, but the flesh still needed a little time. I thought back to her laundry-list of badguy governments. "I was told that this California was a part of the United States. So how did it get to be separate—"

"A different time, Whitey, a very different world. California was a fascist state before the word ever got invented, back in the first century of the Confederacy. It had an Emperor, Norton the First—and Last, thank Gallatin. But the real power was Hamiltonian, kicked out of the Confederacy after the Whiskey Rebellion. We had trouble with them again, the next century, Prussia, the War Against the Czar. They always like someone else do their fighting. They held Hawaii for a while."

I wanted to say that I was a Hamiltonian—it is a name straight out of legend, but this was not the time. Unless I was ready to get dressed and leave her quarters. In any case, another thought struck me: North America seemed to have about twice as much history as it deserved, considering the time involved. This confused me. I said as much.

"Whitey, that's absolutely brilliant! And I hate people who give me answers like this, but I think you lack the necessary background in physics to go any further—with this particular conversation, I mean."

She lay back on one elbow, pulled my mouth down to hers. When I could breathe again, I asked, "What has physics got to do with history?"

"My darling Corporal, the real world isn't divided into subjects, like high-school curricula. You need physics to understand the Second World War—radar, Hiroshima—or to understand the part played by Guccione cells in the Antarctican campaign of the War against the Czar."

I shook my head, weary of answers like that, myself. "So tell me something I do not need physics for—say, something about yourself, Lucille."

She laughed again, but with bitterness touching at the edges of her voice. "My word, you need more physics for that, dear Whitey, than you do for any-thing else we've discussed. But all right, then, I was born on Earth, although just barely: my folks had recently been to the Venus Belt, and they returned there, shortly after I was born. I was raised on a homestead with my sister. We both grew up and studied praxeology."

She lit another cigarette.

"Edwina Olson-Bear?" I asked. "Somebody mentioned her as Chief Praxe-ologist."

"Whither thou goest, honey," Lucille replied enigmatically again, assum-ing a grim expression. "As I was, once, before her. She taught at the same uni-versity we both graduated from. I opted for field studies, aboard the original *Tom Sowell Maru*. Yet somehow, we both wound up here ..."

This initiated another thoughtful moment. Abruptly, she set her cup back on the nightstand, resoftened the bed-surface, got up with a graceful, un-winding motion. The outdoor scene vanished, replaced by white, sterile walls. "To the state with that, Corporal, we're burning daylight."

"But Lucille, I thought—"

"You pissed it away, sweetie. Thinking about my sister too much gives me a severe case of the nuns. I'm not in the mood any more. Just like a man, all action and no traction. Now get out of here, I want to dress."

⋅✺⋅

I FOUND HOWELL—RATHER, he found me—in the hall outside my com-partment.

I had not been back for three days, not since a dreamlike evening on the beach that now seemed like a century ago. I discovered with chagrin that I had not thought of Howell during that time, nor of anybody else. particularly Eleva, toward whom I was not only feeling guilty for what I had done, but for the enthusiasm with which I had done it. In penance, every muscle ached, particularly my lower back. I desperately wanted a shower, despite the con-tinuous cleansing of my suit.

I also needed to talk. In a few well-chosen words—selected during the angry walk back to my room—I conveyed to the coyote the difficulties that

125

I was having understanding a difficult subject. Women in general, Lucille in particular. Or possibly the other way around.

"Over surprisingly few generations," the ceiling was lecturing when the door cleared, "the human brain enlarged without correlative changes in the mechanics of reproduction, which necessitated greater and greater prematurity of birth. Even so, human beings are the only known mammal for whom birth is an agonizing—" Not having known how before my stay in Lucille's quarters, I now waved it off, adjusting the walls to pretend that they were nice clean open interstellar space.

"Well, I can tell you at least one part of Lucille's story ... " the coyote offered as I sagged into a chair. I did not even have the satisfaction of taking off my shoes. The damned things were part of my clothing, more comfortable than going barefoot. He hopped onto another seat, wrapped his bushy tail neatly about his hind-quarters. "... and explain one of her mysterious remarks. She can be very annoying, can't she?"

Beyond a weary, assenting grunt, I did not bother to reply to him, but simply sat there, steeping in the disgusted realization that I felt worse in that moment than I ever had, even in the dungeons of Sca.

"Naturally," Howell continued, once aware that silence was all he was going to get from me, "I would not reveal anything that Lucille would not willingly volunteer. I have known her for a long time, and watched her grow from a lovely child into a somewhat tragic young woman. But this much is public knowledge: Lucille grew up to become head of praxeology aboard the *Tom Paine Maru,* Whitey—and her sister's boss. It was not an arrangement contrived in any pleasant mythological realm. The two sisters have never been on the best of terms."

"Howell," I said abruptly, "I want a straight answer. If you do not have it, then I want to know who does. When, if ever, can I go home?"

"Oho, a change of subject. Or is it? Whitey, I—"

"Please do not string me, as your people say, my furry friend. I have been asking that question, among others, since I first boarded the *Little Tom.* But I have yet to receive an answer that satisfied me."

Howell sat thinking for a moment—if that was what he was doing—then: "I'm afraid you can't go home, poor fellow. Not yet. Events are about to culminate on Obsidia. We also have stops to make at Hoand and Afdiar. There is, as you know, a major operation being planned for Sodde Lydfe. We are sorely pressed for time, and we cannot afford a detour—"

"Howell, stop lying to me! I will not be deterred this time, not by you or by anybody else. This ship is made of smaller ships. Surely one—"

He raised a paw: "The truth, then, although I wish you'd waited until Obsidia. It might have clarified matters. Still, no one ought to operate on faith. My boy, *Tom Paine Maru,* and all within her, rely upon a recent technological revolution so vast as to make the First Industrial Revolution, or what happened in electronics afterward, seem minuscule."

"More physics!" I snorted.

"How's that?" He blinked at me.

"Nothing, Howell. Only I am tired of being offered philosophy instead of substance. Lucille with her politics. Koko's husband with his nonsense about free will, chaos, or determinism. Your own little girl-child with her anthropological dissertations. Just get on with it."

"Elsie's nine, it's true. Rather small for her age, but a typical Confederate person in every other respect. Whitey, all three ancient propositions are valid: the universe is random, but within natural law; its apparent chaos is merely the result of its complexity. It is determined, knowable, orderly. Free will—not an arbitrary set of trivial whims in defiance of what's true or possible—grows from the fundamental nature of the entire universe, and consistently with it. Consider—"

"Howell!"

"Very well, you are aware of the situation on Sodde Lydfe. What do you suppose would happen if either the Great Fodduans or the Hegemony of Podfet managed to get hold of even a fraction of *Tom Paine Maru's* capabilities?"

Those were Sodde Lydfen nation-states I had discussed a little with Lucille. Thinking about her, feeling the strange sensations that merely thinking about her caused me, made this all the more urgent. I had to get home to see Eleva. Yet, equally, I had to answer Howell truthfully, as he seemed to be doing with me. "It would not be very pretty."

"Now, and this is the ethically touchy part, why should we of the Confederacy more sanguinely convey such knowledge to the government of Vespucci?"

It was about what I had been expecting. "I suppose that makes me—also Lieutenant Sermander—something of an embarrassment, does it not?"

He laughed, "Only by demanding what is morally due you. Believe me, we are not kidnappers by choice. No policy has been made with regard to you. We don't know what policy to make. Is it possible you owe us something—for the rescue on Sca? Yes? Then bear with us. When we have a little breathing-space—after Sodde Lydfe—we'll arrive at a solution mutually satisfying to all. That is the point of our of civilization, as you will come to learn with the passing of time."

ELSIE OFFERED TO be "mother", serving hot tea from an insulated plastic baggie until the Lieutenant, the last of us she got to, held a hand up, refusing the drink. Nodding, she placed the "teapot" in the center of a small table where it jiggled, then climbed into her own chair.

"Now," the little girl said, settling in and taking a sip of her own tea, "as the saying goes, I suppose you wonder why I called you here."

"Here" happened to be Koko and Pololo's apartment in what looked like an escarpment wall overlooking a dense tropical forest. Howell had showed up at my quarters to invite me over. At his request I had rounded up the Lieutenant, who had brought me up to date on his own explorations:

"I have continued searching," he had told me on the way to Koko's, "for the uppermost strata of the Confederate hierarchy—to little effect."

I kept on walking, not saying anything. Now we were approaching a transport patch where the coyote, having presently gathered up his tiny scientist daughter, was supposed to meet us. The truth was, I did not much like these devices. I was not looking forward to using one again.

The Lieutenant continued: "I have, however, exacted the promise of an appointment with the captain of this vessel, later in the day. You simply would not believe the lengths that I have had to go to, merely to achieve that barely minimal assurance. Corporal—are you paying attention?"

"What? Oh—yes, sir!"

"Very good. I have just learned, for example, that this great ship has no identifiable control room, as difficult as that may be to credit."

"What?"

"Precisely. No one has an office. There are no stenographers, no clerk-typists, no filing cabinets, no telecommunications devices, save for the ubiquitous wall-displays, or the makeshift arrangement that we witnessed in that canteen aboard *Tom Lehrer Maru*. Whitey, there is no engine room! Just restaurants, shops, parks, other recreational or training areas—some machine shops, if that is what they really are."

I shook my head, my own purely mental filing cabinet of bizarre facts filled to overflowing. Outwardly, I just trod grimly to our destination.

Who were these people, anyway?

Now, while we sipped tea as if nothing out of the ordinary were going on, Francis Pololo grimaced, "Well, don't keep them in suspense, dear. Otherwise, you'll wind up treading on the punchline. It's almost O-hour."

The female gorilla shrugged, causing the pink ribbons in her hair to bob comically. "Lieutenant Sermander, I'm told that you've been looking all over for the captain of *Tom Paine Maru*. I understand that you even rented a diving-rig this morning, and dropped in on the Orca settlement at Seahunt. Well, I have a message from the captain: don't bother any more. She doesn't wield any power you'd be interested in."

"She?" It was a disappointed croak.

"Satisfied?"

He opened his mouth, a puzzled expression on his face, then shut it.

Koko continued, addressing me, "You've been wondering about the mission of *Tom Paine Maru*. I wish I could say that I've arranged events to show you, Whitey. It's all going to look disappointingly simple. But what you're about to witness has been under consideration for eighteen years. I did arrange this tea-party, though. Will that do?"

Overhead, the ceiling starscape cleared.

"Obsidia," Howell announced, indicating the yellow-orange globe above our heads. "We share the viewpoint of a scoutship making her way toward the surface. Williamson's *Little Tom*, in fact, if I'm not mistaken."

It was a dazzlingly brilliant day, the local sun baked down on a dusty continent toward which the little scout ship was now falling. Suddenly, the viewpoint seemed to zoom ahead to a city, primitive but impressive, made of huge stone pyramids. At the flattened top of the tallest of them, a ceremony was in progress, witnessed by tens of thousands who stood on the stepped flanks of the building, looking upward.

"Here we go, folks" Koko chuckled. "I've been looking forward to this—"

A solitary individual, his humanity all but disguised in elaborate feather trappings, stood beside a bed-sized stone across which lay stretched the supine naked form of a young man. In his hand, the gaudily-dressed official held a black dagger raised above the youth's unprotected chest. It glinted as the sun caught its faceted glassy surface.

"Ev should be in range just about any moment, now," said Pololo, excitement overpowering even the well-collected Healer, "I think we should—"

"—of the Sun who is the Sun!" the priest shouted. "We beseech you to accept this unworthy offering from thy miserable and humble servants!"

There followed a great deal of indistinguishable mumbling as the congregation below him made their memorized response. The priest held the glassy knife high. Oddly, his intended victim seemed unalarmed at the prospect of being made into an unworthy offering. Suddenly, a black, circular shadow dozens of meters in diameter—just right for a ship the size of *Little Tom*—fell across the truncated pyramid top.

"HEAR THOU THE WORD OF THE LORD, THY GOD!"

It was Elsie's voice. The child grinned sheepishly at me from across the room. "They offered me the chance, Whitey. I just couldn't resist."

"THOU SHALT CEASE THIS ABOMINABLE PRACTICE IMMEDIATELY AND FROM THIS DAY FORWARD!"

The priest dropped his knife. It missed its reprieved victim by a less than a millimeter, clattering on the altar beside him, shattering into pieces. He fell to feather-draped knees, hands wringing together heavenward. Everybody else on the pyramid had eyes only for the scout saucer.

"I TELL THEE THIS DAY THAT I AM GOING AWAY!" A low moan swept through the crowd, down the sides of the pyramid, dissipating in the crowd on the ground. "FROM THIS DAY FORWARD SHALT THOU HELP THYSELVES, NEITHER SHALT THOU WORSHIP ANY GOD. INSTEAD SHALT THOU RESPECT MY LAW, THAT THOU MAYEST SOMEDAY BE LIKE UNTO GODS THYSELVES. HEAR, NOW, THE LAW:

"THERE SHALL BE NO GOD BUT MAN.

"MAN HATH THE RIGHT TO LIVE BY HIS OWN LAW.

"MAN HATH THE RIGHT TO LIVE IN THE WAY THAT HE WILLETH TO LIVE.

"MAN HATH THE RIGHT TO DRESS AS HE WILLETH TO DRESS.

"MAN HATH THE RIGHT TO DWELL WHERE HE WILLETH TO DWELL.

"MAN HATH THE RIGHT TO MOVE AS HE WILLETH UPON THE FACE OF THE PLANET.

"MAN HATH THE RIGHT TO EAT WHAT HE WILLETH.

"MAN HATH THE RIGHT TO DRINK WHAT HE WILLETH.

"MAN HATH THE RIGHT TO THINK WHAT HE WILLETH.

"MAN HATH THE RIGHT TO SPEAK AS HE WILLETH.

"MAN HATH THE RIGHT TO WRITE AS HE WILLETH.

"MAN HATH THE RIGHT TO MOULD AS HE WILLETH.

"MAN HATH THE RIGHT TO CARVE AS HE WILLETH.

"MAN HATH THE RIGHT TO WORK AS HE WILLETH.

"MAN HATH THE RIGHT TO REST AS HE WILLETH.

"MAN HATH THE RIGHT TO LOVE AS HE WILLETH, WHERE, WHEN, AND WHOM HE WILLETH.

"MAN HATH THE RIGHT TO KILL THOSE WHO WOULD THWART THESE RIGHTS."

"**BUT THIS IS** fomenting sheer anarchy!" the Lieutenant exclaimed, "It is nothing but a declaration of war against everything we know as civilization!"

"Exactly," Elsie said, somehow curtseying while sitting down.

The picture in the camera-eye wheeled as the saucer banked, whirled away heavenward toward its niche in the belly of the mother ship.

The Obsidians were on their own.

"Freely adapted from 'the Great Beast', Aleister Crowley," Howell observed. He bent to lap at his drink. "And omitting—against my specific advice—the Non-Aggression Principle, on the grounds that the Obsidians need to develop that for themselves, which I doubt they will."

"Howell," argued Doctor Pololo, "People can change, a fact of which governments are abysmally ignorant. People can get both smart and ethical in a big hurry when they clearly see a chance to gain by it."

Koko chimed in, "Yes, and Mr. Crowley's 'commandments' ought to help them accomplish all of that and more. All that is necessary to establish the right conditions for that to happen is for oppressive religion—"

"And," insisted the little girl, "government of any kind."

"—which actively prevents such personal growth—" added Pololo.

"It has a great interest in doing so," said Elsie.

"—to go away." Koko finished.

"Which fails to explain why Crowley himself," the coyote growled, "lacking the Non-Aggression Principle, became an admirer of the fascists."

"Them again?" I groaned.

Howell sighed, "Ah, well, perhaps the praxeologists know what they're doing, although I wouldn't attest—I say, what's the matter?"

"You animals!" It was the Lieutenant. He had dropped his cup on the floor, jumped up from his chair. He stood now in a rigid posture, his fists clenched at his sides. "You are nothing but criminals! I have watched you! I know what you are doing! I see the revolts that you are preparing to inflict upon the governments of innocent nations! No wonder that you have no captain! You have probably murdered him in his—"

Howell yawned. "Well, at least the man didn't say 'innocent governments'."

"You're dead wrong, Lieutenant, we do have a captain," It was Koko speaking. "She's more of a manager, really. After all, this vessel is a complex enterprise which she supervises on behalf of its owners. In some senses, they are everyone and anyone, here and there, on or off the ship. *TPM* is a corporation and the property of a corporation, actually commanded by the scientific staff who determine her course and—"

"The captain, a female!" Wounded disbelief was plain again in his voice.

"And a gorilla—me. It's a family illness. The uncle who raised me was the last President that the North American Confederacy ever had."

THE PURPLE HEART APPROACH

"UNGH!"

The front snap-kick was slow, aimed at my solar-plexus. I swiveled my hips slightly, to take the tender arch of the Lieutenant's right foot on my elbow. It was risky, but a very effective maneuver when it works.

This time, it worked.

Hopping furiously on his left foot while cradling the insulted right, the Lieutenant let a single tear of agony escape from beneath each eyelid. "Corporal O'Thraight!" he exclaimed, once he was through complaining to the ghost of Alexander Hamilton, "This is supposed to be practice!" He was so short of breath he could hardly get the words out.

I shook my head to clear away the angry fog. "Very sorry, sir, I guess I got a little too enthusiastic." Despite what had happened on the beach or for three days afterward, the underlying hostility that Lucille had earlier expressed toward me had remained, inevitably to blow up into a terrible fight. It had been idiocy to imagine, even for the briefest moment, that the two of us would ever be anything but enemies.

Taking a series of deep breaths, myself, I tried hard to relax now, realizing that I had been taking all my frustration out on the wrong—

Baaapp!!

Knuckles seemed to come out of nowhere, smashing into the side of my unguarded head above the right ear. I might as well have been sound asleep. Ordinarily, the Lieutenant was so slow he couldn't surprise a freeze-dried rock toad. I stumbled backward, belatedly raising my guard as the Lieutenant moved like winter cactus sap for a second turning back-fist. It glanced harmlessly along the diagonal of my forearm.

"Let that be a lesson to you, Corporal," sniggered my superior. He leaned on a hip-high mushroom protuberance extruded from the mat. The obscenely-shaped things, occurring at random, disappearing in the same way, were intended to make the martial arts practice more demanding. "Proficiency may be a virtue, but it is no substitute for remembering one's place. You have

132

grown lax in this undisciplined environment. You will thank me, I believe, for teaching you better, once we return to Vespucci."

"No, sir."

My head throbbed, a bump began rising where I had been struck. Lucille had offered me exactly the same warning: I risked becoming everything that Vespucci hated. Suddenly, a physical ache to be home, where I knew what was expected of me, overwhelmed me. Without summons, two faces arose in my mind, side by side: Eleva, Lucille. I needed to be home, desperately. Prospects with the girl I had left behind might be unpromising. They were less uncomfortable than whatever I was being inexorably drawn into with this violently unpredictable Confederate female.

Damn her, anyway.

"What is that, Corporal?"

"I meant, yes, sir." Threading around the practice-obstructions, we stepped off the mat together, heading across the gymnasium toward the showers. The place was like an aircraft hangar, with dozens of other pairs sparring, one complement assigned to Sodde Lydfe in heavy desert gear. Lights flashed at random intervals, from random angles, simulating the confusion of battle amidst unpredictable recorded explosions. Many here were practicing blindfolded, perhaps for night operations.

I weighed the advisability of following their example. Sudden flight might bring about the need for such a skill at any time. I had begun to examine everything from one angle: how can it help us get home?

Apparently the Lieutenant had come to much the same conclusion. We stepped through a series of membranous cleansing-curtains on the way to the unnecessary but refreshing showers. Individuals valued privacy aboard this ship. There were no ganged sanitary facilities of the kind military boarding school had accustomed me to. No tiled showers the size of a gameball court. A hundred private cubicle-doors faced us on the other side of the curtains. There was no familiar locker-room smell.

The Lieutenant stopped short of the shower-cabinets.

"Whitey, I have spent days looking for a way off-ship." he stated flatly, in a half-whisper. He glanced around suspiciously. "All of the auxiliary craft are also residences, occupied continuously, defended jealously. Moreover, every one is privately owned, if you can credit that."

I could not think of anything I had seen here that was not. I said so.

"Yes," he answered in bad humor. "But more to the point, Corporal, none of these vessels are for hire at any price we can afford. If that were not enough, checking for possible alternatives, as I have told you, I have determined that there is no other point of vulnerability, no engine-room, for example, that we might occupy and threaten to destroy—"

"Not even any engines." I was repeating something that Owen Rogers had told me earlier that morning. I was not sure whether I believed it.

"Nor even any engines. Whitey, if you are taking measures of your own—"

"I—" I had not been, in fact.

"No, do not tell me. If necessary, make your own way back home to Vespucci with what we know. Meantime, take comfort that I am working, too, toward our liberation, and the eventual salvation of our beloved planet."

"Sir?"

"I have arranged for an appointment with the Chief Praxeologist, Edwina Olson-Bear. You will accompany me, but only initially. She is said to be unattached, so I have every confidence that my subsequent, er ... meetings with the lady will afford me opportunity to learn something of practical use." He leered suggestively. "And if certain rumors also prove reliable, then considerably more than that may be accomplished."

He was the Lieutenant, but I had no idea what he was talking about. "Yes, sir." We went to our separate cubicles, agreeing to meet afterward.

My head still hurt when I was through in the shower.

PLASTIC EIGHT MILLIMETER cartridges squeezed from the strangely permeable face of the autofabricator into the transparency-covered hopper.

"One molecule at a time," observed Owen Rogers proprietarily, "If you could see inside, they start as a faint triangular—pardon me, trochoidal—streak in the matrix, building up in three-dimensions, maintaining a perfect cross-section until closure at the end of the cartridge."

"But how," I asked, not without ulterior motivation, "does it work?"

"There are a hundred and some-odd naturally-occurring elements," said the part-time gunsmith. "I lost track somewhere of exactly how many. From the dawn of time, Mindkind has been limited to permutations and combinations of those few elements to create his entire material civilization."

Some more of the physics, I thought to myself, that everybody said I needed. So be it. I would learn whatever I could, for the immediate project I had in mind, also in the interest of certain longer-range considerations.

"Just as protons, electrons, and neutrons are the building-blocks of atoms, quarks are the building-blocks of protons and neutrons, and therefore of the atomic nucleus. The electrons fill orbital positions around the nucleus, determining the chemical attributes of any given element."

"I understand," I lied. "But what has this to do with your fabricator?"

Sharpening my martial skills, I had mentioned to him a requirement for more ammunition earlier this morning, over a holo-circuit Lucille had shown me how to use. Instead of directing me to another retail outlet as I had expected, Rogers had invited me to his quarters, to see his Rockwell & Decker fabricator. Whole industrial establishments on Vespucci might have been established about this little hobbyist's toy.

"Everything, Whitey. You see, we manipulate those electron shells by—"

"Excuse me, Rog, but I am curious. Is this device good for making ammunition only, or can it be used to manufacture other things, as well?"

He blinked at the subject-change, "Within limits. Like what?"

"Well ..." I had thought this through very carefully. I was my first step in getting out of Confederate jurisdiction, with something to show for the adventure. Now, however, when it came time to start it, it began to feel like a cowardly betrayal of the generous people who—

Stop! You cannot take a hamlet without breaking heads.

"Drawing materials," I told him, wondering how transparent I was being. "Paper or something like it to draw upon, something with which to draw on it. I have noticed that you have artists aboard *Tom Paine Maru*. Their sketches, drawings, paintings hang in meeting places, restaurants. I did some of that at home. I would like to take it up again."

There were no photographs aboard Tom Paine Maru, no writing, but there were watercolors, lithographs, other handicrafted graphics. It made me wonder. But instead of simply wondering, or asking stupid questions, this time I had formed a plan on the basis of this peculiar knowledge.

I was following it now.

The fact was, I needed to make notes.

More, I needed to do it secretly. Each minute, I was being exposed to information of incalculable value to my poverty-stricken culture. Of course that was the reason they would not let us go. But that only gave me greater impetus to escape. Lucille was right. I was becoming an accomplished sociopath. From here on it would be a race: carrying out my self-imposed mission before the total disintegration of my character.

A long pause: "So that's it, is it? Paper. Pencils. You know, I warned Couper about this, too. I'm extremely sorry, Whitey, I can't do it."

Shock: I had been anticipated. There were places on Vespucci one could not take a camera or recorder. Plus the fact all such devices were strictly licensed. Now I was even forbidden to write down what I was learning. It was to be expected. Nevertheless, the surprise was devastating.

Rogers went on cheerfully without me: "I'm just not set up to replicate obsolete organics. Shucks, any industrial-scale fabricator could turn out exactly what you need, with little purple flags on every seventeenth item, if you ordered it that way. Being from a mass production culture, I suppose you don't realize the difference that makes. But there are limits. You'd want wood or rag paper, and, let's see: graphite, clay, cedar, rubber—or were you planning to use ink?"

"What?" I guess I blinked.

"If you had samples—or I suppose I could order the appropriate software. But look, would plastic do, a nice matte that could hold an impression? A smart pen to alter its molecular structure, make it erasable, even manage color, all from this little machine. What do you say?"

135

What I did not say to him was that I could not possibly have been more confused. I simply thanked the nice man profusely, then agreed to stop by later to pick up whatever his wonderful machine created for me.

Who were these people, anyway?

This was more like a real classroom than anything I had seen so far.

Forty assorted beings of various species, at desks of appropriate design, sat in a well-lit room brightly decorated with paintings of what I assumed were scenes—cities, different kinds of wildernesses—on various planets that the great starship had visited. Up front, a lecturer spoke on a definite topic in a linear manner. If you could ignore the pair of glass-fronted walls at the back, behind which various marine-life witnessed the proceedings, it almost felt like home.

There was even something resembling a blackboard.

"We have many names and historical examples for each of the three political systems that are all that are possible," the instructor stated. She was human, female, blonde, adult, showing a strong family resemblance to Lucille Olson-Bear. We had arrived at the beginning of the session. For once it actually sounded like the beginning of a session.

"Each has certain revealing characteristics of its own." She turned to sketch with her finger on the blank surface behind her, an equilateral triangle, pointed end up, indicating the lower righthand corner.

"All known forms of authoritarianism are paternalistic in nature, usually oppressively religious, with an emphasis on law, order, and swift, sure punishment for every miscreant. Majoritarianism, by contrast—"

She swept to the lower left corner.

"—is typically maternalistic, concerned with social 'justice', meaning the survival, above all, of the productively unfit at the involuntary expense of everybody else. Each variation represents an essentially infantile 'adjustment' to cultural and economic reality that prevents further development, either of an individual or society. It's a primary cause of the cyclic rise and fall we observe among the Kilroys."

Now the instructor pointed toward the apex of the triangle: "Individualism is adult in character, representing self-imposed responsibility, steady growth, and both individual and cultural maturity."

I watched the Lieutenant watching the attractive instructor, then caught Howell watching me. Having brought us here on the pretext of introducing us to Edwina Olson-Bear, Chief Praxeologist aboard *Tom Paine Maru*, I was certain that the coyote was much more interested in our reaction to her lecture than in any introductions he intended making.

My own thought was that a "paternalistic", disciplined society, or a "maternalistic" one taking care of its helpless in a responsible manner (both of which were the customary practice back on Vespucci), represented a vastly greater maturity than the lawless hedonism advocated by Confederates, who often struck me as self-indulgently childish.

She continued: "Although there are variations, monarchism is the archetype for authoritarian societies. Modern civilization on Earth, in fact, began with a North American anti-monarchical revolution in 1776 C.E.—that's Zero, Anno Liberatis for those unacquainted with the older calendar. For the first time in human history, government began growing smaller, poorer, and weaker. This was underlined shortly afterward in an unsuccessful counter-revolution by closet monarchists in 13 A.L., which canceled forever the government's power to levy taxes."

Striding across the room, she laid a hand upon a representation of a mountain whose rocky face bore the carved likenesses of men. "Within only two centuries, thanks to the 'Rushmore Four', Tom Paine, Albert Gallatin, Thomas Jefferson, and Lysander Spooner—the revolution had become worldwide. Peace, prosperity, and progress all grew from the concept of absolute individual rights, under a system of unanimous consent."

The Chief Praxeologist stepped further away from the front, toward where we were sitting. "Given the essential tragedy of human evolution—that, as defense against the mortal agony of birth, the dangerous mechanism of repression arose, functioning powerfully both in mother and child, sabotaging while it soothed like any powerful analgesic—the North American Revolution looks more and more to us today like a miracle."

I stirred uncomfortably in my comfortable seat. In spite of the lecture, this was supposedly neither a class on history nor biology. The Lieutenant was here to take advantage of an introduction he had wangled from Howell, I was here as protective coloration, but also for a reason of my own. Only peripherally aware of the Obsidian operation until it was practically over with, now I was determined to watch what happened on the next stop as closely as I could. On a planet rather unattractively called Hoand (pronounced with two syllables, "HO-and"), the warrior-praxeologists of *Tom Paine Maru* intended pursuing an altogether different method than they had employed on the previous world.

This session was supposed to explain it.

Edwina Olson-Bear went on to talk about the three main Hoandian nation-states. Uxos was a mass-society where everything was done by the collective, for the collective, in the name of the collective. In the praxeologist's view, they were scarcely more than a human insect colony.

Obohalu, with a history somewhat like the old Vespuccian Republic, made a pretense of being a free country, was the most technologically progressive, likely the most powerful, but was currently on a steep decline.

Houtty fitted somewhere between, lacking the enormous regimented mindless masses of Uxos, yet possessing much the same potential for mass destruction as Obohalu. All were on the verge of interplanetary travel, each was at constant Cold War with the other two, slowing progress, draining productivity, destroying countless hundreds of millions of lives, not just in terms of mortal flesh or blood, but of human potential. According to the lecturer, in politics, unlike geometry or architecture, the triangle was the least stable of all forms. Something had to give, probably explosively, with lingering radiation.

I listened through detailed analyses of all three cultures. The teacher's questions, directed at the students, regarded how things had gotten to be that way on Hoand, what could possibly be done to change them.

Time passed.

"That will do for today," she said at last. "Be sure that you review F.P. Wilson's *An Enemy of the State*, the listed works of J.N. Schulman, and L.G. Kropotkin's *My Life With Pete*. You'll be asked to make comparisons among Hoand, Earth, and Sodde Lydfe, and specifically Podfet, Nazi Germany, and Houtty, as opposed to Great Foddu, England, and Obohalu. Unlike Hoand, where a relative balance-of-terror has been achieved, Sodde Lydfens are about to use nuclear weapons, after a long conventional war. Using praxeological notation, I want you to tell me why."

After a few more informal questions about the class assignment—where did Stalinist Russia fit in?—the room emptied itself into the corridors. Through glass walls, I could even see the porpoises swim away.

"It's a break in my routine," Edwina nodded over her coffee cup. "I started out as a lecturer. I like to stay in practice." Politely disguised annoyance tinged her voice, replying to the Lieutenant about what a nice girl was doing in that classroom we had just left. I could not have said exactly why I was embarrassed. It had not been my stupid question.

The bizarre restaurant, not far from where we had begun, was filled with the usual colorful, bewildering mixture of species, many wearing costumes I now recognized as native to Hoand or appropriate to Sodde Lydfe. A volume as large as the gymnasium had been filled, from floor-to-ceiling, with man-high transparent plastic tubing, little bubble-shaped alcoves occurred every few meters for tables. The whole thing was darkly lit by candles twinkling in their hundreds, refracted by the plastic, reflected in its twisted, curving walls. Howell called the place "Mr. Meep's In The Belly Of The Whale", a new establishment replacing one that, in the coyote's opinion, had been considerably stranger.

The proprietor, apparently an old friend of his from Earth, led us through the intestinal labyrinth. The chimpanzee entrepreneur wore a long false beard, also an ankle-length striped robe with a matching headdress. Howell said that the language he was addressing us in was Aramaic.

Seen up close, Edwina was pleasant as much as she was pretty, with bright, hazel-colored eyes, a broad, intelligent forehead, an upturned nose that, despite the description, was quite unlike her sister's. Where her sister was almost inhumanly slender without being emaciated or even a bit fragile-looking, Edwina was amply-rounded, without being plump.

"No, Whitey," she replied to quite a different question from me. I had asked her about something that had been bothering me since that day beside the swimming-pool: how the simple act of forgetting could have caused all the "tragedy" the human race was supposed to be heir to.

"It's completely different from simply not remembering. That's what animals do, of course. They're not equipped to do anything else. But intelligent beings never really forget anything. With them it's more a matter of unconsciously refusing to deal with—or of being unable to deal with—certain information that's stored inside you, of suppressing it, sometimes at the very moment it happens, or of pretending that it doesn't exist until you lose conscious touch with it."

"I see," I lied. I was doing a lot of that, lately.

"But enough of that, for the moment—see, there's an example for you. I've done my lecturing for this morning. After the accident, I replaced Lucille in Praxeology." She looked from me to the Lieutenant, suppressed a scowl, then smiled at the coyote. Candle-light at this time of day, was a very strange experience. Mr. Meep, it seemed, also the proprietor of the last restaurant in this location, specialized in very strange experiences. "Each of us, in turn, was the youngest Chief ever—"

"The accident?" I repeated.

Her glance at Howell stopped being a smile.

"It wasn't my place to tell them," The coyote's electronic voice reflected oddly from the curved plastic wall. He turned to me. "During an initial planetary survey some years ago, Lucille was killed—that is, injured so terribly that she could not be immediately reanimated. Yes, even by our medical technology, Whitey. Her remains were kept in stasis."

"Stasis?" It was the Lieutenant, pausing to address Howell during a heretofore uninterrupted campaign of patronizing glances bestowed on the Chief Praxeologist. "Medical stasis. Is that not the condition in which—"

"Indeed you were, Lieutenant," the coyote nodded, an oddly human gesture. "A state of suspension quite unlike refrigeration, sleep, or anything else you are likely to be familiar with, occurring at the subatomic—"

"Interesting," the Lieutenant interrupted boredly, "I recall none of it, of course." He rubbed the shoulder that had been nearly severed. I had seen him do this before—on Vespucci, calling modest attention to a minor wound suffered in the Final War—always in the presence of women. I had privately dubbed it the Purple Heart Approach. "From the Scavian attack on our sleeping encampment to my awakening aboard the *Little Tom*. From what the Corporal tells me, it is just as well."

"That's the general idea." Edwina shook her head. "Although sometimes—for example, in my poor sister's case—it doesn't always ..."

139

"But tell me," the Lieutenant interrupted for a second time. He was getting as bad about that as the Confederates. "How it is that an attractive, accomplished person such as yourself spends all of her time amidst dry praxeological contemplations, wasting all of her most feminine years on graduate seminars more closely resembling military brief—"

Edwina threw her head back, laughing out loud. "Howell, there's rather a good deal that you didn't tell them, isn't there? Lieutenant, what ever gave you the idea that it was a graduate seminar? Simply your august presence at it? Didn't you even notice the visual aids, the—"

"Edwina," cautioned Howell, "I wouldn't—"

"Sorry, Howell. I would like to have the Lieutenant in a graduate seminar—as a textbook example of the authoritarian personality!" She stopped to laugh again. The Lieutenant grew purple in the face. "For your information, that class is one of my charities, for retarded dependents and combat-damaged personnel. Bad brain injuries, most of them."

Before anyone could think of anything to say, the food arrived.

"Aborigines? They're the original inhabitants of Australia. They still are, for that matter. How'd something like that come up in idle conversation?"

Owen Rogers had brought me more than "paper" to take notes on. He'd arrived at my quarters that evening with a freshly-fabricated notebook, the "pencil" he had promised, plus a load of ammunition that I did not really need. It had merely been a pretext for the other items.

Also a mandolar.

If, indeed, there were no such thing as a free lunch, then I was running up quite a tab. I fingered the fret-buttons, idly fiddled with the vane-adjustments. "Howell was telling me something about them that I did not altogether understand, I'm afraid. It was something about their not distinguishing time from space, philosophically. What little I know about physics ... well, physics on Vespucci, anyway, they are saying there is no such distinction. It is supposed to be the latest thing."

Rogers grinned. "I suppose that sort of depends on the context you're stuck with. What Howell meant, I suspect, is that Australian Aborigines confused one with the other in an inappropriate context. They thought that, if you were from far away, then you were also from the distant past. When the earliest European explorers arrived in Australia, the Aborigines thought that the intruders were their own ancestors."

"That is almost appropriate, over interstellar distances, is it not?"

"Whitey, you don't know the half of it." But Howell was working toward a point. "There are a number of different dimensions—call it directions—in the physical universe. There's back-and-forth, for instance. There's up-and-down. And there's side-to-side. Those are the three dimensions of space. There's also back-and-forth in time, the distance from past to future, with the present presumably somewhere in between."

"That seems simple enough."

"Yeah? Well, there's also side-to-side, timewise—"

"So I have been told. Something about different history lines, different—"

"Probability. Look: nobody knew about statistical probability—that's another way of looking at this sideways dimension—before Blaise Pascal. He was a mathematician, philosopher, and a gambler before he got religion, back in the—well, four hundred years ago. It took longer before anyone realized the importance of probability, that time is not only infinite lengthwise—in the dimension of "duration"—but sideways—in the dimension of probability, as well."

"What do you mean, infinite?"

"That there is an unlimited number of universes. That every event that can happen in a number of different ways actually happens in every different way it can happen. And that, as a result, every human choice we make is actually made in every different way that it can be made."

Enough of that. "Owen, there is something else that I have to ask you."

The praxeologist stopped, blinked. "What's that, Whitey?"

"Well, I got involved, today, in a discussion of repression. The fact that intelligent beings never really forget anything, stuff like that ..."

"Now you're more into my territory," Rogers said. "What was the question?"

"This: when scientists dig into the sands of my home planet, they occasionally run across the remains of four-legged creatures very much like Howell. Apparently, they were imported when our ancestors arrived on Vespucci, for food or some other purpose. But they were obviously not intelligent. They were domestic animals of some kind, lacking—as Howell must—the cranial capacity to be an intelligent creature. Yet Howell has mentioned several times that he has 'circuits'. He not only never forgets anything, he seems to remember more than anyone I have met on this ship. No offense intended, I mean." I flushed with embarrassment.

"None taken. You're right, Howell started as a four-legged animal, not even a domestic one. He's from a species of wild prairie-rovers. But he's also different in that he carries several thousand gigabytes of electronic supplementation—data storage-and-retrieval, speed and capacity boosters—attached to the surface of his brain. In a sense he's half dog and half computer and he'll gladly tell you all about it, if you ask him. He's a lot like the Patchwork Girl's glass cat in that regard. But be prepared to stand around listening for several hours."

"Oh." It had been much as I expected. The trouble was, it led to a question that I dare not ask, not of Rogers, nor of anyone else aboard this ship. I had figured Howell out all by myself, then made a leap. No one ever had to look anything up aboard *Tom Paine Maru*. They all knew, at any given moment, precisely what time it was, when the next auxiliary was arriving, what the temperature was, sometimes even what the person in the next room was thinking. Were they all like poor Howell, electronically brain-implanted slaves of some giant master computer?

They certainly all believed the same things, acted cooperatively, accomplished great works (like *Tom Paine Maru* herself) without any visible institution to indoctrinate, instruct, or coordinate their efforts. They acted as if they were under the control of some powerful government somewhere. The problem was that they did not seem to have one.

Impossible!

The Patchwork Girl's glass cat?

OPERATION KLAATU

HANGING IN THE middle of the darkened room, I hooked my left arm under my right knee to fold myself into a sitting position. Holding the notebook against my naked thigh with my left hand, I twisted the business end of Rogers' pencil until it shed soft light on the plastic pages:

Notes from the Asperance *Expedition*

Armorer/Corporal YD-038 recording

Page One:

Along the infinite dimension of "probability", are universes, existing side-by-side ("coextant" is the expression used aboard the Tom Paine Maru), *in which, to name one example, the Big Bang never happened.*

Or happened differently.

Or where somebody in Earthian history named Albert Gallatin talked them out of the Whiskey Rebellion, instead of leading it to the anarchistic victory that Confederates hail as the beginning of their era.

The three principal developments that determined the history of the present era—the 3rd Century A.L., as they call it—were the perfection of catalytic fusion for power production, improvements in the area of interstellar space travel, the discovery of parallel realities.

While searching for a faster-than-light stardrive, the physicist Dora Jayne Thorens, with her partner, Ooloorie Eckickeck P'wheet (I have rendered that last name phonetically as best I can—I will discuss the lack of a written language among the Confederates later) stumbled upon another version of Earth where their Rebellion had been lost, where the state had grown for two hundred years instead of withering.

The examples above are not chosen arbitrarily. The first, somehow a different start for the universe, made what they call the "Malaise Catastrophe" possible. The reference is obscure, yet this, almost as much as the Whiskey Rebellion, seems to be responsible for everything the Confederacy is doing now. It is the reason these enormous ships are exploring the galaxy. It forms the basis for their attitude toward "Kilroys".

The second, Gallatin's rebellion, produced the world we stand in.

Inferences are impossible to resist. There are other universes out there where I was never forced to give up music, universes where I never met or came to love Eleva, or where I never volunteered for the Asperance *expedition, or where I gave up in Sca's dungeons, or where I—*

I stopped, twisted the end of the pencil Rogers had given me to its ERASE mode, then carefully rubbed out the last paragraph I had written.

In its place, I wrote:

Each choice produces a new clutch of universes, entirely complete unto themselves, perhaps differing only by a single human decision. According to Rogers (or others I have begun asking about the subject), this is not some religious notion, but cold, scientifically proven fact.

I have had many reasons in my life for feeling insignificant or inefficacious. Yet, if each choice I make, no matter how trivial, creates an entirely new universe—an entirely new set of universes—what does that say about the power of the human mind? Any human mind?

Even mine?

I stopped writing once again. Belatedly, it had occurred to me that, if I were successful in my self-appointed spying against the Confederates, it might advance me in rank, helping my chances with Eleva.

Now, more than ever, I must get home!

Oddly, that self-serving thought made me feel guilty toward a dozen people at once. As time passed, my friend, my nominal superior, Enson Sermander looked increasingly like ... well, a rather stupid, boring individual, in contrast to those I was meeting here. Yet the man was my Lieutenant, the lawful representative of the planet I had been born on—which was, itself, looking a little stupidly boring to me.

As for Eleva—

A surge of guilt swept through me all over again, along with the thought that any woman who requires something to stir her like the promotion I aspired to, does not deserve to be stirred. I stifled the thought, then immediately felt guilty for repressing it, repression being the root of all evil as far as my new-found friends seemed to be concerned.

Can you feel guilty about feeling guilty? I had asked Howell that very question. His answer had been enigmatic "Only in southern California".

"Writing in your little diary, again?"

I jumped.

In zero gravity, this accomplished a slow rotation about my own center-of-mass. Lucille's voice was sharp as she re-entered the room. Regaining proper attitude, along with the remnants of my dignity, I folded the notebook irritably, tucked the special pencil through its loop, tangled both in the mesh along the wall that I had kicked myself into.

She brushed her freshly-washed hair. "Don't worry, Corporal-baby, I wouldn't dream of peeking at your secret scribblings if you paid me to."

"I do not worry about that, Lucille," I replied coolly, looking around for my smartsuit. For some reason she was keeping to herself, war had been declared between us again. "I only worry about whether I can get my impressions down in a way that will make sense of them later."

She could not know that the notebook was a weapon for the defense of my civilization. I would wrap up my dissertation on metaphysical philosophy as soon as I had provided enough background for Vespuccian Intelligence, then begin on the technological details. They might be useful to our scientists, however badly I failed to understand them myself.

"Okay, write this up in your book."

The walls around us cleared. We were no longer in a warm cavern, but the upper section of a scoutship exactly like the first I had ever ridden aboard. Outside, the stars—the real stars—shone as hard, bright chips. The pearlescent disk of *Tom Paine Maru* appeared to one side like an oddly-shaped moon. The brightest object was the sun of Hoand, illuminating a half-dozen planets, most of them out of sight, with their half a hundred natural satellites. The planet itself hung before us, swirled white-green marble with its own three pock-marked companions.

"Operation Klaatu" was about to begin.

Despite my annoyance with her, Lucille was another individual I felt guilty toward, possibly toward her more than anybody. We were aboard a borrowed auxiliary spacecraft, *John Thomas Maru,* following the giant interstellar vessel that served as its base. This was supposed to be a holiday excursion for us. She had been working hard. Her compatriots had been working my head hard. It was time for a break.

It turned out to be another education, of sorts.

I had always wondered what lovemaking in free fall might be like. Aboard the *Asperance,* there had been neither the opportunity nor the room. Now I was finding out, as often as the two of us could manage, that it is fairly messy, requires considerably more energy than I had expected, plus a modicum of equipment—handstraps and so forth—but that it is interesting, relaxing once you get used to it, oddly satisfying.

As usual, Lucille was irked with me. This time (although she would never admit it), I had not tired as soon as she expected. She had that effect on me. Altogether, we were an awkward pair, our lovemaking always violent. Each seemed to have something that the other needed powerfully.

Almost against our wills, she and I had wound up together again, aboard this little ship. When things went well between us, I saw my life more objectively than I did at other times, measured it less in terms of duty, more by what it had always demanded from me without offering any reward. I entertained uncharitable thoughts about the Lieutenant. I even found myself considering the terrifying possibility that Eleva might even be something of an—well, the proctological reference Lucille used we do not employ much in polite company on Vespucci.

Lucille put her hair up now, snugging it into the hood of her suit which would dry it for her. It was just an ordinary safety precaution—we would soon be docking with the mother vessel in the usual way. With her, however, it also seemed to serve as punctuation, delineating business from pleasure, her ordinary toughness from those rare moments of tenderness that baffled me even more than her habitual combat posture.

"I have to get back to the ship," she informed me. "There's a big conference in an hour, over plans to discredit pro-war politicians in Great Foddu. It's going to be a delicate job. War is always so popular with—"

I shook my head. Even a few minutes away from a crucial operation on an altogether different planet, the planning for Sodde Lydfe continued.

I decided to risk starting yet another fight. "Lucille, how can you people contemplate meddling in the lives of others a scale like this?"

Was that bewilderment on her face? "Why should the scale matter, Whitey? Is it somehow worse than meddling in the life of a single individual?"

She settled to the floor as gravity came up slowly again, produced a self-lit cigarette. I watched her puff ill-humoredly. "And what sort of meddling would you call war itself? Isn't it better to ensure the election of anti-war ward-heelers there and in other democracies on the—"

"Or to foment a violent revolution in the Hegemony of Podfet, or its allies?" I folded my arms, sitting on a wall-couch rising to meet me.

She raised her eyebrows. "You know about that, do you? It bothers you?"

"It bothers me very much. Oh, all right, Podfet is a tyrannical dictatorship. It probably deserves whatever you people decide to do to it. But Great Foddu, that's a constitutional monarchy, Lucille. It's a democracy."

"We'd do the same thing there, if it were pragmatic." She was as close to raising her voice as she could be without doing it. "Get it through your hardened military skull. As someone said, 'a difference that makes no difference is no difference'. Authoritarianism exists in varieties too numerously nauseating to discuss, Corporal. But that isn't the issue on Sodde Lydfe at all. All the governments there are majoritarian."

I threw up my hands, "Political lectures in bed, again."

"After bed. You started this one, don't complain. Look, stupid: just as there are only three ways that people can organize themselves, there are three basic forms of majoritarianism—socialism, fascism, and democracy. Understand that fascism is a majoritarian form. It relies just as heavily on popular support as any democracy. Look at the crowd scenes it's so fond of. What's more, Democracy is just as rottenly dictatorial as the other two. Should half a dozen individuals tell a seventh what to do, just because they could beat him up if they wanted?"

This was insane. "Is voting not better than beating people up? Howell says your system is based on greed. But people need taking care of."

Lucille snorted with contempt. "A free market feeds more people, Corporal, more equitably, than any other system known to history. It's the only system capable of feeding non-productive idiots like you. But you all eventually come to expect it, as a right, and that'll probably be its undoing. That it accomplishes all of this as a by-product of greed is irrelevant—unless you care more about motivations than results!"

Now she had finally raised her voice, only centimeters from my face. Hers was flushed; fire crept up into my cheeks, as well. Howell had told me something like this, about the free market system, more quietly. It was difficult, right enough, separating results from motivations. Right now, I was having a lot of trouble the other way around.

"Idiot?" I asked at the top of my lungs, wishing she could just go back to being nice. Between her and Eleva, I was rapidly coming to the conclusion that I have terrible taste when it comes to women. "Stupid?"

"Stupid! idiot! And a military-industrial parasite on top of that!"

I had never hit a woman before in my life. The slap echoed through the little ship—outside, the vessel was docking, though I did not consciously notice it at the time—as did my voice a second later when she let me have a small, high-velocity fist in the pit of the stomach.

We stood, toe-to-toe, panting, speechless. Curiously, desire for her raced through my system. I could see it on her face, too, along with the embarrassment that such spiritual nakedness leaves in its wake.

"All right, then," Lucille broke the spell. "That settles our account, Corporal O'Thraight. Next time we run into one another, don't bother to speak. I guarantee that you'll never hear another word from me."

The floor rose beneath us, carrying us into the *Tom Paine Maru*.

So much for our holiday excursion.

THE LIEUTENANT WAS not home when I went looking. I could not have said exactly why I did it, except that, suddenly, I felt that I had misjudged him. It was always like this: when things were not going well with Lucille, I grew homesick, overly forgiving, overcome by nostalgia. I was ashamed of letting interest in a woman (a woman like Lucille, at that) distract me from loyalty to my friends, duty to my country. Returning to my stateroom, I found the man waiting in the corridor.

"Corporal!" It was a hoarse noise, trying to be a shouted whisper, or a whispered shout, all at once. He pranced nervously, wrung his hands, spread them, shook them, then went back to wringing them as I approached.

"I have been looking all over for you! I have finally discovered the truth about this ship! It is the most startling information you possibly—"

"Sir?" Somehow, the Lieutenant's face was deathly pale, while the veins stood out on his broad forehead as if he were about to have a stroke.

"Let us go inside ... " He craned his neck to make sure we were not being overheard, " ... where there is less chance of being spied upon."

I could have told him there was more chance of that inside, but he was the Lieutenant. Also, I was suddenly very tired. I wanted to lie down. Entering, he threw himself onto the bed, wiping a hand across his forehead. I sat down in a chair, listening through my personal depression.

"I have been speaking with that Nahuatl ... person this morning. You know him better than I do. Do you think that he is inclined to lie?"

"I think he is less inclined than anybody else aboard this ship. Why?"

"Because if he tells the truth, Corporal, we are in deep, deep trouble. Are you aware that he is half-computer? That he possesses a sophisticated electronic implant within his skull—or it possesses him—that provides most of his intellect. That when we speak to him, we are actually speaking to a device, instead of an intelligent organism?"

"Well, sir, I—" What I wondered myself was what difference it made.

His eyes bulged with agitation. "The truth is that they are all like that! Every one! They are nothing but walking computers: whales, chimpanzees, gorillas—even human beings! They are all controlled by computers stitched in amongst their very brains! Corporal, we are doomed!"

"Sir?" I was not feeling very articulate all of a sudden.

"Oh, I was offered a hasty explanation by the creature himself, to the effect that everybody carries a wholly independent multi-gigabyte computer in his head, and that there is no master machine, no overall program. It was laughable! What society would miss such a chance for control?"

Vespucci would not. I pondered the question for a moment. "On the other hand, would the Confederates, with their fanatic devotion to individual liberty, tolerate such a thing? I find it highly confusing, sir."

He said, "Not at all, Corporal. You see, their desire for freedom, their freedom itself, is no more than a cybernetic illusion foisted on them to maintain their tranquillity. Now that I know the secret—now that we know—they are certain to do us in! This society must have been taken over by an artificial intelligence during a period not much more greatly advanced than our own. They are the prisoners of their own machines! They will kill us before we let their secret out, I know it!"

Notes from the Asperance *Expedition*
Armorer/Corporal YD-038 recording
Page Five:
Quarks may be removed from atomic nuclei, substituted for any or all electrons, thereby vastly altering the character of any element. An early example, "catalytic" fusion at room temperatures, used quark-electron shells less resistant to being squashed together than is natural.

But quarkotopics goes further than "mere" catalytic fusion. Now, instead of permutations of 100-plus natural elements, they have unlimited possibilities based on the number of electron positions in any given element, on whether they choose to leave them alone or alter them.

The door said, "Corporal O'Thraight?"

I put my notebook away. The Lieutenant had departed earlier on some unnamed errand. I saw Edwina Olson-Bear, as the door cleared, standing outside, her suit a plain, pale green. Noticing something in my movements that told her I had been busy, she began, "I'm sorry to disturb—"

"That is all right, I was just finishing up. Please come in, er, Chief Praxeol—Doctor Olson-Bear." I gestured clumsily, embarrassed by what I had been doing, but moreso by not knowing how to address her.

I was turning out to be a lousy spy.

As pretty as her sister in her own quiet way, she leaned on the frame. "Edwina. I came to ask if you want to see the first of our operations on Hoand. It'll only be another ..." She rolled her eyes, looked at me again, " ... twenty-three minutes. We've just time to get there."

"Where?"

"You'll see. It's something that I want to watch in person, rather than by telecom. It's a pet project of mine, really. You see, Hoand has been steeped in warfare for something like three thousand years. There's only one way to end it. All the organizing and demonstrating in the universe never did a lick of good, as long as taxation and conscription—"

"People like war," I defended with a cynicism grown hard inside me. "They will do anything, sacrifice anything. It is instinctive with them."

"Nonsense, Corporal. War is the health of the state, and of nobody else. Put an end to the machinery of war, government, and you put an end to war. Simple, but most Kilroys are blind to it because, as much as they desire peace, they want to keep the state around for other reasons."

I strapped on my gunbelt, then joined her in the hall. After a longer than usual transport patch ride, we were crossing a medium-sized park when the sky overhead went abruptly from blue to starry black.

Edwina stopped because I was gawking. "This isn't what I meant, but it'll be quite a show, I promise. Let's stay a moment. We'll watch it."

Hoand's outermost satellite was a worthless cinder a few hundred klicks in diameter, reminiscent of everything that circled the sun of Vespucci.

Including Vespucci.

Hoandians had reached their other moons by way of clumsy rockets, planted flags, made speeches, returned home when air or courage ran low. They had not yet come this far. Markers on the sky-display showed where camera-landers sat in meteoric dust, one or two still operating. An orbiter relayed signals to the planet, five or six light-seconds away.

Motion in the park came to a halt. Confederates standing around, sitting on benches, going places, as we were, or simply lying in the grass became statues as Koko's amplified voice rang throughout the ship.

"Five, four, three, two, one, commence firing!"

From the broad underside of the mighty vessel came a blast twelve kilometers in diameter, a beam so intense that it looked like pieces might be cut off to build new starships. On the surface of the target moon, an explosion to end all explosions endowed that barren sphere—temporarily—with an atmosphere. Smoke cleared into the airless void, revealing a churning lava pool twice the size of *Tom Paine Maru*.

The beam winked off. Folks breathed again. There was a pause, then suddenly a cheer went up, thundering through the ship, buffeting my ears.

"We'll give the leaders about an hour," said Edwina, resuming her purposeful stride, "to hear from their tame scientists. This spot isn't directly visible from the planet. You need access to telemetered data."

I confess that I did not care. I wanted badly to ask about her sister, anything to help me understand. I did not know how to begin. Howell had said Lucille's period of stasis had been intermittent, interrupted frequently for courses of experimental treatment. Complete "regeneration" (whatever that tantalizing phrase meant) had been prevented for years by a genetic disorder inherited from her father. Finally cured, she emerged from her nightmarish ordeal a changed personality.

I started to speak, but we entered a room at the edge of the park. Koko, Howell, a few familiar others waited. It was difficult to tell, as half of the place was darkened. Lucille was there. The other half, separated from us by a transparency, contained four comfortable chairs, one of them occupied by Geoffrey Couper, freshly shaven from the blunt prow of his massive chin to the polished crest of his great cranium.

The big man's smartsuit was adjusted to metallic reflectivity, its collar turned up high, fastened with a crisp, military appearance—the man would look military in pajamas—I wondered if Lucille ever criticized him for that. On his feet were matching silver boots. A pair of silver gauntlets rested in his lap. He turned toward the partition, which Edwina said was a mirror on his side. "You people ready?"

A pause I thought I was beginning to understand, then: "Fifteen seconds, Geoff," said Koko. "They're having trouble lining up on the Premiere."

"Okay. Sure wish I could have a smoke, but it would spoil the effect."

All the way across the darkened room, I somehow, unexpectedly caught Lucille's eye. She shot a dire glare at her sister, then gave me a rueful, appealing look. I was never going to figure the woman out.

A warning ping. A blinding, brilliant blue at their wire-fine perimeters, broach-openings appeared over the unoccupied chairs, widened, then deposited three human figures in varying attitudes of astonishment.

The first individual was neatly dressed for business. Like Couper, he was a big man. He had been caught, fork in hand, chewing something. He looked up, his eyes widened. He looked down at the fork in his hand, changed his grip to make it a weapon. Then he glanced at Couper, whose rig included a plasma pistol, laid the fork on the arm of the chair.

At the same instant, there was a shout as a fat man in a garish night shirt awoke in a sitting position in the next chair. He rubbed his eyes, snarling in a language that I could not understand. Then he started to get up, but he could not. The chair was holding him fast. He slumped, staring about him like a trapped animal. He did not seem to notice Couper. He had eyes only for the big man in the business suit.

"Get those hamblasted translators on line, stat!" Couper barked. In the back of the darkened half of the room, someone scurried to comply.

The third man—the Premiere of Uxos, my companion told me—was naked, a roll of toilet paper in his hand, the most surprised expression of the three upon his face. Couper tossed him a blanket, then waited for them all to overcome their astonishment enough to listen.

"What we have here, gentlebeings," Couper lectured as he waited, to an unseen audience behind the transparency, "are the three most politically powerful individuals on the planet Hoand. Not terribly prepossessing, are they?" At mention of their planet's name—apparently the only word they understood—all three looked up at Couper.

Edwina whispered: "You're about to see what we call the old Galactic Police gag. I wish he'd stop clowning, he could mess up the whole—"

Clowning?

"Greetings," Couper said suddenly, "from the Galactic Confederacy. As you may have noticed, my speech is being translated into each of your respective languages. I need not introduce you to each other, nor apologize for the abruptness of the summons. The continued existence of your world, and of all the people living on it, hinges on this event."

"What is the meaning of this outrage?" demanded the blanket-covered Premiere. The head of Obohalu, the fellow in the night shirt, nodded belligerent agreement with his erstwhile enemy, glaring now at Couper.

When the others had finished their expostulations, the Houttian Chancellor quietly said, "I would like very much to know how this was accomplished, sir. The lunar explosion was spectacular, yet somehow comprehensible. This is nothing short of magnificent. Will you tell me?"

"In due course, sir, that is but the smallest fraction of our available powers. For now, we have other matters to discuss. Are you prepared?"

"Provided," he said, "the Premiere and the President are likewise prepared."

"Gentlemen? Your attention? We are perfectly willing to confer with members of your opposition, if necessary. Or go directly to the public."

More grudging assent I have not seen concentrated in a single room, before or since. The Chancellor alone seemed collected. The only sign that he was alive was an occasional blinking of his cool gray eyes.

"Very well. Your sun system, while well within our boundaries, was only recently discovered to be inhabited. I welcome you into the Confederacy, and advise that you are in violation—unknowingly, I'm sure—of certain statutes."

He pointed to a stack beside his knee, three massively-thick aluminum-bound books, the first I had seen aboard ship. "This must be repaired. These step-by-step instructions, carefully tailored for your individual nations, will tell you how to begin ... "

YES, OF COURSE, I was back together with Lucille by that evening. We had dinner with Couper's team after the Hoandian bigwigs were sent home with promises this time, not threats, that if they ran into any trouble with heir political opposition, that those folks would be treated to the Galactic Police gag, too, in order to insure their cooperation.

The aluminum-covered books were check-lists, nothing more, for winding government down to its total abolition. Taxes and conscription feed the machinery of war and must be shut off. In one country, the first step was surrendering money-production to private banks. In another, it was opening the arsenals to the people. It all hinged on local conditions, the exact steps, their number, the order they must be carried out in, requiring years of calculation by praxeologists. The people of the planet might never know we had been there. Promising to let word out of an alien invasion had been Couper's last, best lever.

Lucille and I made love again that night, the same violent, soul-shattering act that never failed to frighten us both, that made us irresistible to one another. By morning—also of course—we had another screaming fight. As I wrenched out through the door of her stateroom, she shouted after me, "This time, it's for keeps!" I got back to my own compartment just in time to receive a wall-message from Howell:

"Whitey!" The coyote's fur was bristling in the display, "Get over here as quickly as you can! I'm in your Lieutenant's quarters! He's collapsed! It's brain embolism, they're telling me! In any event, he's comatose. And unless you act immediately, he'll be dead within twenty minutes!"

ACCOUNTANTS OF THE SOUL

BLAAAMM!!

The Dardick bucked in my hand. The repulsive smelly thing that had attacked me dissolved, but another was right behind, fangs dripping saliva.

BLAM! BLAM! The rotor whirled; ivory-colored tround-casings littered the ground at my feet. Claws extended, the monster lumbered closer ...

"Too bad, Whitey," said a disembodied voice, "That one ate you."

How had I gotten into this mess?

Arguing with Lucille, of course.

Z

THE TRUTH WAS, it had disgusted me, the way the Hoand dignitaries—rulers of an entire planet—had been treated like so many naughty children.

Naturally, I had made the mistake of saying so.

"You've gotta be kidding!" She ground out her cigarette, disbelief written on every centimeter of her otherwise lovely face. She turned away from me, pulled the sheet around her shoulders, spoke to the air in the bedroom. "Those criminals? Those mass-murdering butchers? Those ... those ... "

"Human beings," I supplied. "Living on their own little world, not bothering anybody in your overpraised Confederacy." Sitting up, I put a hand on her thinly-covered shoulder, made her turn to look at me as I spoke. "Do you know how mean, how small it looks, taking advantage of your superior technology to press people into frightened compliance with what you Confederates, in your infinite wisdom, regard to be right?"

Lucille did look at me, then, straight through me to the wall behind. It was a trick of hers. I was already sorry I had made her do it.

"I see," she said. "The fallacy of collective self-determination. Corporal, you're ridiculous. Last year, eighty thousand 'human beings' were massacred in Uxos. The socialized farming system failed—again—as it was bound by nature to fail, and somebody had to suffer for it."

153

On Vespucci, when I was only a child, the government had given up on collective farming for that very reason. I opened my mouth to say so—

"In Houtty, every year, thousands of dissenters, petty criminals, and so on are shipped to their antarctic to mine a variety of ice-mold that the *nomenklatura* of the rich nations find palatable. It never seems to bother anyone that ninety percent of them die and have to be replaced."

"*Nomenklatura?*"

"Later. In Obohalu, the tax-rate is sixty-nine percent. For every three people being taxed, two productive human lives are effectively obliterated. If you think economic mass-murder is any less brutal than what happens in Uxos and Houtty, if you think it isn't the right of anyone who happens along to interfere, it's you who're small and mean, Corporal."

I took the hand off her shoulder, folded my arms. "Do not call me Corporal, Lucille. You do not respect the rank, nor the nation that conferred it. My name is Whitey. It is not much of a name, as you have been at some pains to point out, but it is all the name I have. How do I know what things are like on Hoand? My government always says similar things about every country it invades. Is your word any more reliable?"

She hit me first, that time.

Before my angry departure from her quarters, after the short-lived passage-at-arms that had preceded it, two additional things happened: we made love again; she dared me to go see things planetside for myself.

Not Hoand. That was over with for now, the ship already moving on. Which is how I found myself training for Afdiar.

Notes from the Asperance *Expedition*
Armorer/Corporal YD-038 recording
Page Seventeen:

Repression spares us the memory of birth, along with the painful remembrance of many agonies of childhood or adult life, but it has unfortunate side-effects. It creates the subconscious, which is simply a repository of repressed data. According to the praxeologists, a sane person would have no subconscious. It lowers effective intelligence by tying up physiological hardware, intellectual software, also, physical energy.

Worse, by separating the process of cognition from sensation, repression separates the human "life"—which suffers any number of painful experiences daily—from the human mind, in a misdirected attempt at protecting it. The mind—which evolved for billions of years to control a life—naturally looks for other lives to control, instead. The life, because it must, looks for other minds to control it.

This is the essence of the authoritarian personality, inclined to be as fully submissive as it is to be brutally domineering. The praxeologists believe the drive for power is inversely proportional to the remaining operative intelligence, which explains why individuals, climbing up the ladder of society, appear more stupid the higher they get.

Religion serves many functions in a culture. It gives supreme leaders the comforting feeling that there is a controlling mind above them.

According to Confederates, the happiest non-sane human being is a midlevel bureaucrat with lives to control below, minds above for guidance.

I would have to think about that one.

It certainly matched my experience.

Since I was nearest-of-kin within many hundred light years, they wanted my consent before treating the Lieutenant. That had been the only emergency. Once I had told them to go ahead, they simply popped him into paratronic stasis until the proper course of therapy could be figured out. Confederates were great for taking time to think things through.

They certainly had the technology for it. Substituting quarks for electrons, they could selectively tailor billions of new "elements", trillions of new compounds, to suit whatever purposes struck their elaborate fancy, giving rise to exotic capabilities that often did look like magic to others less advanced—present company, for example.

Fundamentally, that was all there was to apparent miracles such as the shower-curtains or the selectively permeable floors. But that is a little like saying that complicated proteins are all there is to human existence. The future still remained unguessable. Already they were looking forward to what they might do with the building-blocks of quarks!

Meanwhile, Francis Pololo had remained in worried attendance upon the Lieutenant all morning. Bad treatment on Sca had been the primary diagnosis. He explained, however, that my superior had not been a young man to begin with, at least not in physiological terms. The gorilla tried hard not to be insulting, yet he had implied that we Vespuccians knew almost nothing about medicine, about nutrition, about extending human lifespan beyond the expectation of mere savages. As a consequence, the Lieutenant was a much sicker fellow than he needed to be.

It was too late now to do anything but try to repair the damage. The Healer would not guarantee it could be done, fancy technology or not.

By now it did not surprise me that my fallen officer was not taken to anything resembling a hospital or infirmary. Confederate medicine seemed to set great store by being able to take care of him in his own quarters. Standing in the bedroom, over a tubular transparent coffin that housed the sleeping Lieutenant's body, trying to make my mind up about something else entirely, I reflected that I had a couple of additional problems regarding the information I was storing up for Vespucci.

First, it was more important than ever that I do the job right. It now appeared possible that the Lieutenant might not make it back to supplement what I was writing down. I had to see, think, keep a record for two. I had to consider what might be possible if I did not make it home, myself. Probably nothing, I reasoned, but I felt stupid for not having thought of the contingency before. My mind had obviously been elsewhere.

Second, everything I tried to set down in writing was inextricably laced with seditious ideas. Yet, how was I to tell what lonely little datum might prove crucial in the conflict presumably to come? Take all that psychological stuff. Maybe it was just garbage. But what if it could make our generals—or even our gunners—just a little bit smarter ...

Even the physics with which Confederates worked their miracles, claimed Howell, could arise only from a unique viewpoint he called "Discordian".

Was I qualified to separate the technology from the politics? I was not. Was there anybody else available to attempt it? There was not. Would anything useful be left if I were successful? If Howell was right, there would not. Yet, if I did not try, most likely I would wind up stockaded, upon returning home—or executed—rather than promoted.

This would not impress Eleva.

Even so, I was stalling. The real burden of Pololo's diagnosis was that, after the unspeakable stresses of our interstellar journey into barbaric captivity, the Lieutenant had collapsed primarily owing to the absence of a cerebral implant to warn anyone about his impending embolism. He must have that implant immdiately, or remain "frozen" forever.

So where had his loyal Corporal O'Thraight been when all of this was going on? What had he been doing, instead of looking out for his Lieutenant? He had been screwing his brains out with a female demon who did not care whether she lived or died herself, let alone anybody else.

Now, if he and I were ever to get home, it was up to me to decide whether I actually trusted these people. I knew the Lieutenant greatly feared becoming a helpless slave of the "therapy" they offered, while the Confederates seemed to take its benign influences for granted. Still, after her "rescue" from whatever world her body had been maimed on, even Lucille had been hideously scarred, down deep inside, by a rather similar experience, by the agonies of intermittent revival and regeneration.

I had learned more, only this morning:

POLOLO FINISHED INSPECTING the stasis canister, wiped his huge—and immaculately clean—hands on his surgical greens, adjusted his wire-rimmed spectacles, then extracted a small cigar from a brightly colored flat plastic can. It had lit itself by the time it reached his lips.

"May the poor old fellow rest in peace, Whitey. He won't age a nanosecond or change in any way that we can measure, as long as the paratronic field is up. A thousand years from now, he'll be just like that."

The gorilla found a chair, dragged it over beside his charge, draped himself on it backward. I stood, hands in my pockets, watching the Lieutenant's immobile features, his unmoving chest. There was no mechanical equipment in sight, the canister was a simple crystalline cylinder. Nor was the Lieutenant actually frozen. Within the field, "temperature" had no meaning. Even the light we were seeing him by now was the product of some very special manipulation at the sub-nucleonic level.

A thought struck me: "Lucille spent a long time, suspended like this."

He nodded, "Off and on. I understand her case was pretty hairy, owing to an unexpected genetic twist. She was down long enough that, when she woke up, her little sister was a good deal older than she was."

For some reason, this touched me, perhaps because birth order can be very important. That is one reason why Vespuccian children are raised in creches. In any case, the natural tensions between the two females must have been unbearably complicated by this weird turn of events.

"Can they feel anything, Francis? Do they think, while they are sleeping?"

The gorilla shrugged, "That would require motion at the molecular and subatomic levels. I've always wondered, though, if going under and coming back doesn't have its effects, just as I've always wondered if the moment of death doesn't—for the dying, anyway—stretch into infinity. I've been in stasis as a part of my medical education, just as I had to spend fifty hours in a hospital bed." He shuddered. "It truly makes you appreciate the things that made hospitals unnecessary. I wouldn't willingly do either of them again, unless it was life and death."

I shuddered, too, but for a different reason. It was in my mind that if Vespuccian civilization were not going to be casually subsumed by these kindly imperialistic destroyers, I must stop worrying about myself, stop fretting over Lucille or anything else. It was all up to me.

Which is why I found it disturbing that, lurking somewhere in my muddled brain, I detected a tiny wish that the son-of-a-bitch would resolve everybody's problems by simply having the common decency to die.

I shook my head, rapidly, as if that could clear it of these vile, unclean thoughts. Somehow—irrationally perhaps—I believed that everything would be all right, if only I could only get back home to Vespucci!

To Eleva.

CRAWLING OUT OF the gully, I spat sand, then jacked another loader of rounds into my righthand Dardick. Somehow, impossibly, a small stone had worked its way into the footpiece of my smartsuit. Hiding down here had not done me a bit of good. I had already been "killed" twice.

Nearby, a diamond-patterned legless reptile whirred out his deadly frustration. Let him do his evil will. I was too damned tired to be frightened.

Staying low, I placed my back against a charcoal-blackened stump, trying in vain to rest. The "sky" was overcast, yet it was very hot. I could not catch my breath. My suit was having trouble keeping up with the sweat pouring off of my body. Except for a few dementedly-warbling birds, not another thing moved on this scorched prairie, grass-covered between sparse clumps of desiccated trees. In the distance, a dust devil managed a few turns before evaporating into the heat-shimmering silence.

The voice spoke again, from a resonator taped to my collarbone. It tickled. "Only fifteen miles left to go, Whitey. Better keep up the pace, or we'll be here all night—and it gets really dangerous at night!"

"Captain Couper," I gasped exhaustedly. "Is this truly what the planet Afdiar is like?" These were not the only second thoughts I was entertaining. I could not believe that I had actually volunteered to assist in the Confederate conquest and domination of somebody else's world—

BLAM! BLAM!

Some nightmarish ... something, covered with glistening barbed spikes had attempted, in a blurry rush, to pin me to the stump. Now the creature lay thrashing in the long grass, only a few centimeters past my trembling toes. In its death-throes, the ends of the spines squirted a vile smelling liquid. Where it fell, the grass began to smolder.

"Careful, Whitey, those things travel in pairs. No, this isn't at all like Afdiar. That isn't too bad a place, actually. There isn't any native religion, for example. Afdiar is just preindustrial. It has an undiscovered, uninhabited continent. True, their leading culture is a matriarchy, and it rains all the time. Count yourself fortunate that you aren't training for Sodde Lydfe, where we're really going to foul the weather up. The idea is, if you want to stop a war, make it harder for the combatants to find one another. No, this is just for practice. Or if you prefer, you can consider it a qualifying course containing replicas of everything nasty and mean that we've ever run across anywhere."

"A simulation?" I panted.

"Or your funeral, if you like. That's real poison there, give it a whiff. That thing would have paralyzed you first, then dissolved your flesh, fed on you itself, then regurgitated your gooey remains on its unborn young—sprinkling Whitey soup over its osmotically precocious eggs."

"This thing is real?" My eyes focused wearily against the noxious fumes. "Then what about those monsters that attacked me down in the ditch?"

"Holos, to make you waste ammunition. Which you did. Get a move on!"

To this day I cannot explain how I got back to my feet, stumbling dully toward the next goal-marker. Two freshly-loaded pistols or not, I could easily have been captured alive by a squad of Vespuccian Young Patriots at that point, girls' auxiliary, junior division, in wheelchairs.

The 'com patch I was wearing was a simulation, too—of the real implants that everybody else aboard the ship carried in their heads. Subject to demonstrating, on this do-or-die survival course, what I was made of—warm lime gelatin, I was discovering—ironically, I owed my highly probationary status on the operations team for Afdiar to the fact that I had no brain implant, nor would I willingly accept one.

It was certainly a paradox. Maybe the Lieutenant had been right, after all. Confederate freedom was an illusion, their liberty loving rhetoric a sick joke. Or maybe they were telling the truth, that there was no central master computer. But it had occurred to me that maybe it was the aggregate network of implants that ran things, a sort of ultimate electronic democracy. The results would look much the same. The participants would never know where "their" ideas were coming from.

The problem was not so much about general freedom, but of knowing whether you were free at any given moment. I thought about Vespucci, but shied away from it. I had more important things to consider right now.

Eventually, I finished the fifteen miles (miles are a lot longer than kilometers) only getting "killed" a couple dozen times more. The sign over the gate said YOU'RE LEAVING HARRISON'S KIDDIE SURVIVAL PARK—COME BACK AGAIN! I had not been wearier, dirtier, or groggier since Sca.

Couper was there to meet me at the exit.

"Well, son," he leaned against the archway, pulling a cigarette from his pocket. His smartsuit was camouflaged to match the hell I had just been through, but it was fresh, clean, unmarked. The man had been sitting somewhere comfortable—probably with the parents of the other "kiddies"—directing me remotely while enjoying a tall cool drink. "You have an aptitude for massacre—your own. What kind of cannon fodder did they train you to be on that woebegone planet of yours?"

Oddly, I had not seen another soul in the park. Now children of every size, every shape, every gender, every species, were tramping through the gate, holstering their pistols, slipping outsize daggers into scabbards, their smartsuits scuffed or dusty, but with grimly satisfied expressions across their grimy little faces. Judging from their numbers, I ought to have seen at least a few inside the park. I wondered how much of that had been real, how much of it holographic illusion.

I planted my behind against the other gate-post, my back bent, my hands on my thighs, trying desperately to blow some oxygen into my lungs.

"I was a musician, sir."

"You shoot like it. And your tactical sense leaves a lot to be desired. One thing I'll say for you, you learn fast. You wound up right on the average line for beginners, even counting your early losses." He struck me lightly on the shoulder. "Congratulations, son, today you are a five-year-old. Take fifteen minutes, we'll crank you back through the course again. It's a little different every time, you know."

I stared helplessly at the waist-high warriors surrounding us. Running sweat still stung my eyes, making it hard to see. "God help me!"

"Somebody'd sure better, or you're going to wind up with your head sticking out of some Afdiarite hunter's trophy-wall. What I'd really like to know is how you managed to take care of those troopies back on Sca."

I had been thinking the same thing, myself, all day. "Dumb luck. Adrenaline."

"Horse manure, son. You've got a natural fighting talent in there somewhere. We just have to find the right stresses to bring it out again."

"Gee, Captain, how can I ever thank you?"

"Call me Coup. And think nothing of it, son, it's my pleasure. Say, what you got wrong with your smartsuit?" He threw his cigarette aside.

"Sir?" I said reflexively. Looking down at my left forearm, I saw that the inset control panel was ablaze with lights. Red lights. They had fuzzy haloes around them. The repeaters on the right arm were the same.

He seized my arm, began pushing buttons. "Great Albert's ghost, boy! No wonder you look like something the government dragged in!" Abruptly, I began to cool off. My vision cleared. Breathing became easier.

My fatigue started slipping away.

Looking at me, Couper shook his head. "This thing's supposed to help you out, Corporal, not hinder you. How long has it been like this?"

"I do not know, sir—Coup. I did not notice."

"You didn't?" He looked at me oddly. "Well, the blasted thing's an antique. It's probably been on the fritz all morning." He stood for a moment, apparently deep in thought, one hand still on my arm. "I guess I'll have to revise my estimate, son, if you fought your way through that course roasting alive and with your body filling up with deadly toxins."

He stepped back. "Whitey, your smartsuit's supposed to maintain correct temperatures, cleanse your system continuously through the pores, take care of sanitary functions, heal wounds, and tend to half a hundred other things. But it can't do it if you don't bother to look at the telltales when they light up blazing red. And it's a whole lot safer if the suit is simply allowed to communicate directly with your body."

Almost without my noticing, my feet had begun to swell up at the beginning of the morning. Now the pain of that, the feeling of an impending explosion in my feet, began to ebb away rapidly. My bladder filled. The suit went through its automatic sanitary cycle without prompting.

I felt a hundred years younger. "Another commercial for brain-implants?"

"Look, Whitey, this suit you're wearing is over half a century old. They hauled it out of mothballs just for you, for nothing, and that's about what it's worth. Like I said, it's your funeral, but in your place, I'd consider an implant. Think about the Lieutenant. Or that you'll never have to wonder what time it is again, or use a calculator—"

I looked around at his oddly wordless world. Across from the park exit, a restaurant was filled with gaily-chattering individuals. There were a dozen shop-fronts in sight. Nowhere a single sign, or simple advertisement.

"Or see a billboard, or read a book," I answered. Or think for myself, I thought. I had been considering little else. I opened my mouth.

"Nonsense, boy!" Couper interrupted, "I'm reading a book this very minute." He closed his eyes, then began to recite: " ... night had already fallen. O was naked in her cell, and was waiting for them to come and take her to the refectory. As for her lover, he was dressed, as usual, in a—" He stopped, reddened, then started a cough that turned into a splutter. "Wrong file," he explained sheepishly. "Now how the state did Pauline Reage find her way in there with ... here we are—"

"... The best-explored alternative universes pivot on Gallatin's decisions regarding the Whiskey Rebellion—or more correctly, on Jefferson's choice to include the phrase 'unanimous consent of the governed' in the Declaration of Independence. Outwardly similar, the two worlds are entirely different respecting their inhabitants' view of life."

He held up a finger. "Third Century interaction between North America and the United States had noteworthy consequences. Millions of refugees began pouring into the Confederacy, which, in turn, began—on a purely private basis—to subvert otherworld governments. The authoritarians struck back, constructing a 230-ship escape-fleet in 223 A.L. One Voltaire Malaise—incredibly, a Confederate native and popular media figure—with Hamiltonian co-conspirators, kidnapped thousands of young women for breeding stock, controlling them through primitive thought-processors. Enlisting statist help, they plunged recklessly into yet a third continuum, the so-called 'Little Bang' universe ... "

He stopped abruptly. "That's enough for now. Malaise and his crew came from one universe—ours—enlisted help from another, and attempted to escape into it. The reading is from the introduction to Grossberg and Hummel's *A History of the NeoImperialist Party*. I find that it never hurts you to brush up on your classics now and again, Corporal."

Primitive thought-processors. "You keep all of that inside your head?"

"Just the introduction—which I happened to write. You see, I founded the NeoImperialist faction of the Gallatinist party, very nearly a century ago. The idea was that government is a disease that nobody has a right to start or to spread. We wanted to declare war on governments everywhere, to wipe them off the face of the earth. I admit I don't think even I ever intended that we'd be out here doing it."

"Do you regret it?" I asked.

"Not a minute of it. But it just goes to show you that intentions count for nothing in the real world, it's only the results that count. There was a fellow in that other universe—the United States—named Henry Ford. He invented cheap, mass-produced automobiles, and put everybody and his brother-in-law on wheels. He accomplished a lot of good, but the main thing he did was take romance out of the front parlor, under the baleful gaze of Daddy Dearest, and put it in the rumble-seat of a Model A, giving sexual Victorianism the deep-six forever. He probably didn't intend for that to happen—shucks, he might even have been against it happening—but it's the results that count."

"In other words," I suggested, "the ends justify the means?"

"Non-sequitur. Intentions constitute a third category altogether, entirely separate from means or ends. And they usually don't have much at all to do with what eventually happens, anyway. Look at the market system, for example. Individuals seeking a profit help others because they inevitably must in order to make a living. However those with an altruistic bent invariably do great damage. They focus on intentions, rather than results, and this represents a severe dissociation from reality that other folks usually end up having to pay the consequences for."

I laughed. "Is that why you are all out here 'curing' governments, trying to end wars? I have been to the lectures on strategy, Coup. I have heard all the plans for Sodde Lydfe, to pass government ciphers, other military secrets between the two sides so that nothing can be a surprise. Why are you doing all of that stuff, if not for altruistic motives?"

He started another cigarette, began pointing me gently toward the watering-hole across the street. Perhaps my labors were over for the day. "For future profit," he explained. "We know from experience that private individuals are always a lot easier to do business with than governments are, so we're liberating the former by eliminating the latter."

The idea of a light meal with an ice cold drink on the side had sudden irresistible appeal. "That is the real mission of *Tom Paine Maru?*"

He grinned. I did not know whether to take him seriously. "None other."

"I do not believe it for a minute." On the opposite side of the avenue, we entered a crowded restaurant. Approximately a hundred delicious smells hit me all at once. My mouth watered. I looked around for an empty table, only paying half-attention to my conversation with Couper.

"Then believe this, son. I just received a bulletin via implant. It was for you. I seems the operations team is planning a twenty-mile orientation hike through jungle mud in a solid, typically Afdiarian, downpour.

"They want you to join them in five minutes."

AFDIAR

Notes from the Asperance *Expedition*
Armorer/Corporal YD-038 recording
Page Thirty-three:
Outline of Confederate History, continued.

The infamous Voltaire Malaise escape plot was only discovered at the last moment. Although it was not fully interrupted, the electronic slave-controls it depended upon to pacify its human breeding-stock suffered deliberate sabotage before departure. Its crude stardrive only operated with partial success, stranding 230 "authoritarian" starships in a partial state of feminist revolt, not only throughout the stars, but randomly distributed over ten centuries by temporal displacement.

The Broach dilated upon a torrent.

Aboard *Tom Paine Maru*, in a comfortable, loungelike debarkation chamber, we could not see a meter past the aperture, its rim a circle of azure brilliance against a curtain of liquid steel gray. Although a perfectly ordinary wooden-planked door—supposedly—lay not much further away than that meter, the other side of this tunnel through reality.

Like a billion tiny hammers on a billion tiny anvils, a relentless roar filled the chamber, broken by a *flash!* The roll of thunder that followed was scarcely louder. A moving wall of chilly dampness swept in upon us, dragging the odor of ancient mildew in its wake. It was an unusually dry summer morning on Afdiar. We had awaited this letup in the regular downpour for thirty hours. It had rained steadily on this horrible planet for a million years. It would rain like this a million more.

So the geologists had maintained, anyway, orienting the team of which I became a part over the next several days. The sun glared down upon Afdiar as mercilessly as that of Sca. The planet possessed more water. In consequence: eternal thunderstorms. Someday, nine tenths of its surface would be ocean. At present, half of that moisture hung as vapor or continually fell as rain, most evaporating before it hit the ground.

"There's no use postponing the inevitable!" I shouted against the mind-numbing, hammering torrent. I freed my brand new shiny shortsword from the tangle of my specially-treated cloak, loosened it in its scabbard, then gave it a hitch where the shoulder-sling cut off my circulation.

Uncomfortable without a smartsuit that I had never worn, or even conceived of, before a few weeks ago, I summoned up whatever courage I possessed, stepped through the Broach. I groped blindly for the door, lifting, then dropping the green tarnished ring of the knocker onto the green tarnished plate that had been bolted to the rough-hewn planking.

The building, of gray stone equally rough-hewn, sat encrusted with a thick carpeting of slimy moss. Others of the team guarded my back—that I had to take on faith—I could not see behind me. Water sluiced down my forehead, running into my eyes. Drenched fabric clung to my body, hampering my movement. I banged again, not quite as happy with my status of "primitive expert" as I had been. It would have been helpful to know whether "primitive" was being used as a noun or an adjective.

It would have been helpful to know a lot of things.

It had been repeatedly suggested during my training that I try one of the brain implants I worried over so much, on the same experimental basis as this mission, especially as we would have to struggle along without our accustomed smartsuits. Afdiar was a "critical" world where the slightest betrayal of superior technology meant death in a number of particularly unpleasant ways. I had considered accepting the offer. If I could overcome the presumed indoctrinatory influences of the device, it would be better than the crude notes that I had been making from hand-fashioned materials in an apparently illiterate culture. A complete knowledge of the Confederate stardrive system alone would be priceless.

But the plain, ugly truth was that I was afraid. By the time I really knew the truth about implants, it would be too late. I could be just another slave, sharing an illusion of freedom with all the other slaves.

Circumstances had forced me, just before departure, to make the choice for the Lieutenant. I could not let him die, or even take the chance. He would have his implant. Or the implant would have him. It seemed prudent to preserve mental independence for one of us, at least.

Also cowardly.

I kept wondering why the Confederates dispensed information so freely. Did they plan to keep us prisoners forever? Or try to subvert us? Or simply kill us? Could they be keeping even mightier secrets in reserve?

I ached for home, where everything seemed so simple.

Also much, much drier.

The door swung, hinges screaming. Even in that constant downpour, the musty smell seemed to take up more space than oxygen. A bear-shaped figure stood silhouetted in a rectangle of flickering yellow light.

I said, "Woodie Murphy?"

164

"Sure, an' if it ain't the blessed *Tommie* herself," said the shadow, "come at long last t'rescue her loyal minions from moulderin' perdition. Dorrie, come arunnin'! Our day of sweet deliverance is at hand!"

The secret word had been "Tommie". Close enough. I felt the others pile up behind me, drawn to the pitiable amount of warmth inside the house.

Carlos Woodrow Murphy—alias "Uberd Ubvriez b'Goverd"—stood only a handspan short of two meters tall. Yet he was constructed with a heavy globularity that made him linger in the memory as squat, even dwarflike. He had long dark hair in the back, no hair at all in the front, a dark full beard and mustache shot through with gray. Behind his primitive spectacles, he possessed the haunted, soulful eyes of a dolphin.

Murphy wore the oiled, handwoven trousers, the high boots, the bloused shirt, the waxed leather jerkin of an Afdiarite city-dweller. A soft, foreign-sounding lilt in his voice—interrupted by an occasional stammer—made me think back to the briefing I had been given.

Murphy, an "Irishman" from that other Earth Confederates spoke of, had fought his share of an 850-year revolution in the cause of Irish independence. But when the opportunity arose, convinced that his comrades had forgotten the idea of freedom, degenerating instead into nihilistic murderers, he had migrated to the world of the Confederacy, Out here, he was fighting a revolution once again, although somewhat differently.

He had surprisingly small hands, one of which he used to seize my own. A voice, female, came from behind him: "Well, y'big lummox, don't stand there gawkin', ask 'em in! It ain't a fit night outside for a magistrate!"

Confederates informally referred to the municipality that we had arrived in as "Mud City". I had expected any soil that might once have existed on this soggy, rain-beaten world to have long since washed down into the sea. Now I faced scraping off a kilogram I had managed to accumulate—on each foot—in ten second's exposure to the great outdoors.

The locals pronounced it "Hobgidobolis". It was the capital of the nation-state of Udobia, the site of Gabelod, the official queenly residence—as it had been for her predecessor, Jagelid XXIII—of Eleador XLIX, whose royal countenance, judging from holograms 'commed to the mother-ship, closely resembled those of the riding-beasts of Sca.

Not that we would be seeing it. Our assignment limited itself to picking up this strangely-courageous deep cover agent, who had spent two decades "inventing" cheap mass-affordable flintlocks, introducing the concept of barrel-rifling, initiating mass-production, while also producing almanacs, newspapers, political handbills, that sort of item, for a living. By local standards, he had become wealthy doing it.

He had also managed to indoctrinate a promising Kilroy genius, one Johd-Beydard Geydes, himself an inventor, colleague, competitor in the printing trade. A member of the upper classes, thus influential in his own right, already Geydes had accepted the "non-aggression principle" that Confederates feel signifies an elementary understanding of basic ethical philosophy. He had even begun writing about it. Assured of other hands to carry the ball of social revolution, the phony b'Goverd looked forward now to "dying", in order to move forward to his next assignment.

Or retiring, if his wife had anything to say about it.

"By all means!" he shouted suddenly. "What can I be thinkin' of? Dorrie, put the kettle on at once, me darlin'. These poor boyos're drenched!"

Murphy ushered us inside: myself, Charlie Norris from the *Peter LaNague*, Owen Rogers, plus a big-shouldered curly-headed martial-arts instructor named Redhawk Gonzales, who had demonstrated to me, during training, that the Confederacy had forgotten more about mayhem than Vespucci had ever invented. We had rigged ourselves out as Udobian sailors.

Inside, a low, heavy-beamed ceiling flickered in the orange-yellow light from a huge fireplace set into each wall. "B'goverd", who was rich by local standards, could easily afford the tons of fast-growing vegetable matter this crude heating-system consumed. In such a manner did Afdiarites measure their relative status. Even so, directly in the focus of the roaring hearths, the chill damp of the planet remained intolerable.

Rogers pushed past me to thrust a gray-silver parcel into Murphy's hands. "Better take this, Woodie. You look like government warmed over."

In the light of four fires, I could see it, too. Murphy, the first Confederate I had met ever to do so, actually appeared old—heavy lines in his face, silver splinters among the ebony. Moving stiffly, he accepted the package, began to unwrap it, both his hands trembling slightly.

"Sure, an' it's the dirty blackmold-spores that've got t'me, after all this time, Owen darlin', 'steada the dirty Black an' Tan. Another year, two at most, an' I'll be subvertin' the Devil's bailiwick for him."

"Six months, more likely," Rogers contradicted him. "Unless you get back to the ship, where they can take proper care of you." He indicated the half-opened package. "In the meantime, that'll help some."

"It will indeed." Ignoring modesty, he peeled off his Afdiarite clothing, slipped into a perfectly ordinary smartsuit with help from Rogers, a look of benediction in his tortured eyes. "I'll be after lyin' down a while, I think. Mind y'keep your Sassenach hands off me wife!"

"You slipped up, that time," laughed Norris. "Sassenach is Scotch Gaelic!"

"Shit!" Murphy answered, his Irish accent mysteriously vanishing, "Any of you guys got a cigarette? Smoking hasn't been invented here yet."

IT HAD COME time for the "primitive expert" to earn his passage.

Envious, I looked around at the other team-members, each huddled, considerably less miserable than I would soon be, beside one of the Murphys' cavernous fireplaces. I set my jaw, then wrapped my sodden cloak about my chilly shoulders, trying to conceal the burden I had been entrusted with. The task ahead seemed very nearly insurmountable. It consisted of nothing more than a short walk through the streets of Hobgidobolis.

In the rain.

Sprawled in a heavy wooden rocking chair, the still-unconscious secret agent snored, competing creditably with the thunderous downpour outside his thick windowless walls. His color was noticeably better already, Confederate medical technology working its now-familiar "magic".

"Up the high street this way," I repeated Dorrie Murphy's careful instructions, shivering with horrified disbelief at the pale wrinkled skin of my pointing fingers. "Then left after that, for two more blocks."

She nodded, lifting a scoopful of coals from one of the hearths, to replenish the supply in a reservoir under the seat of her husband's chair. He stirred, mumbled something about "Outbound at last!", rolled over into what looked like an uncomfortable position, started snoring again.

I shivered again, shot a resentful glance at the others, nodded resignedly, lifted the latch. Forcing my way back into the eternal storm, I was soaked again instantly. So much for Confederate miracles. Shaking my head, I had to think hard to remember which way to turn up the street. The summery respite was over. Visibility was down to mere centimeters.

The Udobian streets were massively cobbled. There was no vehicle traffic; the downpour would drive hauling-beasts insane. Heavily-laden myself, I clambered from stone to rounded stone, attempting to avoid a ruined ankle, ineffectively shielded by the broad overhanging roofs of buildings set apart by swiftly-running gutters. It was impossible to hear anything but the rain, mingled with my own tortured gasping for air.

Suddenly: "What do ye think ye're doin' in this part o'town, Jack Tar?"

He had to shout it in my ear. The menacing demand was made by a hulking shadow deliberately barring my way. Instantly I regretted our choice of disguises. Apparently sailors were welcomed only at the port.

"Officer, I—"

The man stepped back quickly. With a swish even louder than the rain, the constable's quarter-staff swung out in a wide arc toward the side of my head, clanging instead off the forte of my hastily-drawn smallsword, its tip still in the scabbard-throat. My hip took most of the force, although my wrist began tingling with its ferocity, as well.

"Resistin' arrest, is it?" Setting both his hands on the staff, he raised it for a second swing. He never got the chance. Stepping inside his guard, I lifted my elbow, then straightened my wrist, burying half a meter of quarkotopic steel in his throat. He went down to his knees with a horrible gurgle, his blood blackening the runoff between paving blocks.

If he hadn't rushed me I'd have simply given him the pommel on the jaw.

Gravel *skritched* on the stone behind me. I lurched as another wooden weapon sighed through the empty space I had just occupied. The brass-shod staff end slammed to the ground. This policeman had a whistle at his lips. I saw him draw breath to summon help, wrenched the blade messily from his partner's neck, slashed it across his face. The whistle-stub fell to the pavement, whirled away in the torrent, along with most of his nose. The pale blue eyes above his ruined horror of a face were filled with surprise. He grunted with agony. I ended that with a deep thrust of my short, stiff blade through his solar plexus, finishing with a reflexive W-shaped pumping flex of the wrist.

The nightmare minutes stretched into what felt like hours. I tried dragging the bodies between two buildings, but they kept washing back into the street. Finally, I managed to wedge their quarter staves between a pair of walls, knotted their cloaks around them, then left both dead men half-floating, half-hanging, the first policeman's limp arms making reproachful gestures as the moving waters waved them at me.

I staggered back into the street, shaking from much more than the cold. I resheathed a sword cleansed thoroughly by the rain, glancing around for witnesses, thanking whatever waterlogged gods this planet possessed that its buildings were constructed without any windows for busybodies to peer from. Seeing no one, I reoriented myself with some difficulty, resuming what was becoming an endless voyage to the house of Murphy's native friend, the inventor-philosopher Johd-Beydard Geydes.

At the appropriate door, I unfastened the harness Murphy had given me. Attached to it was a fortune in gold, platinum, precious stones, practically everything the agent Murphy had accumulated here, plus a healthy portion of his original operating funds. Not surprisingly, the bulk of it was silica-gel crystals, another "invention" of B'goverd's, the cornerstone of a coming industrial revolution. Geydes was rich, but he would need more capital if the renaissance the little Irishman had started were to continue. Both men had spoken of an academy. This was meant as the seed-money, to be delivered to Geydes with untaxable anonymity.

As quietly as possible, I lifted the slanted meter-square door of the delivery bin around back, accessible from the inside, as well. I laid the bundle on a grill set in its bottom to keep packages as dry as was humanly possible on this miserable planet, then slowly lowered the cover again, eager to retreat to Murphy's—not to mention his fireplaces.

A hand fell on my shoulder.

"Now, now, my dear fellow, that shouldn't be necessary." A strong arm pressed my elbow, slowly forcing my swordblade down and back into its sheath. "I've an idea who you are and why you're here. Shall we make our way to Ubert's place, or stand here in the rain discussing it?"

I turned, looking up. And up. And up. In the rotten light, I could just make out the tall, gaunt, distinguished form of "Johd-Beydard Geydes?"

He shook his head sadly, "Dear boy, if I were in the employ of Her Equality's Peace Police, you'd just have given away the name of a fellow conspirator. Pray so not bother making up an amateur lie with regard to your own identity.

You're one of Woodie's mysterious friends who visit him from time to time. But this visit is the last, is it not?"

I shrugged.

"Let us be off, then. I would have a word with him before he departs."

The journey back was easier, with two of us to hold each other up. Geydes paused momentarily at the alley where blood still ran into the street. "Bardin-Luther Garder and Jibby Ralv-Budge," he shouted into my ear, "They weren't such a bad sort. Rather a pity you had to kill them."

I spat—the effect was lost in the downpour—refusing other comment. The cops had meant to kill me. We trod onward to B'goverd's door.

Inside, the agent was sitting up, now, sharing a meal with the others.

"Johd-Beydard, ye rascal! Caught us up to it, did ye?"

The man nodded solemnly. "And now you're going away to the stars from which you came. It will be most dull here without you, my old friend."

"Ah, ye'll find others to teach, Johd Beydard. That young Walder Boddale Bagdabara is after inventin' repeatin' firearms already, an' a century ahead of schedule at that. Hedry Wallaz Keddedy's foolin' with magnetism."

He sighed. "Just remember to avoid the likeliest paths the comin' revolution'll want t'follow. Each of the major political systems has its own methods of policy-makin'. Authoritarianism, such as ye have here, operates on whim, divine inspiration, the stomach-grumblin' of the monarch. Majoritarian systems appeal to the "wisdom" of the masses—too bad there ain't any—usually a lot of votin' gets done t'everybody's ruination. Individualists, my friend, do 'none of the above'."

"I shall try to remember that, Woodie—once I figure out what it means."

"It means that, no matter how pretty its promises, in order for the government t'act humanely toward somebody, it must first act inhumanely toward somebody else. Because it produces nothin' itself, y'see? The only 'service' it can offer anyone is t'beat people up an' kill 'em, or threaten t'do so. This helpin' an' hurtin'—usually the same people by turns—are inextricably entwined. In a free market system, everybody benefits—this we call 'profit'—because of the marvelous, absolute, an' totally bewilderin' subjectivity of economic value ..."

"Which in turn," he replied, "depends on the Law of Marginal Utility that you taught me about. I shall endeavor to remember, my friend."

"Ye do that—an' someday ye'll stop the rain."

"Someday," Geydes intoned, as if by ritual, "we'll stop the rain. Goodbye, Carlos Woodrow Murphy. Whatever else, I shall never forget you."

"Nor I you, lad. Have a nice revolution." With that, Murphy sighed, fell immediately asleep again. His wife Dorrie barely rescued the half-full soup bowl just in time to keep it from spilling on the floor.

Notes from the Asperance *Expedition*
Armorer/Corporal YD-038 recording
Page Thirty-Nine:

SHIPS OF THE CONFEDERATE FLEET

Tomfleet:	Bobfleet:	Trans-universe:
Tom Paine Maru	Bob Heinlein Maru	Ragnar Danneskold
Tom Jefferson Maru	Bob Wilson Maru	Hagbard Celine
Tom Szasz Maru	Bob Shea Maru	Captain Nemo
Tom Edison Maru	Bob LeFevre Maru	Peter LaNague
Tom Huxley Maru	Bob Poole Maru	Star Fox
Tom Sowell Maru	Bob Walpole Maru	Zorro

Also, numerous smaller auxiliaries such as Little Tom, Tom Lehrer Maru, Tom Smothers Maru, Tom Swift Maru, *and* Bob Phipps Maru.

Some of Malaise's scattered colony-ships, desperately reworked their nearly-exhausted drives. They got back into the first universe. Thus there is a need perceived for two Confederate fleets, Tomfleet, Bobfleet, searching for lost colonies in both continua—plus a third, smaller cadre of scouting vessels traveling between the two universes.

Those notes I made by firelight, unable to sleep, the ghosts of two peace-keepers haunting me. Say their names: Bardin-Luther Garder, Jibby Ralv-Budge. A pair of human beings doing their jobs. Now they were unfeelingly-butchered meat in a flooded alleyway. I had done it myself.

Going to see for myself, as Lucille had challenged me to do, had turned out to be a more complicated, less satisfactory experiment than I anticipated. I could approve—not that any of my teammates cared—that the Murphys had been trying to raise the living standard on this planet for twenty years, struggling against a system that had been deliberately constructed to prevent progress. Now the valiant spy would die if we could not get him back to the ship. I could approve of rescuing him, as I said, not that anybody cared whether I approved or not.

Around me, Gonzales, Rogers, Norris, were sleeping noisily beside their personal fireplaces, wary even in sleep, hands on their weapons. The Murphys were in another, smaller room with even bigger fireplaces. I rolled over to warm my other side, tucked the notebook away, quietly unsheathed my small-sword. Despite its sophisticated alloy, its sheen appeared dulled by the use I had put it to. For the dozenth time that evening, I wiped its length, trying to get it clean. It did no good at all, perhaps because the tarnish was inside me, rather than upon the blade.

It had been child's-play, murdering the two policemen.

On the other hand, hypocrite that I was rapidly becoming, I was still feeling shocked at my discovery during the evening's dinner conversation, that elsewhere—on Sodde Lydfe—relations among the allies of the Hegemony of Podfet would be systematically sabotaged by means of dirty tricks being openly discussed, even laughed about now, while simultaneously communications were to be opened between various warring states. Murphy looked forward to getting "plugged into the program" if he could recover his health quickly enough. Dorrie asked about technical details. She supplied the praxeological expertise on Afdiar.

A long time ago—what seemed an eternity—I had asked "Who are these people, anyway?" The more I learned in answer to that question, the less I liked it. Worse, they were dragging me into it. Surely, I had killed on Sca, in defense of my life, of my comrades. I had killed before that, in the Final War. Tonight seemed different, somehow. I said nothing about it to the others, who would simply have talked me out of it. I did not want to be talked out of that difference I felt, at least not until I could examine it, determine whether it was real, significant.

For some reason it all seemed to hinge on my relationship (if that was the proper word for one long, continuous battle) with Lucille. Either that, or I had spent too much time among these anarchistic schemers. Sitting in the dimly firelit room with the others all snoring around me, I thought back to a conversation I had had aboard *Tom Paine Maru*, just the day before we had Broached down to this planet ...

She said, "You'd better have some more coffee, Whitey dear. Where you're going tomorrow, they haven't invented the stuff yet. They never will—it won't grow down there. They get their caffeine in nearly microscopic quantities from rock lichen. Anyway, you'd better stock up."

I rolled over onto one elbow, waking up slowly, stupidly, with an odd feeling that this was where I had come in. "Coffee, sure. Thanks. Just—please—do not light a cigarette before I am in full control of my stomach, will you?" I squeezed my eyes shut, opened them wide, squeezed them shut again, then shook my head. As usual, I did not help.

She was, I pointed out to myself, an extremely attractive female, with great cheekbones, a very good nose, wide, full lips, and a cute little chin. She was a honey blond with gold-green eyes. Just now, she laughed prettily, "I don't smoke, silly. No bad habits at all, except ... " She laid a hand on the sheet where it covered certain parts of me.

"Except for Kilroys," I said. "What time is it, anyway?"

"Does it matter, darling? Here's the coffee, what do you want in it?"

This one called me "dear" and "darling". I had not seen Lucille—who had had other terms of endearment for me—for several weeks now. Someone

171

had told me she was keeping company with another man, perhaps that tall, tanned individual I had seen her with at the pool that day. Somehow knowing that made me feel sad at the same time that it made me angry.

"Chocolatl," I told my new companion. "If it is not too much trouble."

Not that I had much right to feel angry. In the first place, there had been never that kind of understanding between us, no promises, no plans beyond a pleasant evening's dinner and whatever came naturally afterward.

In the days following our last terrible fight, I had gotten to know Lucille's sister, Edwina, better, attending some of her classes in praxeology as a part of preparing for Afdiar. What happened then was almost inevitable, a warm but not particularly passionate matter involving a lot of mutual misery. I do not know what was wrong with Edwina's life, but I had established an important principle: kissing your girlfriend's sister can be fully as satisfying as kissing your own.

What I could not figure out is why that discovery made me feel so guilty. She was the most open, generous, comforting person I had ever known.

Edwina handed me the brimming cup, then climbed back onto the bed with her own. One thing I liked about her was that she was completely un-selfconscious about her body, which was highly decorative, to say the least. She had large, firm breasts, a narrow waist, a flat belly, rather more womanly hips than I had been used to lately. Good legs, as well.

Some things ran in the family, evidently.

She looked at where the sheet covered me. "Your mind is obviously else-where, Corporal, isn't it? Don't worry, I can be very patient, and I'm not of-fended. My sweet sister has the same effect on practically everybody. She drove away all of her old friends after her experience with medical stasis. She also left Praxeology forever, to enlist with Security, of all things—although she's quite good at it, and rising fast."

"Is that so?" I asked. What that meant was that, despite Lucille's constant harping on the Vespuccian military, aboard *Tom Paine Maru*, she was the closest equivalent to me. "I guess I have the bruises to prove it." I shook my head, sipped at the coffee, tried to shut up, very much aware that I was in one lady's bed, intimately discussing another. It did not seem to embarrass Edwina—but it certainly did me.

"Look, Whitey, deep down inside, Lucille trusts nobody. She won't listen to anybody who could help her to be happier. If you want my professional, praxeological opinion, she drove off any of her friends who weren't capable of exercising the restraint—or the tolerance—demonstrated by Howell and Koko, because she somehow feels she doesn't deserve to be happy. She reacts with a savage hostility to anybody—including her mother and father and sister—who threatens to love her."

I turned to look at Edwina. "What about Couper, then? What is he to her?" In some ways that old war horse seemed like everybody's father.

She smiled, "Her friend, her boss. He keeps a paternal eye on her—but only from a respectful distance. He's much too smart to get mauled."

I shook my head ruefully. "I wish I had been, too."

"So do I, Whitey." She put a soft hand on my bare shoulder. "So do I."

Under the sheet things started happening. I was an hour late for class.

THE MISPLACED CONTINENT

"IN ANY UNCOERCED transaction, 'tis impossible t'distinguish between buyer an' seller, because 'money' is a myth. All transactions are barter, no matter what you're after callin' the commodities bein' swapped."

Returning good health seemed to have had an unfortunate effect on Carlos Woodrow Murphy. As we trudged along through the unceasing rain, he took it as an opportunity to deliver a lecture to me on free market economics. Suddenly I could hardly wait until the Lieutenant felt better.

It had begun that morning, as soon as the Confederate spy had discovered that I was a Kilroy. It continued as we took what he insisted on calling a "bus" to the waterfront main street of Hobgidobolis.

"No such thing as money?" I shook my head. I had been filling it with other, less-lofty thoughts. "Try telling them that where we are going!"

No one looked upward at the sky of Afdiar. To do so was to invite having the eyes washed out of their sockets. People kept their eyes on the mud at their feet. This was not a good basis on which to build a civilization.

I was concerned about the mud in my brain. It made me feel sad and guilty to admit it to myself, but there was something missing with Edwina, no bright magic, the way there had been with her sister, as painful as everything else had been about that brief affair. Somehow this relationship seemed even more wrong. Perhaps I was beginning acquire wisdom of a sort. I was determined to be honest with myself, with her, to break things off as soon as I got back to *Tom Paine Maru.*

Also absolutely never to fall in love again.

The bus "drivers", each bearing a six foot pole that supported the leather canopy over our heads, looked at Murphy oddly as he lectured on, oblivious to the fact that I was no longer listening. As usual, I was thinking that I must get home. The information I possessed would be needed to combat the Confederacy's inevitable depredations against my own culture. This, I was certain, was why they would not let us go home.

Rain fell, making noise like a ripping sheet.

Dorrie walked beside me, taking up the thread whenever her husband fell silent, which was not often. Redhawk Gonzales walked behind us, his eyes never resting on any single object much more than a tenth of a second, his right hand never leaving the curved grip of a gigantic muzzle-loading pistol thrust through the wide belt beneath his cloak. Rogers walked with Norris, at the front, conversing with Johd-Beydard Geydes. Between us, other "passengers" got on or off at intersections in the sloping streets, handing the "drivers" a few coins as they did so.

"The Elephant & Donkey, me bhoy. That's where we're headed, today, although I personally prefer the good old Porcupine. Tis nearer home. They're the principal reason I'm tryin' t'bring enlightenment t'this heathenish balla mud. A free market'll increase the hilk production an' lower prices. Simple as that, or me name ain't Uberd Ubvriez B'goverd!"

He winked at Geydes.

Hilk was a native high-potency brew that Murphy favored. Dorrie suggested that it was how he had contracted the mold. The waterfront hilk-hole he had mentioned was the reason we were dressed as sailors. It was frequented by seapersons, among them Captain Yewjeed B'garthy, half-pirate, half-merchantman, half-explorer. Murphy insisted that I write it that way, adding that B'Garthy was half-again the man any other native of the planet was. One task was left before we broached up to the *Tom Paine Maru.* It could not be done by the agent or his praxeologist wife alone. We had come to bring hope to this miserable planet.

Murphy himself needed no disguise, being a familiar figure there. For more than twenty years he had pestered ocean voyagers, exerting microscopic pressure—a tankard of hilk was all it usually required—to get the sailors to tell their sea stories. Always he listened for news about Tissathi, the "Misplaced Continent". Always he was disappointed.

He would not be disappointed tonight.

"The Elephant & Donkey!" he repeated as we neared the tavern. It looked to me like any other slime-covered pile of stone this planet had to offer. The only difference was the dirty gray waves lapping at its foundation. The agent paid our fare. We ducked from the leaking canopy into the dripping shadows of the tavern's eaves, then went inside.

The aristocratic Geydes was definitely out of place. Noise of the rain was suddenly replaced by shouting, laughing men, the roar of a dozen fires, the clash of a thousand (or so it sounded) tankards of dark, evil-smelling hilk. In a corner sat a sailor, rags wrapped about his eyes, torturing a musical contraption that was half bellows, half keyboard.

Beneath our feet, the floor consisted of a heavy metal grating. I suppose it saved management the trouble of cleaning up after spilled drinks or customers who had one hilk too many. From the looks of the place, they invested their savings elsewhere. Below, waves rolled from one end of the crowded room to the other. Scattered about, seafaring men gambled, drank, sang along

175

with the blind musician, or paid their disrespects to the wenches bringing drinks. The smells of tar, of hilk, mingled with that of the sea, not as unpleasantly as the words suggest.

Captain B'garthy was unmistakable, a tall, trimly-built individual with close-cropped gray hair, he had the hearty look of a middle-aged athlete. He held court at a big corner table strewn with tankards of hilk, maps, weapons, a scattering of coins. A woman sat on each of his knees, skirts hitched up to show their legs. B'garthy paid his real attention, however, to a miserable little fellow standing opposite the table.

"An' what have ye t'say fer yerself, young Chrissie Hockins?"

Stooped over, miserable with terror, Hockins twisted his knitted cap in trembling hands. He shifted nervously from one foot to the other.

"I didn't mean nothin' by it, Cap'n, I swear!"

A great roar went up from B'garthy's tablemates, a threatening-looking collection of peg-legs, eye-patches, dire hooks in place of hands.

"He didn't mean nothin' by it, says he! Hawr! Hawr! Hawr!"

"Now, calm yerselves, bhoys," replied an unruffled B'garthy, once the raucous piratical laughter had died a bit. "Mehinks we'll hear him out."

"Then we'll keel-haul the little bilge-rat, right, Cap'n? Hawr! Hawr!"

Hockins features did, indeed, remind me of a sneaky little rodent of some kind. He even had a ratty mustache. His pointy nose quivered. He twisted his knit cap again, a tear squeezing out from beneath each eyelid. For the first time, I suddenly noticed a dozen or more obvious—angry—non-sailors gathered behind the Captain in the shadowy corner.

"Awrr, Cap'n," Hockins pleaded. "These be only landlubbers an' feather merchants as I was kypin' from. That don't hardly count, do it?"

There came no immediate reply. B'garthy's sudden silence was contagious. Conversation ceased. Even the blind accordion-player stopped. For once there was no braying chorus from the Captain's table.

Then: "By all the saints, you little barnacle, I orta let these here landsmen hang ye after all! A theft is a theft, Chrissie Hockins, be it from lubbers or yer mates. Fer that matter, ye were stealin' from yer mates, in a manner of speakin'—now these worthies'll have yet another reason t'be seein' all us seafarin' folk as untrustworthy dogs, an' every bit of it'll be yer fault. Now what have ye t'say t'that?"

Amazingly, Hockins stood up straighter, a look of defiance on his weaselly face. "Cap'n, I was not alone, pinchin' them chickens. 'Twas both of the Edwards twins helped as me out. If I hang, they orta hang, too!"

B'garthy snorted: "Misery loves its company, don't it?"

There was a general round of "Arrh!" from his table companions.

"All right, then," the Captain said. "Here be punishment—an' the same fer Glarg an' Graid Edwards, do they confess. Do they not, then these townies can have 'em—draw, quarter, hang, stab, shoot an' burn 'em. An' Afdiar hisself have mercy on their non-existent souls!"

176

The captain took a swig of hilk, clearing his throat judicially: "Ye shall go about the town, Christopher Hockins, in every street an' alleyway, an' no umbrelly. There shall ye shout twice in every block 'I am a liar an' a thief an' a betrayer of me friends', an' this ye shall do until we raise anchor from this port, pausin' only fer bread an' water an' two hours' sleep each night. In addition, ye shall pay back the chickens ye stole, an' at the rate we been takin' loot, lately, ye'll be at it 'til ye've a long gray beard. I'll not ask ye what ye say t'that, for ye well know the alternative. Can ye read an' write?"

"Aye, Cap'n, after a fashion," Hockins gulped, fear and confusion flitting across his rat face, mixed with the first faint touches of hope.

"Very well: four hours' sleep shall ye have, an' a spare hour t'write 'I shall never initiate force again' a thousand an' one times. The chickens'll come outa ship's expenses. Dismissed. See to 'im, Sharkey!"

A grim-looking figure rose from the table, possessing as many missing parts as the rest of the Captain's messmates combined, "Aye, Cap'n darlin', I'd be most delighted. Come, lad, ye've yer work cut out."

Caught in the middle of thanking B'garthy profusely, Hockins cringed, was taken by the collar by the unshaven officer, then led away.

The music started again. Soon the room was back to its familiar uproar. "Uberd! Uberd B'goverd! An' if it ain't Johd-Beydard Geydes hisself, come aslummin'! Sit ye down here, ye old philosophizers! What think ye gentles of the disgustin'ly enlightened sentence I've just passed?"

We squeezed through to B'garthy's table. Murphy shook the gray Captain's hand. "Ah, 'twas a fine upstandin' thing ye did, Yewjeed, a fine upstandin' thing. Sounds like ye been listenin' t'somebody we know."

B'garthy winked at Geydes. "Aye, we've both accepted yer damnable Non-Aggression Principle. 'Tis no man's right to inititive force against another human bein' fer any reason. Though it's cut that deep into me privateerin' income. But 'tis the one code fittin' sea-rovers like us. An' 'twill add to our wealth immeasurably in the long run, I trow."

"That it will, Yewjeed, virtue bein' its own punishment, to the contrary nonwithstandin'. An' I'm here to add a pinch more, if ye be willin'."

"Virtue or punishment, Uberd?"

Murphy grinned, removing a long, rolled-up section of yellowed parchment from under his cloak. He added it to the pile on the Captain's table. "'Tis a map, me friend, of the Misplaced Continent, Tissathi."

Raucous laughter circled around the table. B'garthy slapped the other parchments lying there with a hard hand. Flagons jumped, slopping hilk over the scrolls. "Scrounge around in these a while, old dog. Ye'll find another dozen claimin' exactly the same. Hilk for me mates!" the man shouted into the air. "Ye never outgrow yer need fer hilk!"

A tired-looking young woman with large breasts, exposed for the most part by her barmaid's costume, brought the drinks to the table. Murphy took a long draught, looking at me expectantly. I gulped, but I had thought in advance to disguise that reflex with a big swallow of brew.

"Ye will find no such a map in yon haystack, Yer Worship." I said as I had been coached. I still had not gotten the hang of the accent. Now I had to control my stomach as I spoke: hilk did not agree with me.

"It is indeed a chart of the Misplaced Continent—though she be misplaced no longer—as I should know who has lately been there hisself."

There were only two decent-sized landmasses on the entire planet, both of them straddling the equator, at opposite ends of the globe. We had examined the ancient spherical colonizing vessel left in orbit, identical to the one that circled Vespucci. The first arrivals to Afdiar had mapped the world, intending to land in the more hospitable place. Something had gone wrong. Now, sunk into a barbarism they were only just (excruciatingly slowly) climbing out of, their "Misplaced Continent, Where It Only Rained Occasionally", had become a fantastic legend.

B'garthy laughed uproariously. "Tisathee, the land of hilk an' money, is it? Well, say on, then, m'lad, I'm in sore need of a tall tale."

Tall was the word: the map had started as an orbital photo of the other side of Afdiar, altered to look hand-drawn. There were details of closer islands already half explored which only a sailor would know.

The old pirate was impressed.

"Yewjeed, I've a plan," offered B'goverd. "Ye say yerself that yer privateerin' days're over. Explore these coasts, take with ye only those as accept the Principle. Johd-Beydard'll sign on. Build a city, a nation, free of Queens an' rules an' regulations, an' repel all boarders!"

"A dream," sighed Yewjeed B'garthy, "An impossible dream."

"More than that, my friend." He looked directly at me: "There are cures, me bhoy, both individual an' otherwise, for the authoritarian personality. But because the problem's rooted in the evolution of the species, none simple or easy. Birth by low-trauma methods lower the temptation t'use the repressive mechanism that fatal first time. Derepressive therapy can undo damage an' raise resistance, as does use of natural derepressives: vitamin B6, REM, communication with the unborn ..."

B'garthy smiled at me as if he were perfectly used to outbursts like this from his old friend Uberd. All of this talk about ethics bothered me, however. Aboard ship, I had seen people practicing jailbreaks for Sodde Lydfe, rehearsing assassinations, preparing bombs, planning to wreck monetary systems, encourage the growth of black markets. The object, I had been told, was to minimize disorder or loss of life, to leave the surviving real economies intact, while utterly destroying the governments that had fed off them. This was supposed to be a good thing, the absolute right of any being anywhere to undertake. I wondered if B'garthy would still be smiling if he knew.

"Electronic cerebrocortical Implants," added Rogers, "provide users with a warning that their repression 'circuits' have been stimulated."

"What we're tryin' t'do," said Murphy, "is abolish any opportunity t' gain power an' avoid circumstances where folks seek others t'rule 'em."

He hefted a pouch. It was the remainder of the fortune he had not given to Geydes. "I think me that this'll outfit such a voyage, Yewjeed."

Geydes raised the ante, plopping a similar bag on the table.

B'garthy's eyes lit. "An' will ye an' Dorrie be comin'?"

The agent shook his head. "Ye'll need fresh recruits t'replace us. Somebody t'stay here, teachin' an' writin', sendin' more pioneers t'Tisathee."

"All right, then by Afdiar's two-wheeled chariot, I'll think on it, my—"

"Whaddyou shay aboud Afdiar anna Gweed?"

A drunken individual wearing a food-stained uniform had passed by our table several times, the last nearly stumbling across it. Now he stood with both hands planted on his hips, challenging anyone else to speak.

I looked over at Geydes. "Your noble friends, the police."

Geydes looked at the cop, opened his mouth, "Officer—"

Casually, the police officer backhanded the aristocrat across the mouth, drawing blood. Then he raised his staff, brandishing it at the rest of us. "Thaddle do it! Resistin' arrest! I'm runnin the lotta you in!"

Geydes hit him in his swollen stomach with a tankard.

Snatching up the precious map, the bag of money that went with it, Murphy rose while B'garthy overturned the enormous table. Wishing for the pistol I had not brought with me, my hand went instead for my sword-hilt.

Another hand fell over mine.

"Unnecessary, son," said the pirate. "Just go have yerself a grand time."

He smacked another constable over the head with his own flagon, ducked a flying chair, then plunged with a *whoop!* into the melee that had spread away from us in circles. The accordion-player did not miss a beat, simply speeded up the tempo, getting into the spirit of things.

I felt another hand, this time on my shoulder, turned—

Whaaack!

—wound up on the gridded floor, rubbing an aching jaw. A huge civilian stood over me for some unfathomable reason, both his fists raised.

"Hey, get up an' fight like a man!"

I kicked him in the kneecap, heard the cartilage crumble in a satisfactory manner. When he had sunk, screaming, to my level, I let him have a straight shot with my hardest knuckles, right in the nose. He fell over onto his face. I stood, trod over the man's body, found another person sneaking up on Geydes (who was punching the bartender) from behind. Picking up a chair, I lifted it overhead, took careful aim—

"Hey!"

—it was snatched out of my hands. I whirled. There behind me stood another policeman, hanging grimly onto the business end of my chair.

"Naughty, naughty, little sailor bhoy. That there's our fine, proud City Councilman G'neezovig, don't you know. Now come along quiet—Ungh!"

I hit him in the nose while his hands were full. It felt so good I did it again. He fell backward, over someone crawling on the floor. I repossessed the chair—Geydes had finished his debate with the city councilman using a broken bottle—so I used it to hold off a trio of Udobian Navy swabbies who had joined the fun while I watched Redhawk Gonzales.

Gonzales stood in the middle of a knee-high ring of fallen bodies, his back to that of Charlie Norris. The two of them were having a grand old time. I could not decide whether they were an irresistible force or an unmovable object. They seemed the center of considerable attention.

Occasionally one or more Afdiarians would step into the deadly circle. Gonzales would kick, Norris would punch. Or the other way around. They would both whirl about. Before you could tell what had happened, the wall of bleeding, unconscious idiots around them would be a few bodies higher. Each had a flagon in his hand. Neither had so much as spilled a drop. They would take a swig. By then another idiotor two would decide to try his luck. The whole process would repeat itself.

But it could not go on forever.

There came a shout, a whistle. Suddenly uniforms were pouring into the bar from every door, every window. While busy with a half dozen sailors, Norris took a sharp crack on the arm that had just healed. I heard it break from across the room. He sank to his knees. Someone struck Gonzales from behind. Eyes crossed, he joined Norris on the floor.

I used my chair as best I could, unable to see my comrades in the crowd, smashing it over the heads of two policemen who were kicking someone. Someone else jumped on my back. I turned around, smashed that person into the bar, but another pair of hands immediately seized my throat.

Unable to pry them loose, I began to suffocate. The light in the room was growing dimmer, dimmer. I even thought I was beginning to hallucinate.

The burning blue razor-circle of a Broach appeared on one wall. Lucille Olson-Bear stepped out of it. In her upraised hand, she held an object like a grenade. Taking deliberate aim, she threw it at my feet.

Catching in the grating, it went off.

Notes from the Asperance Expedition
Armorer/Corporal YD-038 recording
Page forty-seven:

The North American Confederacy developed a reliable interstellar stardrive around 250 Anno Liberatis. (I have yet to adequately reconcile these Confederate dates to our Vespuccian calendar, but they make mention of another, older reckoning, 2026 A.D.) All they wanted, in the beginning, was to explore freely among the stars, trade among them.

Worried that "degenerate" colonies might make use of the new technologies (inertialess tachyon drive, quarkotopics) to plunge the galaxy into eternal warfare. A minor "party" in the N.A.C., the NeoImperialists, insisted that the revolution must be completed, systematically destroying every post-Malaise government as it was discovered.

Two huge fleets were constructed to accomplish that task ...

My avenging angel Lucille was still there in the bar as I regained consciousness and returned to the world, a surprisingly genuine look of concern on her pretty face. I was lying uncomfortably on the floorgrid, its pattern printing itself into my back. She knelt—probably even more uncomfortably—slapping me in the face with a greasy bar towel.

"Whitey, speak to me!" She was almost hysterical. "Say something intelligent!"

"Something intelligent," I groaned.

There had been some tidying up. Someone, a rescue team from the ship, had sorted out the bodies. Policemen were stacked like cordwood over here. Navy personnel were lying in a corner over there. There was a pile for civilians, another one for bar employees. Somehow, they were being kept unconscious while we Confederates were being brought around.

"That one there's an informer," Woodie Murphy sneered from the chair he was reclining in. "Let's put his carcass over with the police."

There was warm laughter that I recognized. Geoff Couper observed, "That ought to engender a raised eyebrow or two, once everybody wakes up."

"Oh yeah?," the Confederate operative replied. "Well, the other one there. That's right, the little one with all the face-fur an' the naked scalp. He's Navy Intelligence, such as they have. But put him with the cops, and the street-snitch with the Navy. Confusion to the enemy!"

I sat up. "Your accent is slipping again, Woodie."

"What of it, me bhoy? I'm retirin' off this mudball, about t'be listed as the only fatality of an otherwise friendly barfight. Me griefstricken wife'll be after dyin' of the shock. You folks did bring the silicone corpses with you? Orta keep 'em from makin' me a plaster saint like every other conveniently deceased dissenter in Afdiarite history!"

"Well, we'd better be quick about it." suggested Couper, dusting his hands off. "We've got to get back upstairs, and fast. You'd all have been recalled anyway, within the hour, fight or not. There's an emergency."

I looked over at Lucille. "Message from Bobfleet, via Zorro. A planet on their side it's too late to save, now a radioactive ball of lava."

A premonitory chill ran down my spine. "Sodde Lydfe?"

Couper nodded. "Its otherworld equivalent, and a terrible loss to everyone. Tomfleet's own mission has been accelerated. We may be just in time to save their counterparts in this stretch of reality—if we hurry."

"Counterparts?" I echoed stupidly.

181

"And our first alien race," admitted Lucille, "the Lamviin. Nine legs, three sexes, exoskeleton covered with fur. Pretty weird. We didn't know whether to tell you or not. Weren't sure how you'd take it."

I struggled painfully to my feet, the realization dawning on me that the actions of a starship twelve kilometers in diameter, possibly the fate of everyone within it, were suddenly in the hands of a nine year old child, because she had once been the only person interested enough to think about a particular topic. Elsie Nahuatl would be ecstatic.

"Aliens," I repeated, "All right, let us go, then."

Lucille asked, "You're sure you feel up to it?"

"Just fine," I lied.

"Good—"

Lucille kicked me with all of her strength, at the point where my legs join my torso. Red haze filling my head, I went straight to my knees.

"That's for fucking around with somebody else, Corporal! *Anybody* else, especially including my little sister! Now we can go back to the ship."

PART THREE
THE LAMVIIN

WINGS OF AN ANGEL

Wings of an Angel
Notes from the Asperance Expedition
Armorer/Corporal YD-038 recording
Page Fifty:

It has been argued that, while you sweat your brain away over personal choices, there are other "yous" out there, sweating over them equally in alternative universes, but making them differently, every way they can be made. They all cancel out. Therefore, everything is stupidly futile. Confederates call this Niven's Fallacy for some reason, pointing out that you are the only one you have. Only your choices count, since you can only live one life, in one universe at a time.

Now Howell informs me that Confederate physicists are playing with the idea of a third time-dimension, completing symmetry with the three dimensions of space. They do not know what it is, any more than Australian Aborigines saw that time is a different thing from space, or people before Pascal knew about statistical probability (or that it was a fundamental pillar of reality before P'wheet and Thorens). But it will likely be something that we have known about all along, in an entirely different context. After all, people gambled long before Pascal.

It might simply be the way time flies when you are having fun!

"Whitey!" Owen Rogers hissed at me, "Come here a minute!"

His sibilant crackle in my helmet-phones threatened the well-being of my eardrums. I shrugged, levered around to face the praxeologist where he lay like a beached dolphin beneath a wind-weathered overhang. The sun broiled down into my face. As long as I kept my eyes closed, that unmerciful orb shut out of my consciousness, I was comfortable. My smartsuit was more than adequate to any task this planet set for it.

It was only my mind that threatened to bake me to a cinder.

Below, the quarried fortress squatted in a low, marshy depression, a long-extinct caldera atop the isolated monolith locals called Zeam Island. We were

185

just off the south coast of the nation-state of Great Foddu, seat of the world-wide Fodduan Empire. Triangular in floorplan (like most of the buildings on this overheated planet), the place was a low security prison, reserved for the highest-ranking clientele. It was three stories tall—yet broad enough to appear low, forbidding, dangerous.

My thoughts took me unwillingly back to Sca, a full-circle from dungeon to dungeon. It was not the most comfortable of feelings. Over the past few months, I had come to agree with the undisciplined Confederates on at least one point: there is no excuse—ever—for keeping another sapient being in a cage, no matter how he may deserve it.

Far better to kill him outright.

Cleaner.

Elbow-crawling toward Rogers, I kept low as possible behind meager cover, wary of the soldiers posted below. There were six of us, me, Rog, Couper, Lucille, Howell—along with little Elsie—plus the alien who was acting as our guide. We all lay concealed by an outcrop, the Gulf of Dybod behind us at the foot of a sheer, cruel cliff-face. The soggy meadow with its sprinkling of wildflowers, guarded jealously by heavily-armed beings of the same species as our guide, lay before us.

Everything looked *wrong*.

The sky overhead glowed a custardy yellow, cloudlessly clear. The sun on the horizon was the color of dried blood. This would brighten to a dull orange as it rose, bringing local temperatures even higher than the hundred thirty-five degrees Fahrenheit that my instruments attested.

The water all around—an extension, according to my suit-map, of the "Rommish Ocean"—was a brilliant crimson, owing to a variety of algae with a high red chlorophyll content. This far from the mainland, dense growths of equally-red higher-order plants thrust up through the water's surface, their stalks calming the waves to an oily languor. It got on my nerves almost as much as the yellow color of the sky, which on my homeworld would have been a warning of rare destructive twisting storms.

Pink surf pounded on the white sand cliff-base.

The meadow itself was a riot of reds, oranges, yellows. Anything that offered cover lay in a charred heap to one side of the building, but fresh grass, or something like it, a few low shrubs, told a tale of garrison troops grown lax. Overhead, one of the creatures Elsie had dubbed "whirlybirds" circled, looking for something helpless to pounce on.

Like every other advanced organism on Sodde Lydfe, it was built on a trilateral symmetry, boasting three large wings, three eyes, even three sexes, just as promised. Sculling itself around its own axis to obtain lift, how it saw where it was going was anybody's guess. If his went well, Confederate biologists would be scrabbling gleefully over this planet for the next three centuries, asking themselves similar questions.

Provided the natives did not reduce it to radioactive cinders, first.

Settling in beside Rogers, I realized that my inquiring expression was not being conveyed by a smartsuit-face camouflaged to resemble rock-grown cactus. Apparently he needed some help adjusting a setting dial on the fist-sized piece of machinery he had brought with him through the down-Broach. It was identical to the object that Lucille had thrown at my feet in the bar. I held it while he tightened a tiny screw.

Elsie, lying on her stomach, conversed in low tones with Couper who was interrogating our native guide while Howell looked on. As she talked, Elsi played with a small, double-edged knife as casually as she had with her bubble-pipe. Lucille sat up a little higher, keeping watch, a plasma pistol in each hand. I was astonished at the way my attitude had changed toward her. Lucille's personal problems were fairly easily understood, after all—although not so easily dealt with.

Somehow, the alien had contrived to meet us in exactly the correct place when we dilated down from orbit. It was my first chance to see one of these "lamviin" up close. The thing stood over a meter tall, much wider than a human, covered with thick, coarse, blondish fur, shading to a darker tone at the extremities. Its pelt rippled as it spoke, making me suspect that this was not an effect of the offshore breeze.

Each of its eyes, a trio evenly distributed around the inverted bowl-shaped body, was bigger than my hand, dark-irised, protected by a heavy ridge of brow bone. It gazed out from beneath a fringe of furry lashes with calm, unnerving wisdom. An obscenely hairless hemisphere, divided into three sawtoothed sections, formed a mouth atop the alien creature.

Even more disturbing were its limbs. At the rim of its carapace, spaced between the huge eyes, three heavy "legs" emerged, covered with a camouflage fabric spanning the underside of its body, as well. About halfway down, at the cuff of the garment, each limb split into three more delicate extremities, heavily furred like the rest of the alien, terminating in strong, slim, three-fingered "hands"—or "feet". It walked on six of whatever you called them, holding the remaining three upward.

Carrying a large valise made of the same brush-patterned fabric as its clothing, it wore a large handgun in a leather harness strapped to the underside of its carapace. I could see that Rogers itched to get ahold of that weapon. I will admit to some curiosity, myself, not only about the gun, but about the fact that the creature was not an "it" at all, nor a he or a she, but a third sex that human beings do not have. I wondered what pronoun to call it by, also what in the despised name of Voltaire Malaise's miserable navigator, its biological function was.

I had learned that it answered to the name of Mymysiir Offe Woom —"Mymy" to its friends. We were here to break its husband out of prison.

"Okay, here's the situation," said Couper as the conference broke up. Crouching, he slid over to where we were finishing adjustments on the bomb-like object. Behind him, Lucille—how odd to think that she had been

187

born on Earth, the birthplace of all mankind—was examining Mymy's gun, a big three-shot revolver, gray with long use, hard wear. It looked like it used blackpowder cartridges, brass, with big lead bullets.

"Well, our pigeon's cooped up down there on the top floor—he's a Very Important Prisoner, apparently—in a corner cell. They appear to be luxury quarters, considering circumstances, with lots of light, a great view, very dry and warm, the way these people like it. The catch is that he can be reached only through a guard-room. We have to get past the guards. How are you coming along with that stasis-bomb, Rog?"

The gunsmith looked up, "You know that this is a prototype, Coup. There were only two. Lucille used one on Afdiar, and I'm not sure this one's going to work. The Heller effect is a pretty iffy proposition at best."

Couper assumed the grim expression that he felt most comfortable with. "I want to avoid hurting people if we can, Rog. We're here to stop the killing, not add to it. Mymy tells us that rher husband is something of a celebrity down there. The guards here treat him like royalty."

"A policeman's lot, and all that." Howell trotted beside Couper. In his close-fitting coyote-shaped smartsuit, with a pair of small remote controlled pistols fixed to the helmet, he looked like a rubber dog.

"'Rher'? Is that the proper word for this whatchamacallit?"

"Have a care, Whitey old fellow," admonished Howell. "The lamviin have excellent hearing, albeit their atmosphere is rather thin. They evolved in it, after all. I suspect, as well, that Mymy's beginning to pick up a modest smattering of English. Rhe's an exceptionally bright organism."

"I'll second that," said Couper. "Good tactical sense, too."

"Rhe, rher, rhers'," Howell went on. "Those are the pronouns for the third sex. Mymy's a *nidfemo*, a 'surmale', the weakest and the smallest of the three lamviin sexes. Although if that's true, I dread the coming confrontation. Rhe's quite a formidable being, rherself. Rhe's also a physician, and has explained to me how their biology works."

"Oh?" Rogers asked at the same time I did.

"No time now," Howell replied, a malicious expression on the face-piece of his helmet. He turned to look at Couper. "Have we a plan?"

The big man returned the coyote's gaze, unrolled the blueprint—it was ochre, actually, with reddish ink—that the alien had given him.

He shook his head. "If you want to call it that. The only way is through that ground floor arch, with a portcullis either end of the passage. Mymy's been allowed to visit Mav. He's been in a couple of years, local time, since the war started heating up, so rhe knows the layout."

The others joined us.

"I don't know what you got me down here for," said the diminutive xeno-psychologist, tucking her dagger away. She patted Mymy between the eyes, "They may look a little strange, but in here, they're just like us."

"Why, thank you kindly, Elsie Nahuatl," said the alien. I jumped, startled at her—rher—'command' of the language, until I realized it was only our smartsuits translating. Had I dared to strip off my helmet, I would have heard the creature speaking Fodduan. "You look a little strange, yourself. And you say that Howell, here, is your father?"

"More so than most fathers," the little girl nodded proudly, "I was going to spin you a tall tale about being the larval form of a coyote, but the absolute truth is that I was a contract-baby, constructed especially to order, gene by gene, so he could have a daughter."

Mymy said, "I believe that may be illegal in Great Foddu." Rhe glanced down at the map, pointing to the center, "There is the courtyard."

"In fact, the place is little more than three walls about an exercise yard. 'Round the inside, as you may observe on the outside, as well, there is provided a walkway upon each floor, the salient difference being that, inside, these are connected by flights of stairs."

Mymy's voice seemed to emanate from small dilating orifices either side of rher leg where it joined rher dome-shaped body. I could hear rher breathe between phrases. Rher mouth, sort of a flattened beak, had nothing to do with respiration. In essence, rhe talked through rher nostrils.

"We have two choices," rhe observed. "Entering the archway at the front, passing through both iron gates, up two flights to the second floor, through the guard-room and into my husband's cell—or scaling the outer wall straight to the third floor to pass through the same guardpost."

"Not much of a choice," said Elsie. Lucille was being unusually quiet, I thought. I couldn't blame her. She had once died here, after all.

"In any event," Mymy went on, "we shall have to contend with at least an octary of guards assigned to scarcely half again that number of prisoners." Rhe shook rher carpet-bag in emphasis, laid another hand on rher revolver. This left a third hand, with which rhe pointed angrily at the fortress below. "Positively scandalous, that's what it is!"

"What is an octary?" I asked, watching the alien in amazement.

"Eighty-one," Lucille answered for her. "Nine-times-nine. It's the one hundred in their base-nine numerical system. Any more stupid questions?"

"Sure." I refrained from the sarcastic remark that crossed my mind about numbers—or calendars, "We are supposed to get in there past eighty-one guards (or is it a hundred?), then climb three floors past professional opposition, without hurting anybody? Why did we bother coming?"

Couper laid a hand on my shoulder. "Just do your best. I never said you couldn't defend yourself. We've got the stasis-bomb. That's what we'll use in the courtyard. What radius have you set it for, Rog?"

The gunsmith was disgusted. "The marks on the case say a hundred yards. I haven't any idea how truthful they are. How're we gonna play this?"

Couper gathered us all around him, like a kickyball coach, even laying a brotherly hand on Mymy's furry carapace. "Well, here's my plan ..."

189

There had not been any point to our waiting until sundown, after all. Three moons rose, almost simultaneously, flooding the marshy meadow with the reddish reflected light of the Sodde Lydfen sun. You could have read by their glow, if Confederates had ever acquired such a habit. Each of us lay, face down, at the dry edge of the field, our smartsuits telling lies to any eyes that happened to wander their direction.

Suddenly Howell jumped up, his smartsuit suit turning—at Mymy's suggestion—a brilliant lime green, a color that never occurs in nature on this yellow-red-orange planet. At something in excess of forty kilometers an hour, he rushed, yapping loudly in the evening stillness, toward the open portcullis of the prison archway. Couper followed, more slowly, the Heller Effect bomb in one hand, ready to throw.

Mymy ran with Rogers, behind Couper, while Elsie and I followed Lucille with a different task in mind. We angled off toward another wall, hoping the diversion would distract the guards' attention from us. The whole idea was to keep little Elsie from getting shot at, not because she was only nine years old—Confederates simply do not look at things that way—but because she was physically small, could not run as fast as the rest of us. Also, despite her frequent and modest disclaimers on the subject, she was the only expert we had on alien psychology.

From the corner of my eye, I watched the other group converge on the entrance. Howell was already inside, now, making noise enough to raise the dead. The guards inside would be shocked, never having seen or heard anything like a coyote before. The fact that he ran on four legs was enough to make him a monster. In that color they probably thought he was some kind of demon from whatever hell they believed in here.

No one on the planet knew we were here except Mymy, plus whoever rhe talked to via their underground radio network. It was that station—plus half a hundred more like it, planetwide—that had called Confederate attention to the enormous antiwar movement we were now attempting to aid. Not even Agot Edmoot Mav, rher husband, suspected he was about to be rescued, by aliens, at that. Life on other planets was still a speculative concept here, the subject of fiction or fairy tales.

Wait until they saw a killer whale!

Lucille reached the wall ahead of me, began to climb the rough stone toward the catwalk overhead. I still found it odd that many of the cells, on all three floors, had doors connecting directly with the outside of the prison. Lucille would likely reach Mav's cell ahead of everybody.

Responsible for Elsie's safety, I certainly could not climb the same way. I started the little girl up, then began following her, when a bullet zinged past us, striking the stone wall at a shallow angle. I glanced up, flattening myself against the triangular stones, saw a lamviin arm with a large automatic pistol,

190

taking aim again from the guardpost corner. I drew my own pistol, fired three shots. The arm withdrew.

More gunshots rang out, most of them from overhead.

"Whitey!" Lucille shouted, "This isn't working! Shit!"

She had slipped, one smartsuit-covered leg thrusting down between the widely-spaced slats of the second-floor catwalk. Now I understood their purpose: they allowed plenty of room for the guards to aim and shoot through; they were also almost unnegotiable, in a hurry, by human or lamviin feet. Still only a meter or so above the ground-level, trying to shield Elsie's body with my own, I clung to the wall, returning fire to the second-floor corner guardpost, nearly getting myself caught in crossfire between two posts on the ground level corners.

"Keep climbing!" I shouted at Lucille, "I have an idea!"

Tucking our miniature xenopsychologist behind me, I dropped back to the ground, stepped to the door of the nearest cell, fired point blank at the clumsy brass padlock keeping it shut. The tortured metal bent, shattered. I threw the door open, gesturing at the blinking creature inside.

"Come on out, friend, you are free to go!"

I was shocked when the lamviin in the cell picked up what looked to me like a wooden stool. I was shocked even more when he (she, rhe) threw it at me. I could see now why Fodduan prisons were constructed so much differently from Vespuccian ones. Apparently nobody wanted to escape. Ducking, I ran to the next cell, to blow the lock off that door.

Before I could open it, hot lead came whisking through the air from the other corner. Elsie suddenly fired three or four shots. I heard a scream—she must have connected with a careless trio of fingers—then kicked the cell door in. Its occupant, a rather small non-Fodduan lamviin, to judge from the reddish-black color of his fur, dashed outside, nearly knocking me over, began running across the meadow.

Little spurts of dust, water, or turf followed him as the guards reacted.

That was more like it!

The next cell I opened was empty. The next cell after that one was occupied by a pair of Fodduan-looking individuals. "You are free to go!" I shouted at them. "We have come to rescue you! Get out of—*hey!*"

"We may be criminals," one lamviin said, grabbing at my gun. "But we are no traitors! Get it, Byv!" The other lamviin jumped into the fray.

"I'm trying, Toym! It won't hold still! What is it, anyway? It's ugly!"

"Takes one to know one!" I yelled, forgetting all the interspecies civility I'd learned. Hard as I could, I punched the first creature between the eyes. Only my suit saved me from a broken hand. Crowded, hurried, I pulled the trigger when the second prisoner rushed me. It staggered back, only stunned, then came for me again. I fired again—this time it ignored the bullet, began grabbing at me with all three hands.

I shot it in the foot.

191

The lamviin began hopping around, cursing just like any human being, trying to hold its injured foot, yelling at its cellmate to do something. I waved my Dardick at him in warning, deflecting the muzzle toward his toes. "Get out of here, both of you. Right now!" I fired a shot into the floor. It ricocheted once off the flagging, then fell silent.

"We're going, already!" He helped his injured companion out the door.

By now, the guards seemed to have lost interest in the outside of the fortress. My idea of diverting them with escaping prisoners was failing. Finding Elsie, with her smoking pistol, I rushed around the corner to see Couper, Rogers, still outside with Mymy, the bomb in Couper's big hand.

Both portcullises were down.

Howell, apparently, was still inside, trapped.

Our brilliant plan was failing. Poor Howell had been supposed to attract the guards into tight bunch (he'd told me he had border collie genes, whatever that meant) so that Couper, once the coyote had dashed out of range, could knock them all out with the stasis bomb, in theory without hurting any of them. The Fodduans were not cooperating. I ran around, letting several dozen more equally-uncooperative prisoners loose on the remaining two sides of the prison. They all ran out into the field, then stopped a safe distance away to watch what was going on.

We were not impressing them, either.

Leaving the little girl with Mymy for safety, I climbed up to the second level—lamviin stairs are not all that different from those built by humans—tiptoeing gingerly along the widely-spaced slats in the catwalk. There, I opened more cells, skipping the ones without locks.

More gunfire.

I holstered my first Dardick, drew the second, shot back, wounding at least one more guard. Completing a second circuit of the building, I looked down to see that the outer portcullis had been blasted open, most likely with a plasma gun. As I watched, there was an explosion from within the archway. Elsie, Couper, then Rogers stumbled out, his cursing almost coloring the air. He was followed by the surmale lamviin—

—then Howell!

The coyote's suit was torn, the muzzles of his helmet pistols glowed in the midday twilight. Couper cocked an arm, ducked a big-caliber bullet winging at him on a cloud of blackpowder smoke, then threw.

There was an odd, muffled thump, then—silence.

Without watching any more, I climbed up to the next level. I made it over the catwalk rail just in time to catch a three centimeter lead ball right in the chest. Pain became my entire world for a dizzying moment. I nearly slipped as I passed the rail going the wrong way, but grabbed, hung on, managed to pull myself back. Lucille I could not see, but a huge lamviin with a revolver in each of his three hands, was charging directly at me. I took careful aim.

Remembering the hardness of the carapace on these creatures, I shot him right in the eye.

Boom of gun, slap of recoil.

The ruined eye spurted green goo.

The unfortunate lamviin pitched over the railing with the smashing sound of a giant egg when he landed on the cement sidewalk at ground level.

Surprised I was still alive, I glanced at my chest—not even a hole. But it felt like I would have to have my ribs taped. I hopped from slat to slat—they were more like rungs on a horizontal ladder—until I drew even with a guardpost door, not clearly remembering where I was or where this Mav character was supposed to be. There was gunfire inside a large triangular chamber. Peering around a corner, I ran smack into another lamviin, grabbed an outstretched hand, pulled in the direction he had been running. He tripped headlong over the rail.

I did not hear this one hit.

Inside, across the room, Lucille was hiding behind an upturned table of heavy wood, trading shots with three guards. Their soft lead slugs stopped in the table or passed over her head harmlessly to splatter on the wall behind her. She could hardly get a shot in, her small pistol against nine, but when she did, she kept her fire high, showering her adversaries with the hot chips of stone that her plasma gun exploded from the wall. Smoke was coming from more than one carapace, along with the suit-relayed smell of singed fur—plus more cursing.

I picked a victim, shot him in the foot—that seemed to work downstairs. He screamed something impolite which my suit refused to translate, turned all three pistols my direction. I shot him in another foot. He lost interest in me, falling into a toe-massaging heap.

Lucille took this as an opportunity to set a wall-hanging afire. Huge flaky ashes with brightly burning edges swirled and drifted in the air, settling on the two remaining guards. One of them threw his guns away with a sudden gesture, slapped at his fur. He put his hands up.

"I give up! I give up! Peace, in the name of—"

"Shut up, Viideto, you craven weakling!" His companion beat him about the eyebrows with a pistol-butt. "Just because you're a little singed!"

I shot this one in what I think was a knee, just as the entire wall-hanging fell over him. There was a muffled screaming as the creature began running blindly about the room, crashing into the walls.

Lucille flung herself on him, brought him to the floor, flipped off the covering, slapped out the coals in his fur with her gloved fingers. Viideto rushed to his side, did the same thing with his bare hands.

"Zimo! Zimo! Are you all right?" he cried.

"Of course I'm not all right, you vesa! Who are you people, anyway?"

"Yes," said Viideto. "What do you want?"

Zimo and Viideto seemed to have gotten used to the human appearance almost instantly. I could see what Howell had meant by formidable.

"And by the way, thank you for saving what little pelt I have left."

I stepped forward. "We want your prisoner. Is he in there?"

I gestured with my pistol toward the heavy-looking triangular metal door set in one wall of the room. There were three big padlocks on it. The small, barred, three-cornered window through it had been covered.

Couper, Howell, Rogers, Mymy, Elsie rushed in through the opposite door.

"Missur Mymy!" shouted Viideto, his fur standing on end. "So it is you who has engineered this breakout! What a great mistake you're making! Mav is safe here, and outside, there's a war going on. Why I, myself—"

"I am sorry, Viid," Mymy said, not in an unkindly voice. Rher fur lay smoothly flat, which I took for some kind of calm expression. My own fur would have been straight up. As it was, my heart was racing. "You must release Mav. We are about to end this horrible war, right now."

Couper bent down, took a ring of keys from Zimo who was lying on the floor, little wisps of smoke still issuing from his hair. "Be good, now, and you won't get hurt, er ... any more than you have been."

To me he said, "The stasis bomb worked all right, once we got a chance to deploy it. There are about seventy-five unconscious lamviin down there—more, if you count the cells within the radius of the bomb—who'll be awake and hopping mad in a few minutes. We'd better skedaddle."

He reached to unlock the three brass padlocks. Two yielded to keys on the ring. He turned to look at the guards. They looked back at him. Maybe the ripple in their fur was a shrug. Lucille hefted her gun. I holstered mine, reloaded the first with a *(clack!)*, raised it toward them.

"Oh, for Trine's sake, Viid," said a weary Zimo finally, "Give it the trinedamned key. They've saved my life. They're obviously friends of Mav's. And I'm about ready to give up and become a trinedamned Mavist myself. I don't think I can take another trinedamned philosophy lecture!"

Reluctantly, warily, the unwounded guard handed Couper the third key. The big man turned it in the upper padlock. The lock clicked and swung loose. Releasing the hasp, Couper swung the huge iron door aside.

Inside the next room, triple moonlight flooded inside through curtained windows. Some kind of incense burned in a brazier on a table.

On a bed of sand in one corner, the wood of its edges decoratively carved, an elderly lamviin glanced up from the scroll he was reading, set the reading material aside, glanced from Mymy to Howell to Couper to Lucille to Rogers to Elsie to me. Then he took what looked like a long cigarette holder from a pocket on the leg of his jacket, dribbled a little clear liquid into it from a silver flask, thrust it into a nostril.

He rose with an outstretched hand. "I say, alien beings from the stars at long last—hullo, Mymy my dear—Agot Edmoot Mav at your service."

He removed a monocle from the eye that was facing us.

"What the devil took you so long?"

"MY FRIENDS AND GAOLERS..."

Notes from the Asperance Expedition
Armorer/Corporal YD-038 recording
Page Sixty-nine:

From Afdiar to our next stop is about nine hours, some uncounted number of parsecs, also perhaps an entire lifetime—if I choose to believe that people can change. I am writing this—although I will certainly have to erase it eventually—in order to help me decide. The necessity arose some time before we reached Sodde Lydfe, the planet of the lamviin, just after we were whisked up from the bar in Udobia ...

"I've already been briefed," Lucille grabbed my arm as we reached the debarkation lounge. Others of the field team dispersed to various quarters of the ship. I wanted most to go three rounds with a shower curtain, get back into my smartsuit. She said, "There'll be nothing but wheel-spinning the next few hours. We've got important matters to settle."

I tried to conceal the limp that she had given me. "That sounds ominous."

"You should hear it from this side, Whitey." Was that a nervous tremor I heard in her voice? Whatever it was, she passed it by with a rush, pulling me along in her wake. Leaving the lounge, we toothpasted ourselves through a dizzying series of transport-patches, arriving finally at the beach where we had first ... well, gotten to know each other better. This time, no one else was there. It was very hot. I shed my Afdiarite cloak, the swordbelt, stripped down to the trousers, pulled the boots off. The entire ship seemed busy, almost at battle stations.

We stopped, sat down, leaned against a weed-topped dune.

High above us, white birds soared.

Folding her legs under her, Lucille produced a cigarette, inhaled deeply. Momentarily, I envied her the habit. Not knowing what to do with my hands, I wrapped them around my knees, helped her watch the surf.

She said, "Whitey, how old are you?"

195

It was a strange way to begin a conversation between two adults. Keeping my eyes safely on the water, I replied, "I am thirty-seven Vespuccian—"

"That would make you ..." she rolled her eyes back in her head, consulting her damnable implant, " ... about twenty-eight Terran years old."

"About."

"Do you like older women?"

I swiveled to face her, "Look, Lucille, if this is about Edwina again ..."

"No, you moron, it's about me." She buried the burning end of her cigarette in the sand. Her face seemed to be beginning to screw up in a manner that I had never seen before. "I was born in 224 A.L., you see. That's the year 2000, by the Christian reckoning. This would be 2052."

I did not see what she was getting at. I brushed a few sand-grains off the hilt of my shortsword where it lay beside me. "That would make you—"

"Fifty-two years old, Whitey. I spent twenty-three years in stasis!"

Suddenly the tears were streaming down her cheeks. She hid her face in her hands while her shoulders shook. Tentatively—odd, since we had been to bed together so many times—I laid a gentle hand on her. She turned, leaned against me, cried a little more, then, nose running, stifled her sobs, sat stiffly as if awaiting something from me.

I did not know exactly what. I did not have a tissue. Far, far away, the brightly-colored triangle of a sail skimmed across the horizon.

"Constitution, Lucille," It was the first time that I had sworn in Confederate. "If I understand what occured to Malaise's fleet—that parts of it were hurled back in time—you are twenty-five hundred years older than me, like everyone aboard this ship." I put a hand on her silver-colored knee. "Do a couple dozen centuries matter, between us?"

The crying really started then, choked laughter wedged into spaces between gasps for breath. "Whitey, if you really mean that, I ... but it's so hard, trusting ..." She stopped: "I did once, but all it got me—"

Lucille, having difficulty trusting me? Momentarily scandalized, I folded my arms across my chest, looked away. Then I realized that I was a stranger to her, for all of our passionate intimacy, just as she was to me. Even with a computer pasted on her neocortex, she could not read my thoughts, know how I felt, or understand how much I had come to ...

But she was looking out to sea, as well, going on:

"It was the 'accident', of course, the one that got me killed."

She turned to face me. "You know, I've thought of it that way for so long, it's hard remembering it was an attack by stone-age natives ... not even proper Kilroys, really, during an initial planetary survey."

I nodded, urging her to go on.

"I was with Praxeology back then," she produced another cigarette, "So was my husband, who precipitated the attack. Who abandoned me to whatever perversities those savages wanted to commit, using me as the centerpiece."

Having recently been in similar circumstances, I could sympathize. The worst part isn't the pain, which eventually goes away, but the feeling of abject helplessness, which stays with you the rest of your life.

"Ship security didn't believe my husband's report that I was dead, but there were delays locating me. Coup arrived just minutes too late. Happily, I don't remember very much of the really rough stuff—just enough of the preliminaries, believe me—but they tell me I was ... I was tortured to death and ... dismembered over a period of several days."

That is not exactly how she told it. It took a great deal longer. She smoked. She wept. We talked. We touched. We did not make love. That would be for another time. The husband (she never said his name—I later learned it was Dalmeon Geaner) subsequently took their only child while Lucille was in stasis, leaving *Tom Paine Maru* under a cloud.

"I had words with Mac over this," she said at last, "He insisted I tell you this. He told me I'd treated you rotten. He said that I'd better—"

"Hold on a minute: Mac?" I asked, jealousy creeping back in around the edges, "Mac who? I'm afraid that you lost me at the last turn, Lucille."

"You've seen him, darling, I'm sure of it. We had only just found each other, after all these years. The tall, blonde, very tanned young man?"

"Oh. Yes," I said. "The tall, blonde, very tanned young man. Good muscles."

"You perfect idiot," she laughed. "Good muscles. He's my son, MacDougall Bear. He adopted my family's name. He's twenty-nine, the same age I am, physiologically. That's why I asked how you felt about older—"

"My god." Relief coursed through my every capillary, "Anything else?"

She looked up at me, her eyes suddenly very big. "One more thing. An explanation, not an excuse. I've had one particular ordeal to face ever since I came out of stasis. Unfinished business. I thought I was all braced for it, every emotion I possessed shut down in preparation for ... and now this ... you. I was ready to go back, really I was, ready to ... the place where it all happened, where I was left for dead—"

"Sodde Lydfe," I said. "Of course. Just because there is an advanced civilization there does not mean that there cannot be savages as well. Also, you make the same practice that we tried on Sca, landing in the hinterlands. Please forgive me, Lucille, I should have known."

"That's right, Whitey, you should. Now let's talk about this Eleva ... person."

"**What I should** like to understand," Agot Edmoot Mav gazed out the window at the scurrying nine-legged soldiers below, "is why you did not employ this wondrous 'broach', to bring you directly to these chambers. Thus we should have been able to avoid all this noise and bloodshed."

The elderly detective cast his third eye on Couper, who was busy examining the *kood* service on a low table in the center of the room. It had not been incense, as it had appeared, but was used socially like tea. The furry pseudo-crustaceans never took liquid directly, believing water a deadly poison. Mymy maintained that this was a myth, and that water was required by the lamviin metabolism as much as by ours.

"I should like very much to examine your wound, O'Thraight," the alien physician waggled rher carpet bag at me. "Provided you do not object."

Elsie had explained that Fodduans bore three names, one for each of their parents. My full name, so Mymy believed, was "Corporal Whitey O'Thraight". Since I was male, I was to be called by the last third of it. I suppose that it could have been worse. Rhe was calling Lucille, "Olson".

Couper thrust gloved hands into the pockets he'd programmed into his suit, "For a variety of reasons, sir," he answered Mav's question. "The first being that the other end of the broach is in orbit. You understand what that—of course you do. In any event, there are some limits to precision, A minor fluctuation in the mass-average beneath the ship might have opened a broach within the walls of this place—very messy. Now that we have coordinates, we'll be leaving that way, however."

"I see," said the alien thoughtfully. "Mymy, my love, do please stop fluttering about! I'm sure the Corporal would be better off in the hands of his own people. After all, what can you know of his physiology?"

The detective's surwife ... surhusband ... whatever rhe called rherself, stepped back from me abruptly, rher fur crinkling in an odd way.

"My dear husband," rhe began. "I am well aware of my abysmal ignorance—which I had hoped to rectify while rendering aid to a fellow sapient being. My, but you are difficult for one so recently rescued."

Rhe turned to me: "It is quite obvious something that troubles him. Yet he will not admit it forthrightly, male that he is, however sage. No, he would much rather bite my jaws off and those of your companions."

Mav's fur rolled into tight curls. In briefings aboard the *Tom Paine Maru* I had been taught that this indicated laughter. "Guilty as charged, my dear lurry. I throw myself upon the mercy of the court. Wholeheartedly, I might add, it has been rather a long time. Would that Vyssu had come with you. I suppose her *mifkepa* precluded such a journey?"

Mymy gave him a six-nostril snort. "And since when would even so serious a malady keep either of us from your side? We should have long since broken you out of this abominable place ourselves had you not forbidden—"

"Laughing" again, he strode across the room, his six walking legs clittering weirdly along the stone floor, to embrace the surmale physician.

"Nor do I recall lifting that prohibition even now," he told rher. He turned to us. "Do not misapprehend. I am extremely grateful. Prison life was beginning to pall." Back to Mymy: "Where, pray tell then, is she?"

A peculiar fur-swirling: "I cannot truly say at the moment, my dear." Rhe made another half-hearted attempt to practice rher arts on me, picking at the front of my suit, then gave it up, closed rher black bag, then threw it on the "bed"—the sandbox in the corner of the room. "She and her old fellow-conspirator, Fatpa, have smuggled themselves out of the country. She said she'd an idea, but refused me any—"

"Fatpa the tax-collector?" He turned to me again. "She once paid him to remove misbehaving clients from her entertainment emporium. Dear me, what subversives we have all become! Ah well, Mymy, what you do not know, you cannot tell, even under the most stringent duress, correct?"

"My dear husband," shocked scandal filled the surmale's tone, even through our translation devices. "I simply cannot believe that our government—"

He sighed. It was a completely human sound. "History informs us, my overly-patriotic paracauterist, that if the first casualty of war be truth, then the second, only an instant afterward, is civilized behavior."

He paused, "But I am remiss! I cannot offer you kood, since your environmental suits prevent its use. Nor, do I suspect, would you find my inhaling fluid to your liking—it is scarcely tolerable by my surwife (never marry a physician, Corporal). Do you possibly relish juicing?"

"Juicing?" I blinked.

Rogers had finished taking Mymy's revolver apart, putting it back together. It used cartridges of brass, bullets of lead, some white, unidentifiable propellant. Now he looked up from his tinkering with interest.

"What's juicing?" he asked.

"Second to deliberately inhaling the foul vapors of petroleum distillates," Mymy volunteered with a disapproving crinkle in rher fur, "it is probably the nastiest habit known to lamviinity. It leads to—"

Mav had produced a small wooden box with a crank on the top and what looked like electrical terminals at either end. He seized these with his outside hands and gave the crank a turn with his middle hand. For a moment, he froze in place, and a tiny blue spark appeared at one terminal.

Mav said, "Unh!" and then, "Very smooth."

"Simply shocking!" interrupted Howell to the groans of everyone present. Rogers handed the gun back to Mymy, who slipped it into rher holster.

Standing beside Howell, Elsie had been watching both Fodduans with silent interest. Her suit was a perfect miniature of everybody else's, complete to belted pistol which she had used to good effect in the assault. A small dagger hung at her waist opposite the gun. Now she spoke:

"How come none of those people outside are trying to do anything about us? Shouldn't we be getting ready for a counter-attack of some kind?"

The detective stepped to the balcony, shaded his huge eyes against the glare of the moonlight, then returned to rummage through a big carpet bag for an enormous brass telescope. He pulled it open with a *clack!* Elsie peeked over the railing to see what he had been looking at.

199

"I believe they are preoccupied, young human," he said. "Though by what—"

I squeezed into the window beside them, activating the buttons on my arm. Within my field of view, the nighttime darkness vanished, the horizon zoomed nearer. With it, I saw an ominous dark circle growing closer.

"What is black," I asked, "divided into segments, with a—?"

"By the Trine, a riddle!" Mav exclaimed. "I haven't the mistiest notion, old fellow, but coming from that direction it will have been observed first at the other end of the island and its approach quickly reported telephonically. Which accounts for the disinterest of our—I see it now ... it's ... good heavens, I should say we are being invaded!"

The window suddenly became very crowded.

Extracting Rogers' elbow from my armpit, Lucille's gun butt from my ribs, I noticed the soldiers below had lined up in orderly ranks, rifles pointed upward toward the dark object that continued to loom closer.

"What is it?" asked Lucille.

"Indubitably it is an airship of Podfettian manufacture," Mav answered. "Possibly the *Onwodetsa* rherself—ironically enough, that means 'word of hope' in Podfettian, perhaps a salubrious omen. However, such a war-craft is capable of transporting octaries of troops, and a great deal in the way of ordnance. I'm afraid that our escape is about to be interrupted by the very war we had hoped to prevent."

Word of hope—Asperance—Dungeon to dungeon. I had come full circle, A chill went down my spine that the smartsuit could do nothing for.

"Or possibly accelerated," Lucille said grimly, checking her pistols. "This would make a terrific time to get the congress out of here!"

Gunshots rang out from what Mav called the "riflelamn" below us. Unperturbed, the airship continued on course, its gondola visible now as were the engine pods braced on stanchions away from the black fuselage.

Those aboard her were not returning fire.

Closer came the *Onwodetsa*, closer, closer ...

Even for those of us accustomed to the Confederate scale of doing things, the airship was huge. Its shadow in the triple moonlight cast a pall over the entire building. Its engines, driving many-bladed propellers the size of the room we stood in, filled the island with their roaring. Bullets whistled toward it, whizzing harmlessly off its sides. Mav began to say something about fiberglass resins. There was a *clank!*, the engine-noise died off, something began lowering from underneath.

"Attention, soldiers of Great Foddu!" shouted an amplified voice from the airship, "This is a bomb! It contains more explosives than any other bomb ever assembled. It is capable of blasting this end of the island and everything upon it down to sea level!" There was a pause, as if giving the soldiers time to consider. Then: "Drop your weapons!"

Smoke began to issue from one end of the bomb.

I do not know how the Fodduans took it. I was frightened. Progress seemed to have taken a somewhat different path on Sodde Lydfe. In many ways, their culture seemed old-fashioned, but their electrical science was far ahead of what it ought to be, judging from other artifacts scattered about. That caused me to wonder about their explosives technology.

There was some milling about, down below. Finally, one by one, we heard the clatter of rifles on hard pavement. The gunsmith inside me cringed and I saw a similar look on Rogers' face. The Podfettian airship approached the prison. A gondola door popped open, a figure leaped—

—swinging as the slack in its rope was spent. For a moment, it looked like a huge, horrible spider. In a clean arc, a lamviin figure sailed to the balcony, seized the rail, climbed over, cast the rope away.

"I will be triple-damped!" the detective exclaimed. "Also highly delighted."

He turned, presenting the newcomer to us. "Gentlebeings of the starship *Tom Paine Maru*, kindly permit me to introduce our wife, Vyssu!"

"SEVEN OCTARIES, YOU say? Dear me, I'm afraid this complicates matters a bit." Mav had resumed his pacing. The Fodduan ... triple? ... had greeted each other with a characteristically reserved enthusiasm.

In addition to the troops, Vyssu had brought news.

One item was that the combat dirigible outside had been stolen from the Podfettian Navy by its own officers. It was full of Mavist refugees, underground radio personalities, all of them armed "to the jaws".

Another was that the terrible bomb still suspended beneath the *Onwodetsa*, keeping the Fodduan troops on their best behavior, was a fraud.

"Of course we should never have undertaken such a voyage, over land and sea, with that much extra weight, my dear," the female observed.

She was bigger than Mymy, smaller than Mav. Any other differences were concealed by her clothing, basically a pair—a trio—of elbow length trousers, the legs (or sleeves) of which were connected by a span of fabric that concealed the underside of the carapace. Mymy had been dressed similarly, as had Mav, although the texture of the fabric varied.

"We needed the extra lift across the Arms of Pah. That is the range of mountains that embraces Foddu to the north and west, dear humans. So we emptied a bomb-casing we found aboard and stored food in it."

"You know, Mav," offered Rogers, "we could transport the Fodduan soldiers upstairs, via broach, and turn this whole island over to the refugees."

"Who would all starve within a trinight," countered Mav. "You see, the supply boat arrives daily from the mainland, a service, I greatly fear, that would be shut off immediately, in the circumstances you describe."

Rogers shrugged. "Well, it was the only idea I had, at the moment."

"Not a very good one," snorted Couper. "I guess that also takes care of broaching your refuges up, Vyssu. We'd need an enormous cargo aperture, and for that, the courtyard below or the grounds outside the prison. Try that, and somebody down there'll make a heroic move, discover that your bomb's a hoax, and that'll take care of emigration policy."

Mav puffed on his inhaler. It smelled like lighter fluid. "Are you actually capable of swallowing the entire *Onwodetsa* in a gulp like that?"

Rogers waited a while before speaking, consulting the computer in his head. "*Tom Paine Maru* is a little under ten of your *fymon* in diameter. It's a hemispheric section, perhaps a quarter of that height."

"My word. Very well, then, I shall try my own idea."

With that, he stepped out on the balcony, raised three hands in salutation.

One of the soldiers at ground level picked up a rifle, threw it to what served as his shoulder. There was a report, smoke. A huge bullet spanged off the stone over the detective's head. Somebody else grabbed the gun, thumped the shooter across the jaws with it, then threw it down.

Except for a throb of idling airship motors, silence fell over the island.

"My friends and gaolers," Mav began.

The crowd below stirred a little, grew silent again.

"It is time at last for leavetaking. I know that you believe you have a duty to prevent this, although I contemplate harm to no living being."

He paused, then went on. "I am here with you because I endeavored to stop a conflagration that rages even now around our globe. That it was in concert with similarly-minded Podfettians proved intolerable to Their Majesties, who hold it their right to choose our enemies for us."

He laid two hands on the balcony, gestured with the middle one, "I tell now that you we must choose our own enemies—and allies. Our commerce with others must be solely on the basis of unanimous consent. No nation, no king, no group of any composition whatever is entitled to do anything that any individual among their number objects to. That constitutes the sum of what my friends and enemies alike are calling 'Mavism'."

At the same time that I was horrified by the alien philosopher's words, I was fascinated by them. It was as if this Agot Edmoot Mav had been a Confederate all his life. Somehow—apparently all by himself—he had "detected", or reinvented everything Confederates had taken hundreds of years to learn. I came closer in that moment than any before to wondering if there might really be something in it, after all.

He was going on: "Rather than prodigious bodies of law, the only value necessary for all of us to share proposes that no one may obtain his satisfaction by initiating violence against another. Our new acquaintances from the stars—for that is who they be—having made this discovery independently, call it 'Non-Aggression'. In terms of our evolutionary history, we are both

202

predator-species. This Principle is the only way that predators may relate with one another sanely and safely."

There was murmuring below at that, though whether in approval or disapproval, I could not tell. The idea of evolution had its obstinate resistors back home on Vespucci. That may have been the problem here, too.

"I have heard it argued," Mav said, "that unanimous consent, which is a positive expression of this Non-Aggression Principle, engenders inaction at best or a bland mediocrity. I assert this can only occur in the opposite circumstance, where no individual may act without the group's consent. This is the threadbare 'reform' that brought us from a state of absolute monarchy to absolute majoritarianism. It is no improvement."

More mutters. I wondered why it all sounded better coming from an alien.

Mav went on. "Unanimous consent does not require that everyone be constrained to a mindless uniformity, or that nothing ever may be accomplished, simply that no individual be forced against his will to participate. No more natural, decent, lamviinitarian system may be devised."

"In history, his system's first expression was economic, the free market that made Great Foddu the mighty empire it became. But there are parallel social forms whose absence point us all, even now, toward disaster. Social order and cooperation arise neither from politicians nor princes, nor from advances in the technology of communication, but out of the whole aggregate of voluntary exchanges, whose driving-force consists of a no more than desire to better oneself. Elementary greed, dear listeners. There exists no "invisible hand"— that was always an unfortunate turn of phrase—but billions of highly visible fingers, doing, purely for personal gain, what others will freely barter for, with the sole object of improving their lives and those of their children."

The soldiers below were silent now, looking at one another.

"We defy the ordinances of nature at our peril. Taxation, no less than conscription, as both are in contravention to the Non-Aggression Principle, are the very fuel of war. It is obvious in the case of conscription, perhaps less so in the case of taxation. However, no one who favors taxation, whatever intent he claims, can help to end the tragic institution of war, however pious his claims to a desire for peace."

Taxation is the fuel of war. It had a certain ring to it, I thought.

"Are we become so uncertain of our prowess that we must steal, or force what we create upon others at swordpoint? Yet that is the nature of law, which I depart now to combat. I beg you, release me, refrain from injury to others, from bringing injury on yourselves. Destructive engines are about to be employed which will end life upon our little planet."

He paused, then: "In the name of decency, pray help me to prevent that."

Lucille wept openly, as did Couper, to my astonishment. Mymy's fur drooped, a lamviin equivalent, perhaps, of tears. Without opposition, the *Onwodetsa* lowered rher guide-ropes, was pulled down to a mooring on the island by the Fodduans. Somebody thought to throw a bucket of sand over the still-smoldering fuse of the phony bomb. Rhe disgorged rher passengers who began mingling indiscriminately with their former enemies.

Mav turned to us: "I think that we should be about our business, friends. There is a war to stop. Tell me, does this broach contrivance hurt?"

THE PRIME DIRECTIVE

LIEUTENANT ENSON SERMANDER relaxed on the bed in his stateroom, sipping nutrient fluid through a plastic tube from a small-waisted green-tinted glass bottle he held in his free hand. His other hand was busy. The disgusting-looking dark brown liquid fizzed as it was shaken.

A very good month, the waiter had said, what seemed like years ago.

"Whitey!" Sermander shouted at me as I entered, "Come in, come in!"

"Lieutenant," I said. "Doctor."

My own minor injuries had just had time to stiffen. Back aboard *Tom Paine Maru*, I was attending to a pair errands at once, visiting a sick friend, seeing the doctor myself, while he was handy. There was not much time: things were shaping up "downstairs" for a final, deadly battle.

Sermander's voice jiggled in time as he rhythmically squeezed the resilient plastic ball the doctor had given him. "Corporal, it is my understanding that I have you to thank for my rapidly-returning health!"

At the moment, he wore the bottom half of a smartsuit. The rest of the garment lay draped neatly across the foot of the bed. A small round bandage—more of a sticking-plaster, really—was visible at his left temple. Giving my gunbelt's heavy wire buckle a half-twist, I swung it, with its double burden, from around my waist, tossed it into a chair, sagged wearily into another at the Lieutenant's one-handed gesture.

The Healer Francis Pololo released Sermander's other wrist—how strange it was to see a physician taking someone's pulse with his eyes closed—folded up a plastic kit of more sophisticated instruments that he apparently did not trust as much as his own native talents, then turned to his patient. He his wiped broad hands down his pale green tunic. There was a circled red cross embroidered on its left shoulder.

"Your bad shoulder's bad no longer, Enson. It'll take several days to get used to your new implant, and several weeks more to master it completely."

The gorilla removed his wire-rimmed glasses, thoughtfully polished them on his tunic skirt, then arranged them atop his flat black muzzle again.

"In the meantime, take it easy. Don't overdo things. Get lots of rest."

"Ha! You medical people are all alike," the Lieutenant laughed heartily. "Are they not, Corporal? Very well, sir, I shall give your good advice the conscientious attention it merits. Now, will you not see to my loyal associate before you go? He appears a bit out of sorts."

The gorilla examined the indicators on my suit-sleeve, unzipped the seam to finger the painful, slowly spreading bruise across my chest.

"Blue today, black tonight," he muttered as if delivering an incantation. "Green tomorrow, yellow the day after that. You'll live, Whitey. But please have your suit looked at—it absorbed a lot of punishment."

"Gee, thanks a trillion, doc, I will try taking better care of it."

"Don't mention it, I'll bill you. Have a nice day." He gave us a big-fanged gorilla smile. "And next time someone shoots at you—duck! I've already had a report from Howell, he says you saved his little girl's life a couple of times. Are you a hero, or just accident prone?—don't answer, we need all the help we can collect on Sodde Lydfe."

Lighting one of his small brown cigars, Pololo left the apartment.

The occasion appeared to call for a change of subject: "How are you feeling, sir?" He certainly did not look like somebody who had just come out of surgery. His color was excellent, his movements were energetic. There was a light in his eyes that I had never seen there before.

"Much better—almost by the passing minute." He frowned briefly, then smiled. "There are no words for how I feel, Whitey. This is just amazing! It's virtually a religious experience. I wish I had realized before ... look, if I want to know what time it is, almost before I consciously wonder about it, I see a display in my mind, superimposed over the visual field, that tells me. Likewise, if I wish to know where the bathroom is, I feel a sort of tug in that direction, or a voice whispers in my ear, or words appear, scrolling across the bottom of—"

He tossed the little plastic ball through the doorway, striking the bathroom sink precisely, then laughed again. "I do not know how to say it properly, but you get my meaning, do you not?" He was ecstatic—feverishly so—exactly like somebody full of drugs. All of my earlier misgivings flared to full life. What had I let them do to my Lieutenant?

"Yes, sir, I believe so. Sir?"

"Yes, Whitey?" He rose from the bed, put his feet on the floor, picked up the smartsuit top to shove his arms into the sleeves. His voice was benevolent, even friendly. This was not the Lieutenant I knew!

"Sir, I have to ask you a question ... "

Sealing the suitseam, he replied, "Well, in Alexander Hamilton's blessed name, ask away! If I can possibly answer it, my dear boy, I will."

I needed to know: "Uh, how do you feel about the Confederacy now, sir? I mean, about the fact that it is likely to attempt influencing Vespucci the same way that we have seen it influence the other planets we've—"

He burst into deep-throated laughter. "There is nothing to worry about, Whitey, I know these people now. They will do no mischief on Vespucci."

He stood.

"Sir?" It was exactly what I had been afraid of. The Lieutenant had been taken over by the implant they had placed on his brain—with my consent. I was all alone, now, against a mighty interstellar empire.

"That is right, Corporal, because we will not permit them to." He took a few paces, bent his knees, flexed his arms, his fists. "They have made a serious mistake, giving me this device. Every secret of this starship is open to me, every facet of their history." He looked straight at me: "I now know enough to stop them, whatever they have in mind."

"Sir?" Confusion, embarrassment, dawning hope, where despair had been.

He thrust his hands deep into his pockets. "Has anyone ever told you, Corporal O'Thraight, that you are an extremely monotonous conversationalist?"

"Uh, no sir—I mean, yes sir—that is, I—"

"Nor a particularly intelligible one, it would appear. I fear that your little— how shall I put this?—that little *convenience* of yours has already had a distressing effect upon the workings of your mind."

Red heat rushed into my face. "Sir, I—"

"Do not look at me like that, Corporal! It is perfectly natural and normal. That is why the Navy gives hygiene lectures, after all." The pistol belt lying in the other chair caught his eye. "By the way, I believe I will have one of those pistols now—no, do not bother with the holster. I will just carry the thing in a pocket of my own devising."

I got up from my chair, unsnapped the flap of one of the holsters, handed him the weapon, which he tucked away somewhere under his arm. I started to ask him if he wanted a spare cartridge loader, but he spoke first:

"At that, she looks like a palatable little receptacle. Is she any good? Never fear, I do not begrudge you. We shall simply acquire one like her for me, before we leave the ship. Do keep an eye out for a likely one, will you? Dear me, look at the time. Sixteen hundred hours already. We must get moving, Whitey, or you could be compelled to perform an enlisted-man's unpleasant duty. It must be the implant. I am feeling the first animal stirrings I have had for a long, long time."

Imagine the sound of three hands clapping—multiplied by half a dozen octaries. Such a roar enveloped Mav now as he stood atop a large tree stump, attempting to introduce Captain Koko Featherstone-Haugh to the group of lamviin refugees that he steadfastly refused to call his followers.

A thing with poison-dripping spines had tried to kill me on that very stump not too many days before. Now I hoped that the rattlesnakes and various other nasty creatures could take care of themselves. To lamviin, this artificial desert was an overly humid, purely temporary billet—the only place they were even moderately comfortable aboard ship.

"It isn't our custom," Koko was telling them, "to welcome anybody in the name of the Confederacy or any other collective. But I think you're nice, those I've met of you, and I'm very happy that you're here."

For some idiotic reason, I had been asked to stand beside the oddly-assorted pair. I was happy that Lucille was there with me, smiling, holding my hand. The ugly things that Sermander had clearly enjoyed saying about her still rankled, but I had not told her about them.

Mymy was off being fitted for a nine-legged smartsuit so rhe could see the rest of the ship without drowning in an attempt to breathe. I looked forward to seeing rher dressed in the height of Confederate fashion.

Somebody shouted, "Showtime!"

The great ship hesitated, then tipped into the atmosphere. Twelve kilometers in diameter, seven and a half miles across, a world unto herself, with her own mountains, deserts, prairie, ocean, she had never been constructed for such a mission. Inertialess, suspended only by the glare of tachyons from her underside, she skipped, skidded, her leading edge glowing until she was a starship no longer, but a highly improbable gigantic flying thing, high above the scarlet Sodde Lydfan seas.

In an otherwise comfortable living-room recliner, Captain Koko Featherstone-Haugh gripped the arms in grim concentration. I wondered whether, under their fur, gorillas could sweat. *Tom Paine Maru* had no control room—rather, her control-room was inside the captain's head, wherever that happened to be at the moment. I suddenly heard the structure of the chair-arms fracture with the stress which she put on them, in counterpoint to a constant low moaning in the ship's tortured structure.

I sat in the crude, upright wooden chair that had served me so well as a weapon, in the fight in that sailor's bar on Afdiar. My considerate friends had saved it for me, bloodstains and all, as a souvenir.

From the ceiling overhead, strangely enough, came music: some hoarse-voiced woman shouting something about "The Wrecking Ball". I certainly hoped not. Far beneath us, visible through a floor that had become a window, pink-orange foam frothed over the shallow seas of a dry planet. The broad wakes of two mighty warfleets pointed straight at one another, steaming full speed to keep an appointment with racial death.

We were trying not to be late for the occasion, ourselves.

"There she is!" shouted Couper, pointing a finger like an excited child at the gigantic flagship in the center of the great Podfettian fleet.

"Rhe," corrected Mav, "the *Wemafe*. It means 'bird of peace'. Rhe is the largest warship ever constructed in the history of civilization."

He looked out through a real window—at least I think it was a real window—at a bright blue ocean where I had been sailing with the captain not very long ago. "Our civilization, that is, Lamviin civilization. I am still having difficulties absorbing the magnitude of—"

"*Tom Paine Maru* is not a warship," insisted Pololo.

For the first time, Koko opened her eyes. She looked up fiercely at all of us. "Why yes she is, dear. We go now to make war on war itself!"

"The *Awe-Inspiring Refulgence!*" Mymy's voice was louder than Couper's. Rhe had grown up in a thinner atmosphere than rhe was breathing now. Also, rhe had six orifices to speak through. Rhe pointed to the middle of the Fodduan fleet. "Mav, we've got to stop this!"

"I am afraid, my dear surhusband," Vyssu replied, reflecting her husband's calm demeanor, "that it is in the hands, as few as they may be per individual, of our new friends. May I have some more tea, Francis?"

"Yes, certainly." The gorilla poured a few drops onto a silvery rubber pad lying on the floor beside the alien. It would transmit the proper sensations to Vyssu without necessitating the ingestion of fluids.

The giant ship soared lower.

"I'll be a politician's nephew," Couper observed professionally. "It's the battle of Midway all over again, only with helicopters and dirigibles." Having only Elsie's whirlybirds as an example, the aliens had never invented fixed-wing aircraft. I made a note to ask someone about the battle Couper that had mentioned. "Why, this would almost be interesting, if they were playing with anything but atomic bombs down there."

"Nasty ones," Rogers grimaced. "With cobalt jackets."

"I do not believe that the designers were malicious," offered the Fodduan detective. "Please understand that cobalt is a commonly employed metal in our civilization. I, myself, did not realize what effect—"

"Even so, it was a mighty near thing." Lucille toyed with a kood stick, "We have a specific mission out here, Mav, to clean up our own trash. There was a lot of debate over interfering with a totally different species. If those had been plain, old-fashioned low-yield nukes ... "

Mav laughed like six people laughing. "Then perhaps we should be happy that they were not. The danger lasts for thousands of years, you say?"

She nodded, "Base nine or base ten. My mother's culture never did invent them, not for warfare, anyway. But my father's did. We've seen lots of them out here. Or at least their leavings: millions of minds and everything else on a planet, dead above the evolutionary level of a—"

"*Des,*" all three lamviin supplied at once.

"I'll bet that's Fodduan," Owen Rogers suggested, "for Senator."

"Here we go!" said Koko between her teeth.

The mighty vessel banked, bringing us out of the sun from the point of view of the two fleets. They were too far apart to see one another, although their aircraft had begun engaging, but they could certainly see us. The shadow cast by the great starship was dozens of kilometers in extent, a gigantic ominous footprint, precisely as her captain had intended it should be. Smoke poured from boiling places in the shallow sea where otherwise intelligent beings had died for their countries.

Fire lashed from *Tom Paine Maru's* underside, millions of thumb-sized emitters creating a column of raw searing energy many meters in diameter.

"They were just about to throw out the first ball of the season," Koko explained, "employing the biggest artillery I think I've ever seen."

Koko's Podfettian victim began to settle slowly, rher bow burnt off where a cannon loaded with a nuclear bomb had been. We were low enough now to see crew-beings scrambling over the sides into the hated sea.

Instantly, another burst of energy leaped out from the starship's lower hull. An enormous Fodduan dirigible suddenly flashed out of existence.

"Gas-bags to deliver nukes?" Couper shook his head sadly.

"Maybe the last," said Koko. "I'm hearing from the broach crews, now."

The tidy patterns of each fleet had begun disintegrating as commanders realized the new threat they were facing. Despite the gorilla's words, there was a third flash—not from *Tom Paine Maru's* particle emitters this time—within a kilometer of the starship.

"Whew! That was sure close. One of those would've ruined our whole day!" Rogers wiped imaginary sweat from his brow. Personally, I could not help admiring the courage—Fodduan or Podfettian—that had launched that weapon against what must have seemed an invincible new enemy.

"Attention!" Koko demanded suddenly. I looked up, wondering what was going on, only to realize that her eyes were still closed. She was concentrating on her implant readings. "Attention all ships of both fleets! The war is over! Cease your hostilities immediately! This is the Solar Confederacy's starship *Tom Paine Maru* ordering you to cease hostilities or perish! The war is over! I repeat, the war is over!"

Another *flash!* as a Podfettian cruiser emptied its artillery at us. The war might well be over, but it was going to be a long, noisy peace.

THE DECORATIVELY-ENAMELED DECK pitched slowly beneath my feet in a languid swell that was all the thick, blood-colored seas of Sodde Lydfe were capable of generating. Allowing for the traditional lamviin attitude toward water, it may have seemed like a sizable storm to the frightened sailors who had been forced to abandon their vessel at the height of an engagement that had turned, for them, into a nightmarish fantasy.

Adjusting the soles of my feet for medium adhesion, I looked aft, through the haze of battle. *Tom Paine Maru's* tachyon "cannon" (the same devices that drove her through space) had burned a blackened pit three meters across, straight through the *Amybo Kiidetz,* from rher ornately-decorated upper deck to rher specially-stiffened fighting keel.

Rhe was a comparatively new vessel, crisply painted where fire had not blistered the shocking pink that, on this world, served as naval camouflage. Smoke drifted from the smoldering hole that had been rher death wound. From time to time, I heard a muffled sound of small explosions. Only rher deeply-carved water-tight doors kept the vessel afloat this long.

Lucille stepped through the broach behind me.

"Wow, *art deco militaire!* I'll bet that, if Aubrey Beardsley had been a nine-legged furry pseudo-crustacean, he'd approve. Too bad about all this damage, though. She's absolutely beautiful, isn't she, Whitey?"

"Rhe," I corrected automatically.

But Lucille was absolutely right. From rher breathtakingly lovely, dramatic, downswept ramming-prow—embellished with floral scrolls ground deeply out of living stainless steel—to the upswept, equally figured cowling wrapped around rher gigantic pusher-fan, rhe was some three-eyed architect's vision of harmony. Even rher gun-turrets flowed into the structure of the ship without interrupting those graceful lines.

Somewhere below, I knew, there would be a massively-shielded fission powerplant to drive the fan, crew-quarters, officers' country, galleys, mess-rooms, communications shacks, every one of them alien in design, yet streamlined sufficiently in concept to be recognizable, admirable.

I was finding that I liked the lamviin, Fodduan or Podfettian. Maybe saving them from their ultimate fate was a presumptuous intrusion, as the Lieutenant had said, but I was glad we were doing it.

Time enough later for feeling guilty.

Lucille consulted her implant: "Through this door here, across to the other side of the deck, down three flights, and a left turn. Why do you suppose they bolted the nuke so firmly into the ribs of the ship?"

That, of course, was why we were here.

"Upstairs", a dozen very busy technical squads were confiscating nuclear weapons via broach—then slapping them into stasis until somebody figured out what to do with them—those that had not been vaporized hastily because they had been armed. This particular bomb was presenting problems that called for a "primitive expert" once again.

One with training in dismantling the things.

Armorer-corporal Guess Who.

Poking the muzzle of my Dardick through the rainbow-enameled steel hatchway, I bent halfway over, then followed it into a big, deserted, low-ceilinged cross-corridor. Colors really got bright, once you were inside.

"Well, I can see now that my first theory was no good, after all, that rhe was intended as a giant manned—or make that 'lammed'—torpedo ... "

"Fire-ship," Koko said. "A nuclear fireship."

Lucille was right behind me, her suit-top brushing the overhead. I was having second thoughts about that pair of plasma-guns at my back. They did not have a "line" of fire, they had a field, a broad one, at that.

"Rhe is not a fire-ship, then," I said. "Rhe is much too new, much too pretty. Also, it is much too early in the war. Later on, perhaps, when one side or another begins to get desperate ... But just look at how clean rhe is. Rher crew took pride in rher, Lucille. I feel awful about having done this to them. This is an absolutely gorgeous machine."

Traversing the corridor, we passed several open doorways. Bending forward, I examined what could only be an auxiliary bridge: three massively ornate wheels, a clever periscope, binnacles for navigation in the shapes of mythical characters, radar set in expensive-looking framing, etched embellishments encompassing the telecommunications screens.

Aft, across the corridor, was a chart-room.

Lucille said, "It's only a murdering-machine, Whitey, however well-gilded. What do you think, then, that it's a self-destruct mechanism?"

"Not with that yield, the biggest fission-bomb I ever heard of, enough to vaporize a dozen ships this size, along with a major city for dessert. A bomb like that could turn even *Tom Paine Maru* into junk."

"I wouldn't have known. I'll try to remember once we get the thing aboard."

I said, "Do that—also, in case you forget, I will disarm it here."

Stepping cautiously over the low doorsill, we found the ladder, a broad-treaded affair with short risers. We followed it through the smoke, down into the bowels of the vessel. As we went, visibility got steadily worse, even with the contrast enhancement provided by our suits. Occasionally, we passed a video unit, its screen still ablaze with the bright green Fodduan letters that apparently meant "abandon ship".

These lamviin really knew their electronics, I thought, yet they still mixed animal-powered vehicles with motor carriages in their city streets. The sugar-based equivalent of black-powder still found favor in their small arms, although this vessel's artillery seemed to run on natural gas. Mav said his people had not even conceived of surgical anesthesia, yet. Progress in different fields proceeds at different rates, I supposed, depending on the interests of the culture making it.

Rounding the corner, we discovered the remains of a crew-being, recently dead, its carapace perforated, leaking emerald-colored ichor onto the deck plating. We stepped carefully around it, to negotiate the next set of uncomfortably-proportioned stairs.

WHAAANG!

What must have been a thirty-gram projectile flattened itself on the bulkhead next to my shoulder. I ducked back, stomping Lucille's feet, peered out from behind the doorway's protective steel in time to see a pair of lamviin in battledress peering out at us from the next doorway.

One of them had a weapon with a bore the size of my fist.

So did the other one.

"Surrender, monster, or die! Your Podfettian masters will pay for this!"

Before I could answer, there was a roar beside my ear. A ball of white hot plasma streaked toward the Fodduans. One stood up, firing at Lucille. I heard her scream, looked back in time to see her slammed against the opposite bulkhead. I snapped a shot at the rifle-barrel, getting a slug down the center of the enormous bore—it was not very difficult. The weapon exploded in its user's hands, killing him instantly.

His partner retreated out of sight. Keeping a cautious eye behind me, I knelt down beside Lucille where she lay crumpled against the bulkhead, not two meters away from the first dead Fodduan we had found.

"I'll be okay, Whitey," she gasped. "It just knocked the wind out of me, that's all." Her suit-arms both shrieked with blinking scarlet lights.

"Call the ship, Lucille! Bomb or not, we are getting you back upstairs!"

There was a long pause. "I can't raise them. Something's happened to my—Whitey, look out!"

Blam! Blam! Blam!

I had learned by now to aim for the few vulnerable places that a lamviin possessed. He dropped his bigbore weapon, pitched over onto the edge of his carapace. His legs crumpled underneath him. He was still. I felt terrible. I liked these people. I had no desire to kill them.

Stabbing the buttons on my own suit-arms, I was dismayed to discover that I could not reach *Tom Paine Maru,* either. There was probably too much metal wrapped around us this deep in the Fodduan ship.

"We must disarm the bomb," I told Lucille. I could not even strip her helmet away. This atmosphere had plenty of oxygen, but it would suck the moisture out of her tissues in minutes, even this far out to sea. Instead, I used the manual controls of her suit to produce a true image of what lay beneath the silvery rubber. Her face was deathly pale.

"I must go now to disarm the bomb, Lucille, it is being watched by *Tom Paine Maru* on instruments. Then they will know to haul us in, okay?"

She put a weak hand on my arm. "Whitey, please don't leave me ... I—"

I nodded, understanding. "Do not worry, love, I will not leave you."

If I could believe it, her suit was telling me she had no serious internal injuries, no broken bones. Whatever the damage, it would be nothing, compared to being abandoned again on Sodde Lydfe. I collected both her pistols. She would not want them left here. Tucking an arm between her legs, I grabbed the back of her neck, stooped down even further, levered her onto my shoulders. I then gathered ankle to wrist together in my left hand. This would leave me one hand free for fighting.

I stood up, only halfway, naturally, as the ceiling was too low, thinking about the Scavian dungeon where I had met Lucille. Pointing my gun ahead of me, I trudged to the ladder, began taking the steps one by one. At the foot, I rested for a moment, trying to catch my breath.

"Lucille?"

No answer.

Only one more flight, if I could just find where it began. I cast around in the smoky darkness, wishing now I had undergone the implant. As light as Lucille was, not more than forty-five kilos, strain was beginning to hurt me in this cramped, bent-over position. I kept imagining nine-legged things with guns coming out of the blackness at me.

Instead, I saw an angel.

With a blue halo. A broach-circle opened in front of me, its edges glaring brightly like neon in the dim light. Out of the broach stepped little Elsie Nahuatl, fully suited up, a pistol in one hand, a dagger in the other. The broach snapped closed behind her with an explosive *pop!*

She sheathed her knife—it was of the pattern called "rezin"—but kept her pistol handy. "I thought I'd find you here, Whitey. How come you haven't disarmed the bomb ye—oh, boy, are we ever in a mess!"

That was how long it took her to see Lucille's condition.

"Are you in communication with the ship, Elsie?"

"Not exactly, see, I—"

"Get that way! Tell them to get us out of here. Lucille's been shot!"

"Whitey, they're all busy now, and nobody's listening. Besides, I can't communicate through this metal! I came to tell you that they're going to Broach the whole *Amybo Kiidetz*. It's the only thing we can do—"

WHIRRINGGG!

A heavy-caliber bullet ricocheted off the bulkhead from behind us. I fired half a dozen random shots in that direction, grabbed Elsie, found the ladder. We climbed down. At the bottom, a door opened onto a large, high-ceilinged hangar-like hold where I could finally stand up. I was glad we had our suits. The smoke in here was even thicker than above.

THUMP!

A dull explosion. The blow took me full in the face. There was a sickening, disorienting sensation as the ship lurched. I fell atop Lucille—who only managed a little moan at the impact—I felt Elsie's hand wrenched from mine. Her gun clattered to the floor. She screamed.

The hold filled with the sound of tearing metal, as a shaft of daylight burst in upon us. Through a brand new hole in the hull, I could make out the outline of a helmeted head. The smoke was emptying rapidly.

"Whitey! Whitey! It's me, Owen Rogers! Have you seen Elsie? We think she came to find you. Have you wrecked that bomb yet? Where's Lucille?"

I opened my mouth to speak—

BLAM! BLAM! BLAM!

I knew by the sound that it was a Dardick pistol. Rogers ducked as the bullets ricocheted noisily off of the metal plating around his head.

Far away, at the other end of the hold, Sermander stood straddling a bulge in the floor where the atomic bomb had been welded. In front of him, he held Elsie. She screamed and struggled. He slapped her on the side of the head with his pistol. She stopped struggling and was silent.

"Hold still, damn you! It will not be very much longer. Corporal, leave that baggage and get on your feet. Come over here to me. We are going to blow the starship—with everyone aboard it—to kingdom come!"

THE TEDDY BEARS' PICNIC

SLOWLY GATHERING MY feet beneath me, I stood. Lucille still lay unconscious on the deck. Whatever might happen, I would never abandon her.

"That is right, Corporal," Sermander soothed. Holding the little girl's neck in a vise-like grip, he reached up with his gun-hand to peel his suit mask down to his chest. It was foolish, but made good politics.

"Come join me, Whitey. There is no responsible alternative. I have discovered—employing the startling powers that these Confederates have been naive enough to bestow upon me—that they have not felt it necessary, as yet, to notify the remainder of their vast fleet about Vespucci."

Elsie squirmed, "Let me go, you big mammoth-turd!"

He looked down at her almost benevolently, "Is that any way for a child to talk? At home, we would teach you better manners, would we not, Whitey?" He shook his head, "Indiscipline is chronic among these people. It is a sickness, a contagion, a plague. It deserves only death."

He looked up again at me: "It is a great pity that we cannot send a warning home. But we can buy our beloved nation time. What do you say, Corporal?"

"I say that they need more than time, sir. They need that warning—every last bit of the information that you alone can give them, now."

Glancing sidewise at the hole that had been cut in the ship's hull, I could just make out the motion of fingertips clinging to the ragged lower edge. Someone had adjusted his smartsuit to give visual impressions from the ends of those digits, a sort of periscopic effect.

With overly dramatic sadness: "It is we who have no time left. It is required of both of us that we give our lives, unremembered, unsung—the ultimate sacrifice for which our beings were shaped at their incep—"

"Let me go!"

Renewing her struggles, Elsie flailed her arms as Sermander held her by the rubbery nape of her smartsuit. Almost negligently, he slapped the side of her head a second time with his heavy military pistol.

A third.

216

The little girl went limp.

"At long last," he sighed, "blessed silence."

I drew my own gun, pointed it at his face. "If you have hurt her ... Let her go now, Sermander, there is something wrong about your implant. This insanity has gone far enough if it means hurting little girls."

Big ones, too. I did not know if Lucille was still alive.

He laughed. "So they finally got to you after all. I thought that might be the case. How many little girls, do you suppose, perished in the Final War? Yet can you deny that it was a war that had to be fought? Sentimentalism will not alter what has to be done, even now, Corporal."

Carefully, Sermander transferred his weapon to the hand that also held the now-unconscious little girl. Stooping down, he stretched to reach to the glowing control panel of the atomic bomb between his knees.

"Enough debate. So long, Corporal, it has been—"

Firming my two-handed grip on the Dardick, I shouted "I am not fooling around with you, Sermander, let her go now! Get away from there!"

Chuckling at me, Sermander lifted poor Elsie like a coat on a hanger, until her quiet, unmoving form shielded his body from head to knees.

"Are you aware how foolish you appear, Corporal, using a mere pistol to threaten an individual who is prepared to blow himself up with—

"AAAGHHH!"

Elsie twisted the dagger she had slid beneath Sermander's kneecap. In an agony of pure reflex, he tossed the little girl savagely away. With a horrible noise, her tiny body crashed among a mountain of stowage. A barrel burst around her with the impact. Sermander plucked feebly at the knife-hilt where it projected from his ruined joint, looked at me, a sickly smile on his face, then reached again for the bomb.

I pulled the trigger. The ship's hold lit briefly with the muzzle-flash.

Sermander's headless body pitched forward, spewing gore.

Belatedly, Rogers' shot roared through the space where Sermander's head had been only a fraction of a second earlier. His bolt of plasma blew yet another hole, in the opposite side-wall of the *Amybo Kiidetz.*

Unconcerned about anything else, I whirled, knelt, gathered Lucille in my arms. I was cradling her motionless body when they found me.

THE PEOPLE OF *Tom Paine Maru* filled Lucille's stateroom with flowers.

MacDougall Olson-Bear turned out to be a decent enough fellow, after all. A great deal taller than I was—he was perhaps a full two meters tall—he possessed a thick mop of reddish-blonde hair, his mother's sea-green eyes, along with muscles on his muscles on his muscles.

Under the circumstances, I did not think to ask him very much about himself. A fighter-pilot, someone had said. Whatever it might have been, it had given his clean-shaven face a weathered reddish-pink finish typical of people who spend a lot of time outdoors but do not tan well. It looked as if his chin had never seen a razor—or needed to.

I met him in Lucille's quarters where he was busy filling cartons with belongings. The place smelled cloyingly-sweet with murdered foliage.

"I guess it wasn't really much like having a mother," he admitted, continuing our awkward conversation while attempting to control his expression as each item that he packed away evoked a long-buried memory.

Earlier, he had told me that he had grown up aboard the *Tom Jefferson Maru*. He had never gotten along particularly well with his father, from whom he had sought something like a divorce at an early age. He had pursued an adventurous life ever since then, still using his father's name, unaware of his mother's, or even that she was still alive.

They had found each other years later through a fleet-wide survey for people who had blood like hers, rare blood that had been needed after her eventual revival. How ironic life could be. How stupidly ironic.

"It was more," he said now, "like having a sister I had never met until it was almost too late." Was that really a tear he was sniffing back?

I was having some trouble with emotions, too, especially when he found a bedraggled teddy bear in the closet. Peculiar, how similar the customs of two civilizations can be, even separated for so long. There had been a toy like that for me once, back home. It had been my only toy.

"Hamilton take me," he said with a catch in his voice. "Now I remember, this was mine! Lucille must have kept it all these ... " He cleared his throat violently, then wiped a broad freckled hand across his eyes. "Whitey, I've no need of this where I'm going. Neither has Lucille ... any more. Can you think of anybody else who'd like to have it?"

Elsie was recovering from minor injuries at the place she shared with Howell. She had fetched against a barrel of spike-nails aboard the Fodduan warship when Sermander had thrown her. When I could speak again, I said, "Yes, Mac, if you are absolutely sure. I will see to it."

"Thank you very much, Whitey." He walked around the bed where he had placed the cartons, handed me the bear, hesitated, then: "I hope you won't mind my saying I'm very glad that you and Lucille met each other—"

I shook my head, "You need not to say anything. I, er... your mother... "

He grinned ruefully, "I understand, and I hope—"

"Are you two about through with the man-talk?"

Looking at least ten years younger than the giant she had given birth to, Lucille came in from the spare bedroom, another carton of her son's belongings in her arms. There was a pained expression on her face.

She set her burden on the bed—like me, Mac had known better than to offer to carry it for her—rubbed her sternum where that Fodduan sailor's heavy, slow-moving bullet had been stopped by her smartsuit. Looking at both of us guiltily, she slipped her left arm back into the sling that Doctor Pololo had insisted she wear about her neck.

"Mac, I'm awfully sorry to pitch you out like this, just when we'd started getting comfortable with each other, but ... " She tapered off.

He laughed. I do not believe that I have ever seen a human being more relaxed, so completely, unselfconsciously self-confident. "Don't mention it, Mumsie, I have parsecs to go and promises to keep, myself. Besides, it wouldn't do to have your son interfering with your, er, honeymoon."

She blushed.

So did I.

"And since you're running off again so soon, before you give this away," she said, "you might ask me, first." She took the bear from me, plumped up its slightly-leaking body, squeezed it in her good arm. "What's so all-fired important you'd leave your poor old mother and her—"

"Gigolo," I offered.

"I kind of like that—'gigolo'—to go running off for?"

"There's an urgent alarm of some kind out in *Tom Huxley Maru's* investigation sector, something about one of Voltaire Malaise's colony ships that's only just now arriving, thanks to time-displacement, and with its mind-control system still operating. Maybe the old son-of-a-bureaucrat himself is aboard. I want to be there when the plug gets pulled."

"*Tom Huxley Maru?*" Lucille consulted the ceiling for data, then blinked, "Why, that's Brion Bayard's new command. Mac, I hate to disappoint you, but we're beginning to think Voltaire Malaise wound up on Whitey's world. Isn't that right, Corporal darling? Nevertheless, I wouldn't mind being there, myself. Think of it: tens of thousands of freshly-kidnapped women, free to do whatever they want with their kidnappers!"

She held the bedraggled little stuffed bear out at arms' length, sighed deeply, then sat it on the bed, leaning against one of Mac's plastic cartons. "Well, Mac, if you have to go, you have to go. About this ... "

"I think Whitey was going to give it to Elsie Nahuatl."

She grinned, then looked at me. "My daddy gave it to me when I was laid up with a bad appendix. Good therapy. Come to think of it, you'll probably need it yourself, Corporal, after your brain operation this afternoon."

Brain operation. Lovely. The animal stared at me dementedly with its scratched plastic eyes, but refused to offer any comfort or advice.

Nahuatl, Elsa Lysandra: current head of xenopsychology department, praxeology divison, starship *Tom Paine Maru*. Born Cody, Wyoming, Solar Confederacy, May 23, 267 A.L., mostly of Australian Aborigine lineage, [identification of seventeen biological parents under privacy protection except in certifiably appropriate emergency. Adopted parent G. Howell Nahuatl, Operations Division, *Tom Paine Maru*. height 37 inches, weight 53 pounds. Hair blonde, complexion dark brown, eyes blue.

More info? [Y/N]

Elsie's likeness, in full-color stereo, hung before my wondering eyes. Curious, I nodded microscopically. Before very long, I had been told a little while ago, only the subliminal muscular traces of my intention to nod would be sufficient to cue the implant correctly. Until then, it would take a little practice to get to know one another.

Through the ID hologram, I could see another Elsie, chatting with her friends. We were attending something like a wake, except that the nine-year-old guest of honor was sitting up in bed, cleaning her little dagger. Her tiny automatic pistol lay in neatly-ordered pieces on a cloth on the end-table, ready for reassembly after Owen Rogers had thrust them through the room's shower-curtain three or four more times.

She was a tough customer to satisfy. On Sodde Lydfe, she had confided in me that she wanted to be just like Lucille when she grew up.

God help the galaxy!

Associated reference: Nahuatl, G. Howell, Operations Division, *Tom Paine Maru*. American coyote with cyberenhanced cognition. Further info under discretionary privacy-protection at subject's specification.

Contact subj. for info release? [Y/N]

With a microscopic shake of my head, I suppressed any further retrieval from the implant. It was the first thing I had been shown to do, by the implant itself. The arduous "operation" I had dreaded for so long had taken all of three minutes, most of it to dab a little alcohol on the site before injection, a useless procedure medically, but some rituals survive everything. It seemed to make the nurse feel better.

The bright green letters vanished from the bottom edge of my field of vision, along with the picture of the coyote and a map of "North America".

Howell himself, of course, was right there, curled up on one corner of Elsie's bed. Also Francis W. Pololo—along with Mymysiir who was listening intently to the gorilla lecture rher on the subject of alien (meaning human) anatomy. In the corner, Vyssu was showing Edwina how to knit using three needles. My freshly-inserted computer likely would have stripped its gears supplying information on this crowd.

"They're fragile," Pololo was telling the lamviin paracauterist, "unlike you or I, yet somehow they're very tough. This rugged young individual, despite a fractured vertebra, a punctured lung, and three broken ribs, wanted to get up and stomp what was left of Serman—oh, hello, Whitey! I didn't see you come in. Lucille, how are you feeling, dear?"

She gulped. "A whole bloody lot better before I walked into this room, let me tell you! I had no idea little Elsie had been hurt so badly."

Neither had I.

The conversation's subject said, "Little Elsie's gonna hurt *you* badly, Lucille Olson-Bear, unless you stop talking about her in the diminutive third person! Hi there, Corporal darling, what'd you bring me?"

I held up the tattered toy bear with a fresh red ribbon around its neck. "This, sweetheart. It is actually from Lucille, here—also Mac."

"MacBear? He 'commed to say goodbye, but I didn't know he was going to send me—a teddy! An old one! Oh, Cilly, he must have been yours!"

Tears quivering in her eyes, my cast iron warrior-maiden nodded silently. The little girl peered thoughtfully at the gunsmith as she supervised his reassembly of her pistol, teddy bear clutched to her chest.

"Wanna know what I'm gonna call him, Rog?"

The gunsmith/praxeologist smiled, shook his head—then cursed as the sharply-ground end of a coil-spring gouged him underneath his thumbnail.

Elsie giggled, "I'm gonna call him Owen!"

Mymy examined the stuffed animal closely. Howell sniffed at it, confessing that he'd once had a stuffed sandhopper he would not go anywhere without. The gorilla physician closed up his case, extracted a cigar from his pocket, then drew smoke as the smelly thing lighted itself.

"I'll be going. Koko's calling. She's arranging the equivalent of a tea for the royal trines of Podfet and Foddu, and the pleasure of my company has been requested. We're going to show them holograms of the ruined Sodde Lydfe on the other side, so they may not have much of an appetite. Thanks for the smelling-salts, Mymy, we may need them. Now a question of protocol: how are they likely to react when they discover that we won't call people by their authoritarian titles aboard this ship?"

Mymy stirred one of her manipulatory limbs to give the teddy bear an affectionate stroke. "I don't know about the Podfettians, Doctor Pololo, but the crown surprince will be absolutely delighted. Rhe's just finished preparatory school—the very first surmale of the royal family ever to do so—and rhe wants everyone to call rher 'Vuffi'!"

Me, I do not know exactly when I made up my mind about Vespucci. Perhaps in that cargo hold with Sermander, perhaps down on Afdiar somewhere. It is not the kind of conclusion one comes to overnight or all in one piece. I simply began operating on the assumption—before I knew that I had come to it—that I would be acting as *Tom Paine Maru's* "primitive expert" on my own native planet, that Afdiar or Sodde Lydfe were merely practice for what would be to me the main event.

Perhaps it was at this same time that I made up my mind about Eleva. It turned out after all that "acceptably bland" is not my style.

For Lucille, the least bland human being I had ever known, the main event was over for a while. It was ironic that her problem down on Sodde Lydfe arose because Confederates refuse to suppress their unpleasant experiences. Lucille was still in the process of learning how to live with the hideously sharp, clear memories of what happened to her years ago on the same planet, and, under the stress of being struck by that enormous bullet, those memories had simply overwhelmed her.

In the future, for all events, main or otherwise, I planned to train right alongside her. I suspected that our relationship would always be a noisy one, but that, together, we could make sure no demons would ever begin haunting her again. I thought my being beside her from now on would make a lot of difference. At least I hoped it would.

The trouble with being free is that it funnels a lot of decisions your way that you were used to having made by someone else. Mav had made a decision I learned about when he joined his mates in Elsie's room:

"I say, old armorer, this is a bit of all right, what?"

"What?" The alien's breathing orifices had not moved a centimeter. He was "speaking" to me over the implant interlink. "Mav, you have had an—!"

As silently as the "priests" who had rescued me on Sca, he said, "Too right, dear fellow. I loathed and detested growing old, although I attempted to make the best of it. Now I find it won't be necessary. This niggling little operation is only the first step. The Healing staff informs me that, with Mymy's assistance, there will soon be a cure for aging among lamviin much as there are for the various species of the Confederacy. I shall await it with as much patience as I can muster."

I laughed out loud, then: "I take it, then, that one of our starships will be returning you to Sodde Lydfe in the not-too-distant future."

"You take it wrong. Actually, you see, we're going with you."

"But Mav," I said aloud, "You planet is undergoing a revolution. Everything is going to change. Your people will be needing you. There will be all of the things you've fought for so long: peace, freedom, prosperity—"

"And no heroes and no gurus, not if I can help it, Whitey. I am going to be young again and see more of the universe than I had ever imagined possible. My people? They need only themselves. And besides, you see, these," he gestured with his middle hand at everyone in the room. "These are my people—what you all call 'mindkind'. And I am content."

I had already learned that coordination in this culture comes not from cerebral-corticalimplants—they're nothing but tiny computers, after all—but out of sheer self-interest. Here was a wonderful example.

I put both my arms around Lucille. She looked up at me. I winked and kissed her. She went back to watching Elsie playing with the old bear.

"Yes, Mav, so am I."

More Titles from Phoenix Pick

L. Neil Smith
The Venus Belt (winter 2008)
The Crystal Empire (winter 2008)

A. A. Attanasio
In Other Worlds $6.99
Arc of the Dream $7.99
Last Legends of Earth (winter 2008)

Poul Anderson
The Burning Bridge $3.99
Security $4.99

Paul Cook
The Engines of Dawn $7.99
Fortress on the Sun $6.99
Karma Kommandos $7.99

Andre Norton
Key Out of Time $5.99
Voodoo Planet $4.99

Frank Herbert
Missing Link & Operation Haystack $4.99

John W. Campbell
The Ultimate Weapon $4.99

Lester Del Ray
Police Your Planet $5.99

Alexei Panshin
Farewell to Yesterdays Tomorrow $6.99
Earth Magic (with Cory Panshin, fall/winter 2008)

www.PhoenixPick.com

Also download complete books and excerpts for FREE
Phoenix Pick - Great Science Fiction at Great Prices